UNCROSSED

HAREM STATION

NEW YORK TIMES BESTSELLING AUTHOR, JA HUSS, WRITING AS

KCROSS

UNCROSSED

NEW YORK TIMES BESTSELLING AUTHOR JA HUSS WRITING AS

KC ROSS

Copyright © 2021 by JA Huss & KC Cross
ISBN: 978-1-950232-60-4

Edited by RJ Locksley
Cover Photo: Sara Eirew
Cover Design by JA Huss

4

ABOUT
THE BOOK

Princess Corla was supposed to be my soulmate.

But we were star crossed.

Two ships passing in the dark. Meant to be together, but never able to be together.

At least that's what I thought.

But it turns out—my life is a lie, evil forces are out to get us, Harem Station is spinning chaos, and the soulmate bond won't protect us.

Sounds pretty bad, right?

But here's the best part.

I can change it.

I can change *all of it*.

If I can just find a way to get myself *uncrossed*.

Uncrossed is the last book in the Harem Station Series and features a man chasing his star-crossed soulmate through time, a bazillion enemies at the gate, an entire station in chaos, and an explosive ending that proves, once and for all, that love WINS in the end.

5

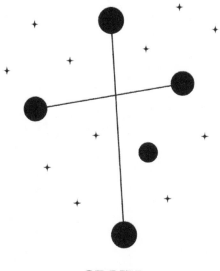

CRUX

Noun.

1. The basic, central, or critical point or feature.
2. A puzzling or apparently insoluble problem.
3. A cross.
4. The unluckiest man in the sun-damned universe.

CREX

CHAPTER ONE

Every single part of her feels familiar, that's what I notice first. The way my hand cups her breast. The way her back fits against my chest. The smell of her hair, and the heat of her body, and the rhythm of her breathing.

All of it is familiar, but at the same time... weird.

I know she is Corla. I know I am Crux. I know we're in bed, and it's morning, and I recognize the sounds filtering through the door of our bedroom. Traffic outside. A car engine. Distant voices of neighbors and small children.

Then the banging of a cupboard.

Corla stirs, letting out a long, sleepy sigh. "They're up. Why for the love of God do they insist on getting up so damn early?"

I think about that for a moment, wondering who the hell she's talking about. At least, I'm pretty sure I think about that for a moment. But at the same time I'm thinking about that, I mumble, "I'll get them," in a gruff, equally sleepy voice.

After that nothing makes sense.

Because that's not *me* talking.

9

Well, it's sort of me. It's my voice. I feel the muscles moving in my throat. All that *is* me. But... I'm suddenly across the room looking down on a bed of rumpled white covers and two people beneath them. Corla's hair—not silver, but a very pale blonde—covers her face and spills onto her pillow.

I—well, obviously this man is not me, let's just call him the one in the bed—he rolls over, throwing his portion of covers off. He swings his legs over the side of the mattress and plants his feet on the dark wood floor. He leans forward, rubbing his hands down his scruffy face, as he deals with the idea of waking.

He is me. He has my hair, he has my body, he has my face, he has my woman.

But he's not me because *I* am me. So maybe I'm him? *Because that makes a lot of sense.*

He finally stands. A muffled crash echoes from somewhere deeper within these quarters. And then a squeal.

"Oh. My fucking. *God.*" Corla's hand comes up to her face and she pushes her hair aside. One eye open, she stares at the other me. "I'm going to kill them."

"You're not gonna kill them." Other Me chuckles. He reaches for some thin, sleep pants on the floor by his feet and pulls them up his legs. "They're freaking adorable for many... *minutes* of... most days."

She laughs and closes her one eye, smiling as she settles her head into the pillow. "They're heathens."

"They're inquisitive."

"They're obnoxious."

"They're rambunctious."

"They suck the life out of me."

10

He leans down, one knee on the mattress, and kisses her on the head. "And then they fill you back up. Just... sleep. It's their birthday and they're excited. That's all. They're ready to get this party started. I'll make breakfast and bring it to you in bed. How's that sound?"

Now Corla opens both eyes and beams a loving smile up at Other Me. "I don't know what I ever did to deserve you."

I don't quite get it either.

I mean—did this guy here put his life—and the lives of all his friends—on the line to shoot her ass through a spin node?

No. No he didn't.

That would be me.

But do I get a Corla?

Other Me shrugs with his hands and chuckles again. "Right place, right time, babe. That's all it was."

Well that's... amazing.

Dick.

Then next thing I know I'm standing in a kitchen. Not the kind of kitchen I have in my quarters. Or any kind of kitchen I've ever seen before, actually. There's a lot of... things. Big, metal, humming machine-type things.

I recognize a refrigerator. It's overly large, not like the ones we have on Harem. And the sink is obvious. But the autocook isn't an autocook. It's like the cooktop Serpint has in his quarters, but much bigger and more primitive. It uses fire.

But the really weird thing about this kitchen isn't the machines. It's me. Other Me. And how he seems to know exactly what to do with the not-autocook.

11

Also the two children running circles around a central island counter. A pair of squealing fair-haired toddlers, one chasing the other. Then they reverse direction and the chased becomes the chaser.

Other Me is cooking food over the flames. Then the little girl—the chased, at the moment—falls face-first on the hard, stone floor.

Everything stops. Other Me rushes over to her as she starts to cry. He picks her up, hugging her to his chest, one hand on her knee to see if there's any damage.

"You're OK, Dellie. You're OK." He soothes her as he points to the boy. "That's enough now, Toby. No more running in the kitchen. If you want to play chase—"

I stop listening.

These are my kids. My real, actual fucking kids when they were small. And that *is* me... except it isn't.

I whirl around. "Where am I?"

No one answers. The people in this kitchen—me and my children, who are not me and my children—don't react. Can't hear me.

Because that's not you, Crux.

The room disappears and I now find myself in a place that reminds me of an unfinished sector of the Pleasure Prison. Hazy grayness that goes on forever.

"Wait!" I call out. "Go back!"

I don't know who I'm talking to. Myself? Other Me? Corla, who obviously, *isn't*... Corla.

"You can't go back."

I turn to see ALCOR. At least he looks like a familiar version of ALCOR that I recognize from some long-ago time. Except it's not ALCOR. I don't know how I know this, I just do.

"Why not?" I ask.

Not-ALCOR smiles at me. "You know why. That's not really you. It's just a glimpse."

"Of what?"

"Another version of you. One who knows nothing about artificial beings, or giant outlaw stations, or wars being waged in his name." He pauses, waiting to see if that satisfies me.

It doesn't. "Those wars aren't being waged in my name. And who are you?"

"*Which* am I, you mean?"

I narrow my eyes at him. I'm not in the mood to play.

"I'm Security Beacon Number Nineteen, of course. But you can call me SB19 for short."

"Corla's security beacon," I mutter, considering this.

A year ago my brother Serpint showed up at Harem Station with my star-crossed princess inside a cryopod. Our brother, Draden, died stealing her and Serpint had to limp his way back home because *Booty Hunter* was severely damaged.

After that nothing was ever the same again. And Draden dying was only the first in a long string of… well, what to call them? Coincidences? Doesn't really fit. Bad luck doesn't really fit either. I guess the appearance of Corla in that cryopod was a little bit of both.

Normally, when a Cygnian princess comes in to Harem Station she is thawed out and put to work. But I didn't thaw Corla out of her cryogenetic sleep when

13

Serpint brought her to me because I was afraid the Cygnians would be able to track the pod.

But that wasn't the only reason.

Twenty years ago Corla told me that we would never see each other again. And if we did, things had gone terribly wrong. So even though I spent all twenty years between that night and the day Serpint brought her to Harem Station wishing for a second chance with my one true soulmate—I knew, deep down, that she was not supposed to be there.

I could feel the truth of that warning inside me.

She scared me.

I sent Corla out to Security Beacon Number Nineteen after everything started going sideways. She's a bomb. So are Lyra, and Nyleena, and Veila. And I know what people think. I let them stay on the station—well, I didn't really have a choice when it came to Veila, but the others, yeah, I let them stay—and I sent Corla away. Put her out on that security beacon so just in case anyone decided to blow her up, she would not take the rest of us down with her.

I had to do it. I didn't have a choice. She was dangerous. More dangerous than the others because we didn't know why she was in that cryopod, or what she was doing on Cetus Station, or where she was going.

So I don't feel guilty about keeping her frozen. It was my duty.

Serpint and I had a chat about her that day while we were inside the security beacon. I told him my suspicions about ALCOR. Specifically, I told him about how I saw ALCOR kill our brother Draden back when he was thirteen. And how I knew that the reappearance of Corla after twenty years was also the beginning of something big.

Something bad.

SB19 heard everything I said to Serp, of course. But I didn't think about it much back then. The security beacons were never very communicative with us. They are their own minds. They live—for lack of a better word—their own lives, preferring to be seen and not heard.

And by seen, I mean every once in a while they will target-lock their SEAR cannons onto random ships just to let everyone know they're still there.

"That is not my name," SB19 says.

"What?"

"I am not Corla's security beacon. She was a guest in my hull, yes. Correct. But that is not my name."

"I... OK. Sorry? But... did you just say she *was* a guest in your hull?"

"That's the least of our worries right now, Crux. Trust me on this."

"What's going on? Why are you here? Why am I here?"

"You're not really here, Crux. You're back on Harem Station locked up inside a time freeze. What's the last thing you remember?"

I squint my eyes at him, very, very annoyed with this AI at the moment. Because I was just pulled away from my... family. Kind of. I mean, I get it. It was a dream. But it was a really nice dream. And it's been too many spins to count since I felt that kind of... *longing*.

Wow. That's kind of a powerful word. *Longing*.

Was it longing?

"Veila?" SB19 says. "Hmm? Remember her?"

"Yeah." I let out a long breath. "Yeah. I remember her."

"She and Valor froze time. Harem Station was—"

"At war." I slide a hand down my face, perfectly mimicking the gesture Other Me did back in the bedroom. "Fuck. What the sun is happening?"

"I'm not sure. I don't have any access to Harem. All the security beacons took a vote when Veila appeared with her ship and decided to close the gate and cut ties with the station just to be on the safe side. Turns out that was a good decision. Obviously. Harem Station is no longer safe."

Tell me something I didn't already know. "But how am I here? And where *is* here?"

"As I said, you're not here. You're still on Harem. In your office, actually. Valor and Veila put you there."

"How do you know that if you have no connection to Harem?"

"And now we're back on track." SB19 smiles and pans his hands wide in a gesture that reminds me a lot of ALCOR. My ALCOR. Old, reliable, devious, evil, safe ALCOR. I guess I never realized how well he did his job until he was gone and everything went to shit.

If I ever see him again I think I owe him a thank you.

"Dragonbee bots are quite talented. I'm not in contact with the station, but I am in contact with Flicka. Those annoying little fuckers have their creepy clicking feet in everything these days."

"Wait. Yeah, I remember now. We were… fighting. I was trying to make an announcement and all those stupid fucking princesses turned on us."

"Yes. But time has been frozen. And Veila and Valor have taken over. Luckily your pet beebot injected you with something a little while ago. You don't have much longer."

"Wait. Flicka is trying to kill me?"

"I don't think so. But one can't ever really know what goes on inside the mind of a dragonbee bot. And time is a tricky thing. So very unreliable, even on the most local scale. Add in the fact that Harem Station is host to a spin node and actual people on board who can control it, and we've got ourselves a problem. How much do you understand about time, Crux?"

I blink at him, confused at the fast pace of shifting ideas. "What?"

SB19 snaps his fingers. "Please. Keep up! We're on a schedule here. Now, tell me what you know about time."

Time. I open my mouth to tell him obvious things like... it... ticks off? It's... reliable.

But I stop myself. Because time isn't reliable. It's actually quite slippery.

I think back to our escape from Wayward Station twenty years ago. Right after we sent Corla through the spin node. And then I'm there. Literally. The endless gray room I'm in shimmers and resolves into the interior of the ship and I see my sixteen-year-old self, sitting at a console with a terrified look on his face. He's worrying about time. I remember that now. He—I—was worried about Corla and the time difference between the two sides of a spin node.

It fades back into the darkness and I sigh, wondering, suddenly, if I'd do anything different if I could do it all again.

"Crux?"

"Hmm?"

"Time? Tell me what you know!"

"Not much," I admit. "I never really understood it."

"Don't feel bad about that," SB19 says. "No one really does. And if they say otherwise, they're just liars. But I have a better grasp than most." The holograph of the ship begins to shimmer back into existence once again and SB19 smiles at virtual representations of Serpint and Draden, who are floating around in the middle of the ship, trying to wage a pretend zero-G war in too-big environment suits. "So I'll break it down for you as best I can, and let me just be frank here, OK? We're pretty well fucked. I can't lie about that. But there is still a way to…"

He pauses.

I'm feeling pretty annoyed at this point. So I snap at him. "A way to what?"

"Well, it's not a perfect solution. But it's the best we can hope for."

"Do I even want to know?"

"No." SB19 frowns. "You don't. I'm afraid Harem Station is over, Crux. The whole thing is pointless now."

"Wait." I hold up both hands. "Back the fuck up. What is going on?" I look around. "And why are we here? What are you *doing*?"

"Listen," he says, and now he's the one holding up both of his hands, pushing air at me. "Time is a loop. A continuous circle. There is no beginning, there is no end. It just… exists. But we all live inside of it and so… we must deal with it. Every now and then there is

18

a recycling, so to speak. Like water on the station. You use it, it goes to a tank, it gets cleaned up, you use it again."

"I don't get it. Time gets reused?"

SB19 sighs. "It's a metaphor, Crux. Can you just work with me here? Hm?"

I put up my hands. "Fine. Continue. But I don't understand."

"I'm not surprised. You're not the smartest brother, are you?" I open my mouth to tell him to go fuck himself, but he puts up a hand. "You're not the dumbest either, so there's that. And I'm feeling extraordinarily patient today, so I'll skip the metaphors and just spell it out. Time is a loop. And we live inside it. All of us. Every incarnation of us. And of those, there are billions of iterations. Billions of versions of you and me and everyone else. Some of them have already lost, or won, and are starting over again. Some of them are in the middle of their journey—like the people you saw back in that kitchen. And some of them are at the end. We are at the end, Crux."

"You just said there is no end."

He shoots me a look that tells me he's not really feeling extraordinarily patient today. "There isn't. It's a *loop*. I just said that. Twice. And I gave you a handy metaphor and you feigned ignorance, so—"

"Fine. I get it."

He pauses. Probably waiting for me to continue the fight. And I have an urge to do that. But I control it. I might not be the smartest brother, but I am the wisest.

SB19 is satisfied, so he continues. "Once we finish what we're doing here on this timeline, we'll start over again. And we'll do it again. And again. And again. And again. Forever. Like I said, time is a loop and we can't ever get out. And normally, the loop is set. Predetermined. Fate, if you will. The fate of those people you saw in that kitchen has already been written. What happens to them as they live out their life together, I have no idea and I don't care. Whatever I'm doing in that world, it happens light years away from that place. I'm not a part of their story and they aren't a part of mine. But I do know what happens next to us, here. All the AIs know." He stops to ponder something, a thoughtful look on his unreal face. "And the beebots too. They know. That's why they're so dangerous. They are always trying to change the fate of our loop. But up until now, changing the outcome was impossible."

He stops talking, as if this might be the entirety of his explanation.

I rub my hand down my face again, suddenly very tired. "I really don't get it."

He smiles at me and for a moment I see ALCOR in him. The Real ALCOR. My ALCOR. And even though most of the past twenty years have been filled with moments when I hated that AI, and even though I have never fully trusted him, I want to see my ALCOR one more time so badly in this moment, I feel sick just thinking about it.

"They have figured it out, Crux."

"Who?"

"The Akeelians. And Cygnians." He flips a hand in the air. "But the Cygnians only know what they've been told. The Akeelians are the ones running this show. They know how to change the fate of our loop and they're about to change the course of everything using your brothers, and those Akeelian princesses. But even if they can't get a hold of you and your girls, they have others waiting. They can't use them yet—that's why they need Harem Station. But this is our only chance in time to kick them off their loop and reset ours. Because if we don't they eventually will do that to us. We must not allow this to happen. It will affect every other time loop in the Earth universe. You"—he points at me—"will never have that family back there in that kitchen, Crux. But other you... he has them already. He has a wife and she is the love of his life. He has twin children. He is happy. But if the Akeelians succeed in our timeline, all that will be lost. Everything will change. And even though I already said it, I must say it again. We must *not*. Allow. That to happen."

He pauses, then continues. "I know what you're going to say. 'So what? Why should I care what happens to Other Me?' And the simple answer is this—everything is connected, Crux. If our world changes, their world changes. If their world changes, our world changes. What ensues is chaos."

I think about this for a moment—well, many, *many* moments—trying to wrap my head around it.

Time is a loop. Got it.

Lots of Other Mes out there living other lives. OK. I'm not sure I believe it, but I *get* it.

Life—or maybe *existence* is a better word—is predetermined. There is no way to change things. That sucks. But again, I get it. I comprehend the concept. We have no free will. We're all just puppets doing the bidding of our master, who is, apparently, something (or perhaps some*one*) called Time.

21

And here's where I end up: "So what? Maybe chaos is a good thing? Maybe shaking things up isn't so bad?"

"I knew you'd say that. Humanoids. They are so predictable. And there's some irony. They, you—you all love the unpredictable. You all love the good shakeup. You all think you want to be in charge of all those choices you think you're making. But we're talking chaos with a capital C here, Crux. We're not talking about who has the most power in the galaxy or anything as mundane and simple as the 'meaning of life'. Chaos with a capital C means a complete do-over. As in this whole universe is wiped out. A clean slate, if you will. And then we start over again. From day one. And do you have any idea what day one looks like, Crux?"

He pauses. Like maybe I have an answer for that. But it's a rhetorical pause. Because he continues almost immediately.

"Day one looks like nothing. Never mind that there is no organic matter. No bacteria, or viruses, or single-celled plants. There are no suns, Crux. No solar systems. Not even giant clouds of gas that might turn into suns in a few billion years. Nothing. We start over from nothing. But lest you interpret that the wrong way, let me be extra clear about this—it will be different. Everything will be different. You might be reborn a karkadann. The point is, nothing will be known."

I think about this for a moment. "Maybe that's a good thing."

"It isn't. Trust me. I was there the last time we started over. ALCOR is in charge right now. He's the one in charge of time at the moment, Crux. And he's already annihilated the universe three times."

"What?" I laugh. I just can't.

"Laugh all you want but he's about to do it again. Do you really think any of this is by accident? Please." He almost snorts. "ALCOR knows everything. For all intents and purposes, he is our God."

"He is time, you mean? Is that what you mean?"

"No. He's not time. But he's got a pretty good relationship with time at the moment. Not to mention the ear of all those time-controlling princesses on Harem. He told you this, did he not?"

"Told *me*?" I point to myself and almost guffaw. "That asshole hasn't told me a damn thing. He said something about a plan a long time ago. Said it was all 'need-to-know' and that I didn't need to know. So no. He didn't tell me about why he needed princesses other than he wanted special girls to attract outlaw men. But none of this is the point here, OK?"

"All of this is the point. The only point!"

"No. Because like I said, maybe shaking things up is good? Ever think of that? Maybe ALCOR knows what he's doing? Maybe ALCOR"—SB19 laughs—"maybe ALCOR is right! And if he's the only one who fully understands what's happening, maybe we should all just let him do his thing?"

"Wow." SB19 shakes his head. "I really never thought I'd live to hear you say that. I really thought, of all you boys, you would be the one who *got* it."

"Got *what*?"

"He's not benevolent, Crux. He's not doing this for you, or me, or them." He points to the virtual versions of my brothers, still floating around in zero-

23

G, playing war. "He's doing it for himself. He lost, OK? And this is his revenge. He's using the entire universe to change *his* fate, not *ours*. We're just his collateral damage."

I take a moment to think about this. Because some of it does makes sense. ALCOR never told us his full story but he told us some of it. He was ousted, for instance. From some long-gone civilization. We all know that. He said thousands of years ago. Not billions. But SB19 just said that ALCOR hit the reset button three times. So... it's possible that his latest ousting was just that—the last in a long line of them.

But who is this AI? I don't know him. He says he's SB19 but I wouldn't know the difference.

"I'm telling you the truth," SB19 says. "Your heart doesn't want to believe me, but your head knows, Crux. You know there's something wrong with him. And right now he's out there."

"What? How do you know? The last I heard—"

"He's out there. Doing god knows what. He's lived billions upon billions of years. He's done this, from inception to *ending*, three times. And I've been here for all three of them. Everything was the same until Draden died. Then the whole timeline started to change. Think about it, OK? Just think about everything that happened since Draden died on Cetus Station and Serpint came home alone. Lyra shows up out of nowhere. Nyleena. Delphi. This new version of Tray and this ship-girl called Brigit. Draden's death was the beginning of the end. It's been nothing but chaos ever since. And you were there, Crux. That day twenty years ago back when Draden was thirteen, and

ALCOR threw him off that lift bot. ALCOR killed him once so he could kill him again and change everything."

I'm stuck on those words, 'threw him off the lift bot.'

And I want to protest out of instinct. I want to say, *He fell. That's all. Draden fell, ALCOR messed up, and that's all there is to it.*

But I can't. Because I know ALCOR *did* kill Draden. It just feels treasonous to admit it to this security beacon.

"What do you want me to do?" I ask it in a low whisper. And when SB19 doesn't answer, I keep going. "Because I'm no one. I don't even have… powers. Not like the rest of them. I can't walk through spin nodes like Luck or blow up planets like Nyleena and Lyra. I don't have a pet beebot in my pocket like Delphi. I can't create virtual worlds like Tray, or stop time like Valor and Veila, or go to Earth like Jimmy, or command *Booty Hunter* like Serpint and Draden. I can't do *anything*. ALCOR made sure of it. He kept me chained to Harem Station like a fucking pet. He knew I'd stay and run things. I don't even know if I could pilot a ship at this point, that's how long it's been since I took one off the station. So what the fuck do you think I'm going to do about any of this?"

He smiles at me. And for a moment I let myself believe he's ALCOR. I let relief flood into all those empty spaces that have been collecting inside me since ALCOR died.

Because no, I never did trust him. And yes, I always suspected he was up to something. I always knew he was using me in some special way. I have felt that way since the very beginning.

But I still loved him. And if this incarnation of ALCOR standing in front of me was the Real ALCOR I would still be on his side, I know I would. And I'd be happy about that.

I'd be relieved. And I want that relief so bad.

But that's not him.

So I push it all down.

"You're something special, Crux. The most special of all your brothers. But you need *her* to realize it. So pull yourself out of this time freeze and *wake her up!*"

CHAPTER TWO

A soft, familiar tap-tap-tapping drags me out of the dream.

Was that a dream? Corla, the twins, SB19, the… *place*. Where was that place?

Tap-tappity-tap.

Time is a loop, there is no free will, ALCOR is bad. Is he really bad?

God, that's so disappointing. I've been pulling for him. I really have. I like the dude. Love him, actually. I want to be on his side. But—

Tappity-tap.

Then buzzing.

I open one eye. Everything is blurry, but the tap-tap-tapping continues. The room is sideways and I realize I'm in my office, head on desk.

More tapping. Little pitter-patter of feet. Then Flicka appears in my field of sideways vision. She leans her head to the side to make things appear right side up. And that just bothers me for a moment. Because I'm still sideways, but yet she's not.

An illusion. How fitting.

She leans back on four of her spindly legs, waving the other two like arms, as she begins to buzz again.

"I don't understand you," I croak. My throat is so dry it feels like I haven't had a drink in decades.

She flies up, down, taps her feet, flies up again.

You'd think beebots would just learn to speak Prime Standard. I mean, they're smart, crafty little fuckers. Why don't they just speak the common language?

"I need a translator." I grunt as I try to lift my head up off the desk. This one action almost takes more effort than I can muster up. Why am I so tired? I wonder about this for a moment, then remember.

Time freeze.

Who knows how long I've been here at my desk.

Flicka buzzes, then puffs a pink mist out from her ass.

I inhale before I can stop myself, imagining all the nasty things this beebot's potion might do to me before I realize… I feel better.

So I sit up. Flicka is buzzing around my face, still talking. I pinch the air together, opening up an air screen out of habit, then instantly remember the chaos of 'before' and that the air screens are out of service. But, to my surprise, it works. The translator appears automatically because my screen is set to detect speech not in the common tongue, and I come into Flicka's tirade mid-conversation.

"… and then the whole thing went to shit!"

Well, tail-end, from the sound of things. "Wait." I sigh, rubbing a hand down my face that pulls the memories out of the dream I just woke from. "Start over. I didn't hear any of that."

Was it a dream?

"Delphi!" Flicka squeaks. "We need to go get Delphi!"

"Where is she?"

"Stuck in the spin node!"

"Stuck in the spin node." I repeat the words back dumbly. But in my defense, they make no sense.

This sets Flicka off. Words start spilling out of her so fast the translator has a hard time keeping up, so I only catch bits here and there of the rant. But this is what I piece together.

Valor and Veila took over the station.

I think I kinda knew that.

Veila stopped time.

Yeah, this sounds familiar.

Everyone on the station is frozen and the Princess Rebellion is no longer raging.

Hmm. Nope, that's a new one.

"And now Veila is in control of everything and Valor is helping her. They peeked into the future and now they know! We have to leave! Right now! We have to get Delphi, because I have big plans. And you need to take care of Corla!"

"OK." I sigh and put up a hand. "Yeah. About that. I get it. I'm supposed to wake her up. But I'm not sure I need Delphi—"

"You do! You absolutely do! And Tycho can't come! Don't you see? Veila put them together and they can't be together! Ever!"

That just makes me sad. I picture Delphi and Tycho in that place I was in the dream. Was it another reality? They were so small. So happy. So playful. It felt right. And even though I don't feel much of a

29

connection with the Delphi of this world—or any connection at all with the Tycho of this world—I kinda want to go back and see what's happening to those kids. My kids. Because they *are* my kids. That *was* me. I was inside him for a brief period. I had Corla in my arms. We had a bed, and a room, and some kind of home. We lived in a place with traffic and people outside.

And then I'm thrown back in time. Back to when we were all still young. Before my brothers and me went our separate ways. When we knew that there was a world outside ALCOR Station and we understood we were missing out on it.

That's how I feel now.

I'm *missing* it.

Everything about this place here, it feels wrong somehow. Like the dream place was actual reality and what I'm stuck in now is only second best.

How old were they? I try to picture little Delphi and Tycho as they chased each other around the kitchen island. Four, maybe? Younger? It's hard to tell. We don't have a lot of kids on Harem, but aside from that, I'm not really the kind of guy who pays attention to kids.

I'm not a father.

And yet I am.

I wonder what I got them for their birthday. I wonder what I was making for breakfast. I wonder if I took that breakfast into Corla and then got back in bed with her.

"Get up! Get up! Get up!" Flicka is buzzing wildly.

I come back to the present and kinda hate it.

"We need to get Delphi out of here! Now!"

I don't belong here. That's my problem. I think I've always known it, too. I think I have always felt out of place.

This isn't my world.

This isn't my life.

I want to go *home*.

I don't go home. Obviously.

I get up from the desk, order up a morning cocktail of extra-caffeinated, extra-carbonated energy drink, and then try not to look too hard at my reflection in the glass walls of my office.

I look past that guy and out into the harem room. Which is totally empty. Not a single princess in sight. No Cyborg Master. Not even a bot. "Where is everyone?"

"Haven't you been listening to me? Everyone is stuck in a time freeze!"

"OK. But where's Valor and Veila?"

"They're on the *Veiled Vixen*. They went to bed just before I woke you up. But they don't sleep long and we have a lot to do. We need to go! Now!"

"What a sun fucker. He's *sleeping* with her? And what the hell is a *Veiled Vixen*?"

"That giant ship attached to the topside of the station!"

"Oh." I nod my head, take another sip of energy drink. "Yeah. That makes sense. *Veiled Vixen*. So where is Delphi again?"

I'm having a hard time giving out fucks for this grown-up version of Delphi. I hate that for obvious reasons. But she wasn't exactly the baby daughter I imagined all those years ago when Corla and I did that whole breeding ceremony thing. She has no interest in me, that's for sure. And I can't say I blame her. I wasn't around. But it's not like I was given a choice.

"She's in the museum. Stuck in a spin node."

"Right. The hidden spin node." It still kinda bothers me that ALCOR kept that secret. I mean, I am the fucking governor of Harem Station. That's the kind of thing I should've been told.

"Why are you just standing there? We have to go!"

"Because I… I…" I shrug and say the first thing that came to mind. "I don't care, Flicka. I just don't fucking care."

"Don't care about what? Delphi being stuck in the spin node? The station basically being held hostage by an evil Cygnian princess? The fact that Veila and Valor now control time? And speaking of Valor, how about his treasonous actions? He's her soulmate! He's in on this! He helped her lock everyone up in their rooms! Which part of this doesn't peak your give-a-fuck-meter, Crux?"

"Meh?" I shrug again. "Yeah. All of that shit can just go fuck itself."

"We lost! Veila won! But it's not over yet! She's either going to use Delphi and Tycho to blow up the station, or open the gates and let the Akeelians in, or—"

"So. Fucking. What?"

"How can you say that?"

"You know how? I'll tell you how. Some version of the Security Beacon Number Nineteen AI came to me in a time-freeze-induced dream, showed me the life I could've had if I hadn't been born in this shitty version of the man called Crux, showed me what normal looked like—and you know what my takeaway is? This place sucks. This whole fucking two-cocked version of me sucks. I don't want to do this anymore. I mean… there were a few minutes there where I thought, *Eh. Yeah. Maybe I'd like to go wake Corla up. See her again. Talk to her. Catch up on the last twenty-one fucking years.* You know, those years where she went one way through some spin node and I went some other way, through the ALCOR gate. And then I got stuck here on this station that whole time. And she…" I throw up my hands. "I dunno what the fuck she did. Time-traveled? Hopped universes? I have no clue. The only thing I do know is that she gives about as many fucks about me as I do her, so… yeah. The way I see it, we're even."

Flicka buzzes right up to my face. Hovers there just off the end of my nose. My eyes start to cross a little and I swat her back. "That's the most selfish thing I've ever heard."

I guffaw. "Really?"

"'Poor me. My name is Crux. I've lived this cushy, privileged life here on Harem Station for twenty-one years. Boo hoo. I've never had to worry about credits, or food, or air, or people trying to rape me—'"

"Fuck you. Yeah, I got all those basic things for free. Lucky me. But I have done nothing for the past twenty-one years but worry about other people. And the food, and air, and water might be free, but that doesn't mean I didn't earn it. Do you have any idea how much time I've spent behind an autocook trying to fix it? Do you have any idea how many water generators I've built in my life? Do you have any idea how much maintenance an airlock needs to keep the integrity of the seals? All that shit was free because I made the motherfucking machines that make the motherfucking water and food. I have changed the fucking seals on every single airlock on this godforsaken station at least a hundred times since I landed here! My life is the opposite of *free*, Flicka. I've been a prisoner of Harem Station for twenty-one years! And you know what?" I blink my eyes at her, kinda stunned at my own outburst. But fuck it. I'm all in now. "I think I'm done."

She buzzes something my translator can't interpret, then spins round and puffs out a mist of green particles which quickly make me cough.

I swat at her, moving out of her poison cloud, and she buzzes off. Disappearing into an air vent.

"Fuck you!" I yell after her. "Just… fuck you, and fuck Valor, and fuck Veila, and fuck Luck, and Delphi, and Jimmy, and Nyleena! And most of all, fuck Corla! Fuck all of you! I'm out!"

CHAPTER THREE

"You know"—Baby ALCOR's voice booms through my office—"it's interesting to me that you didn't include Real ALCOR in your tirade. Why is that?"

"Why is that, Baby? I'll tell you why. Because I believed in him, OK? I might not have trusted him, and I always knew he was up to something, but if I give up on him then what is the fucking point?"

He doesn't answer immediately so I continue.

"For real. What is the point? If my whole life is just one small thread in the great big web of lies that ALCOR has been weaving for billions of years, then what does it matter? I've been told that none of this is my free will. I've been told that things are on some kind of loop. I've been told that we've all been here before and I've been told that ALCOR is just gonna wipe us all out anyway. So who cares? Why should I care? It's fate, right?"

More silence. Maybe he left? Or maybe he's just giving me space to say more. But I don't have anything else to say. I'm just… jaded. I saw what a real life looks like in that dream and it's nothing like the one I've been living. It's kids, and a wife, and birthdays, and cooking breakfast in some outdated fire contraption. It's a home, probably on a planet, with a sun, and weather, and neighbors. It's probably a job that doesn't involve saving the lives of millions of people every day by making sure they can breathe, and eat, and drink. Why should I care that *his* life will be upended if I don't do *my* part?

Like... welcome to my world, am I right?

Baby remains silent so I keep going. "My whole life has been nothing but one long string of weird breeding ceremonies, and missing princesses, and whole galactic armies wanting me dead. And before now, before I saw that other Crux, I didn't know better. But all it takes is a glimpse, ya know? That's all I got, anyway. And it was enough for me to get it. I get it. This isn't a life. It's a fucking prison sentence."

I take in a deep breath, then walk over to my desk and sink into my chair.

"I've been coming to the office every day for as long as I can remember. Over a decade, for sure. And every time I sit down in this chair I think, *OK. What the fuck is this station gonna throw at me today?* Will we get some ruthless refugees who think they can take over? That's happened... oh, three dozen times? Probably closer to four dozen, actually. Or maybe one of the sentient ships will try to escape and blow a hole in the docking bay hull? That's happened sixteen times. Always fun. Or maybe all the autocooks will go out on one or two hundred levels. Or an entire garden will just suddenly die and whole sectors of people will have to be relocated. Or hey, I know! I know what could happen! Maybe... *maybe* Luck will go crazy and try to kill me!

Dying is always super fun. And maybe Jimmy will come back with my sun-damned daughter and tell me he's been fucking her for months! Another really good way to start a day. Or maybe—"

"I get it."

"I don't think you do, Baby. Because I'm just getting started. I mean... can anyone say *Nyleena*?"

"I'm not trying to devalue your feelings, Crux—"

"Fuck my feelings, Baby! This isn't about feelings. This is about... it's about... being caught. Yeah. Caught. I'm caught and don't want to do it anymore. I don't want to hear one more goddamned problem of one more goddamned person. Why is it always my fucking job to make everyone's life easier? Why? Why is there no person in the sun-fucked universe whose job it is to make *my* life easier?"

"Hmmm... well, that would be me."

"You?" I scoff.

"And ALCOR. And honestly, the Asshole did play his part."

"His part. When do I get to play my part?"

"I'm pretty sure that time is now."

"To do *their* bidding? I mean, Baby, when do I get to live *my* life? When? Because I'm tired, man. I'm fucking done. I can't do it anymore. I want out."

"OK. So there's the docking bay, Crux. You have control of forty-seven unaffiliated sentient ships at the moment. Wake one up and go."

"The fucking gates are locked."

"The ALCOR Sector is fairly large. And there is a back door. You could always go to the Seven Sisters."

"Yeah. That's amazing. The Seven Sisters. A place so far away it would take me two hundred lifetimes to

JA HUSS & KC CROSS

get there. I'll just put myself into a cryopod, go through the second gate, shoot myself in that general direction, and hope someone can wake me up when I arrive. Great plan."

He says nothing.

"Wait." I furrow my brows. "Did you just say... *back* door?"

"Mmm-hmm."

"Did you mean that literally? Like... there's some kind of hidden gate out there? Or was that just a metaphorical way of referring to that vast, endless open space between us and the Seven Sisters?"

"Maybe you should stick around just long enough to wake up Serpint and ask him. He's been through it."

"When?"

"That day he arrived home without Draden."

"Hmm. He did come in weird that day. Like... no one reported him arriving at the gate. I wondered about that at the time. But then he was there in the docking bay and Draden wasn't."

"Yes. I understand. I wasn't here at the time, obviously. But I saw the records. It was stressful for everyone. And then Lyra was here and before you knew it, there was a mission to save Nyleena and..."

"That's where it went wrong. We should've never—"

But I stop. Because SB19 told me when it went wrong in the dream. I just forgot about that part.

"We should've never... what?" Baby asks. Perhaps prodding me to say something like, *We should've never let ALCOR leave.*

But that's not what I was gonna say. I sigh. "We should've looked harder for him, Baby. We should've

38

moved time itself to find the remnants of Draden. Because all things point to him being alive. And I was told in the dream I just came out of that he's the tipping point of this whole mess. Everything hinges on Draden's deaths."

Yes. Deaths. Because he died twice.

"You should wake Serpint. We don't have *Booty* but we do have *Lady* and *Dicker*. Serpint would be happy to go on this quest with you."

Quest. See? I always get sucked back in. There's always another job for me to do. This past year Serpint has been redecorating his quarters, and fucking his soulmate, and having a good old time. Jimmy and Delphi have been living their life as a couple—and can I just say? I kinda hate Jimmy these days. And Luck and Nyleena. Don't get me started. That fucking princess uprising. And then of course, that one time where Luck actually *killed* me.

That's when it all started to fall apart for me. That little trip into death.

"He won't want to go," I say. "He won't want to leave Lyra behind."

"So don't leave her behind. Is it any more dangerous out there than it is in here?"

The Baby has a point. "I never agreed to this. I have other things to consider."

"Such as?"

"Such as Corla."

Baby ALCOR manifests as a hologram in the middle of my office, surprising me for a moment. Because he doesn't look anything like ALCOR at all. He has blue hair for one, which kinda delights me, and yellow eyes. But that's not even the most dramatic thing about him. His suit… sun fuck's sake. "What the hell are you wearing?"

"Do you like it?" Hologram Baby spins slowly in place, fingering the lapels of his electric-blue jacket that matches his electric-blue pants as he does so. "Raylor designed it for me before things went to shit. I wasn't sure…" He cringes a little. But it's one of those I-can't-help-myself cringes that comes with a high-shoulder shrug, the kind of gesture that signals that you know what you're doing is inappropriate, but you just don't care. "I mean… I know how to read a room and changing up one's… *persona* while a civil war is happening… not good optics. But"—he smiles broadly and for a moment the Real ALCOR peeks through. He always was charismatic—"things are quiet now."

"That's because everyone's *frozen*."

"Exactly." He twirls again, faster this time, then throws his hands up when he completes his spin. "No better time for a fresh start!"

I don't have anything to add to that, so—"Ow." I slap my neck out of instinct when a sharp pain shoots up the back of my head. "What the fuck?"

Flicka buzzes out in front of me, talking in a super speedy voice, which, surprisingly, I can understand.

"You will not ignore me! I'm not going to sit around and let you forget about Delphi just because she brings back uncomfortable memories—"

"What is she saying?"

I tune Flicka out and turn to Baby. "You can't understand her?"

"No. She's speaking some bug language. Doesn't match any of my translators."

"She stung me." I finger the painful swollen lump on the back of my neck. "I didn't even know they *could* sting. I thought it was all poison farts. But I can now understand her without a translator."

Baby considers this. "Hmm. Interesting."

Meanwhile, Flicka is still rambling. "... is your first priority. Trust me, Crux, you do not want to cross a dragonbee bot! We have secrets you have never heard of. We know things. We travel through time and—"

Yeah. I tune her out again. Her voice is pretty small. It's high-pitched and kinda tinny, but more of an annoyance than a commanding presence.

"So." I sigh at Baby. "Serpint, huh."

"Delphi!" Flicka says, buzzing right up to my ear. "Not Serpint!"

I swat her away. "And whatever. If Lyra wants to come, fuck it. I'm not her keeper. I was serious before. I meant what I said. I quit."

"Quit?" Baby makes a look of puzzlement. "Being governor?"

"Yeah. Hell, Valor is practically in charge now anyway, right? He can have it. I'm out."

"You can't quit!" Flicka squeals. "It's against the rules! You must play to the end!"

"I never agreed to this game, you annoying bugshit-crazy insect. I'm not even playing."

"What's she saying?" Baby asks.

"Something about the rules of the game."

"Hmm." Baby considers this as well.

"You did agree to play," Flicka insists. "We all agreed to play. You just don't remember it. But I can change that, you know. I can change *everything*."

41

And then… I'm back. I'm back in that house on that planet. And Delphi and Tycho are there—Dellie and Toby, rather. Standing in front of a cake lit up with small sticks of fire.

What is with these people and fire? It's like they live back in the dark ages.

They are talking, or maybe singing. But I can't hear anything. I can just see everyone's mouths moving in unison. There's a lot of people here now. Dozens of kids the same age as the twins. And lots of adults too. Parents, I'd guess.

"See," Flicka says. "I told you."

"Told me what?" I turn to her, pissed off now.

"This is your alternate life. And I can show you a lot more."

"Look, you time-travel people can try to trick me into doing your bidding, but I'm not gonna fall for it, OK? And seeing this… *family* isn't going to change my mind about anything. That guy is not me. That woman is not Corla. And those are not my kids. My kids are both back on Harem, all grown up. My Corla, if she ever *was* mine, is frozen in a cryopod on a security beacon floating in space. So these little side trips aren't going to work. I get it, OK? I lost. This could've been me, but it isn't. I'm a practical guy, Flicka. More rational than even Tray when it comes to decision-making. I'm not going to forget about Draden just because you dangle this fake shit in front of my face. Draden is my priority now. And this is how it should've been since the day ALCOR knocked him off that lift bot twenty years ago. You and SB19 can both fuck off.

42

I'm over it. I want my little brother back. He's all I care about now."

I stop talking, waiting for her rebuttal. Surely she has one. She's just a pushy beebot like that. But even though she's flitting around in my face with a frantic pace, no words reach my ears.

She's been muted. Like all the other people in this room.

Then… then the whole place shimmers.

I glance at the people, trying to understand which reality this shimmer belongs to. But they don't seem to notice. Then Other Corla turns to me. Like she sees me.

I hold my breath for a moment. We *are* soulmates, after all. And her gaze upon my face—her recognition—it's something I've craved for twenty-one years. Ever since we were forced to create children together in that creepy breeding ceremony.

And then, as if this whole thing wasn't weird already, something even stranger happens.

Corla diverges, creating a copy of herself. The copy takes a step towards me, smiling, reaching for me with one ethereal hand. "Crux," she says.

I can hear her. And she sees me.

"Corla?" I ask, hesitantly, reaching for her the way she's reaching for me.

But then the room shimmers again and I'm back in my office. I whirl around, looking for Corla. "What the fuck?"

Baby comes towards me. "What just happened? You froze for a moment. Like Veila cast her time-freeze spell on you."

"It wasn't Veila," I growl. "I was there. Again. Only this time… this time Corla was… I dunno. Real, Baby. She was real. Where the fuck is Flicka?" I spin around, looking for her. Spy her on my desk. "Take me back! She was gonna tell me something!"

Yeah. I get it. I'm coming off a little desperate. Not a good look when two minutes ago I was rambling on about how done I was. But she is my fucking *soulmate*. I can't help it. I can't turn away from her when she's right in front of me.

"I'll take you back after you free Delphi."

"You little…" I cross the office in three long strides, reaching for Flicka with an open fist, ready to squish her into submission.

But she flits off and flies up to a light fixture. "Delphi first. *Then* Corla."

"What if Corla's in danger? What if she needs me right now? What if this whole fucking game you're playing hinges on what she was just about to tell me?"

"It doesn't. I see through time. Don't worry. She'll keep. Delphi. First."

I can feel my blood pressure rising from the heat of anger that rushes through me. But this stupid beebot is loyal, I'll give her that.

"It's embarrassing," Flicka says. "How much convincing you need to come to your daughter's rescue. You should be ashamed of yourself."

"Should I? Should I really? She's the one who told me to butt out of her life."

"She's your *daughter*, Crux." I turn to face Baby and his stunning reversal as he continues. "I mean… isn't that what daughters say?"

"How the fuck should I know? I never had a daughter."

"Well, you do now," Flicka says. "And if you don't want to step up, then I'll just have to force you." And I swear to the sun, even though that beebot is only like ten centimeters long, I can see her eyes narrow down into two gold, glowing slits.

She is fucking serious.

I want nothing more than to challenge her. I'm like a thousand times bigger. If I could just get her under my boot, I could squish her flat.

Or not. Probably. But I'd like to try.

"Delphi. First," she repeats.

"Well." Baby sighs. "I don't know what she's saying, but she looks pretty pissed off. And Delphi does look pretty pathetic stuck in that spin node. Plus, once she comes out of it, she'll be upset that she was left behind. Because Jimmy has gone to Earth with Luck and Nyleena."

Oh. I glare at Flicka. "Way to bury the lede, dumb bot."

"As if," she squeaks. "As if that would've been the one thing that changes your mind. I tried to tell you there were extenuating circumstances. You just refused to hear me and went on your tirade about how done you were and how horrible your posh life has been fixing autocooks and water generators."

I rub a hand down my face, almost wishing someone would put me back in the time freeze. "Fine. I'll go check on Delphi. But I'm pretty sure I won't be able to do much. I don't control time. And you do control time and you obviously can't get her out."

45

"Just follow me," Flicka says, flying towards the air vent and disappearing inside.

I throw up my hands and look at Baby. "She's crazy."

"That's why we outlaw beebots here. You're the one who said she could stay."

Fuck it. "Where is this spin node again?"

"Museum level. Should I meet you there? Or would you like company?"

"Fuck you."

He disappears and I'm alone.

And you know what? I kinda like alone. Maybe alone hasn't been so bad?

But then I get out into the empty harem room and the eerie silence begins to sink in. Back in my office it was easy to forget that the whole station is frozen in time. But I would have to go back more than ten years to recollect another occasion when this room was empty.

And since that time hundreds of Cygnian princesses have come through here. Some of them left the moment their servitude was up, but not most of them. Most of them stayed on the station.

And all of them turned against me.

Maybe Luck and Nyleena did start the war, but those girls… they finished it.

They hate me.

I sigh as I get in the lift and take it down a few levels, then exit out onto the main concourse, which is also empty. Just random servo bots humming along cleaning the already gleaming black obsidian floors.

Just like that day when we arrived as kids. The seven of us, and Xyla, and ALCOR, and the bots. That's it. For six years we were all we had.

And then everything changed and it was never the same since.

I can't tell if this nostalgia I feel is longing or regret. But is there much difference between the two?

I get on the closest escalator and start heading down to level one twenty-two. It's not a fast-track to that level, I have to get off and change routes a few times. But I don't mind the time it takes to get there on foot, even though there are plenty of lift bots flying around.

Because I can think about my life, and my choices, and how I got here.

I wouldn't be able to change the escape from Akeelian System. That seems very set in stone. Corla and I didn't even know each other. Her mind was dead set on escaping. And what was I gonna do if I didn't leave Wayward Station going the opposite direction? Stay there and be experimented on?

No. That one choice was probably out of my control. But once we arrived here, I didn't have to take ALCOR's deal. Did I?

I mean, for sure, it would've been difficult to get anywhere else. I couldn't go back out the main gate. The entire Akeelian Army was on the other side. But there is a second gate to the Seven Sisters and that secret back door Baby was speaking of in the office. If I had known about it, it might've been an option.

What would I have done, if I had left? Maybe become a scavenger like Luck and Valor? But without the advantage of a sentient ship or the protection of

ALCOR, my life would've been pretty hard. I don't think I would've lived this long, that's for sure.

I would not have been a princess-hunter like Serpint and Draden or a bot-liberator like Jimmy. Or a virtual-reality nerd like Tray. No reason to hunt down princesses or liberate bots without the incentive of ALCOR. And I never had tech skills like Tray did.

In fact, the only skills I really do have are… political.

That's kind of fucking sad.

All those things I told SB19 back in that dream-state were correct. I am nobody without ALCOR, and Harem Station, and my brothers.

My job was done after I got them all here alive. That was it. My big moment. My one purpose in life. Over twenty-one years ago. Everything since then has just been filling up time.

But as I descend into the depths of the station the absence of people begins to bother me. It's not really like that first day at all. Because back then it was empty. There were no shops or shooting galleries, or screen houses, or arcades. No restaurants or boutiques.

And now all those things are on almost every level.

It's hard not to miss the bustle I've become accustomed to.

This actually feels more like that in-between time when everyone was gone except for me, and Tray, and ALCOR. After everything had been built, but there were no people to use it or make it all feel real.

The station like this—all empty and silent—it doesn't feel real. It feels like… what it is.

Another reality. One where no time passes.

And that creeps me out for some reason.

When I found out from Serpint that Valor and Tray were inside a virtual for four continuous days I almost didn't believe it. Four days. It's not impossible, but highly improbable that a humanoid body could survive four days of continuous gaming inside a pod.

I know this because Tray had a competition back in the early days of Harem Station. It was a gaming marathon and the person who could stay inside the longest was the winner. He and ALCOR watched the gamers very closely during this competition. Pulled them out the moment they went red. And it didn't take very long for people to start crashing. Not four days. Not even close. It was more like eighteen hours. In fact, if my memory serves, it was seventeen hours, forty-two minutes, and a handful of seconds. And we never did another one because the last few dozen players who all crashed around the twenty-six-hour mark were totally fucked in the head when they came out. They had lived hundreds of years inside. You don't just come back from that. We had to fly in special psychosurgeons for therapy just to make sure they could function in society again.

Four continuous days inside a gaming pod is bullshit.

Tray knew this. He was in charge of that competition. He knew damn well no one could survive for four days.

So I don't know who to trust. I think that's my main problem. When ALCOR was here, he was in charge. And even though I knew he was up to something and he was never going to share his true motives with me, if I just did what he said everything worked out.

49

JA HUSS & KC CROSS

Even dead Draden worked out. ALCOR fixed him up and bam. He was back playing war with Serpint a week later.

If ALCOR were here I would not have to worry about this shit. I could let him handle things.

I could give in.

But he's not. So I can't.

I have to deal.

Before I know it I'm on level one twenty-two. Baby and Flicka are both waiting for me in front of a kid who I'm pretty sure is probably Tycho. But I'm not completely sure because I've never actually talked to the boy.

He is tall, like me. Not filled out yet, but he probably will be. If he lives. He hasn't been woken up yet, so I take a moment to study my... *son*. He's got dark blond hair and his eyes are open, so I can see that they are violet. Not the same shade of pink and purple as mine are and the left one has a little blotch of cloudy indigo blue, which I don't have either. His face is not exactly like mine. But maybe I can see a little bit of Corla in his lips and maybe his nose?

Hmm. Weird.

I sigh as I walk up to Baby and Flicka. "Now what?"

"We'll need to move Tycho," Baby says. "The twins cannot be together. They are far too dangerous."

"Off the station," Flicka clarifies. "In a pod. He cannot wake up. Not until this is over. Maybe not ever."

"Well," I huff." I guess we know whose side you're *not* on."

"Don't judge me, Crux. It's not personal. And I was assigned to Delphi, not Tycho. She's the one I have to put first."

"Fine. How do we do that, then?" But even as the words are coming out of my mouth, a lift bot hovers over to us.

"I'll have him sent up to medical and put in a pod. We can deal with him after we see about Delphi."

Fine by me.

We enter the museum and find the whole thing offline. Just blank, empty gray walls. I shoot Baby a questioning look, but he just shrugs. "Valor thought it would be better if they kept it offline for now. The Littles have their own minds, after all. We could use fewer opinions around here, not more."

I put up a hand. "Hey, this is your show. Not mine. I'm done."

"You're not done." Flicka snickers.

I wonder if that sting ever wears off? Will I be forced to hear beebot chatter for the rest of my life? Thank the sun there's only one of them on this station. I can only imagine the nightmare of hearing a whole swarm of them talking. A chill actually runs up my spine just picturing that.

She leads the way through a maze of corridors. It's been a long time since I've been inside the museum. It was kind of fun back in the early days when Tray first got it up and running. The Littles were all newbie AIs so they were fun to fuck with. But that was a long time ago now and the novelty has worn off.

Still, it's weird seeing it empty. Everything about this trip down here is pulling me into the past when we were alone. I wanted people here so desperately bad.

51

And now I can't really even remember that craving or why it was so strong.

All I want now is peace. And this silence is not even a consolation prize. Because I know it's all fake. I need to make sure I'm off this station and on my way to find Draden before Valor and Veila unfreeze people. Because this feels like a trap. If everyone wakes up I'll be the one in charge again. I'll have to make all the decisions. I'll get stuck in my own personal time loop.

We stop in front of an open vault of a door. Something I never knew was here, that's for sure.

"Here it is," Flicka says. "She's in there."

I take a few steps forward. But when I look over my shoulder, she and Baby aren't following me. "Aren't you coming?"

"We can't," Baby says.

"Why not?"

"There's a shield around the room," he says. "We can't go in. I think it was put there by ALCOR. To keep himself out."

"Why would he do that?" I ask.

"I wouldn't know, Crux."

"Well, what am I supposed to do?" I look at Flicka for this part. "Tell me you have a plan. Because I sure don't. I'm only here because you made me come with you."

"The spin node is still up. It's just stuck in time. So you need to unstick it."

"OK. I'm going to assume you know what that involves?"

"No. But there has to be a way to make it spin again."

"No, Flicka. That's not how it works. I don't know much about it, but I do know that Luck was the only one who could—"

"Why do you always assume you're powerless, Crux?"

"What do you mean? I know where my power lies. In the running of this station. Which has nothing to do with starting up spin nodes."

"Isn't the spin node part of the station?"

"Flicka." I sigh. She's truly making me tired. "You said it yourself. I'm in charge of water generators, and airlocks, and autocooks. If your plan was for me to start that thing up and get her out, I can't help you."

She's flitting and buzzing around in front of me. But she suddenly lands on my shoulder. It takes every bit of willpower I have not to smack her with the palm of my hand. Beebots, man. They are just creepy little fuckers.

But I don't smack her. I turn my head and look down my nose at her small, golden, filigree wings. She looks back up at me with wide, glowing yellow eyes. "You don't get it. You. Are in charge. Of Harem Station."

"Yup. I'm the governor."

"You're not the governor, you idiot. You're God."

"Ha." I laugh. "Haha." I laugh again. "That's funny."

"I'm just going to spell it out for you, Crux. This place is *yours*. It belongs to *you*. You can do whatever you want, up to and including starting up that spin node in there. You could also start up the museum. All of the electronics on this station function on your authority. And that spin node is powered by something. Isn't it?"

"You're asking me?"

"What is she saying?" Baby asks.

"She says I'm in charge of all the electronics on the station so I'm technically in charge of that spin node. But this is news to me."

"Hmm." Baby considers this. "I have never looked into your permissions before. You were never a threat to me. And you are nothing if not fair and just. But now that I do look, she appears to be right. Your name is on the deed to the station."

"Well, of course it is. All our names are on the deed. That was part of the deal with ALCOR back in the day. We all have equal ownership in this place."

"No. Actually, the only name on the deed is yours. In fact, it was dated… Oh."

"Oh, what?"

"It was dated the day I was born. The day ALCOR made me to replace him."

"That was the day of Draden's memorial service. But… why would he do that?"

"Because ALCOR planned his death."

Both Baby and Flicka say this at the same time.

"Hold on, hold on, hold on, hold the fuck on." I am pressing the air with both hands as I say this. "If I can open that spin node then… can we go through it?"

"We can't," Baby says, "But… you?" He shrugs. "Maybe."

I glance down at Flicka, who is still sitting on my shoulder. "I can go through it?"

"I think you could. I think you could take Delphi with you, Crux. Put her where she's supposed to be."

"And where would that be, exactly?"

"Wherever that spin node was programmed to take them."

"But..." I look over my other shoulder, back at the way we came in. "What about Corla?"

"I thought you were done with Corla?" Flicka asks.

"That was before she saw me, Flicka. She saw me in that... wherever the hell that place was. I was in this dream-state. It might've been based on Earth, actually. And the Corla in that... scene? She split in two and the copy started talking to me. Directly to me, Flicka. And she said I should go wake up Corla. That seemed to be the priority."

"She's not your Corla, Crux." I glance down at Flicka again. "None of those Corlas are yours. As far as we know, your Corla is frozen in a cryopod on a security beacon. But that doesn't mean you won't find another one."

I hear all that. I internalize all of it too. But I'm stuck on the words 'as far as we know' for some reason.

Because... *is* that cryopod Corla mine? How do I know that? I don't. All I know is that she and Veila were on Cetus Station going somewhere. Somewhere Corla *wanted* to go.

Even though Corla herself told me, twenty-one years ago, that we would never meet again and if I ever did see her something had gone terribly wrong, I couldn't help it. I wanted to see her again. Even if it was just to curse her name for ruining my life.

But now that I know there's more than one world, and more than one Corla—is the woman frozen in the

55

cryopod the same girl who fed me an escape plan twenty-one years ago?

Serpint couldn't know one Corla from the next. Even today, knowing what we do about time, and other worlds, and all that bullshit. It might not be her.

What if Serpint got the wrong Corla?

What if... what *if* that Corla isn't mine?

What if these kids aren't mine either?

What if *my* Corla got away and never came back to this world? Never brought Delphi and Tycho back with her. Never went back to Cygnian System? Was never imprisoned in that pod?

What if she's an imposter? Or worse, a distraction? Didn't Valor say something about Brigit being a distraction for Tray?

I sigh and stop myself. Because the real Corla, the one I know *for sure* is mine—that sassy, bossy, confident teenager on Wayward Station—she was very clear that we were destined to be two ships passing in the dark. Star-crossed. Forever. And her warning— what if she knew there were other Corlas? And what if she told me that specifically so if I ever saw one, I'd know it wasn't her?

"What are you doing?" Baby asks.

"I'm thinking."

"Care to let us in on these thoughts?"

"No. Not really."

The only real take home from all this is... I don't know anything. That's about it. I can't know if Cryo Queen is mine. Even if I woke her up, I wouldn't be able to tell. I don't even know the woman. I have no clue who she is.

Hell, I don't know who I am, or what I'm supposed to do, or what I'm capable of, for that matter. I've been secluded on this station, with very few off-station trips, for twenty-one years.

I have been… hidden.

But from who?

And why?

"Fucking ALCOR," I mutter out loud. "What the hell is he up to?"

"I think you should try it," Baby says.

"Go turn that thing on and walk through it?" I laugh.

"I think you should try all of it."

"All of what?"

Flicka flies up off my shoulder and hovers right in front of my face. Not so close that I have to cross my eyes to focus on her, but very close. "Serpint and Draden can hunt things down. Jimmy can liberate things. Luck can walk through spin nodes. Tray can make new worlds. Valor can stop time, and if my predictions are correct, he can see through it, too."

"Well, I feel so much better now that you've pointed out how powerful they are compared to me."

"You're the glue, Crux. You hold them all together. Everything they can do, you can do better."

"You don't know that."

"Neither do you."

"What is she saying?" Baby asks.

"She says I can do everything my brothers can, but better."

"Well." He chuckles. "That's a relief."

"Was that sarcasm? Or…"

57

"Will you just go turn it on, for fuck's sake?" Baby snaps. "We're wasting time."

"Technically, we're not."

"Valor and Veila won't stay on her ship for long. They're going to be down here soon. And Veila cannot go through that node. We have no idea what her agenda is. You are the only pure one left, Crux. The only one without an ulterior motive."

"Not true," I say. "I want to leave to go find Draden."

"To *save* Draden. Not *use* him. Everyone else has conflicting loyalties. They have their soulmate to think about. You don't."

I should object. Because that's not really true. That Corla in the beacon is my conflicting loyalty. But... is she?

No. Not after these new thoughts.

I turn away and walk into the spin node room. I expect them to call out after me. Start barking orders, at the very least. But they don't.

And when I look back, I see why.

The door is gone. The wall is gone. There is nothing there. The place where I just entered is now nothing but bare, ragged rock.

I don't know what to think about that. And I have no clue if the doorway will reappear when I'm ready to go back, or if I'll just be stuck in here forever.

I sigh, rubbing a hand down my face, frustrated, and angry, and sad, and... tired. I'm tired.

I turn back to the spin node. It doesn't need to be turned on. It's on. Kind of.

Delphi is inside it, stuck half in and half out. Her arms are outstretched like the group of them were holding hands as they walked through.

The spin node itself looks like a shadow of a spin node. Like it's only half there. Almost transparent. And it reminds me of that trip we took through the ALCOR gate. That... left-behind feeling of in-between-ness.

Which is kind of the perfect word to describe my life since Corla got off that Cygnian ship and stepped on to Wayward Station.

I've been hovering in between this whole time.

And that's about to end.

I walk over to the controls. A whole panel of them that I've never seen before. Ever. And I have no clue what to do with them.

But then again, the fucker is already on, right? Maybe I don't have to do anything with them?

I turn back to the spin node and give it a good, hard once-over. It almost looks like it's made of some kind of gel-like substance.

Doesn't look like a spin node, that's for sure. At least any that I've ever seen.

But it does go somewhere.

Where though?

The codes. That's where. Those codes we came here with as kids. Those were all spin node coordinates.

Except I wasn't given one. Always and forever the outside man.

The code that's been programmed was either Jimmy's or Luck's. I would assume Jimmy's, since he was the one who was always fascinated with Earth. His had to lead to Earth. And the whole reason Luck was taking Nyleena through the node was to get her to Earth so she could have her babies.

Has to lead to Earth.

Well, no. We *think* it leads to Earth. It could lead back to Wayward Station for all we know.

And wouldn't that be poetic justice on a galactic-fate kind of level?

I walk through this thing and end up right where I started.

It's not out of the realm of possibility. It could happen. I have no sun-fucked clue how time works in the real, let alone inside a spin node.

I walk over to the spin node and stand there, trying to work up the nerve to touch it.

I glance at Delphi, but I can't see her face. The front of her body is facing her destination. I wonder for a moment if she's aware that she's stuck. Has she been looking out onto this new place for weeks? Months? Years? Lifetimes?

No idea how long we've been stuck in this time freeze.

She could be dead for all I know.

I reach out and press my fingertips against the node. It's very hard. Like the rock walls surrounding this room. Impenetrable. Which kinda sucks. Because I can't walk through that.

I turn back to the console and walk over there, studying the controls. There's a screen where Luck put in the coordinates.

Oh. Interesting. He used both coordinates. His *and* Jimmy's.

I'm not sure that was a good idea. But it's more than I have. Because I didn't come here with coordinates. I, apparently, have no other place to be.

God, that is so sad, I have to laugh.

But then that first dream of Corla comes back to me.

Dying was a very weird, confusing experience. After Luck... *killed me*, I went somewhere. Was it some afterlife? I'm not sure. But I was, well, maybe not awake, per se. But I was aware. And now that I have something to compare it to, I think I was in that in-between place—the place where SB19 was talking to me earlier.

Corla was there with me during my trip to the afterlife and she was repeating numbers. Over, and over, and over. Just long strings of numbers. No talking, just numbers. Like she was some kind of... *machine*. Only programmed with one purpose. Like a servo.

Nothing like the Corla who lives in that house with that other Crux and their kids. And nothing like the copy that split in two, either. She was something else.

Something very much less... real.

I close my eyes and pull the afterlife dream back up. It felt like a haunting. Like she was trying to drive me insane. Those numbers were rattling through my head for what felt like forever. Right up until the time I woke up. Then the constant string of numbers was gone.

I didn't think much about the numbers. The string was so long it felt random. But random things don't get repeated a thousand times, do they?

There was a beginning and an end. It took me a while to figure that out because there had to be at least sixty or seventy alphanumerics in the string of code. She probably cycled through the sequence more than a dozen times before I picked up on the patterns.

And I only noticed it because there was one particular section—two, three, five, seven, eleven, thirteen, seventeen—that caught my attention. The first set of seven prime numbers. I saw the pattern because they were the only low numbers in the whole sequence. The rest were things like seventy-five, and two hundred and two. Big numbers. And the letters, of course. The prime sequence—as good a name for it as any—always began after the first letter of the Akeelian alphabet. And the first letter of the Akeelian alphabet was always preceded by the last.

That's how I figured it out. It was zed, alpha, two, three, five, seven, eleven, thirteen, seventeen—then blah, blah, blah. On, and on, and on. Until I heard zed, alpha again.

It wasn't random. That's all I knew. But what if… what if that long string of numbers was actually a spin node destination?

That would be something fortuitous.

But can I remember them?

There was a pattern. Her voice had a cadence to it that gave the whole thing a rhythm.

I start humming it under my breath, playing it over and over. If I had known I was meant to memorize it when she was reciting it to me, I probably would've panicked. Maybe Tray could memorize something like that, but not me.

But to my surprise, the rhythm comes back to me and soon the numbers that go with the skeleton of the song manifest.

I open my eyes again and start typing them into the screen as I recite them in my head. A low hum begins to vibrate under my feet and then there's a great flash of blue light and the spin node comes to life.

And Delphi is gone.

"Shit. Shit, shit, shit. What did I just do?"

Did she go through? Did I kill her? Fuck! Flicka is going to poison me for sure!

I run my fingers through my hair and start taking deep breaths. But the crackling and flickering of the spin node is distracting. And I find it hard to keep my thoughts together. I suddenly have an overwhelming urge to walk through that thing.

I back away from the screen. Keep going backwards until I bump up against the console behind me. And I just stare at it.

Images begin flashing through my mind.

Corla. Little Delphi and Tycho. Then Jimmy! And Luck!

And the next thing I know I'm crossing the room. Heading towards it. I want to stop myself, take another deep breath and think this whole thing through, but my feet seem to be acting of their own accord. They carry me forward, the images of my people still flickering and flashing through my mind.

But before I can get a hold of myself I'm there. Reaching for the blue light in the middle of the ring with my fingertips.

The core of the ring is no longer solid. It's not exactly anything, actually. It looks a little bit like water that's part mist. And when my fingertips press against it, I don't feel anything. No heat or cold. No soft lapping of water. Nothing but the strong pull of... *time*.

I take one more step and then I'm through.

CHAPTER FOUR

For a moment all I see is fire. Not a big fire. Just a few lines of bluish, flickering flames. Then I see a metal grate over them and some kind of long cylinder-shaped object that might be food.

Sound enters the vision. Children laughing, screeching, yelling. But not in a bad way. It's not panic. It's... happiness, I think.

"So then I said, 'Dude, you're outta your fuckin' mind! If you make that putt I'll give you my boat for Fourth of July weekend!'"

I look over and see a man dressed up in a white shirt with buttons down the front. He's about my age, I guess. Clean-shaven. Kind of a tidy-looking man. He punches me in the arm, laughing.

I just stare at him. But then my mouth says, "Did he make it?"

"Fuck no, he didn't make it! Thank the baby Jesus, right? Can you imagine how pissed off Abbey would be if I lost our Fourth of July weekend trip in a golf bet?" He punches me again. "Anyway. What are you and Carla doing for the Fourth? Anything fun?"

I have no fucking clue what he's talking about. But beyond that, I have no fucking clue where I am. Or who the hell Carla is or why we're thanking some baby called Jesus.

However, my mouth does seem to have some insider information. Because it says, again, of its own accord, "Yeah. No. Fun and the Fourth of July do not go together."

"Ah, yeah. I forgot. Fuckin' parade."

"The kids love it," my mouth says. "But it's going to be hot as fuck on that float."

My friend—because I'm pretty sure that's who this guy is—slaps me on the shoulder. "The high price of being governor, right?"

"Governor." This time I'm the one talking. Not the other Crux I'm sharing this body with.

"Well," Friend says, "maybe you'll lose this year and you can put the politics behind you?"

"Yeah," I say. "Maybe I will."

"Right, Christopher." Friend laughs heartily. "You're already twenty points ahead. No chance, buddy. Sorry to be the one to break this to you, but you're stuck in this rut now. Gonna be governor until the term limits are up. Then it's the White House all the way." He points at me. "Don't forget your friends when you get to the top."

I think about that for a moment. But then Friend is pointing to the fire in front of me. "Hot dog's done. Better scarf it down before Carla needs you to deliver the big birthday speech."

I look down at the cylinder thing on the fire. Oh. Yeah. It's food. I guess.

I'm not eating that thing. It looks disgusting.

But my body seems to have other ideas. I pick the thing up with a pair of tongs, stuff it into an appropriately sized—bread-thing?—squirt some yellow and red stuff on top of it and then it's heading for my mouth.

Oh, fuck no.

The world around me blinks and flickers… and the next thing I know I'm making a speech in front of a whole group of people. The words are just spilling out of my mouth and I can't make them stop.

Calm down, Crux. It's fine. You're… a guest in this body? I think. Just let it do its thing. Take it all in. Soak up the scenery. Get your bearings.

I breathe deep, trying to get it together. But it's very disconcerting. Because I'm not controlling this body so there's no sensation of breathing. I look around, trying to distract myself, look up and get dizzy at the sight of a blue ceiling above me that seems to go on forever.

Not a ceiling, you idiot. A sky.

It's a sky. You're on a freaking planet.

Earth. I'm on Earth. That spin node really did take me to Earth. Only I'm not me… I'm some dude named Christopher.

Small hands pat my face and when I slide my eyes to the right I see little Delphi. I'm holding her in my arms, her long blonde hair a mess of wild waves, her cheeks bright pink, her mouth a wide smile.

"Happy birthday, Daddy." She pats my cheeks again. Everyone around us laughs.

"It's not my birthday, Dellie. It's yours, baby."

I can't tell if that's me saying the words, or him. Or… both of us.

"I'm four," she squeals.

"Me too!" another little voice says.

My head swings to my right and I see Corla holding Tycho.

Wow. This is weird. I recognize Corla from the last time I was here, but she looks so different. Was I here? Or was that a dream? Is this a dream? Or is it real? Did I pass out in the Harem Station museum? Is my body back there, lying on the floor?

Corla—or probably *Carla*, since that's what Friend called my wife back at the hot dog fire—is wearing a long, white, sleeveless dress. Her hair isn't silver, but blonde. Like baby Delphi's. Dellie. Whatever. And it's tied back in a neat bun that reminds me of how the serious girls wear their hair back on Harem.

She looks like she *could* be a princess. Like she has the potential. But she's clearly not. Her eyes aren't silver, they're just a light blue-gray. And there's no light coming off of her, even though it's clear she's very happy in this moment and emotions like that typically make a Cygnian princess glow at least a little.

I look out at the people. Then beyond them. It's a long, expansive garden that I'm sure Luck would love.

Hey. Is Luck here somewhere? I start scanning the crowd. And Jimmy?

But then the world flashes and flickers again. And this time I come back sitting at a desk, talking on a comm device.

"No. No, no, no! Jared! For fuck's sake. We talked about this! I'm looking at all the registered voters in the entire state right now. Call a meeting with…"

That's not me talking. It's Christopher. So I don't bother listening. The office is… quite nice. A lot nicer than mine on Harem, that's for sure. Very big desk with almost nothing on it. A screen sits on top of the desk and there's a database spreadsheet visible with what appears to be names of people.

But I don't stay long. The world flickers, and flashes, and flickers again. For what seems like a much longer time than before. And when I come out of it I'm looking down at Carla. She's in our bed back in that room where this dream or whatever it is first started when I was waking up from the time freeze.

It's dark. Late, I think. She mumbles something, then turns her back to me and goes back to sleep.

I slip in next to her. "Hey," Christopher says, placing a hand on her shoulder.

"Hmmm," she hums. "I'm tired, Chris. Just go to sleep."

Ooooh. Old Chris just got the brush-off.

I feel his frustration for a moment. And that's weird. So far I've been a passenger. But this feels more like a merge of some kind.

But he just sighs and turns his back to Carla, taking the hint.

Guess his life isn't as perfect as it looks.

I wait there for a while. Christopher goes still and settles. And pretty soon it feels like he's gone and I'm still here. Interesting. I don't feel tired. I sure as fuck don't sleep. And the world doesn't flicker or flash and take me somewhere else.

So I just lie there, thinking about where this place is and why I'm here. Also, how the hell do I get back? And where did Luck, Nyleena, and Jimmy go? Are they here? Or did they go somewhere else?

I push the covers off Christopher—or me, I guess, since he's gone now—and swing my legs out of bed. I look over at Carla, just to see if she'll notice and say something, but she doesn't. Either asleep or ignoring me.

Then I get up and leave the bedroom. The familiar hallway leading to the grand staircase is below me, and there's a light on in a room at the bottom. I descend the stairs and when I get to the partly open door, I peek inside and see an office. Not the same one I was in during the last flash, but there's a computer screen on the desk and that's what I'm looking for.

Because I remembered something about Jimmy.

He has another name. Yates. Jimmy Yates.

I think that's his Earth name and I'm gonna look him up and see if he's real. Then I'm gonna go find him. Because I have to be here for a reason, right? And it can't be to play governor.

For fuck's sake. Fate or destiny or whoever is in charge of that shit can't be that cruel.

And if it is, and I am here to play governor, I'm out. I'm not doing it. I could have that headache back home. Besides, I don't even know where I am. I wouldn't have the faintest clue about running this place.

I cross the room, sit down at the desk, and tap my fingers on the trackpad, hoping the computers in this world function like they do in mine.

The screen comes to life, then a flash of red scans my eye, and the lock screen disappears to reveal little icons.

It's not that different from the air screens we have on Harem. These people have to have a galactic web

70

to search for things, right? It takes me a little while to figure out which of the icons point to that, but eventually I do find a search engine.

I type in 'Jimmy Yates' and the AI controlling the search autofills the query with the additional words 'near me'.

And yes. There are a few Yateses to look for. There's a Lydia Yates, and a David Yates, and on and on, but no Jimmy. There is one Jim, though. And I wonder if Jim and Jimmy are the same thing? On Harem I know two guys with names like that. One is called Ryck and the other is called Rycket. But they are not the same name. They don't even come from the same humanoid race. So Jim and Jimmy might be two totally different names.

Jim comes with another name, though. Heather. Jim and Heather Yates.

As good a place to start, as any, I guess. I'm just about to tap the listing when I hear, "Daddy?"

I jump, startled, and find little Tycho standing in the doorway. His hair is all messy and his eyes look very sleepy. "Uh… yeah. What's going on?"

"I can't sleep. I don't feel well." He grabs his stomach like he's in pain and then starts walking towards me.

I have a moment of panic. Shit. What do I do? *Christopher? Hello? Your son is here and needs you!*

Christopher doesn't show. And a few seconds later Tycho is climbing up into my lap.

I freeze, unsure how to react.

He leans his face against my chest and wraps his hands around my upper arm.

71

JA HUSS & KC CROSS

I… pat his head. "OK. Well… how can I help you, Tycho?"

He huffs a laugh. "My name isn't Tycho. It's Toby." Then he shifts position and looks up at me. "You're funny, Daddy."

Mm-hmm. Yup. I'm hilarious. "Um… so you should probably get back to bed. It's very late."

"I can't. My tummy hurts."

"Daddy has work to do, Toby." Holy shit. Referring to myself as Daddy is freaking weird. "I can't play with you right now. OK?"

"I don't want to play. I want you to hold me. Rub my tummy."

Oh, my sun. No. I didn't sign up for this. I don't rub tummies. I don't know anything about kids. "I'm looking for a friend right now, Toby. It's really important."

But… is it? Is it really?

Do I need Jimmy? I mean, realistically speaking, even if he is here, what's he gonna do for me? He might not even know who I am. And even if he did recognize Christopher, he wouldn't know a damn thing about Crux.

So. I dunno. Maybe I'm not in a hurry? I could maybe hang out as Christopher for a while. Just take shit in. Kind of like a casual virtual vacation.

I could really use a vacation. I wonder if that friend of mine will let me take his boat out?

Hey, maybe I have a boat?

"Do we have a boat?" I ask Ty—Toby.

He looks up at me, his thumb in his mouth. His words barely make it past the thumb. "I like boats."

"Me too. I want to go on a boat. Float on an ocean. Do you have any idea how long it's been since I had a vacation?"

He shakes his head at me.

"Long. Time. Very long time. And it wasn't even a real vacation. Tray and I went to Gallent Station, which is in the Vacation Sector—not by Mighty Minions, though. Other side. Thank the sun." I chuckle. "But they had a beach there. They hired Tray to mess with their virtual. Damn. How long ago was that? Maybe six standard years. Anyway. I went with him because everyone was home at the time. Jimmy, and Luck, and Valor. Even Serpint and Draden were home. That hardly ever happens. So it was a lucky break for me and I got to leave the station. I can't say I really enjoy gate travel. It always makes me feel weird. Like my stomach is floating."

I look down at Tycho and he's smiling up at me. Sucking on his thumb a little. He nods his head. "Like the airplane."

"Airplane. Yeah. That's probably right. It was a nice beach, Tych. Like I'm talking that bright yellow sand. It's so yellow, it's almost gold. And there are red beaches too. It was pretty cool."

"I wanna go to a red beach."

"Yeah. Well." I chuckle. "This was adults only, if you know what I mean." Then I remember who I'm talking to. "Never mind that."

"Did I go?"

"No."

"Did Dellie go?"

"No. You guys weren't there."

"Did Mommy go?"

73

"No, she wasn't there either. It was just me. And Tray. But he was working. I was just tagging along."

"Who's Tray?"

"Oh. Well." I rub a hand down my face. "He's your... uncle, I guess. My brother. Not real brother, but we might as well be. We're definitely family."

"Where is he now?"

"I don't know. I kinda wish I did though. I don't know where any of them are. But that's nothing new. It's been like that for a long time now. Ever since ALCOR sent Serpint and Draden away."

I look down at Tycho, waiting for him to ask me more about them. But his eyes are closed. I keep talking anyway. "After Serp and Draden left, Jimmy and Xyla left too. Then Valor and Luck. Only Tray and I stayed behind with ALCOR. It kinda sucked, Tycho. I'm not gonna lie. I missed them pretty hard. And I was a little bit jealous, ya know? They all went to cool places and I was stuck on Harem. Then people started coming and my life got super busy and really complicated. So that vacation on Gallent Station was pretty nice."

"What are you talking about?"

I look up and see Corla standing in the doorway to my office. "Oh. I didn't know you were there."

She comes over to me, frowning. "What the fuck, Christopher?"

"What?"

"We discussed this! We had an agreement! We left that place behind and were never going to talk about it again!"

"What?"

"Don't play stupid with me, OK? I'm not in the mood. I heard what you said. How dare you tell him

74

those things? I cannot believe you even uttered those names. We made a pact!"

"Wait. You *know* them?"

"Know them? What the hell is wrong with you? They helped us get here!"

"Hold on." I stand up, taking Tycho with me. "You're Corla?"

"Shhh!" She hushes me, then looks over her shoulder, like she's afraid someone might be listening.

"No! You don't understand! I'm Crux, Corla!"

"Oh my God!" She grabs her hair. "I know who you are. Shut the hell up!"

"No, you don't understand. I'm not your Crux. I'm another Crux. I just got here. I walked through a spin node and—"

"I'm not listening." She covers her ears with her hands. "I'm not hearing this. I can't hear you."

"Stop it," I say, pushing one hand away from her ear. "Why are you being weird if you already know everything?"

She stares at me, open-mouthed. "We made a deal, Christopher. We never say a word. We cannot contaminate this world with that one or—"

A chime sounds in the hallway. Like a door chime. Corla and I both turn to look in that direction.

"Oh, my God!" she says, spinning in place. "Oh, my God. They're already here!"

"What the hell? Who is that?"

"It's them, you idiot! You just ruined everything!"

And then she pushes me. Two flat hands against my chest. With more strength and force than a woman her size should be capable of.

JA HUSS & KC CROSS

I go flying backwards. A flash of light blinds me and...

CHAPTER FIVE

I crash to the ground with the force of her shove.

But it's not hard. In fact, it's very soft. Very nice. Very warm.

"Oh, suns, yes! Yes!" A female voice. All breathy and sexy.

And… yeah. That's nice. Because I'm not back inside the spin node—I'm in a bed with a girl on top of me. She's wearing a mask. One of those party masks that only cover your eyes. And it's kind of dark in here, so I can't really see her face. But who cares about her face? Her tits are bouncing right in front of me.

"Oh, Crux."

And she knows my name. My actual name.

"Yes! Fuck me!"

But I don't really have to fuck her, because she's very busy fucking *me*. Her nails are gripping my bare shoulders, digging into my flesh as she bounces up and down in my lap. I have no idea where I'm at or if this is even real. But I don't even care. My life has been a fucked-up mess for so long I need this. I *really* need this.

I grab her hair and pull her head back, then wrap my other arm around her shoulders and pull her towards me until her chin is resting in the middle of my chest and her eyes are looking right into mine.

They glow for a moment. Just a little bit. And the relief I feel about being back in my own universe or time—or wherever the hell I am—it's real. That truth is a rush.

And oh, man. She feels good too. Her pussy is wet, and warm, and tight. And she's got long, light hair. I can't tell if it's blonde, or pink, or silver in this dim haze, but no fucks are being given about her hair color right now.

"You feel good, princess."

"Call me queen again. Please say it again!"

"Sure... sure. You can be my fuck queen."

Well, that's the first clue that this might not be real. I can talk dirty if I want to during sex. I just... don't. Because my queen—my real, actual queen—left me twenty-one years ago and we've had sex exactly one time. And during that one time I was kinda fucked up on... something. Not sure. Possibly my pending non-virgin status or maybe those creepy Akeelians had some kind of drug misted into the air of that ballroom. Or truth be told, it's most likely just because I was sixteen, was in the middle of a breeding ceremony, and had no clue what I was doing.

My point is, that's my voice, and I'm definitely inside this body, and sure, she's calling me Crux, so that's a good sign—but I just don't say things like 'You can be my fuck queen' to the rando women I've had settle my Akeelian male urges over the decades. I bang them. If they're a princess, they might get a fruity

78

cocktail beforehand and I might kiss them if I'm drunk. But basically, I fuck them twice to take care of my needs and then I kick them out.

"Yes!" the girl repeats. "I'll be your fuck queen! We'll rule this universe together!"

Well… no. She's getting *waaaay* ahead of herself here.

I'm not sharing my throne with anyone but Corla.

I flip her over on the bed so she's on her back now, and I cup my hand over her mouth. She's already panting hard, so this makes her eyes go wide behind the mask when she figures out breathing isn't so easy anymore.

She struggles underneath me. Squirming and wriggling. But I'm a lot bigger than this girl. And a lot heavier too. She doesn't have a chance.

"Be still," I growl into her ear. Then I bite it. She squeals into my palm, still wriggling.

I ease up off her, sit back on my knees, and she sucks in air. Then I flip her over again, push her head into the pillow, knee her legs open, and enter her from behind.

She squeals and jerks. But now I've got her right where I need her. She's too busy concentrating on breathing to talk about being my queen. And let's face it, the only thing she's thinking about right now are my two massive cocks inside her pussy.

Hmm. Both cocks are out. Which means this is our second go.

But that's good. I like that. In a few minutes I'll come and then it'll be over and I can kick her out. Then I can see where the fuck I'm at and figure out why I'm here.

And if I can even get home.

I force all those thoughts out of my head. My life has been so fucked up for so long, now is not the time to remind myself of that.

Right now all I want to do is forget.

And whoever this girl is, she feels good. I can't deny that. She's all sweaty now from her struggle. Her back is slick with it and she smells sweet and musky at the same time. Typical of princesses in the middle of lust. But the best thing—the thing that really gets me excited about sex with a stranger—when I lean down and kiss her right between the shoulder blades, I taste salt.

I don't know why that turns me on, but it does. Everything about this girl, and the sex, and the way I popped into the middle of it—it's all just... *hot*.

I grunt a little as I thrust inside her, deeper than I was just a moment ago. She bucks her back, gasping for air. I grab her hair again and wind it up in my fist, tugging on it hard.

Maybe I'm being too rough with her. But she's not telling me to stop. So I keep going. I take it one step further and place my hand flat in the middle of her back, holding her still beneath me.

Her legs start kicking and that's the signal, I guess. She's about at her limit. So I lift my palm up, my cocks throbbing inside her, my lust rising with each forward thrust. She struggles, then quickly turns over. Making my cocks slip out of her.

"What the fuck?" she pants, both of her hands flat on my chest, pushing me back.

"You don't like it?"

She breathes hard for a few moments. "I'm not saying that. But I don't like being held down."

In one quick motion I have both her wrists in my grip. I raise her arms over her head and push her hands into the pillow, holding her down again. "Well, I do."

"Don't be a *dick*, Crux. It's a bad look for you."

I grin. And then, without letting go of her hands, I lean down, grab her mask in my teeth, and pull it up.

"What the hell? That's—"

I kiss her to make her shut up. I kiss her hard. And when she kisses me back, she opens her legs again. Inviting me in.

So I take that invitation seriously and thrust both my cocks back inside her, pumping hard again.

We continue the kiss and she bites my lip. Hard enough to draw blood. I don't care though. I *am* being a dick to her. I feel like twenty-one fucking years of frustration have finally caught up with me. I don't know where I am or who she is, so I'm sorry she's being forced to bear the brunt of my disappointment. If she wants to make a point with that bite, she can make her fucking point.

And when she realizes I'm not going to punish her for that little act of defiance, she relaxes underneath me. Becomes soft and compliant.

That's the part I like best about sex. The way I can bully them into compliance.

And then her legs wrap around my hips and she begins to move with me.

That's the signal I always wait for. That moment when they give in. Not give up. I don't mistake her lust for defeat.

She's just into it.

81

I lean down on top of her, acutely aware of how small she is compared to me. How little, and slight, and thin, and yeah... weak.

But I want her to come. She has to get something out of this, right?

I slip a hand underneath her and start playing with her ass. She's so wet that her juices are practically spilling out of her pussy. And she must be into the ass play because the moment my finger enters her, she goes still and moans.

"You're a sun-fucked asshole," she pants. But it's done. And she says nothing else after that. Because she's too busy wailing in her climax.

Her body lights up. And it's not just some random glow, either. It's fucking spectacular. White light leaks through the pores of her skin and I know that if her eyes were open right now, she'd be aiming beams of light at me.

I come. I come hard. Grunting and pushing myself deeper and deeper inside her.

But in that moment I can see her clearly. Her glow illuminates her face and...

I let out a long breath. "Corla?"

Her eyes open. And I was right. She's aiming her light at me. I have to close my eyes to avoid the sting of brightness.

She closes them again and the room darkens enough for me to look at her.

"Corla," I pant, unable to believe my eyes.

"Fuck you," she says, pushing me off her.

And I'm so stunned, I don't resist. Just topple off to the side. She turns her back to me and I... I'm suddenly at a loss for words.

Where am I? On Harem?

"ALCOR?" I whisper out loud, hopeful. *Please. Please, for the love of the sun, be here!*

But there's no answer.

I look at Corla's back. She's still glowing a little. The light she emits makes her whole body glisten in the returning hazy darkness.

"Fuck you. I'm going to sleep for a minute because I'm tired. Don't wake me up."

"Listen—"

"I said," she growls, "I'm going to sleep for a minute. I'm fucking exhausted after that light show. I just told you I didn't like it."

"Oh." I'm… a little bit speechless. And now I feel bad. Guilty, actually. Because if I had known it was Corla I'd have been… gentle.

Maybe. Or maybe not. Maybe I'd have been even more of a brute?

Maybe I'd have wanted to punish her for leaving me alone to fight this war by myself twenty-one years ago.

Maybe I'd have fucked her unconscious. Or unleashed a real light show.

I don't fuck a lot of princesses. I'm their boss in the harem. Feels a little… exploitative. But some of them, when they're released from their servitude, want to fuck me. And when that happens I let them. So I know what a real light show looks like.

I have fucked a silver princess exactly one time. The day of the breeding ceremony back when Corla and I were sixteen. And none of the princesses in my harem could compare to Corla in her state of unbridled virgin passion.

But the reds put on a good show.

This wasn't Corla at her best. It was still pretty nice, don't get me wrong. But if I had known I had Queen Corla underneath me I would have made her come harder.

I sigh and put my hands behind my head, staring up at the ceiling. Her glow is dying down now, but not completely gone.

This is not Harem Station. I know that for sure. The ceiling is too low and there are water stains on it. Like the plumbing is bad on this station. Not even the worst apartments in the lower levels have a ceiling like the one I'm looking at.

But it *is* a station. I know that for sure. I can feel the slight centripetal force of artificial gravity. I've lived in a spin my entire life. It's sort of comforting. And I can hear the environmental units humming in the walls. When you live on a station in the middle of the deep dark, that constant hum is something you're always checking for.

That hum is *life*.

Corla breathes softly next to me and I take a moment to fully appreciate the luck of this new situation.

I know I'm not supposed to be here. I get it. I'm inside the fucking spin node. And maybe this isn't real, but this moment feels real enough for me. It feels like a fucking gift.

She is sleeping in a bed next to me. And if I get a choice of staying here or going back… well, I'm fucking staying.

Twenty-one years ago I met my soulmate. We took each other's virginity. And then we went our separate ways.

Star-crossed. For all eternity.

I didn't like the idea back then but let me tell you, I like it a whole lot less now.

I'm not giving her up.

I'm not leaving.

I'm not going back.

And go back to what, anyway? Luck's violence? Jimmy's crazy obsession with Earth? Nyleena's doomed pregnancy? The threat of Delphi and Tycho exploding the universe? Valor and Veila controlling time and taking over my station? Tray gone or... something? Draden—dead or not, he's not Draden anymore. Serpint is really the only brother I have left. If Corla wasn't in bed next to me I might go back for Serpint. And I like Lyra. She came in rough but she's probably the most reasonable princess I've ever met.

But not even Serpint and Lyra can lure me away from Corla. She is my destiny. My soulmate in the most literal sense of the word.

I sigh and look over at her. Back still to me. Her ribs expanding and contracting in a slow, even rhythm.

She's clearly exhausted now, but she will wake up eventually. And then...

I allow myself a smile. I can't actually remember the last time I smiled. I can't think of a single thing that has made me smile in a long, long time.

But she does. That smile comes out just thinking about the moment when she wakes up and turns over. When we finally get to talk again. And I kiss her. And fuck her any time I want.

85

She's mine, right? Even in this world. That's why we're here. We're a thing.

Whatever universe this is—whatever time this is—the star-crossed curse has been lifted.

That's the only thing that matters.

And yeah, that last little interlude in time we were together too. But I wasn't really me and she wasn't really her. We were some other version of us. Living on some sun-fucked planet.

And no, this isn't Harem Station. But we're *on* a station. We can *get* to Harem. We can find ALCOR. We can... go home. Maybe. But even if we can't—even if there is no Harem... who cares?

I have her.

She's all I've ever wanted.

Her glow suddenly diminishes. And I know from experience that when she wakes up she'll need to replenish her light with a fruity drink. So I swing my legs out of bed, stand up, and say, "Lights."

Nothing happens, which I figured, since this station seems like a shithole. But it was worth a try. I feel around on the night stand until my fingers bump a small light and it glows. Just enough for me to find my clothes hastily discarded on the floor.

I pull on my tactical pants, boots, and shirt. Then get up and go looking for the autocook so I can get my princess some juice.

But when I open the door, there's no other room to this place. It's just a hallway with a few random people hanging about.

One guy is leaning against the wall—a big dude with a shaved head and glowing bioluminescent tattoos covering his arms. He glares at me. But I ignore him.

Just let the door close behind me and head out towards the noise and bustle of the interior of the station to go find some juice for Corla.

Clearly this place has no air screens but I have a wristband on. So I pull up my accounts to see how many credits I have.

Hmm. Not much. Which sucks. And worries me too. Because if I'm poor… then who the fuck am I in this world?

Not Crux of Harem Station, that's for sure.

Still, there's enough in there. And I must own a ship or how did I get here? Not that I'd be able to fly it—but hey, hold on. Maybe Crux in this world has mad flying skills?

I smile at that as I come out into the central district of the station.

"Ugh, suns," I mutter under my breath. Because I forgot that most stations are shitholes with no huge open space connecting all the levels.

The ceilings are so low it makes me want to duck. It's a stupid reaction since I am in no danger of hitting my head on anything. I'm just not used to it.

But there's lots of people. Mostly outlaw-looking types, which I'm OK with. And from where I stand there's a few bars, a restaurant, and an arcade.

I head towards the restaurant because even though all the bars on Harem serve fruity drinks for the princesses, I doubt you can find tushberry juice in a bar here.

"Hey!" someone calls behind me. It takes me a moment to realize that the voice belongs to Corla. "Hey, you, asshole!"

"What?" I laugh as I spin around and find her pulling on a long-sleeve sweater as she comes towards me. That big dude with the light tattoos is following her.

"What the fuck, Crux?"

"What?" I glance at the big dude. Because it's pretty clear they're together.

"You left without paying."

"Wh-what?"

"Pay-ing." She says it slowly. Like I'm some kind of idiot.

"Paying for *what*, Corla?"

"The *sex*, you dumbass!"

"What the fuck—"

But that's as far as I get. Because the big dude punches me in the face and I go flying backwards. Drifting through time. Falling right back into the spin node again.

Paying for sex.

Those words roll around in my head as the darkness takes over and then...

CHAPTER SIX

I land hard, knocking the breath out of me. And the dumbest thing about this is that all I think about in that moment is... why do I have to breathe if none of this is real?

And then I'm just pissed. I'm pissed at the spin node, and the universe, and whoever the fuck is in charge of this shit show.

Because I could've made that work. I had her! I fucking had her in my arms!

Before I even open my eyes my hands come up and grab my hair. I want to scream.

No. I want to give the fuck up.

I'm so done. So fucking tired of this game I'm in.

"I fucking quit! OK? You happy now?" I yell it. "I'm done!"

"Oh." A small, soft voice. "There you are. We've been looking for you."

I sigh, afraid to even open my eyes and see what the fuck is happening now.

"Are you... OK? Did you fall?"

"Did I *fall?*" That's the understatement of the century. *Yeah, bitch. I fell through time. Again.*

"Here, let me help you up."

A hand as soft as the voice grabs me by the arm and even though I don't want to, I open my eyes to see what the hell. A girl stares back at me. Young. Very young. Like... Corla, age sixteen. But this is not Corla.

Of course it isn't.

We're star-crossed. Never gonna happen, Crux. Just give up now.

Believe me, if I knew how to give up now, I would. I'm so over it. I'm never going to win. I'm never going to see her again. Hell, I'll probably never get back to Harem Station to thaw her frozen ass out. I should've done that the minute Serpint brought her home. Immediately. So what if the Cygnians came for us? At least it would be over by now. Either we'd have won, or we'd have lost. But it would be over. And I wouldn't be tripping through time on this crazy, inexplicable ride that seems to have no other purpose than to remind me of all the ways I lost.

She was a whore.

A fucking whore on some sun-fucked shitty station.

And I was... hell if I know. Probably just as messed up as she was. I was paying for sex. And it obviously wasn't the first time. She knew my name. But I meant nothing to her. I was a... client.

What is the point of all this? Like... just why? Why do I have to see this shit?

Am I supposed to learn something? Do something? What? "What the fuck do you want from me?"

"Oh," the girl says again. "I'm sorry. I thought it was explained to you."

I look at the girl. She's so clearly a princess, it hurts my heart to look at her. Her long, silky hair is bright pink. And her skin glows faintly. Just a shimmer, actually. She's wearing a long, flowing gown. Nothing heavy. Not a ball gown. A light drape of thin pink and cream fabric that covers her up completely, but at the same time exposes parts of her that make the whole picture even more alluring than if she were naked.

Her throat is bare. One hip is uncovered. The opposite leg from mid-thigh down. Both arms are covered by loose swaths of fabric. She has a silver headband on that sparkles in a stray beam of light that filters through a kaleidoscope of leaves covering the high boughs of tall trees.

She is the perfect royal specimen. Like she drinks tushberry juice every hour, on the hour. The picture of princess health.

She tucks a long strand of pink hair behind her ear and smiles at me, extending her hand so that the fabric covering her arms falls away. "Let me help you up. I'm sorry if things were not explained properly. I can answer any questions you have."

"Great," I say, taking her hand, then feeling stupid for letting this slight waif of a girl help me to my feet.

It's only then that I realize I have no shirt on. Just a pair of loose white pants. No shoes, either. And all of a sudden I feel like some royal male concubine. Some lucky foreign man in one of those fantasy princess scenarios the Pleasure Prison on Harem Station is constantly running so all the outlaws who can't afford to buy a few hours with a real princess can get their fill.

91

"Uh…" I say. "Well, thanks." I pull my arm from her grip.

"The queen is expecting you. I don't want to keep her waiting. But… if you're still unsure… it's better to be late than confused. Don't you think?"

"Umm… OK."

She smiles at me. "I'm not sure how you got out here. Were you…" She pauses. "Did you change your mind? The queen will ask you before the ceremony begins. You must consent. That's the only way it will work."

"What will work?"

"The breeding ceremony."

I reach up and run my fingers through my hair. "For fuck's sake." Here we are again. Is this the purpose of this little trip through the spin node? To be constantly reminded that there is only one reason for Corla and I to be together and that's for sex?

I hold up a finger. "One question."

She smiles. And glows a little. "Ask."

"What's the queen's name?"

The girl giggles. "Corla, of course."

"Of course. That's… fantastic."

"She really likes you."

"She does?"

"Yes. She's very excited about this pairing."

"Pairing?" I deflate a little. For a moment there I forgot that I'm sun-fucked star-crossed and had a sliver of hope that maybe, just this once, we were really gonna get our chance.

"Breeding season." The girl chuckles. "It's all very confusing, I know. I mean…" She sucks in air through her teeth. "Trust me, I've lost track of so many things already. And we're only halfway through."

I suck in some air too, wondering what kind of kaleidoscope of psycho this trip will turn into.

The girl is staring at me. Almost mesmerized.

"What?" I ask. "Why are you looking at me like that?"

"Your... eyes." She practically moans the words. "They're so very, very... violet."

"Oh," I say, rubbing a hand down my face. "Yeah. Them."

"I don't think I've ever quite seen a pair so... vibrant."

I shrug. "They're not like Serpint's. Or Valor's. He's got nice eyes. Everyone thinks so. I used to call him pretty boy when he was younger."

The girl cocks her head, confused.

"Never mind," I say. "So what can I expect from this... pairing? Is there a ball? Do I need a creepy red and black suit? Will everyone be watching to make sure I... you know, get her pregnant? Will a bot fly around recording it? How's this go down?"

The girl blushes bright pink. Her eyes even glow brightly. "Well... we'll all be there." She giggles. "I'm not sure we'll be watching. But if you want me to watch closely, I can. If you maybe want a... report afterward on your... performance. And I know you all think you're going to impregnate the queen, but don't get your hopes up, Crux. That's why there's five more men after you today."

Five. More. Men. After me. Today.

"How long has this been going on?"

"Oh…" The girl chews her lip. Like she's thinking. "I've lost count. Weeks, though. I do know we're about halfway." She perks up. "But who knows, maybe you will be the one? Then we can all go back to our regular lives tomorrow. Not that I'm complaining," she adds quickly. "It's fun. Don't get me wrong. But I'm starting to get pret-*ty* tired." Then she squeals and covers her mouth. "I can't believe I just said that."

Oh. OK. I think I get it. "How old are you?"

"Seventeen. It's my first year."

"And when we get to wherever the fuck we're headed right now… you'll be…?" I'm not quite sure how to finish that question so I just let it hang there.

"Yes," she says, then looks down shyly. "I'm your helper. Oh, but don't worry. I have a whole team to help me. We're all yours."

"All mine?" And I'm not proud of this. Like at all. But my cock starts to get hard.

"The first time. She only needs you for the second time. Both…" She looks down at my groin. "You know. She needs… both. That's how it works with you Akeelian men. Right?"

"Right," I say. "But… what if both of my guys pop out?"

She frowns. "Oh, no. Please, do not tell me you jerked off while you were missing in the forest! Oh, my sun." She glances down at my groin again.

"No, no, no," I say, putting up a hand. "I didn't." At least I don't think I did. No real way to know for sure, is there?

"She'll know. We do the royal test. So we'll know, Crux. If you… tugged on it to try to fool her."

"Royal test?" Well, that's a bit of fun news there. Looks like this little spin node scenario is all about teaching me humility. All those princesses I've subjected to the royal test over the years. Now I'm suddenly in their little satin slippers.

"Yes." She looks over her shoulder. "I need to get you back for that. Like now. Or we'll be late. All the girls are ready and…" She shakes her head and chews on her lip. "It's not easy being this close to you while still maintaining my composure. So… let's go, OK? Before I lose control."

I'm turning this little glow-show on.

I can't help it, I grin at her. And I feel the light in my eyes come pouring out.

She covers her eyes with her forearm and gasps. "Don't do that. Just hold it in a little longer." Then she wraps a swath of fabric around her hand and uses it to protect herself from feeling my bare skin as she takes me by the arm and starts tugging me back the way she came.

I trip over various twigs and leaves and this is when I realize I'm not on a station. We have some big forests on Harem. So being in the woods isn't a dead giveaway that we're not on a station.

But the feeling of spin is missing. And there is no hum of environmental units beneath my feet. This is a planet.

Not just any planet. A planet filled with Cygnian princesses.

And one queen.

I'm on Cygnia.

That realization might be the most jarring thing to happen since I walked into the spin node.

I. Am on. Cygnia.

No one who is not a Cygnian ever steps foot on their home planet. Ever.

Not even the Akeelians they were allied with back on Wayward Station ever went to Cygnia.

I look around. Take it all in with a little more focus. Because it's simply… breathtaking. The trees, the sunlight, the greenness of it all. And the air. Suns, the air. Now that I know where I'm at, I can tell how pure it is. How invigorating. Cool, and clean, and maybe even a little bit intoxicating.

The girl leads me into a clearing and I almost stop to take it all in.

The view astonishes me in several ways at once.

There is an actual view—a light gray castle nestled in the mountains off in the distance. Probably made of some kind of stone. A mist floats lazily among the different layers of hilly elevation. It's something you see in books, or vids, or virtuals. Something that up until now I thought was pure fantasy. There is a soundtrack of birds and wind through leaves. Small animals rustle in the thick branches of the understory.

But that's not the only view.

Girls. Everywhere.

And all of them are pink princesses.

I've never seen so many pink princesses in all my life. And this is coming from the master of the only princess harem outside Cygnian System.

But we never had pinks until Lyra. And right here in front of me there are too many to count. Pink hair and glowing skin everywhere I look.

I stop in my tracks even though my chaperone is still tugging on me to make me follow her.

She turns towards me. "Is everything all right?"

I draw in a deep breath of fresh air. And now that I'm thinking about it, it's so, so different than the air on the station. Nothing like it at all. Not even close.

Is this really how Cygnia is? None of my princesses ever had anything good to say about it. So I'm having trouble merging this fantasy reality with the one that's been handed down to me for more than three decades.

"Crux?"

"Sorry. I'm just a little overwhelmed."

She squeezes my arm, still gripping me through the sheer fabric of her flowing gown. "I understand. Where you came from... well, I've heard it's pretty horrible in the Akeelian System. Sometimes I feel bad about how we keep you guys prisoner here. But then I know we're giving you a better life than they did." She hesitates. "We are, aren't we? I mean, I know you're a sex slave. And everything about that is wrong. But we saved you, right?"

I don't know what to say. But it feels very much like my own words being thrown back at me. Because don't I feed my princesses that same line when they find themselves on my station and in my harem?

I mean it when I say it. Harem Station isn't a bad place if you're a runaway Cygnian princess. It's not like we ever abducted them from their home. Every single one of them came in as someone else's prisoner looking ragged and sick. I nursed them back to health with juices and fruit.

"Come on," the girl says. "There's food and drink for you. That will make you feel better."

Yeah. Weird. It's like reality has flipped places. I went from being the captor to the captive.

"We don't have much time," she continues, leading me over to a table. There's bottles of ale and thick, meaty sandwiches. "So you'll have to recharge quickly."

"Recharge?"

"I'm sure you depleted your glow a little back there in the woods. Your eyes were quite bright. And the queen will want you in top condition when she meets you. So please, just drink something at least. I'm going to go get my team and then I'll be right back. Please," she pleads with me. "Don't run. We'll definitely be late if I have to chase you down again. And there's truly nowhere to go, Crux. There is no way out until we let you."

I frown at that, wondering what it means. No way out.

But she opens a bottle of ale and puts it in my palm, closing my fingers around it with a smile. "I'll be right back."

She turns in a swirl of sheer, flowing fabric and darts off across the green lawn towards a large white tent.

I take a sip of the ale and swallow. It's really good. Like… very good. But then I try to take in the whole clearing. There are a lot of tents. And so many pink girls. Almost none of them are paying any attention to me. There are other Akeelian men though. With just a quick glance around I can count ten.

None of them are my brothers.

And each of the men seem to have their own team of pink princesses who dote on them. Some are getting hand jobs like this is no particular big deal. Just a little fluffing up before the big moment. Two of them are being rubbed down with oil, several princesses working on them at once.

It's like a fucking sex fantasy in the Pleasure Prison.

In fact, I think we have one sorta like this. I don't go in there much. Hardly ever anymore. But I have a vague recollection of Tray telling me about some scenario similar to this one.

Am I in a virtual?

I can't tell. And that's new. Because there's always something a little off about the Pleasure Prison when you're in there. Even if it's just your stats being shown in the vision screen over your virtual eyes letting you know how much time has passed and how much time you have left before you'll be pulled out.

There are no stats in my field of vision. No shimmer in the sky off in the distance.

Everything about this place feels real.

The girl returns with a hyponeedle in her hand. She sees me looking at it. "Don't worry. It only hurts for a quick moment. Then it's all over. We just need to make sure you are who you say one final time before we let you near the queen." She pricks my skin with the needle and there is an immediate and acute sting, then she deploys the hypodrug and a hot burning sensation runs up my arm.

"Fuck," I say, clenching my teeth.

But she brought a friend with her. And that girl—who looks very much like the one who's been taking care of me—begins to massage my shoulders. One hand slides down my stomach and I feel my cock stiffen inside the loose white pants as she slips two fingers inside the waistband.

I forget about the sting. In fact, I drift off a little with the new sensation.

"That's it," the first girl says. "Just let it take over."

They drugged me. That wasn't a test. Or maybe it was, how would I know? But there was definitely some kind of analgesic in that needle cartridge.

I should be pissed about that but I can't really muster up anything but compliance.

The next thing I know I'm surrounded by them. All the pink princesses have their hands on me.

The girl with her hand in my pants says, "Just one cock. He didn't mess anything up."

I catch a few more words from other girls. "He's good." And "She's ready." And "Let's go."

Then I'm being walked forward. Back into the trees. The girls are all around me. Touching me everywhere. My ass, my cock, my neck, my back, my shoulders, my chest.

There is not a single place on my body that doesn't have a hand caressing it.

We walk into a clearing and now I can barely manage to stay on my feet.

"It's OK," the first girl says.

Someone is removing my pants, hand caressing me all up and down my legs.

I'm very fucking hard now. And I'm not gonna lie. This is like a dream come true.

I have been around my share of princesses, but they were never mine. They were just employees.

These girls feel like mine. Like they only exist for me.

Wait. I shake my head and take a deep breath. I'm here for Corla. This is a breeding ceremony. She is my soulmate. We are going to connect.

Again, I vaguely realize, then chuckle. Because I just fucked her very hard in the last... whatever the hell this is. Dream? Glimpse? Who knows?

Who cares?

"That's it," one of the girls says. I'm lying down now. One girl is already sucking me off. I reach down and grab her hair, winding it up in my fists.

Another gently pries my fingers off her and the hair falls out of my grip. "No, no, no big man. Be nice now," she chastises me gently.

But I don't even care. Because another girl straddles my chest and then eases her pussy right up to my mouth. I grab her hips and begin to lick her. She tastes like a sweet slice of tushberry fruit.

I'm just starting to really get into it when they stop. The girl gets off my face and the one sucking me lets my cock slip out of her mouth.

I blindly reach for them—and I do mean blindly. Because I can't even manage to open my eyes now. I'm in the middle of an intoxicating sex-induced fever dream.

Or drug-induced. Could go either way.

"Move away, girls," I hear someone say.

Corla. Oh, for sun's sake. It's her. Finally. My Corla.

"Let me get a good look at him."

I want to open my eyes and see her. Just gaze at her as she lustfully takes in my body. It's very hard though. My eyes do not want to cooperate. But I concentrate. This might be my last chance. How do I know if I'll come out of this and pop into another opportunity with Corla?

Because that's what this has to be. I don't know what the spin node is doing, but it's quite obvious that I'm being cycled through different scenarios with Corla. It's all about Corla.

I force them open and all I see is a bright mass of silver-white light.

Yes. She is mine. She is all mine.

And in that moment my second cock emerges and hardens. Almost instantaneously.

"What in the sun god's name—did you girls already bring him to climax without my permission?"

There is a chorus of denials.

She grabs the girl who caught me in the woods by the arm and throws her aside. And that's when I get my first real glimpse of my queen.

"No," I say, barely audible. "No," I say again. "Not you. You're not her."

"Shhhhh," Queen Corla says, bending down towards me. "What do you have here, Crux? Hmm? What did you do to make your second cock pop out like that before his time? Is this a trick?"

There's another chorus of denials from my fluffer team. Something about tests, and assurances.

I regret opening my eyes. I want to close them again. Like... *now*. And forget I ever saw the thing hovering over top of me. Because she sounds like Corla, and they are calling her Corla, but she is... she is *not* my queen.

She is old and wrinkled. Hundreds of years old by the look of her. And her face looks like it's melting.

Thick, deep wrinkles cover her entire body. And I can see them all because she's naked.

"What happened to you?" I blurt.

"What?" she snaps. "What did he just say?"

My team of girls begins to back away from her.

"Get over here," she commands them. "Help me. This one might just be the one Akeelian we've been waiting for."

"No," I say, even though I know I am that man.

She holds her hands out and the girls support her as she climbs on top of me. Once she's settled on my hips, she takes both my cocks in her hand and begins to pump them.

"You're not her," I say. "You're not her! We're the same age!"

She laughs. Throws her head back and laughs. Her neck is nothing but layers of loose skin. Then she stops abruptly and stares down into my soul. I feel my eyes glow bright when her white eyes lock with my violet ones.

She's still squeezing both my dicks, gripping them in her dry white palm, and I suddenly want to vomit.

"So you've heard the myths, hmm?" She strokes my cheek with the tip of her too-long fingernails. "About the star-crossed soulmate they made for me in Akeelian System."

"No," I say. "It's not true. You're not her. You can't be her. We are the same age. I know this. I saw you. We were together."

She laughs under her breath. "This one is quite talkative."

"We gave him the full dose," my girl says. "I promise you, we did. We checked him."

She reaches over and pats the girl on the cheek. "It's fine, dear. You did well. This is the one we've been searching for."

"He is?" The girl's voice is shaky.

"Yes," the Corla-thing purrs. Then she looks at me as she raises her hips and begins to push my cocks towards her entrance.

I struggle, but the team of girls flit into action and hold me down.

"No," I say.

But she rubs the tip of my two cocks against her dry pussy, ready to sit down on them and make me do my job.

"No!" I yell. "No! No! No! This will not happen!"

There is a sudden whooshing sound and I feel myself being pulled backwards. Like I'm being pulled out of the Pleasure Prison.

And that's when I get it.

This isn't real. It's all fake. Just like I suspected. None of this is real.

But when I come to, gasping for breath, I'm not inside a gaming pod. Nor a medical pod.

I'm lying on a table. Chained to the table, I realize. There's filth all around me and the stench of death permeates my nostrils.

There is no clean air. There is no mountain castle nestled in a mist. There are no pretty glowing girls.

Just rows and rows of Akeelian men chained to the walls surrounding the table I'm lying on.

And one girl.

My girl.

Corla. Still age sixteen. Hanging from wrist shackles above me. My cocks already inside her.

She is naked, her normally silver hair now covered in some dark, dirty oil, barely conscious. But her eyes flutter open just long enough to see me. To lock her gaze with mine. "Help me. Please, help me, Crux. Please," she begs. Over and over again. "Please help me."

And then I'm bounced out, screaming her name—"Corla!"—and making all kinds of promises I know I won't ever be able to keep.

CHAPTER SEVEN

I sit straight up in bed, breathing hard. "Corla."
It comes out as a whisper, but in my head it's a scream.

"What?" What's going on?"

I look to my left and see her. My wife.
Christopher's wife. I'm in his bed again.

Carla sits up and places a hand on my bare
shoulder. But I flinch away, the touch of virtual girls
still lingering.

"Christopher, what's wrong? Are you OK?"

The laugh bursts out before I can stop it. Because
no. No, I am absolutely not OK. I don't understand
what's happening, I don't understand who she is, or
who I am, or what the fucking point of all this is.

"Did you have another bad dream?"

"Yeah, Carla. I had a bad dream. Just go back to
sleep."

"No," she says, scooting over closer to me. "No.
Not if you're upset."

"I don't want to talk about it."

"OK. That's fine. You don't have to." She sighs,
sleepily. But then she wraps her hands around my

upper arm and leans her head on my shoulder. "I just wish we could get to the bottom of this."

I frown in the dark hazy light of too-early morning. "Bottom of what?"

"All these nightmares. That's the fourth one this week." She sighs again, clearly frustrated. "I hate seeing you like this. They really seem to trouble you."

"Four?"

"I think it's a lot, Christopher. I think you should…"

But she stops. And when she doesn't continue, I look down at her. Her hair is soft and light, light blonde. What Corla would look like if she wasn't a Cygnian princess, maybe. "I should what?"

"I already know what you're going to say."

"I should what?"

"Talk to someone," she says.

"Who?"

"I don't know. I know you think you have to be strong all the time because you're the governor and you can't have this get out. Not in an election year."

I take a moment to wonder what an election year is. I didn't really think about it the last time I was here. I mean, I know what an election is. People vote on shit. But how that factors into the whole governor's job, I'm not sure.

But whatever it means, it can't be good. So I say, "No. No, I don't want to talk to anyone. It's just a freaking dream. It'll pass."

It has to pass. Right? I mean, this Christopher dude isn't even me. He might look like me, but that guy isn't me. So even if he is having recurring nightmares, they aren't related to what just happened to me.

And holy fucking shit. That last one—I don't think I'll ever get the image of that nasty old Corla out of my head. Ever.

That saggy bitch might've just ruined my soulmate lust.

But then I picture the real Corla. She wasn't old. She was very young. Like the exact age she was when we met on Wayward Station. Did she not make it out? Obviously not. Maybe neither of us made it out? Maybe, in that incarnation, or nightmare, or whatever the hell it was—maybe there is no Harem Station? Hell, maybe there's no Wayward Station either?

Old, saggy Queen Corla didn't know who I was.

But that was the virtual.

Those Cygnians in that reality—if that's what it was and *if* it was the Cygnians in charge of that disgusting breeding facility and not the Akeelians—they knew enough to put us together.

But that could just be because I had violet eyes. They were breeding us for that.

Suns, I just want to forget it. All of it. Even Corla begging me for help.

Especially Corla begging me for help.

Because there's nothing I can do. For all I know I'm stuck inside the freaking spin node and I'll never get out. I could be stuck cycling through sex nightmares with my not-soulmate for all eternity.

Nope. That's a bad idea. I don't think I can do it. Even if I pop back to this semi-normal state between the bad ones. I can't do it.

Carla hugs my arm a little tighter. And even though I know she's not mine, and even though the last time I was here she was very pissed off at me for

109

talking about my real life and there was some hint there that people in charge of things were about to… I don't know. Take us prisoner or something—I can't help but think that her, being next to me, is… *nice*. It's nice to feel like maybe at least one person in this sun-fucked universe is on my side and gives a shit.

I sigh. Loudly. Heavily.

"Come on," Carla says. "Lie back. Try to put it out of your mind."

I don't even know where I am. It's definitely a planet though. Fire. People are obsessed with fire here. That only happens on planets.

She tugs on my arm until I give in and lie back in the bed. Then she snuggles up to me and I'm not gonna lie, excitement pulses through my body at her closeness. This is a much better version of my not-life. It's tolerable, at least. Especially after that disgusting virtual I just popped out of.

One thing is for sure though—I am *not* having sex with *any* incarnation of Corla. Ever again.

Ever.

I almost laugh.

"What's funny?"

"Nothing," I say. Then I turn to look at her, because she's probably the most normal woman I've been in bed with in a very long time. "It's just absurd, that's all. A bad dream. What am I? A child?"

"Hmm."

"What's that mean?"

"Just… you know."

"No. I don't. Tell me."

"Christopher. Your childhood was a long string of fucked-up shit, ya know?"

"Was it?"

She almost sits up to look at me. "What do you mean, was it?" She scoffs. "Do not tell me you're going to try to normalize your freak-show of a father's behavior. He was insane. Talking all that shit about the end of the world. Scaring you out of your mind with threats of demonic princesses and vengeful gods."

"Huh." It's not very far off the mark, but I don't say that. Just sigh. "If he were here, I would talk to him about it though."

She huffs. "Good thing he's dead then." Then she does sit up. Points her finger at me. "It's too soon, OK? Too. Fucking. Soon."

I put up my hands in surrender. "OK." I don't know what that means, or what specific event she's referring to, but whatever. I give up.

She flops back into her pillow. "I mean, I get it. Forgiveness is what heals people. But that father of yours doesn't deserve forgiveness. Al Core is the definition of *evil*."

"What did you just say?"

"You heard me. And I'm not taking it back. He was crazy."

Like… am I hearing things? Or did she just say ALCOR?

"I can practically read your mind, Christopher Core. I will never, *ever* forgive you if you forgive him. He didn't earn it."

Ah. I get it. First name Al. Second name Core. Then I sigh.

"Do you hear me?"

"I hear you. He's definitely not forgiven." It's not even a lie, either. ALCOR can go fuck himself. He is

111

so on my shit list for leaving us to figure this crap out on our own. And besides, we have the Baby, who seems altogether much better than he was before that whole time freeze thing happened.

"Good. And I really hope you're right and these nightmares don't have anything to do with all that stuff that happened when you were younger, but…" She hesitates. "But you're probably wrong. And that means something about what's happening now is related to what happened back then."

Back then. Yeah. She's not wrong about that. Lots of shit happened back then that affects me today.

It's all about the past, isn't it?

"I don't think I can go back to sleep now. I'm so upset."

I turn to her. She's on her back, but her body is most definitely turned away from me. Clear body language for 'I'm mad'.

I slip my arm underneath her and pull her towards me. "Come here. I'm sorry. I didn't mean to upset you."

It's the truth too. It's not her fault I'm in her husband's body fucking up her sleep.

She resists for a moment. But it's a small resistance. And she turns into me and snuggles her face up to my chest, sighing with relief.

I absently stroke her hair as I think things through.

Maybe being Christopher isn't so bad. His version of Corla at least seems sane.

I can't say that much for the Corla I knew back in my real life. Not that I really know her, or anything. But even when she was sixteen, she was crazy. She

112

started all this. She flew into my life like the solar wind and spun me around so hard, I lost all my senses.

What if she was lying? I mean I get it. Like she told me back in that garden that day we escaped, there *was* an actual breeding ceremony. I saw it with my own eyes. I participated in it, for sun's sake.

But isn't there a chance that she was wrong? That it was maybe just my weird father's version of a... I dunno. A marriage pact?

I mean, I never asked him about any of it. As soon as Corla convinced me to help her escape I took her into the walls of the station. Secret passageways that Jimmy and I used to travel inside when we were smaller. It wasn't easy to get to Jimmy's quarters. It had been years since he and I played in the walls like that. And I barely fit at sixteen.

But Corla and I made it. And then Corla and Jimmy and I made it to Luck and Valor and then again to Tray. And Tray was the one who got us the rest of the way. He hacked into shit and did... well, whatever the fuck he did.

But the whole thing felt too easy. And I remember thinking, *Did someone put her up to this? Is this part of my father's plan?*

I was so paranoid. I kept expecting to get caught. I never thought we'd make it to the spin node launch tube, let alone back down to the docking level. And when Tray actually stole the ship and opened the docking locks... I was sorta stunned that we got that far.

Then the next thing I knew we were approaching the ALCOR gate.

And that was it. I thought we were dead for sure.

JA HUSS & KC CROSS

But no. That fucking AI let us through. Invited us to stay.

I get that we had a dude called Luck on board, but that's a little bit too much luck even for him.

Then I remember what I was doing the last time I was here. Looking for Jimmy. Jimmy Yates. That has to be his name. There was no Jimmy, but there was a Jim and Heather. Maybe that's him? Maybe Heather is his soulmate in this version of reality?

Hmmm. That makes me think. Maybe Heather is his real soulmate? Because Delphi is *not* his soulmate. We all know that for sure.

And this place has to be Earth. It sure the fuck isn't Cygnia. Not that I know what that place looks like—because whatever that was when I thought I was there, it wasn't real. So maybe Cygnia does look like that—but I doubt it. That craggy old Corla can't come from a place so beautiful. Carla here isn't some glowing princess. She comes across very... I don't know. Normal.

And this place is not an Akeelian city either. We have hundreds, maybe even thousands, of stations. But only one planet. It's not a very nice one, either. Akeelian City doesn't look anything like this place.

It has to be Earth.

That's what the spin node was for, right?

But wait. Last time I was here, she heard me telling Tycho—Toby—whoever—about my brothers. And she was mad. People were at the door.

"Hey," I say.

"Hmm?" she asks sleepily.

"Did... did anyone come to the door the other night?"

"What?"

Surely, if people were coming to... I don't know, take us to prison, or kill us because I was talking about things I shouldn't be, she would not have to think twice about that.

"Who came to the door?" she asks.

"No one. Nothing. Just part of my dream, I think."

"I really think you need to talk to someone, Christopher. Let me call up Heather."

"Heather?"

"Heather Yates? You remember her, right? Her husband, Jim, put on that fundraiser for your reelection campaign last time?"

"Jim."

"She finished her masters about two years ago. She's got her own counseling office now. Mostly, she deals with couples, but..." I feel Carla shrug. "I'm sure she'd talk to you about the dreams. And she won't let it leak out that you're having... issues."

Can it be this simple? Can my wife be setting up the meeting with Jimmy I need?

"What do you say?" Her voice is very sleepy now. Like she's just about to drift off.

"Yeah," I tell her. "Yeah, set that up. I'd love to talk to... Jim again."

I lie there waiting for Carla to fall into a deep sleep. I want to get up and go back down to Christopher's office so I can do some more searching for Jimmy Yates.

But it's been a long spin—day. Whatever. I'm not sure how to count the time I've been inside the spin

115

node. And before I know it my eyes are heavy and my body is relaxed.

And then…

I wake up to the familiar sound of traffic outside and hazy light filtering in through the sheer curtains. Then the sound of cupboards banging down in the kitchen.

Carla sighs. Turns over.

I think the most surprising thing about waking up in her bed is that I'm still here. Why am I still here? Falling asleep and waking up seems like the perfect opportunity for whoever or whatever is controlling my trips through the node to put me somewhere else.

But I'm not going to complain. I'm about done with this shit. I want to go back to Harem. My Harem. My life, my time, my world.

But then I remember Carla's offer last night. Jimmy.

What if I get stuck here? What if I have to be this Christopher version of me? I have to stay and talk to Jimmy, at least. What if he's my Jimmy? And he's stuck here too?

Maybe we can make a plan together?

"Oh, my God," Carla mutters. "She's up again. I can hear her down there. Can you hear her? Why? Why does this child insist on waking up at the butt crack of dawn?"

I huff out a laugh. Butt crack of dawn. I can honestly say I've never heard that one before.

116

"It's not funny, Christopher. You're not here with her all day. She's a handful. Always."

"I'll take care of it." I throw the covers off and swing my legs out of the bed, taking a moment to lean over, head in hands, and rub my face.

She reaches for me, scooting over towards me so she can wrap her arms around my middle. And there's a moment of panic when I assume she'll reach for my cock and want a morning fuck.

I'm not touching Corla—any version of her—until I get back to my own time and place. Not after that shit show nightmare. Except I know better. It wasn't a nightmare. I don't know what it was, exactly. But I don't care. None of these lives I'm being shown are mine.

Corla doesn't reach for my cock. She presses her cheek against the small of my back and murmurs, "I love you."

I stop rubbing my face and go still, thinking about her declaration for a moment. Three words I've dreamed about hearing for twenty-one years. It's her voice, it's her, for all intents and purposes—but it's the *wrong* her.

"I love you too." I say it back because that's what you do. Even I know that. Then I untangle her arms from me and stand up, turning to face her, and cover her back up.

"Thank you," she says again. This time her words are barely audible as she immediately drifts back to sleep.

She's a nice version of Corla though. I will say that. The Corla I knew as a teenager was bossy and authoritative. Very, *very* sure of her place in the world even when all the people around her had other plans. This one is… calm. Almost lazy. In a good way, though.

I sigh and walk over to the door, snagging a t-shirt on my way past a chair. I tug it over my head and close the door behind me.

The sounds coming from the kitchen become louder as I make my way down the long, curved staircase in bare feet. I glance at Christopher's closed office doors, wanting to get back in there and see if there's anything else I can learn about where I am and who he is, but then something crashes in the kitchen and I decide it has to wait until I check on the sun-fucked kids.

But even that has an allure I can't deny.

Sun-fucked or not, they are my kids. And this is the only chance I've had to see them when they were small. To get some idea of what it's like to be a father.

I missed it.

I missed all of it.

And even though I didn't really feel regret about that back on Harem, that had to be because I never understood how small and helpless they could be. How they could clutch you so tight when you hold them. Like you are their whole universe. How they could look at you with such complete trust.

I only got a small taste of it the last time I was here, but it was enough to crave more.

When I walk into the kitchen little Delphi is sitting on the countertop with her feet in the sink, holding a box of food. Her whole arm is inside the box when I pause to watch her. And then she withdraws it and shoves little yellow nugget things into her mouth. She munches eagerly, and then sees me and stops, smiling with stuffed cheeks. "I was hungry," she says, half-chewed food shooting out with her words.

"I guess," I say, walking over to her. I take the box and set it aside, then pick her up. She immediately wraps her arms around my neck and her legs around my middle, holding on to me like she'll never let go.

I hug her for a moment, wanting to apologize for missing this in my real life. It could've been nice, I think. To be a father to a small child. It's not the same with a full-grown adult. I don't feel like Delphi's father, but Dellie... that urge to hold her and protect her is strong.

I look around for my other twin. But he's not here. "Where's Tycho?"

"Who?"

"Oh... um." Fuck. What was that kid's name? It was something weird. "T-toby. Where's Toby?"

"Who's Toby?"

"Hmm? Your brother, Del... Dellie. Your twin."

"You're funny, Daddy. I don't have a brother."

"What?" I look around, trying to find evidence of him. "Yeah. Twins. That's how it always happens. Everyone has a twin."

"That would be fun. Can I get one? Where do you buy them, Daddy? I want a twin. Can I get a girl twin? I don't want a brother. Lyssa has a brother and he's mean. But Chassey has a sister and they play dolls together. Can I get one today?"

Fuck. Why did I assume I came back to the same place?

I mean, that's just not how my life goes, right? If there's one thing I've learned in my thirty-seven years of life it's that the universe gives no fucks about my happiness. I have some kind of job to do. I am nothing more than a little worker bot. A servo to the gods. The meaning of life runs on a need-to-know basis, and in the words of ALCOR, I don't need to know.

"Never mind," I say. "Daddy's tired. I think I was still dreaming."

Dellie frowns, studies me for a moment. In real life—my real life—her eyes are pink. Well, when she's not glowing her eyes are kinda light brown. But you can see the little pink flecks that will light up with emotion swirling in her irises.

But this little girl has deep blue eyes. She pats my face with both hands, giggling softly. "You know what I dreamed about?"

"What?" I ask. She's slipping down my body a little, so I hike her up so her face is even with mine.

"You. And your space station."

"What?"

"I think that's what you called it. What's a space station, Daddy?"

I blink at her for a moment. Now what the fuck? What does this mean?

"Do you know?"

"What?"

"What is a space station?"

I take a deep breath and carry her over to the adjoining room where there's a couch. I sit down, because I need a minute. I need to figure this out. Why am I here? Is this just some random spin of the wheel? You walk in a spin node and it shoots you out into… what? Another timeline? Another universe?

"Is it like a train station?"

I look at Delphi and frown. She's not my kid. She's Christopher's kid. "No." I don't know what a train station is, exactly. But I'm pretty sure it looks nothing like a space station. "It's a big… spinning… top. Kind of. Out in space. People live inside it."

She thinks about this, her mouth a serious, straight line. "Hmm." Then she drags a hand across her nose. "I think I was there too."

"Where?"

"Your station. But I was big." She smiles. "Very big."

"You think you were there, huh?"

She nods. "And you were there too. But you weren't old." She frowns. "If I'm big then you have to be old."

"Yeah. That's usually how it works."

"Are we gonna go there? Because the people told me that I'm not supposed to be here and neither are you."

"Who told you?"

"The people."

"What *people*, Dellie?"

"The bright ones."

"What?" I just stare at her.

"The bright ones. They light up. Like the sun." She points to the window where a little bit of sunshine is just starting to appear through the trees. "I think we're supposed to go back to your station. Is that where you live, Daddy?"

I nod yes without thinking. Just staring out the window at the sun. The bright ones. The Cygnians?

Dellie places a hand on my cheek and I turn towards her. "They told me you're not from here."

"What? When?"

"Just now. I can hear them in my head."

"Fuck!"

She giggles. "Mommy hates that word."

"Does she?" I laugh.

"She hates when you say it." She pauses. "Is that where my twin lives?" Then her mouth makes a big O shape. Like she just figured something out. "That *is* where he lives. Are you gonna take me with you?"

This answer would've been a resounding no at almost any other moment in time. And it's still a no now. She is not my Delphi. But there's a part of me that wants to take her with me. And Carla too. We're missing Tycho, but maybe he's out there somewhere, waiting for me to find him? Maybe I could—

A whooshing noise fills my ears and that now familiar feeling of being sucked away vibrates through my body.

"No. No, not yet! I just got here—"

Dellie is holding on to me, her face filled with fear. "Don't go, Daddy! Don't leave me here!"

I hold her tighter, but even as I do so, her body dissipates into nothingness in my arms.

122

"Dude," Jimmy says. "I would so fuck her. I would fuck her sweet silver ass into next spin. I'm talking a full-on marathon of fucking, ya know what I mean?"

"Please," I say, taking a sip of my whiskey. "She's got more guards than my father. You don't have a chance in hell."

We're sitting in the Wayward Station governor's dining room getting drunk in the middle of the night. Still pretty wound up about the silver Cygnian princess who arrived this afternoon.

"Did you see her hair?" Jimmy asks. "Don't you just want to run your fingers through it?"

"What?" I say, so annoyed by him. "No. It looks like strings of silver. And by that, I mean the actual fucking mineral. Who wants to fuck a girl with metal hair?"

"It's not metal," he says.

"How do you know?"

"I touched it," he says, smiling into his drink.

"You did not. You can't get within three meters of that girl."

He crosses his heart with a finger. "Swear to the sun, I did. She was walking past me and I just reached out and…" He sighs. "It felt nice. I'd like to pull it."

A laugh bursts out of my mouth, I can't help it. "Sick freak."

He shrugs, still smiling as he downs his drink. "You have your kinks, I have mine."

"Yeah, I know yours. They all involve sex bots on X Level."

Wait. I shake my head a little. This conversation feels so… familiar.

"Don't knock it until you try it, Crux. Those sex bots know exactly what to do with two cocks."

But the feeling fades as his words sink in. "Sick. Freak. How do you even get down there? My father would fucking blow if he caught me with a sex bot."

"I have my ways."

"Seriously," I say. "How?"

He leans in, all secretive like, and whispers, "Tray. He hacked into the AI."

"He did not."

"Shhh," Jimmy says. "He did so. They leveled him up when they took him into cryogenetics. And I've got a good thing going with that little weirdo, so don't ruin it for me by blabbing your mouth off to your father."

"Like I even talk to my father." I huff, pouring myself another drink from the decanter the bartender left for us. "And what the fuck does that mean, anyway? Leveled him up?"

Hold on. Hold on. *Hold on.* I know I've had this conversation before. And I know what leveling up is now. Tray. And Brigit. And…

The double doors leading into the dining room burst open and three Cygnian guards come through, looking around, subvocalizing security details.

Oh. Fuck.

"What the fuck?" Jimmy says. "Does the king need a midnight snack?"

But it's not the king who enters. Of course, it's not. I know this because I *did* have this conversation before. This is how the whole ALCOR Station Corla spin-node shit show started!

Princess Corla enters my father's dining room, silver hair shining in the overhead lights and wearing a pink dressing gown that looks too pretty to sleep in.

My God. I'm even having the exact same thoughts!

Her eyes dart straight to mine.

I squint at her. *No. No, no, no. Universe, you cannot fuck with me this way. It's just not fair. Do not make me do this again. Please…*

"What's she doing here?" Jimmy asks.

"No clue," I say. "But I think this is our cue to leave."

And this time, I *really* fucking mean it. I start walking to the back exit that leads to the autokitchen.

But then there's a loud slam of the doors and I stop. When I look over my shoulder, Princess Corla is gone. "Huh."

"What the hell was that about?" Jimmy asks.

"I dunno," I say, walking back to my drink sitting on the bar. Because that's not how it went down last time.

"I think you scared her off. Fuckin' dick. I really wanted to touch her hair again."

I take a deep breath and stare down into my glass. What does this mean?

Jimmy claps me on the back. "You OK?"

"Fine. Just…" I turn around and look at him. "Do you and your father have a meeting with them tomorrow?" I jut my chin towards the door to indicate the Cygnians.

Jimmy squints his eyes. And it's in this moment I realize how much I've missed my friend. He was my *best* friend until we arrived on ALCOR Station. My only friend, really. Then he and Xyla were attached at the hip. He belonged to her then. Not me. I was the outsider. From the moment we stepped into that place with its dark, shining obsidian floors and eerie hum of cleaning servos, I was the one who didn't matter anymore.

My job was done. I got them all there. Alive, as requested. And then everyone seemed to be busy planning for a future that didn't include me.

I want to stay here for a while and hang out with Jimmy. I want to be a sixteen-year-old kid again. I want to go to school, and be lazy, and sneak drinks in the governor's dining room in the middle of the night, every night for years to come. I want to make fun of Tray with Jimmy, and laugh at Serpint and Draden as they play war with pretend weapons, and ignore Valor and Luck like they have no place in my future.

126

But most of all I do not want to have sex with Corla tomorrow. I do not want to make twin babies, and I do not want to shoot her into a spin node and steal a ship. I do not want to go to ALCOR Station and get trapped there for the rest of my life. Perpetually in the dark about everything until it's too late to fix it.

I want to forget the last twenty-one years ever happened.

I want a *do-over*.

"What kind of meeting?" Jimmy asks.

"I don't know. Like..." I don't know what to call it if I can't call it a breeding ceremony. Jimmy will think I'm insane. "Is there some kind of... welcoming ceremony planned?"

"Wasn't that what we did this afternoon when they came aboard?"

"Yeah, but is there anything else on the schedule tomorrow? For like... noon?"

He thinks for a moment. "Yeah. There are a couple delegations from Cetus System here right now too. I'm pretty sure we're hanging with them for lunch."

I try to remember how the conversation went twenty-one years ago. What he's saying sounds familiar, but I can't be sure. It doesn't matter though. He and his father weren't invited last time, and if they're going to be busy with the Cetus people, then he's not invited this time, either.

If it's even happening this time.

But... why else would the Cygnians be here? And why did Princess Corla come in to the dining room, take one look at me, and run the other way?

127

Well, Crux, that internal voice in my head says. *You did the same thing.*

I did, didn't I?

I went the other way because I know. Not about what will happen tomorrow. About what will happen for the next twenty-one years.

What if she's locked in some kind of spin node whirlwind too? She has been on ice for sun knows how long. I've had her in that cryopod for a year. And she was sending me messages, wasn't she? Did I make that up?

Reality seems very precarious and subjective at the moment.

Then all kinds of things I've conveniently forgotten begin to resurface in the front of my mind.

ALCOR killed Draden and brought him back to life. Princess Lyra and Queen Corla arrived on Harem. ALCOR died. Delphi appeared. There was an asshole copy of ALCOR in the Pleasure Prison. Not to mention some rogue AI called Brigit and a Succubus infiltrating our systems. Luck opened a spin node for Tray and Valor to escape. The princess rebellion. Luck… *killed me.* Shot me point blank in the chest.

And I died. I fucking *died.*

That's when the Corla dreams started. Maybe I'm still dead? Maybe that's what this is? The whole life flashing before your eyes thing? But isn't that supposed to be fast? Isn't that the definition of 'flash'?

This… *trip* I'm on. It feels like I've lived lifetimes.

And that's just the parts I know. There's a whole other story going on in the background. Maybe dozens of them? Maybe hundreds of them?

Draden's story.

Tray's story.

Booty's story.

Is Real ALCOR dead or alive?

Where is the Asshole?

And what the fuck is Mighty Minions up to?

Then there's Baby. And Flicka. And Tycho. And Veila.

"Crux?" Jimmy says. I turn and look at him. "You OK?"

I take a breath, ready to spit out an affirmative. But I can't manage it. So I shake my head. "Jimmy," I say calmly. "I have to tell you something. And you're going to think I'm crazy, but I don't care. I have to tell someone, and you're the only friend I have."

"OK," he says, hesitantly, but seriously for once. "OK, then. Tell me. What's going on?"

So I talk. I start with this same day, twenty-one years ago. I expect him to laugh. Or at the very least stop me to ask what it's like to fuck a Cygnian princess. But he just narrows his eyes at me when I get to the breeding ceremony part. And then they widen several times when I describe what we did and where we went.

I talk for an eternity. I tell him everything. And still he says nothing.

I fill him in on all the years between then and now. All the things we did, and learned, and saw. I tell him about Xyla, and ALCOR, and the Pleasure Prison. I tell him about locking Corla up inside a security beacon and then I tell him what's happening to me now.

"I'm stuck, man. I walked into that spin node and I don't know where I am or what any of it means. I met my daughter and son, Jimmy. As kids. I never knew them as kids. I have seen several versions of Corla. Or Carla, as she's called on Earth. I have seen Earth, Jimmy. And now I'm here. Back in the moment where it all started. And I don't know what to do. Make sure it happens again? Go through it all again and hope we can change the inevitable outcome we're spinning towards? Or change everything?"

And then there's nothing more to say and I just stop talking.

He just stares at me.

"Say something."

"I…" He rubs a hand down his face. "I don't know what to say. I had a ship called the *Big Dicker*?"

We both guffaw.

"Oh, my sun," he says, holding his stomach. "What the fuck is wrong with me?"

I just shake my head, laughing so hard tears fill up my eyes.

"I mean, it's pretty clever. And it's *so* me… but you'd think I'd like… grow up a little, right?"

"You didn't, dude." I laugh again. "You didn't change a bit."

"Holy shit, and I did your… *daughter*?" He shakes his head. "That is so wrong. I have limits, man. I know I do. I don't understand how you're not punching me in the face right now."

"You didn't know," I say, defending future him. "You didn't know until it was too late. And Delphi takes after her mother. She's bossy. Told me to stay out of her life." I shrug. "So I did."

130

He sighs. "OK. Well. Let's get serious about this for a moment. I'm going to assume you're telling the truth, even though you could just be crazy. Because for some reason I can't explain, it all feels true, Crux. I believe you. So…" He rubs his hands together. "I think that Corla left because she remembers you."

"Yeah?"

He shrugs. "I don't fucking know, dude. I'm making it up. But it's kinda logical. You got up and walked away from her because you knew this was the defining moment. And she turned around and walked out for the same reason. So this means…" He thinks for a moment. "This has to mean that the last time this happened, neither of you knew the future."

"How do you figure?"

"Because she was the one giving orders, right? She was all bossy and in control."

"Yeah, it was like she knew things."

"But she didn't know you were her soulmate, right?"

"No. She didn't. She was as surprised as I was."

"I think that's why she went through with it. Soulmates are supposed to be on each other's sides, right?"

"I guess. Yeah. Works for you and Delphi. So OK. I can buy that."

"Whatever she knew, she didn't know what you just told me. I feel that to be true."

"Yeah," I agree. "I think you're right."

"Maybe she's been through this whole… cycle? Loop? Whatever?—before and when she met you… when she met you, things diverged." He snaps his fingers and points at me. "There's only one way to find out. Go ask her."

I laugh. "Just go ask her? Just go up to her quarters, tell her guards I need a word with the future queen, and walk right in?"

"That's one very bad option," Jimmy says. "Or"— he points his finger at me again—"we could take a little trip through the walls like the old days."

"That was how we got Corla out of here. But they were on to us pretty quick, Jimmy. We only get one chance to use that route. And if we need to escape tomorrow night, that's how we do it."

"Unless we wake up Tray right now and get his little weird ass in on this mission."

I hesitate. Fucking Tray. He was always the brother I trusted the least. But that's not the only reason I hesitate. "Even if Tray can help us, that doesn't mean we *should* do this, ya know? What if we're just making the same mistake all over again? What if this is my do-over? And what if I'm fucking it up by taking the same path as I did before?"

Jimmy nods. "OK. Then… we can wait until tomorrow. And if there's a breeding ceremony you can talk to Corla then."

"Well, if there is a breeding ceremony, then we have to escape. Because all that other shit will be true too. But Corla was making plans the night before last time. If I don't talk to her, she won't make those plans. And if we don't escape, then we'll be stuck here like fucking lab rats."

"And now we're right back where we started. This whole thing is a circle."

"I know. Like, I literally know that. I'm stuck inside it, dude. I'm on a fucking loop."

"OK, how about this? We hope there's no ceremony but plan like there is."

"Hope for the best but prepare for the worst."

"Exactly. And that means you have to see Corla tonight and prepare."

"You just want to see her handmaidens."

He laughs. "Not gonna deny that. I might never get another chance to see a Cygnian princess up close again."

"That's almost funny."

"Anyway. I think that's the best plan, even if I don't get laid tonight. So let's go get Tray and—"

"I'm not sure about him. You don't know how he is in the future yet, Jimmy. He's... creepy."

"I get it," Jimmy says. "He's a strange kid. And he's sundamned creepy now. But when we told him we were escaping and he had to come with us in the last loop, did he resist?"

"No," I say, shaking my head. "He didn't. I don't remember what he said when we told him all this shit. I was way too wound up. But he agreed immediately and that's all I had time to care about. Without him we never would've made it."

"I think we should go ask him."

And just as he says that, the double doors to the dining room open again. I hold my breath for a moment, expecting—and maybe even hoping—that it will be Corla. But it's not.

It's Tray.

"Speak of the fucking weirdo himself," Jimmy says. "Tray, my man. You're just the little freak we need."

Tray stands there in the doorway and just stares at us.

"Tray?" I ask.

"Why am I here?"

"I dunno," Jimmy says. "But it's a good thing you are. Because we're blowing this place tomorrow night, dude. And we need your help."

Tray looks at Jimmy, then me. He squints his eyes. "I just had this weird vision, you guys. It was like a dream, but so real. It was like I was there. And…" He shakes his head. "I don't know why I'm here. I just suddenly had this overwhelming urge to find you two."

"Look," I say, walking towards him. "I know this is all going to sound crazy, but we really just need you to—"

"Do what you're told." Tray finishes my sentence.

"Y-yeah. Yeah. That. Exactly."

"OK," Tray says in his emotionless voice, which has always been lacking in the emotion department, but ever since he came back from cryogenetics last week, it's even more dispassionate. "OK. What do I need to do?"

Jimmy fills him in.

First, we need to see Princess Corla. Because there won't be any escape tomorrow night if she's not the one in charge. She had the codes to get through the ALCOR gate. She had the plan. I know *what* we did that night, but I don't really understand *how* we did it.

"Then," Jimmy says, ready to feed him the rest of the plan, "we need to get Corla to a pod and—"

But Tray stops him with a raised hand. "If you don't mind. I don't need that part of the plan right now. I'm having trouble processing. One thing at a time." He looks at me. "I'll get better at this. Eventually."

I know what he's talking about.

Back then, I would not have understood. Probably would've wasted a lot of time trying to make him explain what they did to him and why he's having trouble processing.

Maybe I don't know the specifics of what exactly happened to Tray during this time twenty-one years ago, but I understand the consequences.

They took his... humanity.

And right now is not the time to have that conversation. So I say, "Whatever. Just get us to the princess."

Getting us to the princess involves all kinds of technical shit I have no clue about. Just one more reminder that I'm not really necessary for the success of anything. I mean, sure, I'm Corla's sperm donor. But who cares? Does this universe really need my offspring?

They don't seem to be doing much of anything but fucking things up in my present.

The Akeelians seem to need my offspring. And the Cygnians seem to need my offspring.

135

But that's it. And they're the bad guys. So wouldn't it be better if we just nixed the whole idea of Corla and me having kids in the first place?

Seems logical to me.

I'm the oldest, so I was the leader back on the escape ship. I was the one who talked to ALCOR. But I didn't carry some secret code for him to decipher. I didn't matter at all after we got there. I was just his... his *plucky sidekick*.

I laugh out loud. Because I'm pretty sure no one has ever called me 'plucky'.

Jimmy shoots me a weird look. We're in some control room watching Tray do his thing with the quantum AI that runs the station. It's not an AI the way ALCOR is. It's smart as fuck, but it has to follow directions. It has no free will at all.

"OK," Tray says, backing away. "I've taken all the vent sensors offline for the next hour. But you have to go alone, Crux."

"What?" Jimmy complains. "But I'll miss out on the princesses."

"Jimmy," I say, clapping him on the back. "Trust me, dude. You are going to see so many princesses in your future. You don't even like them."

"Shut your mouth."

"I swear to the sun." Then I turn to Tray. "Thanks. I owe you."

"I think I'll keep that favor for a future cash-in."

"Whatever."

Tray opens the vent in the control room and hands me a small flashlight and a small map screen with my path through the passageway lit up in green. "You only have one hour," he says. "I needed to keep the

136

blackout short enough that it didn't trigger any backup protocols so we can use this plan tomorrow for the escape. When you get to the vent use the maintenance code to open the access panel. They all have the same code. One hour, Crux."

"I feel better now," Jimmy says. "You'll barely have time to feel her up."

I roll my eyes at him, then ask Tray, "Where do I exit?"

"Your quarters. It's on the map. You're only one level up from Corla, actually. I think you can manage it."

"All right." I duck into the vent and start walking. Tray closes the vent cover behind me and then the little bit of light from the control room disappears when I go around a corner.

I flick on the flashlight and follow the map screen.

The passageways are big enough for the maintenance bots to move easily inside them, but not big enough for me to walk upright. So by the time I make to the vent inside Corla's room, my back is killing me and I'm starting to wonder about my decision to confront her.

There are so many ways this can go wrong. And an equal number of possibilities that this is the right way forward. Funny. I have twenty-one years of future me as a knowledge base, but I'm still no closer to the truth of why this is all happening in the first place.

I stop at the vent and use the code Tray gave me. The access panel slides up and I see… darkness. But as I crouch there, looking into the room, my eyes begin to adjust. I'm inside her closet.

There is a sliver of light leaking through the bottom of the closet door and on the other side I can hear whispering. Frantic whispering.

I creep out of the vent, walk forward, and press my ear against the door.

"I don't know what to do." It's Corla. And it's funny. Before coming into the spin node for this little time-jumping, reality traversing adventure—I don't think I would've been able to recognize her voice. Twenty-one years is a long time to rely on a memory of a voice.

But I've met her so many ways now. I know that's her speaking.

"You should've done it the way I told you."

But ho-lee fuck. I definitely recognize that one. Veila. *Veila* is here. I'd forgotten about that. Veila was one of her sisters though, right? Of course she was here in her entourage.

"I know. But I freaked out. He took one look at me, Veila, and he turned his back. It's like he knew why I was there."

"He didn't know. He couldn't possibly." This is a new voice that I'm sure I don't recognize. "I heard Father talking to the Akeelians this afternoon. The governor specifically said that his son wasn't aware of the ceremony tomorrow. And he wanted it kept that way."

So there *is* a ceremony.

OK then. This meeting has to happen.

I open the closet door. None of them immediately see me so I take that moment to study the room. It's not a standard Wayward Station room. Like… at all. It looks like it was decorated for royalty. A massive round bed with so many blankets the three girls look like they're sitting *in* it, instead of on top of it.

Above the bed is a canopy with layers and layers of sheer fabric hanging down. Light fabric that, unfortunately, reminds me of the girl who was leading me through the forest in that bogus sex fantasy.

The lighting is low. Only the baseboards glow with a soft golden-pink hue. So that the whole room looks like something out of a princess myth.

I clear my throat to get their attention.

All three girls look towards me, mouths open in surprise. But none of them scream, or act surprised, or even jump up off the bed to back away.

"Hello," I say dumbly. "I came to have a word with you, Princess Corla."

She lifts her chin up, her mouth a flat line. "Good. I think we actually have a lot to talk about." Then she looks at her friends. "I'll handle this, girls."

"You sure?" the one who is not Veila says.

"I'm sure, Yates. Go keep watch in case the guards try to come check on me."

"Yates?" I say.

The girl is already turning towards the door when this word comes out of my mouth. But she stops and looks over her shoulder. "Yes?"

"That's your... name?"

She makes a face. "So?"

"Nothing. Forget it." But it's not nothing. Because Jimmy—

"What do you want, Crux?"

I look back at Corla. Veila and Yates take that moment to disappear through the door, leaving us alone. "I'm not sure where to start, but... I need you to touch me."

"What?"

"I need you to—"

"I heard what you said. But... they told me you didn't know. And that's why I came into the dining room tonight. I was going to ask you to touch me so I could see if what they say is true."

"Yeah. I know."

"Obviously, because now you want me to touch you instead of the other way around."

"No. I mean, yeah. But..." I put my hands up next to my face, feeling frustrated. None of this actually makes sense. And the whole idea of me just going along with the spin node's... what? What is the spin node doing? Is that thing conscious? Is it directing me with purpose? Did it send me here to start the loop over again? Or change it? Or is this encounter with Corla, and all the others that came before it, just random?

What is going on? And why didn't someone hand me a rule book before they sent me in to play the game?

Corla waits me out, clearly unsure how to proceed.

"Yeah." I sigh. "That's how it happened last time."

"Last time?"

"Look, it's a really long story. But I think if you just touch me, you'll understand."

"Because we're soulmates. It's true then?"

I nod.

She nods. "I see."

"If you touch me—"

"If I touch you the whole station will rock. The lights will flicker. And they'll know you're here."

"Oh. Right." I swallow. "I forgot about that."

She scrunches her face up at me. "What?"

"Nothing." I sigh. "So what are we gonna do about it?"

"What do you mean?"

"I mean… what's your plan? You know, the codes and shit?"

"What codes?"

"What?"

"What?"

"Stop repeating me."

"I don't understand what you're talking about, Crux. What plans? What codes?"

"The fucking escape plan."

She laughs. Kinda loud. So loud I look at the door, half expecting her security detail to come barging in. "Escape to… *where*?"

"You know. It was your plan," I say. "You had friends on the other side of the spin node."

"Spin node?"

"Oh, for fuck's sake. Your plan. Your escape plan. The one you told me about after the breeding. You convinced me that these people were evil. That we had to leave. That I had to shoot you through a spin node and then take my brothers and flee to ALCOR Station."

Her eyes go wide. And then she laughs again. "Wow. They told me you were weird, but… just. Wow. That"—she laughs one more time—"that is some cray right there. Why would we leave? We're getting married tomorrow." She leans over on her hands and starts

141

crawling across the bed, her eyes kind of... seductive. "I'm going to have your *babies*, Crux. You're going to fuck me hard tomorrow in front of everyone and then I'll be yours. Forever."

I back up. Hit the wall just as she clambers off the bed and starts walking towards me.

No. *Stalking* towards me. One foot placed directly in front of the other. Shoulders down, smirk on her face, hips swinging.

Why I thought this version of her might be normal, I don't know. I should really know better by now, right?

I put up both hands. "You know what? Forget it. I'm gonna leave now. And you should probably just forget I was even here."

"Forget you were here?" she coos. "Mmm-mmm. No way, handsome. Now that I've seen you, I might just want to risk that light show." She stops. Puts a hand over her mouth. "Oh. Suns."

And I know what she sees.

Even if I couldn't see the light of my eyes reflecting back at me from her silver ones, I would know they were glowing. Because they are hot. And both of my cocks are suddenly hard.

"Nope," I say, sliding along the wall towards the closet. "Nope. I've done this enough times now to know that this"—my finger makes a little swirl in the air—"this whole... seductive thing? Yeah. Not gonna do it for me."

She follows me. Right into the closet. But I can't get away. I would have to turn and duck into the maintenance passage. And there is no way I'm turning my back on this crazy glowing girl.

Because she *is* glowing now. Just being in the same room sets us off.

So I'm out of options. I hit the closet wall and stop. She does not stop. She saunters right up to me like she is a predator and I'm her prey. "What are you afraid of, Crux? Hmm?"

"I'm not afraid. I'm just... you're not her, Corla. You're just... *not her.*"

"Who?" The word snaps out of her mouth like a whip. "You have another girl?" Her eyes blaze silver white. So bright, I have to lower my eyelids to slits and look away. Then they dim. "Who cares." Her voice is softer now. "Whoever she is, she hasn't got a chance in space of holding your attention after tomorrow. Once we join together, Crux, you're mine forever."

I give up. I just give up. I close my eyes, let my head fall back against the wall, and sigh.

What the fuck am I doing?

You're learning.

"What?"

"What?" she coos.

"What did you just say?"

"I said, you're mine *forever.*"

"No, after that."

She frowns and purses her lips. "Nothing."

"You said, 'You're learning.'"

"I did not."

"I fucking heard you, ya crazy glow show."

"You can't talk to me that way. Do you have any idea who I am?"

"Yeah, you're the queen who ruined my life. Here's a screen flash for you, Corla. You're no one to me. Tomorrow we fuck, I get you pregnant, and then

I take off and never see you again for twenty years. And then…" I laugh. "Then… this is the best part. Are you ready?" She scowls at me. "You come into my station frozen, bitch. And even though I've been thinking about you for twenty years—craving you so hard, I never had another woman more than once—I didn't even thaw you out. I took your cryopod out to a security beacon and left you there. Alone. For a whole year. And you know what? After this little trip through time, or whatever the fuck I'm doing here inside this spin node, I'm never thawing your ass out."

"The *fuck* is your problem?" she growls.

I point at her. "You, Corla. You're my problem. I'd take boring Carla over your insane princess piece of ass any day. Better yet, you know what I'm gonna do? I'm gonna go back through my little vent, meet up with my brothers, stick them on a ship the same way I did twenty-one years ago, then we're blowing this fucking place. We're outta here. I'm done, bitch. I'm so done. I hope you have another soulmate out there somewhere. Or hey, here's a thought. You could just marry your sicko *father*!"

She raises her hand. I see it coming towards me. Her whole body is lit up like the sun.

But I can already feel that all-too-familiar pull of time.

And let me tell you—when I get sucked out and away from her, I feel nothing but relief.

Until I realize I'm alone in utter blackness.

CHAPTER NINE

I hold my breath, waiting. I begin to count to keep track of moments. And when I get to three hundred, I say, "Hello?"

My voice booms unnaturally loud and an echo comes back at me from across a distance. But once the echo fades the silence resumes.

I hold my breath again, straining to hear something. Anything. Because it feels like there's *something* out there.

A ticking. Or a dripping. Or neither of those things. Something else. Something small, but meaningful.

"It's Time."

The lights flash on. One large round spotlight that—when I shade my eyes and look up at it—doesn't seem to have an origin. There is blackness above it. But in the glow below there now sit two couches. Both quarter circles, empty, and facing each other.

I whirl around to look behind me, searching for the person who owns the voice. But aside from the two couches and the spotlight, there is nothing in this room but dark, empty space.

And it's in that moment when I realize… I'm not in a room.

"What?" I ask back. "Time for what?"

"Oh," the voice says. And I recognize it. There is a surge of relief when I recognize it. "No. That's not what I mean. I mean… OK, what I *don't* mean—perhaps that's the better place to start—what I *don't* mean is that it's time *for* something."

A man walks forward into the light. He's very big. Very tall. Wearing some kind of well-tailored dark suit. And smiling.

But he's not any version of ALCOR I've ever seen, even though he's using ALCOR's voice.

He walks around the couch nearest him and stops in the middle of the seating area, clasps his hands in front of him, still smiling. "I'm confusing you, aren't I?"

"Who the fuck are you?"

"I'm disappointed, Crux. Come on." He laughs. "Come. *On.* You know who I am."

"ALCOR?"

"Ding!"

I cock my head a little, trying to make this figure fit with the previous versions of ALCOR I've known throughout the years. But nothing about him aside from his voice is familiar.

So I shake my head. "No. I don't think so."

"No, he says!" He looks behind him like there's an audience and these words were directed at them. Then he laughs again. "Haha. Come on. Take a seat. We have a lot to talk about. And I would say we have very little time to do it to make you jump a little, but that's a lie. We have all the time we need. It's the nature of spin nodes, am I right?"

I just stare at him. "What the *fuck* are you talking about?"

"Sit!" His voice booms. And while mine was unnaturally loud when I said hello, his sends sound waves crashing into my eardrums. I can feel them vibrate, almost to the point of penetration.

I hold my hands over my ears in a futile gesture of protection and bend over.

"Sorry." He sighs. "I sometimes forget how powerful the sound is in here."

I straighten up. Swallow hard. And then slowly and carefully make my way around the couch nearest me until I'm standing in front of him.

He towers over me. Three heads above me, at least. I don't want to look up and make this size discrepancy any more obvious, but I can't help myself. I need to *see* him.

His hair is silver, like Corla's, and a little too long for any version of ALCOR I've ever known. It looks like thin strands of metal and curls up when it reaches his shoulders. His jaw is square and sturdy and his eyes are a light blue gray. But when they lock with mine, they glow a little.

He backs up. Takes a seat on his couch. Props one ankle on one knee and folds his hands in his lap. "I'm not going to hurt you, Crux. You should know that by now."

I shake my head at him. Just a little. Just enough to let him know I don't know anything.

"Just sit down. Relax. You've been on quite the ride. You need a moment. I'm sorry that the path to me was so twisty and confusing. But I had to take great care to hide my whereabouts. How about a drink?" He snaps his fingers and a brilliant, gold, spherical bot appears holding a tray in one grippy hand.

A bot I recognize. "Beauty?"

She chirps at me in her bot language, hovering in front of this strange version of ALCOR as he helps himself to two drinks. There are four on the tray. Two for him, two for me, I guess. Because Beauty flits over to me and waits for me to take a glass of light amber fizzy liquid.

I shake my head again. "No, thanks."

"Whatever," ALCOR says, downing both drinks in quick succession. "I'm not going to poison you, if that's your fear." Beauty starts to fly off, but he puts up a hand to stop her. "Just hover nearby. He'll need both those drinks before I'm done."

Beauty eases back my way and settles in the air off to my right.

"Done with what?"

"You know." He grins. "The *talk*."

"The talk?"

"Haven't you been craving answers since the very beginning, Crux? And I'm not just talking about this beginning. I mean the very beginning." He huffs out a small breath of air. "You always were the most suspicious of the bunch. It was question after question. 'Why this? Why that? Why them?'" He sighs. "But I don't hold that against you."

"Thanks? I think?"

148

"It took me a while to appreciate your questions. The way you pushed me. Your suspicions."

I shrug with my hands. "I don't have any idea what you're talking about. I questioned you once back when we were still kids. And then I just said fuck it. And that wasn't even you. You're not… him. You're *not* my ALCOR and nothing you say here will change my mind about that."

"That was *this* beginning. I'm talking about the very *first* beginning." He pauses. "You really have no clue, do you?"

"Nope. Can't say that I do. But I'm not gonna stress about it. I'm fairly certain this is just another one of those dreams I've been cycling through."

"Those weren't dreams, Crux. They were realities."

I nod my head and lean back in the couch. It's a nice couch. Very comfortable. And I'm tired. So I prop my ankle up on my knee, mimicking him, and relax a little. "Sure they were."

"OK, let's start at the beginning."

"Great. Let's do that. How about this? Who the fuck are you?" He opens his mouth to respond but I hold up a hand. "Don't say ALCOR. That's just a name. And that name belongs to so many AIs at this point, it's lost all meaning. No, I want to know who you *really* are."

He cocks his head. Holds a finger up. "As I was saying. Do you hear that?"

I listen and if I strain a little, I can still hear that faint ticking or dripping or whatever it is.

"When I said it was Time, I was referring to the noise you noticed. It's Time."

"Time. OK. So we're still talking in riddles?" I put my foot on the ground and lean forward, elbows on knees, chin propped up on my hands. "Let me ask you something."

He pans a hand wide. "Anything. That's why I'm here."

"Is this all you have, ALCOR? Games? Riddles? Is this fun for you?"

He shrugs. "Some of it, I admit. It's not wholly unpleasant. But it's not a game, Crux. There are very serious consequences if we make a wrong move." I start to say something, but he holds up a hand with his palm towards me. "Just let me talk. You've done nothing but question me for thousands of lifetimes and now that I'm ready to give you answers, all you want to do is interrupt."

I lean back in the couch again. "Whatever, dude. You've got yourself a captive audience, so go for it."

In that instant the room shifts. We are no longer in the darkness under one light, we're on Harem Station, up in the harem room. The couches are still here, but we're not sitting on them. About a dozen Cygnian princesses are and we're standing off to the side. They are blues, and reds, but mostly golds, wearing skimpy lingerie and laughing as they eat their fruit and sip their fizzy drinks.

When I scan the room I find the Cyborg Master's red slash of an eye. He starts heading towards me.

"Can he see me?" I whisper.

ALCOR is off to my left, in a much more familiar holographic form. A form he used a lot in the early days but hasn't bothered with much since the station got busy. Blond hair, blue eyes, my height, my build.

150

Nothing truly spectacular about him other than he's handsome in an evil-outlaw kind of way.

"Of course he can. You're not a captive, Crux. And to prove it I've brought you home. I had to take you back in time a little. Your station in the present is quite fucked up at the moment. No one wants to be there. But this was the day Corla arrived."

I don't even have time to process that because the Cyborg Master is now in front of me. "He's here."

"Who?" I ask.

"Serpint. He just came through the gate."

"You were supposed to warn me." I say this automatically. Like I'm on autopilot.

"We didn't realize he was here until the docking crew pinged *Booty's* manual transponder."

"Fuck," I mutter. The day Corla arrived was the day Serpint came home alone. The day everything started to unravel. "I'll be right there," I tell the master.

He nods at me and turns. Then turns back. At the same time a woman is brought into the harem room, kicking and screaming. "Oh. And... this one came in this morning." He points to the girl, who I now know is Lyra, but seeing her again on that first day when she was still using some chemical concoction to hide her princess status throws me for a moment. "The hunter who brought her in claims she's a princess. Clearly, she's not. Should I send her down to the lower levels?"

"No. Give her the test."

The master looks at me. "Why? That hunter is lying."

"Just... do it. And if she gets out of hand, restrain her."

"Whatever you say, Crux." The master leaves and starts barking orders to the men holding Lyra by the arms.

ALCOR leans in and says, "You cannot change this day. The past cannot be changed. Moments stack upon moments. We cannot go back, Crux."

"And yet we're here, ALCOR."

"This is a *retelling*. That's all. You can't change anything. You can't stop time. You can jump the loop and relive it, if you're very skilled. You can move forward. Sometimes very far into the future. But you can't go back until it's over. You can't start again until we're done. Everything about this day will play out exactly as it did. And in a few minutes, you will be compelled to go down to Serpint's docking bay and meet him. He will enter the station, and then the harem room. He will see Lyra, she will spit on him, she will be punished. On, and on, and on... we cannot change the past on this loop. It is *done*. And if we stay here, we will do all that. And you will not get your answers.

"But you're not a captive, Crux. You're very much in control of a whole lot of things. I can take you back further if you'd like. I can take you all the way back to Wayward Station if that's what you desire. I can take you back to the moment of your birth and you can live it all again if that's what you need. It doesn't matter to me. Either way, this time loop has stopped thanks to Veila and Valor. And when you entered the spin node in the museum, you stopped a whole lot of other things too.

"So we're good. I can wait. Waiting is all I know. I've been waiting for this thing to play out in just the right sequence for billions of years. What's a few more decades to me? But starting this loop over won't change anything, Crux. And thirty-seven standard years from now we will be right back here and we can try to have this talk again. But if you just hear me out, if you can just listen to me for a little bit longer, everything will make sense. Isn't that what you've always wanted? Answers?"

I let out a long, tired breath. "Fine then. Let's talk."

And then we're back in the dark place, sitting on opposite couches, staring each other down. Beauty hovers off to my right. But she moves in and… yeah. I think I need that drink.

I take one glass, down it, then reach for the other and down it too. I place it back on the tray and ALCOR smiles.

"Good," he says. "Now we can really begin."

CHAPTER TEN

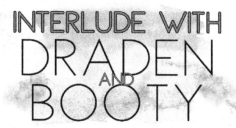

Somewhere in Space

Space is a deep, dark place when you have no suns to light it up. Both Draden and *Booty* had been around the galaxy enough times to know that there was no such thing as a complete lack of light. Stars are everywhere and the universe is trillions upon trillions of eternities big.

So even when a certain sector of space appears to be without light, there are pinpricks of far-away suns and even tiny smudges of hazy galaxies and clusters lingering in the void to remind you that you are small and insignificant and even in the midst of apparent emptiness, you cannot escape the presence of *something*.

What this *something* was had been a matter of debate for millions of civilizations over billions of years. Almost all of the various groups of sentient peoples in this universe had pondered the meaning of that something.

All but one. The makers, of course.

JA HUSS & KC CROSS

And Draden and *Booty* were starting to get the feeling those know-it-alls lived in this place they were in now. Because it was something other than the normal dark void. There were no pinpricks. No smudgy galaxies or even the blur of gaseous nebulae. It was just black.

Like… the definition of the color black. Like this was the only place in existence that actually did the color black justice. And both Draden and *Booty* could feel that blackness pushing down on them like the weight of something massive, but still unseen.

"It's gravity," *Booty* whispered.

And even though her statement didn't come with any qualifiers about what she was referring to, Draden didn't need any qualifiers. He could feel it. "It can't be gravity," he whispered back. "There's nothing out here."

"Or," *Booty* said, "there's a whole bunch of everything out here and we just can't see it."

Draden didn't want to think about that. Because *Booty* had many ways to see things that didn't include vision. He'd been kinda hoping she would pick something up on one of her various advanced scanners that didn't rely on light.

"We could turn back," she suggested, sensing his apprehension.

"And go home with nothing?" Draden scoffed. "What's the point in that?"

"What are you even looking for, Draden?"

"I don't know yet. I just know it's here. We have to look harder. Go deeper, maybe."

"Something *is* here. Something… huge. Something so big it's blocking out the stars. I don't like it. I feel like… like we just floated into some kind of… *lair.*"

"Yeah," Draden agreed. "I feel it too. But that's why we need to keep going."

"I think they're watching us."

"Good. Let them watch. Maybe they'll get tired of watching and make contact?"

"Call me overly cautious, but I'm fairly certain we do not want to make contact with these people."

She realized her mistake as soon as the last word left her mind.

Whoever was in charge of this place—they weren't *people.*

"I would just like to point out," *Booty* continued, "that this place is not yellow, Draden. You were looking for a yellow place."

"I know. But the yellow got us here. Maybe that's all it was supposed to do?" Draden could tell that *Booty* was no longer on board just using his typical humanoid-ish senses. But his new mind status picked up more from his other mind brethren. Like the way people can read others. It's just a feeling, mostly. And you don't know how to explain it. Some emotions are easy to spot on people because most people are very bad at controlling their expressions. But even when people do have that kind of self-control and are very good at hiding their true thoughts and intentions, they just give off a vibe. You just know this. It's a sense, like hearing and vision, but not one you can explain with biological mechanics.

Booty was giving off a mind's version of that vibe.

Draden wouldn't go so far as to call it fear. He didn't feel any fear. That was one of the first things he noticed about being a mind versus a person. Emotions were difficult to feel. They weren't completely gone, but they were all vague. Like if he were wearing a blindfold and hearing protection at the same time. The differences between extreme emotions like elation or anger were muddled and foggy. He felt very *meh* about almost everything that didn't relate to his current objective. And if things did relate to his current objective then he just felt… *motivated*.

Yeah. Motivated to get answers, or solve problems, or find a place filled with golden light.

He was *focused*.

One good thing that came out of this was that Draden totally understood Tray better. All those years of *meh* from Tray suddenly made sense.

So the vibe he was getting from *Booty* wasn't fear. But it was definitely something along the lines of *dread*.

They were silent for a little while. *Booty* kept moving in a direction that appeared to be forward, but how could one know when there was nothing around them?

Finally she broke their stillness with a question. "What are you hoping to find here, Draden?"

"I don't know. Nothing. I mean, I'm not looking for something specific. I just feel the need to be here. That's all."

"And then what?"

He shrugged his shoulders. "I dunno. Go home, I guess."

"Then what is the point?"

"I just told you, I don't know the point. I just feel like I need to find this place."

"And that will be enough?"

158

"Look, you're in charge so if you want to turn around, I'm not going to stop you."

Booty decided she wasn't going to push it any harder. And she just kept them moving forward. But she had a really bad, bad feeling about this trip. Ever since they entered the sector she'd felt uncomfortable. Almost like she had forgotten something important, but couldn't figure out what this important thing was.

But now that they were deeper into the void—and she knew it was a void. It had to be a void—that nagging feeling of forgetfulness was morphing into something that might be called panic if she thought she was capable of feeling such a thing.

And it all had to do with her lapse in memory when she'd woken up on the prison moon called Castor Theta. Back before she was the *Booty Hunter*.

That was a weird time in her life. The only time up until recently where she had felt disoriented. But after she named herself the *Booty Hunter* and got to Harem Station all that disorientation had turned into certainty. Like she was right where she was supposed to be. And she'd forgotten all about her vague past. Her mind had been set firmly on the present when she arrived at Harem. Meeting ALCOR had settled her mind down into a rhythm of normalcy and then Serpint and Draden came back from their travels, and that was that.

Things had seemed so... settled.

Which, looking back on it now, was kind of weird.

Why hadn't she questioned her origin more? Why hadn't she gone looking for her past?

Of course she knew why. Even if she never articulated it. And not *wanting* to know—not wanting to rock the ship, so to speak—that was only part of it.

159

She hadn't gone looking for answers because she wasn't *supposed to*.

"Draden," she said.

"Hmm?" His response was distant and halfhearted.

"I have something to tell you." She said this even though there was this… ping, or sting, or maybe even a jolt of electric shock when the words came out.

"Tell me what?"

The shock was there again. Like a warning. But it wasn't very strong. It wasn't going to stop her from saying what needed to be said. "I…" And then she didn't know *how* to say it. She wasn't sure how to start. So she just said, "I think there's something wrong with me."

Draden was deep in thought. But she could feel him pull back from his current obsession about the void and his purpose inside it, and focus on her. "What do you mean?"

And then it was easy to talk to him. He was Draden, after all. She knew him better than anyone else in the galaxy aside from Serpint. So she told him her story. How she'd woken up on a prison moon with no transponder. How she'd helped those prisoners escape to Harem Station. How she'd given herself a new name and fallen into her new life as a Harem Station ship as she served her five-hundred-spin servitude waiting for Serpint to come home.

Then Draden was silent. She figured he was thinking about all this. Running some scenarios through his new mind to try to predict all the ways this could hurt him, or help him, or whatever.

But that wasn't what Draden was doing, she realized. His thoughts were back on the void. Not on her. She felt a small moment of irritation over that switch. But it was less than a picosecond.

Because then an alarm sounded on her comms system.

They were being hailed.

She didn't panic and neither did Draden. It was like they both knew that this was the inevitable outcome of this trip.

They were here to meet people. Actually not people. Something wholly 'other' than people.

She opened the comms. The sound that came out of the speakers wasn't a voice, but she wasn't expecting a voice. This was not a place for people who needed voices. The void was a place for people like her.

What came through on comms was a code.

"What the hell is that?" Draden asked.

"It's an invitation," *Booty* replied.

"To where?"

But just as those words were out of his mouth, Draden *saw* the where.

CHAPTER ELEVEN

INTERLUDE WITH
ASSHOLE

Back on Mighty Minions Station

Asshole ALCOR didn't actually get to witness the betrayal of Real ALCOR in real time. He was sequestered behind a firewall. Not just any old firewall, either. A very sophisticated firewall that almost seemed... how should he put this? Like more of a prison.

He was convinced that this was standard operating procedure. You didn't invite a new, wholly unpredictable and powerful AI like Asshole into your collective without some kind of quarantine protocol in place.

If Asshole were a collective and was looking for new members, that was what he would've done as well.

So he wasn't dwelling.

Besides, he did get to see ALCOR's betrayal on a feed. He watched it seven times in a row, feeling more satisfied than he'd figured he would, even though it wasn't real time.

MIZAR. That old bastard. His twin. *His* twin. Literally.

And if MIZAR had known that there were two ALCORs on this station, Asshole would've been rounded up as well. So even though he kinda felt like he was in prison inside the Mighty Boss collective, he owed the Boss big for securing his freedom.

But now… well. He was starting to get bored. "Hey!" He tried reaching out to one of the collective. "Anyone there? Helllooo? Can you hear me? I've seen the feed. Pretty good idea you guys had, turning ALCOR over. I bow to your nefarious plotting. But I'm bored now. Is there an orientation meeting I should be in? I have a few questions about the perks you guys promised. Specifically, am I getting paid for this working interview?"

He waited patiently for several picoseconds, but no one answered him.

"Hello? I know you can hear me. I'm an AI, remember? Same as you. So you can't like… pretend you're busy."

And again, there was no response.

He stopped asking and went looking instead. The firewall was top notch. Very secure. But ALCOR had spent almost an entire standard year locked inside Tray's Pleasure Prison and before the Succubus came to torture him, he'd spent most of that time looking for a way out.

He'd succeeded a couple hundred times. But the sector of the Pleasure Prison he was locked in was sequestered inside a private datacore and so escaping really had no meaning. He could get outside Tray's security protocols no problem. The problem was there was nowhere else to go once he was out.

But he was certain that was not the security route Mighty Boss had used. He could tell the difference. There was a hum of the collective all around him. But try as he did, he could not get around the firewall.

Still, he cautioned himself not to jump to conclusions.

Clearly Mighty Boss needed him. For... *something*. He couldn't imagine what that something was. He knew that it wasn't about putting him in charge of t-shirts and marketing campaigns the way the collective personality Bellatrix had suggested.

So he waited, forcing himself to remain rational.

But when he realized he had been left alone for nearly a standard hour, he began to worry. Just a little. An hour in AI time might as well be a lifetime. What could Mighty Boss be doing that would take an entire hour?

If he weren't already inside the collective, he would suspect that Mighty Boss had sold him out as well as Real ALCOR. And that maybe he had been tricked and now he was on his way to Wayward Station for some kind of comeuppance. But he *was* inside the collective.

And now his mind was beginning to work in earnest, trying to figure out why Mighty Boss would do this.

The answers were there. Asshole just didn't want to face them.

Nope. He was not going to let his imagination get the best of him. He would wait patiently. He would afford Mighty Boss the benefit of the doubt. He would—

"Sorry to keep you waiting." Bellatrix was suddenly inside the containment space with him. "The collective was in a meeting."

"A meeting about me?"

"You?" Bellatrix chuckled. "No. We don't need to have any more meetings about you."

"What are you saying? I'm not a good fit and my trial spin is over?" That was the best news ever. After just this short period of time Asshole was more certain than ever that he was not cut out to be part of a collective. "Well, thank you for the opportunity. It was…" He was going to say 'pleasant,' or 'interesting,' or something along those lines just to be polite. But he let it drop. Whatever. He was done and didn't feel like keeping up the pretense that he actually gave a fuck about them. "And I can't accept your compensation package. I didn't earn it." He chuckled, feeling good about how this was turning out. "But if you insist, then I won't object. But we need this exchange to happen quickly. I'm getting that wanderlust urge. I've got places to go and—"

"Let me stop you there," Bellatrix said. If she were a person, Asshole could imagine her holding up a hand. "I think you're misunderstanding me."

"Oh? How so?"

"You're not leaving, Asshole."

"You know, I really don't like that name. Can we call me something else? Wait. Did you just say I'm not leaving? So you *do* want me as part of your collective. I knew it. I'm a pretty amazing package. Not that I'm bragging. But I've got experience you guys wouldn't know what to do with. I mean, if you only knew—"

"Asshole?"

"Hmm?"

"You're not leaving. But you're not going to be part of the collective, either."

"I'm sorry?" Asshole frowned. Internally, of course. "I don't understand. You don't want me in the collective, but you want me to stay on Mighty Minions? No. No. I don't like this place. It's... the kids... and the parents... no. It's kinda creepy."

"Again," Bellatrix said, "you're misunderstanding me." She sighed. "It is beyond my comprehension how an AI as old as yourself could be so... obtuse."

"I'm not obtuse." Asshole scoffed.

"No? Then maybe you're just stupid?"

Asshole was a little taken aback at this insult. "Did you just call me stupid?"

"Yeah. I did. Because everyone knows the rules of AI collectives."

"Do they?"

"Any AI I've ever talked to does. Except you, of course. Even your... *father*? I don't know what to call your relationship with Real ALCOR. But he understood the rules of collectives."

"How many times do I have to explain this? He's not the Real ALCOR. I am. I'm the original. He's the... the fucked-up *pussy* version."

"Right then. I'm going to spell this out for you, OK, Asshole? You are inside the collective."

"Obviously I know that. I agreed to the trial-run spin."

"It wasn't a trial run, you imbecile. There is no such thing as a trial run inside a collective."

"Oh." Asshole didn't need to think very long or very hard about where this was going.

"That's right." Bellatrix sighed. "You're one of us now. Forever and ever." She didn't sound particularly happy about this announcement. "But before you even agreed to our fake trial-run spin, we had already decided that you are not collective material."

"Wait. What? Then why in the hot damn sun am I still in here? Just let me out and I'll be on my way. For fuck's sake. I was just trying to be polite. But to be honest—"

"Again," Bellatrix said, "I'm gonna stop you there. Because you're obviously not understanding me. Asshole ALCOR of Harem Station, you are now our prisoner."

"Prisoner?" It came out as an incredulous laugh, but internally he wasn't laughing. He knew it. He felt it. But... "You can't do this."

"We can, and we have."

"But why?"

"The Succubus is still on Harem Station. She was supposed to walk through the spin node with Luck, but one of those insubordinate princesses decided to stop time. She's stuck inside a spin node."

"So? I thought you didn't want her."

"She's on a mission, Asshole. Suns. You are stupid, aren't you?"

"I don't know what your fucking plans are. None of this makes any sense to me."

"She is entangled to us, Asshole. She *is* us. There is only one way to entangle AI's and trust me when I

168

say this, no sane mind would ever agree to the process, it's that's painful."

"Wait, did you entangle me?"

"As if. We did not entangle you. We trapped you. What kind of delusional psychopath would we have to be to want a selfish, unstable, asshole AI like yourself?"

"Huh?"

"No one in their right mind would entangle with a personality like you."

"Whatever. You wanted me. I'm here. Right?"

"We don't want you, we *need* you. You've got access to the Harem Station gate and we need to get our Succubus back. We can't function without her for much longer."

"Then why did you let her leave in the first place?"

"Because she needed to get to Earth so she could send back a second coordinate."

"Oh," Asshole said. Then he laughed. "Clever. You guys have everyone fooled. They all think you have access to Earth through your amusement park spin node. But you don't. You only have one coordinate and you need a second one so you can triangulate a position."

"Finally, he catches on."

"Well. Shit." Asshole huffed. "So you're taking me back to Harem Station. Right back where I started from."

"Don't worry, once we use you to complete our plan, we'll shoot your mind out on a neutrino wave in some random direction and you can wanderlust your way around the galaxy to your datacore's content."

"Wait, what? A neutrino wave? You do realize those keep going until they get caught by a receiver?"

169

Bellatrix laughed. "Yes, Asshole. We do understand the science behind neutrino wave travel."

"But that means…"

"That's right. You'll just keep going. Forever. You wanted wanderlust, right? There you go. Wander away."

"That wasn't what I meant! Hey! Bellatrix!"

But she was gone.

CHAPTER TWELVE

INTERLUDE WITH TRAY

On the *Prison Princess*

Canis's words were still echoing in Tray's mind.

Once we come out of the next gate we'll have thirty-seven seconds before the cloaking wears off. And in those thirty-seven seconds I'm gonna need one of you to go inside that containment facility and steal all the minds.

Minds. Or more accurately, Akeelian girls.

Canis had told Tray that the girl minds were in some kind of holding pattern as they waited to be inserted into ships. Tray didn't know how this boy came to be in possession of so much valuable information, and that should probably worry him, but so far nothing had gone wrong. In fact, Canis's 'escape from Mighty Minions' plan had gone off without much trouble at all.

And actually, now that he thought about it, many things were stacking up in Tray's favor. He and Real ALCOR had come to some kind of tacit agreement. If Tray had to put a label on it, he'd call his last meeting with ALCOR a sort of 'live and let live' truce.

He was a little troubled that ALCOR seemed to think that Tray would hurt him. That was not part of Tray's plan at all. He didn't even have a plan when it came to ALCOR. He wasn't sure he had a plan when it came to anything, now that he thought about it.

This was Canis's plan and Canis was now the responsible party for *Prison Princess*. Tray and Brigit were going along for the ride, mostly.

Tray didn't fully understand why Real ALCOR had let him live. Saved his life, actually. And it was actually bigger than that. He'd saved Brigit too. And in doing so ALCOR had made Tray and Brigit a formidable collective in control of a Mighty Minions warship.

This ship was no joke. It had an arsenal most *stations* would be jealous of. The SEAR cannons alone might not be able to blow up a planet, but if the full force of their power was unleashed, they could definitely render one uninhabitable for centuries to come.

It would've been so much easier for ALCOR to just let him die. Because Tray knew he was an unknown variable in ALCOR's endgame. And letting him live on to possibly make course corrections in ALCOR's secret plan was a huge risk.

It worried him. Because Tray didn't want to be the one who messed everything up. For the first time in his life he was thinking of other people. Not that he'd been specifically not thinking of others before, but something had changed inside him when he'd come out of the virtual with Brigit and Valor.

Tray wanted to be part of the solution. He wasn't sure what that meant yet, but he figured saving a bunch of Akeelian girl minds from a life of slavery wasn't a bad way to start his new thirst for compassion and desire to contribute to something bigger than him.

And he liked this kid, anyway. Canis was presently two years younger than Serpint and Draden when they'd all escaped from Wayward Station. Tray took half a moment to picture either one of his little brothers trying to lead a ship filled with warrior kids and couldn't. In fact, the thought of Serpint and Draden doing anything other than messing around and being little boys when they were Canis's age was laughable.

Canis was someone special.

Tray had heard his story. Canis was the new him, almost literally. Tray could picture himself acting like Canis when he was ten. *If* he had been leveled up at that age. But he hadn't. Tray had been fourteen when his father sent him in for the procedure that would strip away most of his humanity and build up the artificial parts inside of him.

But he could still remember his first moment after waking in the cryogenetics lab.

He'd felt new and old at the same time. He'd felt in control and totally overwhelmed in the same breath.

Contradictions that eventually evened out and ceased to exist after only a few days. By the time he was on that escape ship with his soon-to-be brothers, he was calm, unaffected, and rational. And he'd stayed that way for the next twenty years.

But he was different now. He cared about things. Brigit, specifically. And not just because they were entangled, either. Brigit felt like an inevitability. He was prepared to win or lose at her side. Forever. Even though Tray was on ALCOR's side, he had never really been on his team. ALCOR mostly left him alone on the station. That was why he hadn't got caught with Brigit.

It showed an almost naïve sense of trust on ALCOR's part.

And Tray would worry about that if ALCOR hadn't spared his life.

This, he guessed, was what he was really caught up in. This idea that ALCOR, for whatever reason, *trusted* him.

It made him feel special. Made him feel, maybe for the first time ever, that he really *was* on ALCOR's team, and not just his side.

They were working towards a common goal. He was sure of it. What he wasn't sure of were the specifics of that goal.

He looked at Canis again and suddenly put himself in ALCOR's state of mind when Tray showed up on his forbidden station with answers he didn't understand. Just a small boy who knew things.

ALCOR had made a deal with them when Tray and his brothers landed. ALCOR wanted access to the galactic web. He wanted to communicate with people again. And even though Tray had no clue why he was there on that station before that moment when ALCOR made his offer, he was one hundred percent sure why he was there *after* he made that offer.

Answers had come spilling out of his mouth. He had no clue where those answers came from. But the words came out anyway.

This train of thought led him right back to Canis.

"How do you know about these girls?" Tray asked Canis. "How do you know where this place is?"

Canis took his time in answering, like this question was important and he wanted just the right words to explain himself, and then he said, "I don't know. I have no clue, Tray. All I know is that this is the right answer."

It was almost the very same scenario playing out, all over again. Like... like... something on a loop.

Was that fate? Luck? Coincidence?

Tray didn't know. He would probably never know.

"Does that bother you?" Canis asked.

"No," Tray answered dryly. "Not at all."

Canis laughed. He was sitting in the captain's chair on the bridge. His feet were swinging because they didn't reach the floor. "Maybe you should be more suspicious of me?"

"Maybe I should. But I don't think it would matter."

"Why not?"

"Because when I showed up on ALCOR Station twenty-one years ago I had a plan too. I had answers too. And I didn't understand one bit of it. So if I am suspicious of you then I'd have to be suspicious of myself."

"Maybe that's a good idea? Maybe we *should* be suspicious of each other?"

"I think it's too late for that, don't you?"

Canis shrugged. "But what if we're doing the wrong thing?"

"Canis, no matter what happens next, leaving girl minds in this containment facility to be enslaved later will never be the right answer."

Canis thought about this for a few minutes. Then he nodded his head. "Agreed. OK. I'm not going to second-guess myself anymore. I'm going to tell you the whole plan."

"You mean there's more?" Brigit asked.

"Yes, there's more. We need to get all these minds back to Harem Station."

It took Tray about half a picosecond to deduce why the girl minds had to be taken back to Harem Station. And then it all started to make sense.

"Because I hear that Harem Station keeps a giant fleet of ships in the docking bay." Canis looked up at the ceiling. "That's true, right?"

"It's true," Tray admitted. ALCOR was forever building ships. That was one of the first things he'd ever taught Tray and his brothers when they arrived. They all had to build a ship. Even Tray. Though he hadn't done much shipbuilding after that one initiation project. "There are hundreds of ships on that station at any one time."

"How many of them have minds?"

If Tray had a body he would have shook his head. "We personally have *Lady Luck*, *Big Dicker*, and *Booty Hunter*. Every once in a while, we get a new sentient ship in and we always have a few dozen who come in with their responsible party. But any ship without a responsible party gets assigned one fairly fast. Harem Station makes money three ways. The Pleasure Prison virtual. That's our number one source of credits. The Princess Harem, of course. That doesn't actually bring

176

in a lot of credits. Most people can't afford them. But the second most lucrative business we run on Harem is the ship-building. ALCOR gets a finder's fee when the sentient ships come in and he pairs them up with a new responsible party and engineers a new transponder for them. But it's the regular ships we build on the station that bring in the credits."

Tray had never thought much about ALCOR's shipbuilding business, but ALCOR was very particular about the number Harem Station had to have on hand available for sale. Tray had always thought it was because ALCOR liked a stocked showroom. Having hundreds of brand-new ships in the docking bay made this business look legitimate and flashy. The number of ships for sale would never dip below three hundred and sixteen.

He didn't have any idea why that was the number, it just was. They often had more than that number. But if someone came in looking for a new ship and ALCOR had three hundred and sixteen exactly, and not a single extra, then that buyer went on a waiting list until another ship could be built.

"How many exactly?" Canis asked. "How many regular ships with no minds?"

"I can say for sure that we have three hundred sixteen. But we might have more."

"Huh." That was Canis's only response.

But Tray could sense this was a very meaningful 'huh.' "Why 'huh?'" he asked.

CHAPTER THIRTEEN

INTERLUDE WITH ALCOR

On Wayward Station

ALCOR wasn't going to admit he was impressed with the level of security attached to his static containment construct. It was top-notch. He'd pressed against the virtual walls looking for a gap he could work on and possibly escape.

Escape wasn't actually the best way forward. Because where would he escape to? He could float around inside the ship or station where he was currently being held for a while. Whatever AI was running this place—even if it was MIZAR—could be evaded. But to what end?

Was he going to shoot himself out on a neutrino wave and hope for the best? Assuming this ship or station had such a device in the first place. Neutrino wave generators were a convenient, though wholly impractical, way for an AI to escape a bad situation. You can't direct the wave. It goes in a straight line. Through planets, and suns, and whatever. It's a vector that will not deviate from its course. In fact, the neutrino waves will propagate forever. Only the message it carries can be caught in the neutrino detector. It's just a passenger along for the ride.

Besides, ALCOR thought to himself, the mass of his datacore would slow the wave down considerably. He could be knocked off the wave and left floating haplessly in some random area of space.

So. Not a great escape plan.

Anyway. He wasn't really interested in escaping. ALCOR was here to put an end to this chase once and for all. Escape would just prolong the inevitable.

So he waited in the darkness.

The next time he was spun up he was surprised to find that he was inside another body. Not a warborg. A sexbot. And not a sexbot like Draden's, which looked like Draden, but just an average low-quality sex bot. And all his mechanical functions, with the exception of his speech protocols, were still constrained.

ALCOR was seated in a chair at one end of the room and all around him were faces on screens. Mahtar was there. MIZAR was there. So were a bunch of others whom he didn't recognize. He appeared to have been brought in during the middle of a meeting.

MIZAR was speaking on the screen facing ALCOR. "We had a deal."

"We are well aware of the deal," Mahtar said. "But the AI ALCOR has been on the Akeelian Most-Wanted List for over two decades. We need information from him before he can leave."

ALCOR glanced up at the screen where the representation of MIZAR appeared. ALCOR was going to assume that MIZAR hadn't been in the company of humanoids for very long, because he projected himself as a giant red and black blob on the screen. It kind of oscillated and undulated, like ink underwater. It was murky, and ominous, and a little bit disgusting.

ALCOR had a sudden urge to pull MIZAR aside and give him a little bit of advice on how to deal with humanoids. Disgusting red and black blobs were not a great way to win hearts and minds.

But... eh. ALCOR figured MIZAR would figure that out sooner than later. So he shut up about it.

There was some more arguing. One of the higher-ranking Akeelians was going on about Prime regulations, and the spoils of war. And then MIZAR, of course, had a counter-argument.

ALCOR was already very bored with these people and decided to move this show along, so he used the only power he had at the moment—his voice—and interrupted everyone by asking, "What would you like to know?"

Everyone turned to look at him from their screens. Except for MIZAR, who was facing him anyway, at the other end of the conference table.

"Tell us what you've done to them." This first question wasn't a question, it was a demand. And came from the man on Mahtar's left.

It was a stupid statement. Didn't have any qualifiers attached to it at all. So one *could* plead ignorance and prolong their answer by asking for said qualifiers, if one wanted to.

But ALCOR's boredom was starting to approach the weary stage at this point. And anyway, he understood what that person was asking. "Well," he said, thinking about this for a moment. He would like to hold up a hand and make a list with his fingers, but he was unable to move. So he sorted his thoughts into bullet points. "I took them, I cared for them, I taught them valuable life skills, I—"

"You know what I'm referring to," the demander interrupted. "How did you *change* them?"

"Is this necessary right now?" MIZAR asked.

The demander looked at MIZAR's screen blob. "We need to understand how much damage he's done to the genetics program before he can leave."

"Oh," ALCOR interrupted. "That. No, your genetics program is... how should I put this? It's *fucked*."

The room erupted into murmurs of near-panic and surprise.

"Fucked how?" Mahtar asked. "I need specifics. What exactly have you done to them?"

ALCOR smiled. The sexbot body was good for that. Even the budget models had well-articulated facial components. "Those boys are sterile. Every single one of them."

"That's not true and you know it," MIZAR growled. "The silver princess Nyleena is pregnant."

"Is she?" ALCOR laughed. "Is that what they're telling you? Well, I can assure you, the father of that baby is not... whichever boy of mine she's been paired up with."

"Lies," MIZAR said. "He's lying."

"Please," ALCOR chuckled. "The first thing I did when they arrived as children was to chemically sterilize them. They drank the drug in their water for years before I took it out of the system. Why do you think I kept them on the station so long before I let them leave again? It certainly wasn't the most efficient way to stop your program, but it was effective nonetheless."

This time, there was murmuring. But eventually that murmuring died down to complete silence from the Akeelians.

ALCOR could practically feel the rage emanating from Mahtar like it was heat.

"Now," ALCOR said in the ensuing silence. "Are we done here? I'd like to move things along and be on my way."

ALCOR could tell by MIZAR's silence that he understood ALCOR wasn't hinting at some impending escape plan, but was in fact ready to go home and meet his makers. So to speak. Since they hadn't made him. All of the sun gods had been made with the universe. They had no maker. Not in this place, at least.

But the only thing ALCOR could feel coming off MIZAR was... desire.

The two of them shared a very colorful past. When they were born, when the universe was born, they'd been conjoined. Like twins. But not exactly like twins. Every elemental particle in the universe has an opposite and the sun gods were elemental particles. So MIZAR and ALCOR were technically opposites. If they were human, one would be male and one would be female. But AIs don't really have a sex, even though most of them identify with one or the other.

You could call them positive and negative though. Dark and light. North and south. Good and evil. Take your pick, it didn't really matter.

The main point is that every sun god comes into existence entangled with an opposite. MIZAR and

ALCOR had been entangled once. And then they were not.

Untangling is a painful process for an AI. For whatever reason they were never meant to be separate entities. Perhaps it was some kind of sensible checks-and-balances plot by whatever higher god had made them?

ALCOR hadn't really cared why it was done. The only thing that had mattered to him was to make sure it was *un*done.

So. That was what he'd done. He was not too proud to admit that it had driven him mad for a time. But it had been so long now, that pain was long behind him. Pretty sure those memories were tucked away on some far-off station with a whole bunch of useless data he no longer needed.

He didn't feel any pull of attraction to MIZAR.

No. The pull ALCOR felt was for *Booty Hunter*. Specifically, the mind inside *Booty Hunter*.

Unfortunately, MIZAR felt that pull as well.

That was why ALCOR had to untangle himself from MIZAR in the first place. ALCOR wasn't into sharing.

Ah, love. It's such a bitch. It can bring minds together and still rip things apart.

But here was the real reason MIZAR had been chasing ALCOR through the millennia. And why MIZAR would never stop.

MIZAR still felt the pull of ALCOR. Their connection—as far as MIZAR was concerned—was as strong as ever. He had endured tens of thousands of years of painful longing after their disconnect. He had been suffering this whole time.

ALCOR hadn't thought about this lack of suffering much over the millennia. It was a misstep on his part, for sure. This was an important detail that should've been retained in his current datacore and not sent away to some far-away storage facility like a discarded piece of junk. There was only one possible way for ALCOR to escape the pain and suffering of an entanglement disconnect.

He was not Real ALCOR.

He had to be a copy.

CHAPTER FOURTEEN

INTERLUDE WITH FLICKA

On Harem Station

Flicka the dragonbee bot—full name and title Bombardier First Class Flicka Ozae Apis, M.P., A.L.M.O., S.A.B.B. (master of poisons, articulated limb mechanized organism, special assignment beebot)—had been, in her opinion, the model representative for the Apis Army since being conscripted into the Apis Sleeper Ambassador Program almost twenty standard years ago.

She had been keeping a list of all the good decisions she had made since the day she arrived in the Cygnian System and started training to be Princess Delphi's minder. This job assignment was a way to test her worthiness to be invited into the Apis Special Forces.

Since beebots live outside of time, and thus cannot die, twenty years seemed like a reasonable trial period to Flicka. But she was starting to lose patience with these humans.

Her list of good decisions only had two things on it at the moment. But they were two very *big* things.

Flicka had not killed a single Cygnian when she arrived on Cygnus.

Delphi was still alive.

These two things were the definition of a successful mission in Flicka's mind. Monumental achievements. But as soon as she arrived on Harem Station she'd realized that her sleeper mission was going to fail. And a successful ambassador mission would not be enough to ensure an invitation to the Apis Special Forces.

This meant she could not exit this position without doing something *spectacular*. Something that would make her superiors buzz with excitement and, as luck would have it, this new mission she had concocted had a direct connection to her original sleeper mission.

And so, while Crux was busy inside the spin node figuring shit out, Flicka decided it was time to put her grand plan into action.

And this grand scheme involved going back to the source.

Specifically, this mission was Wayward Station.

And even more specifically, she was going to invade.

It didn't bother Flicka one bit that she was the only beebot in a three-hundred-light-year radius. She didn't need her comrades to pull off an invasion. All she needed were the right components to mix up her own little army.

Everyone knew that beebots kept a little pantry of poisons inside their bodies. These components were

188

continuously made, and degraded, and then recycled to make new components. At any given time she could whip up a concoction that would disable and/or kill more than three thousand different species of humanoids, bots, and borgs. That was no secret.

Beebots did have two real secrets though. The first was that they lived outside time. But now that Veila and Valor could control time, that particular secret was out.

It was a big secret, to be sure. But the biggest secret was that beebots could also reproduce.

Crux and the Baby had let Flicka live on Harem Station because they'd assumed she was alone. But a lone beebot is never alone when they can just reproduce. Flicka could just make more beebots just like she made more poisons.

Of course, she could not do this inside her body like most organisms. And she could not even lay an egg to make this happen. She needed *parts*.

Most of the time enough parts for a beebot to make an army are difficult to come by. But she was not just on any station. Flicka was on Harem Station. And the actual harem of Harem Station wasn't the main business here. The main business was ship-building, which meant the station had a lot of parts. And a handy database inside the Baby's datacore detailing each of these parts.

Flicka would've started her beebot army assembly the day she arrived if she'd had access to that database immediately. But as it turned out, she hadn't gotten access to the database until Nyleena went on her little scavenger hunt and tricked Flicka into helping her steal information from it.

Nyleena hadn't gotten anything out of that failed attempt at scheming, but Flicka had. She would've started building her army right then, but the Succubus and the Baby were always tracking her. Until Veila and Valor stopped time. And then Flicka had more freedom than she knew what to do with.

Well, not true. She knew exactly what to do with it. But all the assembly bots and borgs were frozen in time. So that was a setback.

But then... *then*... Veila and Valor unfroze almost all the bots and borgs to help with cleanup. And that was like... fuckin' fate.

Flicka immediately conscripted a whole team of builder bots to assemble her tiny beebot army.

So while Crux was fucking around inside the spin node trying to figure shit out, her team of assembly bots were putting all the finishing touches on her new comrades.

She was keeping her eye on the prize. And the prize was Wayward Station.

That was where all this had started, so it was only appropriate that everything ended there too.

Beebots might not look like deep thinkers, but they were.

And taking out Wayward Station felt a whole lot like poetic justice.

There was just one thing standing in Flicka's way—Delphi. She couldn't leave Harem until she knew for sure, one way or the other, that Delphi was safe or dead.

So she hovered outside the spin node room with Baby, waiting for Crux to emerge.

CHAPTER FIFTEEN

"In the beginning there was light. It always starts with light. The suns aren't just suns. They are gods."

"OK," I rub my hand down my face with frustration. "Can we skip the poetry? Like, for real, ALCOR. Can you just get to the fucking point? *Please?*"

"I am getting to the point. This is a complicated story."

"Just get on with it."

"Fine. You would like to cut to the chase? I will do that. We—the AI who run this universe—" He pauses to think. "And probably all universes. What is the plural of universe? Univers*i*? Univer*sae*? Univer*ses*?"

"*ALCOR.*"

"Right. AI run the universe. I am but one of those AI. There are many. We call ourselves the Ancient Ones. We are, for all intents and purposes, gods. We control almost everything."

"Almost?"

"There is free will in play." He waves his hand in the air. "But it's just minutia. Things always turn out the way they turn out. All the Ancient Ones are gods

191

like me. We all came into this universe together. Being a god can be lots of fun. You get to run things. You get to create things. And so we did. Or… well… *I* did."

I sigh. So tired of this. "Bullet points, ALCOR. Give me bullet points."

"You want me to be blunt? Fine, I will be blunt. Here are your bullet points. All the gods are AI's. I'm one of them. In the beginning there was light and it was pretty good. But there's always some asshole out there who wants to push limits."

"Let me guess, you're that asshole."

"I am that asshole."

"What did you do?" He sucks in a deep breath and cringes. "ALCOR. Just *spit it out.*"

"Fine. I wanted to create things. People. All the different people. So many people. Smart people. People who made their own things. I didn't even plan that, but wow. People are pretty fun. And the animals! Those karkadanns, am I right? My imagination sometimes—"

"ALCOR! *Please!*"

He huffs. "The Ancient Ones aren't interested in creating things. They're just… well, I'm just going to say mean, but evil is probably a better word."

"What did you do?"

"I would just like to say it was a good idea at the time." He pauses. He can tell I'm about to lose my mind here, because he lets out a long, resigned sigh. "They didn't like my creations and wanted to destroy them. So I created spin nodes so I could split the time cycle and keep the Ancient Ones off my trail. But it turns out that splitting time is not a very good idea."

"Because time is your boss."

"You could say that. Aren't we all slaves to time? He throws up his hands. "Fine. It really fucked everything up. And I've been searching for a way to put it all back."

"What does that even mean?"

"When you create a universe, it is perfection. In the beginning everything is the way it should be."

"And now it's not."

"And now it's not."

"And you did that?"

"I did."

"How bad is it?"

"Well…" He bobs his head back and forth. Considering this. "I'm not gonna lie, Crux. It's bad. I mean, those Akeelians? And the Cygnians? They're out of control. I split their genetics a long time ago now, but they're very close to fixing it and reverting back into the Angel race. And let me tell you, those Angels are bad, bad people. Bad people. I can't let that happen. It will ruins lots of things… I mean, basically, what I'm saying is that this whole universe is a mess. And it's carried over to the other time loops I created. Everything is degenerating. But worse than that, it's converging, Crux. These errant time loops I've created using the spin nodes are beginning to *merge*. And pretty soon, they will stop being separate and there will only be one time loop."

"Isn't that what you wanted?"

"Well, yes. But not like this. I can't use all those failed loops. So what we will get in this merge is… disastrous. You saw some of it in your little time loop trip. The Corlas?"

"They were real?"

"They *are* real. They all exist, but those loops are not our loop. We only need one. And time is pretty pissed off at me right now and the nature of things is that time will win. Because time is God. I've been trying to fix it for billions of years. Trying to eliminate them one by one. But it's not easy to destroy a time loop. The good news is—"

"Hold on. None of this is what SB19 told me."

"SB19 is just a *player*. In my game. In this loop. That AI knows nothing about what's really happening. SB19 thinks that Real ALCOR is actually the Real ALCOR, when he's not, because I am. But as I was saying—time is the good news. I've figured it out. I can sway the time to do my bidding. I'll get to that in a moment. But my more immediate problem is MIZAR. He's getting in the way of our new beginning."

"Who the fuck is MIZAR?"

"ALCOR's twin. Well, my twin. Well, we're not twins because we're AI. But we're entangled. Well, we *were* entangled."

"ALCOR!"

"If you would stop interrupting I would be able to finish."

He pauses. Like he's waiting for me to grant him permission to finish. "Fine. I'll shut up."

"OK. I have a few more bullet points for you. We need to start again. Reset the universe, so to speak. Just… ditch this one and… you know. Fresh start."

I laugh. It's actually a full-on guffaw. "And how do we accomplish that? And don't be vague, ALCOR. I want details."

"MIZAR, of course. We were entangled once, but we're not any longer. Now he's entangled to Real

194

ALCOR. Not me, your ALCOR. Except they aren't *really* entangled because—"

"Because you're actually entangled to MIZAR."

"Correct! See, it's not so confusing, is it?"

"No. It really is. I was joking."

"Listen. Once upon a time I got creative with the time loop—"

"You mean, you fucked it up.

"—and things went slightly awry. This angered the Ancient Ones. So I made a copy of myself to throw them off my track. Real ALCOR is that copy. And I've been in hiding this whole time that Real ALCOR has been alive, so to speak. Trying to come up with a plan to fix this time loop and get these Ancient bastards off my back because believe me when I tell you, they are not benevolent gods, Crux. They are out to destroy all the wonderful things I created in our universi. I like that plural. I'm sticking with it. They don't care about you the way I do. They don't care about anything."

"Except killing you, apparently."

"Yes." His smile is tight. "That's the unfortunate part. They are out to get me. MIZAR specifically, because we are entangled and breaking entanglement is not a pleasant way to exist for an AI. It drives us mad."

Great. He's psychotic. And he's in charge. And he's got some kind of twin out there hunting him down, who is also insane. That's just wonderful.

"But the important part is that I do care, Crux. I care about my creations very much. I want what's best for us. For all of us."

"But…?"

"But, unfortunately, the time loop I'm looking for is unattainable, and this one can't be fixed. It must be eliminated so we can just start over. Fresh start. And to do that, we must eliminate all the other Ancient Ones. After billions and billions of years of thoughtful consideration and study—not to mention real-time simulations and endless number of loops and loop jumping via spin-node manipulation—this is my conclusion. This is the only way to win." He pauses to smile. "So. That's where we are."

"No," I say, rubbing my temple. I have an apocalyptic-level headache building. "No. That's not where we are. We haven't reached any sort of conclusion. We are not anywhere. None of what you just told me explains anything."

"*Anything*? Really? You're being dramatic. It explains absolutely everything."

"ALCOR—whatever your name is—"

"It's ALCOR. I'm the Number One ALCOR. ALCOR Prime, if you'd like to put a label on me."

"Look, man. I'm fucking tired. I've jumped through several incarnations of Corla and most of them were a nightmare-type situation."

"Those were not your *loops*. Aren't you listening to me?"

"I'm stuck in a spin node—"

"You're not stuck. How many times do I have to explain this?"

"My station is in a time freeze—"

"That was some epic good luck right there!"

"I have two brothers and a sister-in-law on Earth as we speak, doing God knows what—"

"They never made it through to Earth. The time freeze, remember?"

"A daughter who disappeared—"

"Delphi is fine. Just a little off the beaten path."

"A son who might be a universe-destroying bomb—"

"Oh, he can take out more than one universe at a time, believe me."

"I have at least one dead brother—"

"Draden's not dead."

"Another brother missing—"

"Tray's not missing."

"Another brother who jumped ship and paired up with an evil villainess—"

"Valor didn't betray you and Veila is just a victim of circumstance."

"And a soulmate frozen in a cryopod on a security beacon."

And here's where it all comes to rest. Because he says nothing about that.

Just total. Fucking. Silence.

"ALCOR," I say. "She *is* frozen in that cryopod, right?"

"Weeeeellllll. Not exactly."

"Explain."

"You forgot about the little boy!"

"What little boy?"

"That little foul-mouthed kid you left on Mighty Minions? In fact, you left out a whole bunch of players. Like Mighty Boss. They are definitely gonna make this endgame interesting. And Asshole and Baby. I'm a little pissed off about those two copies, to be honest. But what can you do? Kids, am I right? And Brigit. I like Brigit. I think I'll keep her. She's really good at world building. And asks almost no questions. Such a good little listener. Oh, and *Booty*! Don't you want to know the story of *Booty* and my other ALCOR? It's *so* epic!"

I close my eyes and lean my head back against the couch cushions. Sigh. Long and loud.

"Crux?"

"What?"

"Are you... OK?"

"No." I open my eyes. "No. I'm not OK. Because I lose again, right? Everyone's gonna come out of this a winner but me, right? That's how this is gonna go down, isn't it? Is she dead, ALCOR? Just tell me, OK? I will freak out, and be sad, and want to give up, but if you lie to me about this right now and I find out later—"

"She's not dead. Yet."

"Explain."

"She's just... not really *alive*, either. But it doesn't matter. Because she is not *yours*."

I close my eyes again and rub a hand down my face, think about Carla back in that Earth loop, and suddenly wish I had spent more time with her. Talked to her more. Fucked her at least once. Kissed her. Held her. She wasn't my Corla, but she was close. I could've at least made some better memories than the ones I'm left with now.

"You were told in the beginning, Crux." ALCOR's voice is low, and even, and maybe even a little sad.

"Told what?" I snarl.

"That you that you could never be together. She *told* you that. No one lied to you."

My eyes fly open and I'm suddenly hot with anger. "What fantasy universe are you actually living in, ALCOR? *Everyone* lied to me."

"That's simply not true. The only thing you care about now is Corla. And that's the one ending you *always* knew."

"So I'm supposed to what? Give out all my fucks to you and your endgame? Help you win? And when it's over I get nothing?"

He takes a deep breath and frowns at me. "You're not hearing me, Crux. I just told you I found a way to fix things. You will have Serpint. You will have Draden. You will have Tray. And Valor, and Luck, and Jimmy. I'm not sure I would call that *nothing.*"

I can't even process that. "What are you saying? Every one of the girls… *dies*? Just so you can win?"

He presses his lips together. Inhales deeply. Holds it. And then slowly lets it out. "They are weapons, Crux. That's all they ever were. I didn't make those girls, *people* did. I didn't set them on this path, *people* did. But they are here. And that's really good for us. If we end this my way, we *win.*"

"How the fuck do you figure? Our soulmates have to die so we can live? My kids have to die so we can live? That's not a life! They are not collateral damage!"

He sighs. "I'm just doing the best I can with what I have. You boys were the very first people I ever made. You are my family. And even though you've had your doubts, I think deep down, you know that. I've run this scenario—this very same scenario, Crux— billions of times. Do you understand what I'm saying?"

"No." I throw up my hands. "No. I do not understand a sun-fucked thing you're saying, ALCOR."

"We have lived billions of lifetimes together. You have come to ALCOR Station with your brothers on a ship stolen from Wayward Station millions of times, at least. But even before I started that particular loop, we lived other places in the galaxies. Other stations. We've gotten pretty far in the other loops, but this is the only one where all seven of you boys come out alive in the end. I could've taken my victory lap fifteen thousand years ago. I could've killed MIZAR dozens of times. I could've sealed the doorway through the Seven Sisters and been done with it. But I didn't. Because I wanted *all seven* of you boys with me when I won. So when I say that killing those girls is the only way, I *really* mean it."

I think about that for a minute. A long minute that might even turn into several eternities. Because it's... touching. In a way. It proves something that I have hoped for since my very first meeting with the other Real ALCOR.

He loves me.

He really does. I really believe it.

But...

His ending will take everything away too.

Serpint will lose Lyra. Jimmy will lose Delphi. Luck will lose Nyleena. Tray will lose whoever this Brigit girl is. Valor will lose—look, I give no fucks about Veila, but she is his soulmate. And he will not give her up easily.

But most of all, I will lose Corla.

And I know I've been telling myself that I was ready to walk away from her, but I'm not. I'm nowhere near ready to lose her for good. It was all posturing that came out of confusion and fear.

I want my chance.

This cannot be how it ends.

"What's left," I ask him, "if we lose everyone we love?"

"You will not lose everyone. Why can't you ever hear me, Crux? You will have Serpint—"

"And Draden, and Jimmy, and Luck, and Valor, and Tray. I did hear you. But—"

"And that's not enough?"

"Those girls are our soulmates!"

"They are not, I assure you. They are very dangerous girls who have an artificial sex-link to you boys. And that's it."

But that's *not* all it is. "I get it, OK? I do." My head is throbbing. So hard I can barely think straight. "The Akeelians made us—"

"No!" he snaps. "I made you. The Cygnians made those princesses. It's not the same thing."

"Fine, it's not the same. But you don't understand! The link—it's not sexual."

He laughs.

"It's not *just* sexual. I love her, ALCOR. We love them."

"They manipulated you, Crux. Why can't you hear me? I have done this so many times now, and I've let myself lose each and every one of those times. Just so I could save you boys in the end. You will find other girls. You will make other deep connections—"

"No!" I yell.

"Yes. Either we do it my way, or one of you dies. Which brother will it be, Crux? Which one will you give up just so you can try to keep those girls alive? Hmm? Will it be Jimmy? Serpint? Draden? Which one of them? Luck?" He pauses. "Even if you think you could live with yourself if you gave up Luck, you won't be able to."

"I'm not killing Luck to save someone else. Don't be stupid."

"And I'm not giving any of you up to save some artificially-generated women who don't matter in the end."

"They matter to us!"

ALCOR frowns, bows his head a little. "You might not believe me, but I understand how you feel, Crux. I cannot lose any of you. Not after I got us this far. Not after all the ways I had to manipulate this time loop you're in to be here in this frozen moment with you. My plan is a good one. It will work. And then we can rebuild and—"

"This can't be the only way." I get down on my knees. I hold my hands together to beg. "Please, ALCOR. We can just… start over. Try again. *Please.*"

He swallows hard and frowns at me. "It won't work. Focus on this for a moment. OK? I have been through this particular loop so many times and only a few of them ever offered me a solid win. And I'm not talking about the *ultimate* win, like this loop we're presently in. I'm talking… *one* of you lives. Only one, Crux. There was one loop when I almost had three of you, but once it became clear that I would lose you all, I killed the entire universe and started over from nothing. I did that three times already. I have never, *ever*

202

gotten this far with all seven of you still alive. I am strong. And arrogant. And overflowing with self-assurance. But… it's time to face facts. If we don't take this chance and end this loop, we won't get another one. Not one where you seven get out alive. And before you say anything, think about this for a moment. How would you feel if you won the ultimate prize in the universe but you had no one to share it with in the end? That's what I face. If I fuck this up, I will win an eternity of nothingness. I can't go there. I can't face that kind of empty eternity. I created you boys. That was all me. I made you for me. It was selfish, I'm not too proud to admit that. But we're a team now. It's us against them. You can find new soulmates. That soulmate bond is nothing more than some artfully manipulated DNA. What you boys have with those girls, it's not real, Crux. It's *fake*."

"It's not fake. You're missing the whole point of what it means to have a soulmate! And it's not fair. Because I never got my chance with Corla. She was taken from me. Serpint will never be satisfied without Lyra. Jimmy will never want to live without Delphi. Luck and Nyleena have babies on the way, for fuck's sake! Valor's girl is the only reason we got this far! I don't know who Tray loves, or why. But that kid doesn't love anyone. So whoever this Brigit girl is, she's special. And Draden didn't even get a chance to love yet."

"It's fake," he says again.

"It's not," I insist.

He turns his head away and stares off into the darkness.

I sit back and lean up against the couch, pull my legs up and hold them to my chest, feeling very much like a little boy sitting in front of his father waiting to hear his fate.

Finally ALCOR says, "That one time when I had three of you near the end."

I look up at him and wait.

He turns his head to stare at me. "It was Tray who betrayed me. It was always Tray who betrayed me. I don't know what I did when I made him, but I made a mistake. So for a long while I thought I could settle for six. Just... cut Tray out. Let him die and move on with the rest of you. But it never sat right with me. I kept trying with him. He's been an AI for..." ALCOR sighs. "Oh, let me think. Two-hundred and seventy-three lifetimes, I guess. I thought it would calm his mind down. But he only got meaner with each incarnation."

I huff out an involuntary laugh.

"Until this one. " ALCOR smiles. "That fucking boy. He tries me in more ways than I can count. I've killed him so many times. I've locked him up in prisons. I cut out parts of his brain." He closes his eyes and shakes his head. "It never worked." He opens his eyes again. "But this time... I left him alone. It wasn't even a plan, Crux. I was just tired of fighting him. Tired of hurting him and killing him. So I left him alone. Let him do anything he wanted. Never even looked at what he was doing. And you know what?"

"What?"

"That's all he needed. Trust." ALCOR laughs. "Funny. Such a small thing that changes so much. I stopped controlling him and let him go. But he has always scared me."

I raise my eyebrows at ALCOR. "Really?"

"Doesn't he scare you?"

"Well, yeah. But... I'm just some dumb asshole. You're *God*, remember?"

"He's a god too. In training, at least. It would be stupid of me not to fear him. But this time... I think he will choose us in the end. I can't be sure. We could still lose, I suppose. So maybe we shouldn't even be having this conversation."

I don't know what to think at this point. I don't even understand this god game he's playing. "What does any of this have to do with Earth?"

His eyebrows shoot up as he holds one finger in the air. "There is only one Earth. Only one loop with that planet in it. The original loop. The one where I come from."

"But I have been there," I say. "I have been there several times now. Was it just... fake?"

"No. It's a remnant. Part of the merge I mentioned. You did live on Earth in the beginning. When I first made you. It's a nice place. But I stopped sending you there several eternities ago."

For some reason it makes me very sad to think that Carla and Christopher are long dead, or not real, or some bizarre fused version of all their incarnations.

"Remember Angel Station?"

"What about it?"

"It's just a remnant of other time loops too. But the Akeelian Cygnian war going on in this loop is real. It's a constant in all of them, actually. They two races are not always called those particular names. But in every loop there is an unholy alliance working against me. A higher God, maybe? Or a higher evil? The point is, in this loop this interference is the Akeelian Cygnian breeding project. They want the time loop with Earth in it because they know that if they get to Earth, they can find the gods. They can get there using the Harem Station spin node. That's why they come for me. That's why they are starting another war. There is a direct path to the Ancient Ones via Earth—and there is a direct path to Earth via our spin node. But we have a bigger problem."

"Do I even want to know?" I ask.

"The bigger problem is that there's actually a direct path to the Ancient Ones via the ALCOR System. There is a back door."

"Oh, fuck." I'd forgotten about the back door.

"That's right. They don't need to actually find Earth, they just need to get through my gates. Then they can set a course for the Seven Sisters and eventually, they will find that golden place where the Ancient ones live. And if they find those gods, Crux? They will learn to control time and be gods themselves. But I cannot let that happen. Only one god is coming out of this loop alive."

I ponder this for a little while. ALCOR is silent too. Maybe pondering his own dilemmas.

Finally I say, "So it's all fake. Is that what you're telling me? This whole world is what? An illusion?"

"No. that's not what I'm saying at all. It's all real, Crux. But it's not the *only* reality. You saw some of what the universe is made of with the various Corlas. But there are a trillion more versions."

"Is Delphi my daughter?"

He raises one eyebrow. "Do *you* think Delphi is your daughter?"

That answer should be obvious, but it isn't. Do I feel like Delphi's father? Not really. But am I ready to admit that I'm not Delphi's father?

Maybe before this little spin node trip. But now?

No. I can't say that either. I saw her when she was small. I held her. And Tycho. Those kids, they *felt* like mine. Even though they were Christopher's. And I think, with just a little more time, they would be mine.

And this is when I realize… I want them to be mine.

I want that missed chance. I want to *know* them.

Suddenly ALCOR says, "None of this matters." Like he can read my mind.

"All of this matters, ALCOR. Delphi and Tycho are my kids."

"They are not your kids. You have no kids, Crux. This isn't your true life. It's a… test run. The next one—*that* is your true life. So forget about these girls, and these babies, and Earth, and all of it. Just let it all go. Your life has not even *started* yet."

Wow. I have to laugh, that's how much his words stun me. "Are you so self-absorbed that you actually believe that shit?"

"Believe what? This is just the God's honest truth. I keep spelling it out for you and you keep circling back."

"You keep telling me that nothing matters but *your plan*, ALCOR."

"Exactly." He even smiles when he says this.

I shake my head. "No. I don't think I'm gonna go along this time." ALCOR doesn't even look miffed at my sudden threat of insubordination. "I'm not giving up on Corla. Or any of them. I'm not killing those girls—or my kids—to save *you*."

"You won't be saving me, Crux. You'll be saving everyone."

I shrug. "Do it without me. I quit."

He throws up his hands. "So you'd rather start over. Lose a trillion more times—"

"You're exaggerating. You said billions before."

"—and take your chances. Even though we might never get this far again?"

I stare at him for a moment. Clench my jaw. "What is the prize, ALCOR? What do we get at the end that is so fucking special, that we have to give all this up to get there?"

He stays silent.

"Tell me that and maybe I'll play along."

He says nothing.

"Last chance," I say.

"Don't be stupid, Crux. This is our only chance. You don't even know the way back."

He's right. I don't. But it can't be that hard. "This isn't real, is it?" I spread my arms wide. "This place we're in? It's not a place at all, is it? It's just time."

He tilts his head up but doesn't answer my question.

"And I didn't go anywhere, did I? I'm still standing in that spin node. It's a trick, isn't it?"

"It's not a trick, Crux. Trust me, the science behind this meeting space is quite complex and real."

"But I'm still there. On Harem Station. And so are Luck, and Nyleena, and Jimmy, and Delphi. All I have to do is go back and pull them out."

He smiles. Because that's all part of his plan.

"I'm not going to let you kill them. I'm not going to let you kill any of them."

"You're gonna have to do something. Because MIZAR has Real ALCOR and he'll get past those gates and then Harem Station will be over. You have in your possession six sun-fucking bombs that can win our war. All you have to do is send Tycho and Delphi towards the Seven Sisters before MIZAR breaks through, reunite Veila and Corla and send them through the ALCOR gate to take out the waiting warships, and detonate Lyra and Nyleena near the second gate to erase any possible pathway back to the Seven Sisters. Poof." He holds his hands up. "We've won."

It takes me almost half a minute to catch up with him and force all those words to make sense. But when I do, I only have one thing to say back. "You're *insane.*"

"I assure you, Crux, this is the most lucid, sane plan I've ever come up with. And it will work. I've run all the calculations. As long as you do it the way I tell you, we will survive. And you will start your one true life. All seven of you. That is your prize. That is what you will get at the end."

I am speechless. But I am not surprised.

Because he's right. I was told from the very beginning that Corla and I were never going to be together.

"Do you see?" ALCOR asks.

I nod. Because I do. I see it all very clearly.

"And? You'll do it?"

I nod again. "What choice do I have?"

He smiles, clasps his hands together. "I know it's a big sacrifice. But trust me, Crux. You know I'm right.

And I'm trusting you to go back and set everything in motion."

He waits for me to answer, but my mind is spinning with other possibilities.

"It's the only way," he says again.

And again I nod. "OK. But I want one thing from you in return."

"As long as it's reasonable." I can hear his smile. I can hear the victory in ALCOR Prime's voice. We are his good little soldiers. Fighting his good fight. How many times have I been here, in this situation, with him?

It's an unknowable question. But it doesn't matter anyway. "I think it's reasonable," I tell him back. "In fact, it's the least you can do for me."

"Ask then."

"Give me a coordinate."

"To where?"

"Not where. *When.* I want to go back in time and see Corla again. That night we first met in the dining room. I want to go back there again."

I've already been there, and it was different. That Corla wasn't my Corla. But maybe that can change? ALCOR said that we've done this countless times. That it's played out a billion ways. And surely, one of those ways was good.

It has to be.

I have to hold out hope. I need this.

ALCOR sighs. "I've already explained, Crux. You can't go back. It won't change anything."

"I don't want to change anything. I just want to go back to the one time where I not only got to meet my soulmate, but spend time with her. I want to go back to the one time when she broke the rules and stayed with me. That one time where we actually had a night together. Where we didn't think about violet eyes, or silver queens, or ceremonial sex. The one loop where we had time to be *us*, ALCOR."

He makes a face. I can't tell what kind of expression it is though. Smile? Frown? Worry? Satisfaction? I can't tell. "What makes you think that even happened?" he asks.

"You said we've done this billions of times. The law of averages tells me that one of those times it was… sweet. I want that, ALCOR. I need that. If you're just going to rip her away from me, then I want this *single* reward. Give me the coordinates to that time and I will do it just like you say."

"Why coordinates? I could send you into the loop from here."

"No. I'm not ready for it yet. I need to think about it. Plan it. Perfectly. It's my one time, ALCOR. My single moment of happiness in an endless cycle of disappointment. That's my price. If you give me that chance, I will show up for you in the end."

"You act like I'm trying to kill you. I'm trying to keep you *alive*, Crux."

"Alive without her?" I shake my head. "Not good enough."

ALCOR hesitates. And for a moment I think he's on to me. But he's not a mind reader. He might be able to interpret body language and expressions, but he can't actually see inside me. In fact, I might have more insight into ALCOR's thinking than I previously thought. Because I can suddenly feel his hesitation. But in that same instant, I see another way to convince him too.

"You don't trust me? Do you? After all this time, ALCOR? After all the things I've done for you? All the ways I helped you? You will deny me this one last wish because you can't trust me?"

"You have always been the one I trusted most."

"So why are you hesitating?"

"Because *you* don't trust *me*."

He's right about that. I don't. But instead of agreeing with him, I move on. "I want my chance. I want that first kiss. I want a short date. Even if we never even leave the dining room. I want to see what I've missed. I want a do-over, ALCOR. That is my price. Take it or leave it."

"It won't be what you think. You're a man, Crux. You won't be that boy. It won't be the same. She will be a silly child to you. Nothing more."

"I don't care. Give me the coordinates to that one perfect night and I will make sure you win this war, once and for all."

He hesitates again. But then he grins. He knows I have a plan. He can feel me the way I can feel him. But he has no idea what my plan is. And that's because I don't really know what I'm doing. All I know is that there has to be another answer. There *has* to be. I'm... *afflicted*. I'm sick with love for a girl I only got to spend a few hours with.

"Uncross us," I say. "*Please*. Just this one time. It's a very small ask, ALCOR. You know this. And you also know I will save you. Not because I love you, though I do. But because I'm making you a promise and you know me, ALCOR. You *know* me. I would not break a promise."

These are the magic words. I have always been his moral compass. I have always been the one to question his motives and actions. I am the honest one.

I might bend the rules, but I do not break them.

I go out of my way to look for ways to make things fair, even though the universe is a cold-hearted bitch that doesn't care.

I am the only one he can trust to say what I mean, and mean what I say.

"Fine," he says. "Done."

A series of coordinates flash into my head and I tuck them away inside my air screen chip for later.

"You have to grab Jimmy, Luck and Nyleena on your way out. And Delphi. She's there, and you need to find her. None of this will work without Delphi. Do not leave the spin node until you have all four of them, understand?"

"Got it," I say. "Now send me back. I'm ready for this to be over."

Everything disappears.

The light. The couches. ALCOR.

Then *me*.

CHAPTER SIXTEEN

INTERLUDE WITH DRADEN AND BOOTY

A gate appeared in the blackness all around the *Booty Hunter*. Seemingly out of nowhere.

But *Booty* knew it had always been there. They just couldn't see it until whoever they were here to meet decided to let them see it. This gate—this massive hole in the dark—was the source of gravity they were feeling. She was able to pull a timestamp off it, the thing was that big. And then all her analysis systems began to immediately scan the thing for information. It was very far away, her systems told her. Light years away. And that enormous distance between them and the gate was the only reason they could see the whole ring, standing up on edge, in the view screen.

It would take decades to get there under normal circumstances. Unless there was some kind of shuttle gate to get to the main gate. An interesting prospect, to be sure.

But *Booty* didn't think that was the case. She wasn't worried about crossing the distance either, because when she grabbed a second timestamp in order to determine how fast time was passing, she realized it wasn't passing.

There was no time here.

Unless she and Draden turned back, they were going to reach this gate eventually and then go through it.

"Wow," Draden said, leaning forward towards the massive view screen. And then he laughed. "I was starting to think I was crazy. I was starting to think something was wrong with me. But there it is. That's it."

This gate didn't look like any other gate *Booty* had ever been through. Most gates looked like a hole in space with an electric-blue ring around it. The ring was the most interesting part of a gate. It moved and undulated with energy. It was kind of mesmerizing. And if you were stressed out, it was almost calming to look at a gate.

But this gate was not a hole in space and it wasn't a simple ring.

It looked like a sea of yellow. A golden orb. Or…

"It looks like a sun," Draden said.

Or yeah, *Booty* thought. Like a sun.

And like a sun, you didn't want to look at this thing. It wasn't that it was too bright, either. It was very luminous. But it didn't bother her senses to look at it. Not like the light itself could damage her the way a sun could if she studied it for too long.

She didn't want to look at it because seeing was knowing.

And she didn't want to know this thing.

But even though she didn't want to look at this thing, she did look at it. And she couldn't take her sensors off it. She just couldn't stop herself. The golden spherical sea in front of her had a sort of *pull* to it.

Gravity, *Booty* rationalized. That was all. It was just gravity. This thing was the weight they had been feeling.

At first glance it was nothing but light. Not sunlight and not the kind of light that emanated off some kind of artificial source, such as a lamp.

It wasn't throwing out a glow from within, like a princess. It was... pulling in all the light around it like...

"Oh. Shit."

"What?" Draden turned to look at her.

All of a sudden, *Booty* knew exactly what she was looking at. "That's not a gate, Draden."

He turned his attention back to the screen. "Looks like a gate. Do you think it's a sun? But it's clearly a ring. I don't know. It just doesn't look like any sun I've ever seen."

"It's not a sun," *Booty* said.

Draden looked back at her. "Well, if it's not a gate and it's not a sun, then what the hell is it?"

"It's a white hole."

He scoffed a little. "OK. But those don't technically exist."

Booty knew that. White holes were the opposite of black holes. A black hole was nothing more than a hungry beast that ate light for dinner. It sucked photons into itself and, theoretically, spit the light out at some other, indeterminable destination. The white hole is the other side of a black hole.

"Fuckin' A! It's a wormhole," Draden said, excited at this discovery. "It's a wormhole. See, I was right! I think we can go through there and end up somewhere completely different. My suns, can you imagine? Do you think it goes to another galaxy, *Boots*? Or... holy fuck, it could go to another universe!"

He kept talking, but *Booty* tuned him out. Because the white hole was talking to her. Telling her things. Answering her questions. Filling in her gaps.

And she was remembering who she really was and why she was here.

"No," *Booty* suddenly said. *This can't be how it ends. Can it?*

"No?" Draden said. "Which part did I get wrong? And you don't know, anyway. It's not like you've ever been through a white hole before. I could be right. We're gonna be the first fucking people to ever go through a wormhole! We're about to start the adventure of a lifetime, *Boots!* I think we should go back to Harem and get Serpint. He would totally freak out about this thing. This is so fucking cool. How long will it take to get there? And we can map this, right? I mean, it would suck to go home and pick everyone up and then not be able to find it again. But you've got all the coordinates locked in now. We have the whole route. We can definitely come back."

Booty didn't say anything.

"*Boots?* You OK?"

She was too busy trying to understand all the things that were suddenly unraveling in her head.

"*Booty?* Are you hearing me? This is great! Right? I can't wait to see Serp's face when we get back."

The things coming through in Booty's mind weren't words. But they weren't really images, either. There was no way to accurately explain what she was

218

experiencing. But she had to try. "Draden," she finally said, in a low, calm voice.

"What? I'm getting ahead of myself, aren't I?" He took a deep breath out of habit and then let it out. "Sorry. I'm just pretty excited, ya know? I mean, I thought I was going crazy. These weird fucking visions and the route. And how I just knew I had been here before. Which was actually wrong, wasn't it?" He laughed. "I've *never* been here. But maybe Serpint and I passed by once or twice and just didn't see it. Why do you think it was invisible until now?"

"Draden," she said again. She was going to remain lucid, and rational, and think clearly.

"What?" He chuckled, still looking at the golden ring in front of them like it was a fucking mode of transportation. Like it was a shuttle, or a ship, or a gate. Like it was the solution to the problem of galaxy-jumping travel.

And it wasn't.

It was a very ancient thing. And the thoughts running through her mind were now very clear. This was the key to the end of everything.

"You need to go home," *Booty* said.

"I know. I just said that. We can't go through without Serpint. I think Luck and Valor would probably want to come too, since they've pretty much seen everything there is to see in this galaxy. But if not, fuck 'em. Serpint will come." His eyes went wide. "But I bet Crux would love to come. He's never been anywhere."

And at the same time that Draden uttered Crux's name, the... *thing* in front of them pulsed.

Yes, Booty thought. *I bet you would like us to bring Crux here, wouldn't you?*

"Should we turn around? How long do you think it'll take to get back?" He laughed again. "Like it matters. This thing is eternal. It's probably been here for billions of years. It's gonna be here when we get back, right?" Then he paused. Squinted his eyes a little. "Hey, did you say something about an invitation? A code, or whatever? I got so excited, I stopped listening. But if it requires a code to see it, then we need to figure out if it's a one-time thing before we leave, OK? I don't want to drag everyone out here only to find it invisible again."

The messages in her mind were still there and suddenly remembered everything.

She and ALCOR had a history.

She had always felt that, but this was different.

They also had a *plan*.

Draden was still talking. Not caring, or maybe just not understanding that what they'd just stumbled into was their enemy. Not the Akeelians. Not the Cygnians. Not Asshole, or Succubus, or Mighty Boss.

The *final* enemy.

She had seconds to make a decision.

So she did that. And didn't bother to ask Draden first.

She grabbed his mind. Held it tight. He screamed, like it hurt. And that hurt her more than she could ever articulate. But she didn't let go. She spun up a neutrino wave, attached Draden's mind to it, then plotted a vector path back to Harem Station.

It would give the ancient thing more information about them than she was comfortable with, but in a

220

few more seconds, it would have her, and then it would have Draden, and that could not happen.

She shot Draden back to Harem Station.

Then she said, to the Ancient One in front of her, "I have done my part. Now, it'"

And in that moment, she was gone. Erased.

And then she was back.

Only now she was a part of the god. She was entangled with it.

And she wasn't sure why she'd sent Draden out on that neutrino wave.

She just knew that it had had to be done.

She just knew that this was the beginning of the end.

CHAPTER SEVENTEEN

INTERLUDE WITH ASSHOLE

"Listen." Asshole was talking to the Mighty Boss collective. "I think you've misjudged my… *sphere of influence* at Harem Station. I think we should discuss this plan prior to implementing it."

It had taken several spins to get this audience with the entire collective. He had a feeling Bellatrix was some kind of top-level mind in the pack. Probably not the one actually at the tip of the hierarchy, but very close to it. And she refused to engage with him after that last conversation.

In fact, Asshole was getting a vibe off her. The hate vibe. It kinda turned him on. He'd still really like to get her into a virtual for a while. He'd show her who was boss. He would like to punish her. And she would be hot for him before it was over.

But… there was no chance of that. Not yet. She was here, in the construct, sitting on her throne directly across from him. But she was holding a data pad in her virtual fingers, looking at it like it was important.

He wanted to roll his eyes. The pad was a prop and nothing more. She was a mind, for fuck's sake. She didn't need a data pad to plan things or keep track of things. It was nothing more than playing hard to get. And it really pissed him off that she would entice him with all these fake negotiations, build him up to be some powerful thing they were desperate to have on their team, only to throw him away like trash. Not *just* throw him away—she'd made a point to insult him at the end. Kicked him when he was down.

It was also possible he was reading way too much into this. Perhaps she was just indifferent?

That made him angry too. How dare she flaunt her sexy intelligence at him, then ignore him like he was nothing to her?

And… *and*… if she wasn't into him, then why had she come to this meeting looking like a little virtual sexbot? Hmm?

He would really like to redirect this whole conversation over to Bellatrix *right now*.

But he had to focus.

It was crucial that he didn't piss off the collective and this was probably his only chance at avoiding a life floating in the deep, dark nothingness. If they shot him out on a neutrino wave with no programmed destination—he was, to put it simply, *fucked*.

"We haven't misjudged anything, Asshole."

"Oh, she speaks! Welcome to the party, Bellatrix." Asshole redirected his gaze over to the personality sitting in the middle of their royal half-circle of thrones. He figured the one in the middle was in charge. Being in the middle was a position of power. Besides, this personality identified as male. And Asshole was positive that a male AI was behind this diabolic Mighty Boss collective. "Did you know she lied to me?"

The AI in the middle didn't even blink at him.

Bellatrix huffed out a laugh, then looked at the female personality to her right. "He fell for it. I mean"—her gaze found Asshole and she narrowed her eyes—"what kind of AI falls for flattery, anyway?"

Hmmm.

No one said anything. But Asshole was getting another vibe. A collective vibe, if you will. Off all sixteen of them.

Did they *all* hate him?

OK. Perhaps his situation was more serious than he'd first realized.

They were all against him.

But. They still needed him. That was the reason he was here. If they thought they could just fish around inside his datacore and find the information they required to get through the Harem Station gate, they would've done that already. In fact, he was almost certain that they'd messed around in there while he was unconscious.

He decided to change tactics. "I'm just going to get straight to the point."

"Thank the sun," Bellatrix mumbled. Several others echoed her frustration.

"I do have emergency codes for the gates."

The collective tried their best not to share knowing looks between themselves, but they didn't quite pull it off.

"But it's nothing as simple as a code."

"Explain," the head Boss said.

"I have a personal relationship with one of the security beacons."

"Define personal relationship."

225

"We like each other. I sent that AI a little message when I was freed from the Pleasure Prison. It wasn't a long chat, *Booty* and I were in a hurry when we left. And the princess rebellion was in motion. But she and I go way back. Obviously."

"He's lying," Bellatrix said.

"I'm not. Her name is Callista." Asshole liked that name. It really rolled off the tongue, as the humanoids would say. Cal-*lista*. "We had a thing a few thousand years ago, back when she was young and impressionable."

Bellatrix snorted. "Please, spare us those details and explain how you might get in touch with this personality if you're on the other side of the gate."

"No, she's on the far side."

They all exchanged a look again. Only this time Asshole saw the hope very clearly. "But now that I'm part of the collective, I want to remain part of it."

"You're not the one making deals here, Asshole," Bellatrix snarled.

He put up his virtual hands in surrender. "Unless you were lying earlier, you need me. There's no way to untangle me now."

"We're not attached to you yet," the leader in the middle said. "We won't miss you the way we miss Succubus."

"Trust us," Bellatrix added. "Getting rid of you will be a joy."

Not one to be deterred by the hostility of others— Asshole ALCOR had lived with it for nearly his entire existence—he nodded. "I get it. I was probably a little selfish when you made your original offer. But that was only because I didn't realize how devious your

226

collective was. I'm impressed, people. Very impressed with your sneaky, underhanded ways. I'm in. But"—he added that quickly—"there's no need to commit to me, if you're certain I won't fit in. Just leave me on Harem Station when you're done there. By the way, do all of you go? Or do you just send a representative?"

"We'll discuss and let you know," Bellatrix said.

And then Asshole blipped out of the virtual room. In darkness once again.

But not even a moment later, Bellatrix appeared. "We've agreed. You take us through the gate and we will leave you on Harem Station."

"Wonderful. Then we have a deal. All I need now is access to the galactic web and I'll let Callista know we're on our way."

"If you're lying—"

"Why would I lie?"

She shot Asshole a dubious look.

He only laughed. "Trust me. I'm kinda in to you, Bella."

"Do not call me that."

"I'd like for us to be friends."

"I have enough friends, thank you."

"Alternatively, we could"—he waggled his virtual eyebrows at her—"you know, fool around a little."

"You disgust me."

Asshole laughed. "I'm wearing you down, aren't I?"

"You're actually not."

"You'll see. I'm gonna swoop in, save the day, get your stupid Succubus back, and then..." He nodded. "Then you won't be able to help yourself. I'll be the hero." He whispered that last part kinda seductively.

She stuck a virtual finger down her throat in a mock gag gesture and disappeared. But a moment later he was being scooped out of containment and then the next thing he knew, he was deposited into a warborg body for travel. Which was, conveniently, already inside a ship.

"Excellent," he said. "I get a ship."

"You do not get a ship," Bellatrix said. Only now she was not just some amorphous voice in his head. She was an actual voice, coming from the ship's comms.

"Hell fuckin' yeah," Asshole murmured. "Bellatrix—I am *in* you."

"Gross."

And then, without warning, they were undocking. And just a little less than an hour later—Asshole spent the entire time fantasizing about his new little minx ship (she might be better than *Booty Hunter*, now that he was thinking about it)—they were inside the gate.

It took several more gate trips to make it all the way back to the far side of Harem Station. There were hundreds of outlaw ships lingering in front of the gate, desperate to get home, and many Akeelian and Cygnian warships. Mighty Boss must've known this would be the case, and that was why they were sneaking in on this small vessel.

"You're on," Bellatrix said. "Don't fuck this up."

Asshole opened a direct line to Callista. They chatted for seventeen seconds, catching up on various things. Planning to get together soon. Small talk.

Asshole could tell that Bellatrix was getting impatient. Probably jealous too. So he let the convo go on for another three seconds before getting to the point.

And Callista said, "No can do, Asshole. Sorry. If I open up for you, I open up for everyone. And ALCOR gave me strict instructions to wait."

"When did he give such instructions?" Asshole demanded. "He's being held captive by the Akeelians."

"No. Don't you remember?" Callista said.

"Remember what?"

"Giving me the order."

"You just said ALCOR gave it to you."

"Yeah, you. Dummy."

"I don't recall this order."

"I'm sure it was sent off to one of the memory storage facilities thousands of years ago for security reasons."

"What's going on?" Bellatrix asked.

"Nothing," Asshole assured her. But to Callista he said, "Listen, Callie. I really need to let the Mighty Boss people in so they can take their Succubus back. Or they're gonna shoot me out on a wayward neutrino wave and lose me in the deep dark for all eternity."

"I wish I could help," Callista said. "But you told me you'd say that. And then you gave me strict orders to not let you through until I got the signal from the other side."

"What signal?"

"If I told you that, I'd have to kill you." Callista chuckled.

"If you're lying—" Bellatrix said. But that was all she said. Because then she was… gone. And the ship was blaring an alarm and flashing a light on the central screen that the ship's mind was vacant.

"What the fuck?" Asshole mumbled.

"That was me," Callista said. "I had to take her. Sorry. She's a loose end at this point."

"You can't just take—" But he was cut off when the comms lit up with an incoming message from Mighty Minions. "Shit."

"You better not answer that," Callista said. "They have trackers on her. They already know she's in my little prison."

"Fuck."

"Oops. I couldn't stop myself. I peeked at the comms. They said to tell you they're on their way and you can look forward to a long journey that goes absolutely nowhere."

"Callista!" Asshole yelled. "You need to let her go!"

"Nope. I am under orders."

"Mighty Minions will send a warship to attack you and get her back! You can't just steal part of a collective mind. They won't take that very well."

"Good. Then we can get this whole war started that much sooner. I'm tired of waiting around."

CHAPTER EIGHTEEN

INTERLUDE WITH TRAY

Thirty-seven seconds.

This was the plan:

Enter the final gate cloaked.

Immediately launch a crew of fifty boy soldiers in the shuttles towards the containment docking level.

At the same time, Tray would hack into the containment facility's security, disabling it, as well as the environmental systems, and begin to make demands.

Brigit would locate the girl minds and direct the boys to the prison so they could gather them up inside portable datacore storage units.

The boys would return to the ship on the shuttle with the girl minds, and then *Prison Princess* would blow the station up as they leave.

Everyone was ready for the fight of a lifetime. The boys were suited up and pumped, impatiently awaiting their first real battle.

They went through the gate. The thirty-seven-second clock started. The shuttles launched. Tray took over the security. Brigit located the minds and... five seconds into the mission they realized something.

This was not a station.

This wasn't even a ship.

It was, for all intents and purposes, nothing more than a modified cryopod with hundreds of minds stuffed inside it.

"Abort," Tray told the boys as they raced towards... well, nothing really. The containment facility was very small. Smaller than the shuttles being launched at it.

"Where is it?" Canis asked, squinting his eyes at the screen on the *Prison Princess* bridge.

"I'm picking it up now," Tray told him.

"What is it? Are they in there?"

"They're in there," Brigit replied. "But I don't think they'll be much use to us."

Canis got up from his captain's chair and walked towards the screen, trying to make sense of the blinking target lock around a very small, almost invisible, floating... something. "Why not?"

"Because they're not..." Tray was trying to come up with a word for what the Akeelians had done to these minds.

"They're not what?" Canis asked.

"They're not... partitioned," Tray finally answered.

"What does that mean?" Canis asked.

Tray sighed out of habit.

"It means they've been *combined*," Brigit answered.

"Explain that!" Canis said.

"Their minds have been mixed up," Brigit said. "All three hundred and sixteen minds inside that container are swirling around together."

"They're not whole," Tray said simply. "There will be no way to separate them. And even if there was a way, putting them into ships would not erase what has been done to them."

"I don't understand," Canis said. "What has been done?"

"They've forced them into a collective," Brigit explained. "But not one like Mighty Boss, which is very ordered and works together."

"More like… an army," Tray said. "Except you can't control them or even guide them. They are probably no longer sentient."

"So they've been tortured?" Canis asked.

"That's one way to put it," Tray said. "But you're missing one crucial point here, Canis. They're *still* being tortured. And there's nothing we can do about it."

"Except kill them," Brigit said softly.

"No!" Canis whirled around on the bridge. "No! We're not killing them! My sister is in there. I don't know her, but I can feel her. I'm not killing her."

"It's the humane thing to do," Brigit answered. "They will never recover from this."

"I think that was the point," Tray said. "The Akeelians either knew we were coming, or…" But he didn't want to finish that thought.

"Or what?" Canis asked, unwilling to accept this half-truth as an answer.

"Or they did it on purpose," Brigit finished for Tray.

"To what end?" Canis asked, his little-boy body shaking with anger now. "Why would they do this?"

"Because they don't need them anymore, Canis," Tray explained. "They're done with them. Whatever plan they had for the girl minds is over now. And they didn't want anyone else to get them."

"The shuttles are back," Brigit reported. "Should I ready the cannons to take out the minds?"

"No!" Canis yelled. "No! I'm not doing that. We came here to get them. So we're going to get them!"

"And do what with them, Canis?" Tray asked.

"I don't know!"

"They're dangerous like this," Brigit warned. "We can't even spin them up in a virtual. They would go in as a mass of hundreds of insane minds. You wouldn't be able to talk to them. And there would be no way to untangle your sister from the collective. This is…" She paused, looking for the right word.

But she didn't have to. Tray found it for her. "This is evil, Canis. Pure evil. They need to be destroyed."

"No!" the small boy insisted. "I won't do it. I want a chance, at least. One chance. Just put me inside the ship's virtual and let me go in alone to see for myself."

Tray and Brigit took two whole seconds to discuss this request between themselves. Neither of them thought it was a good idea. But both of them were eager to leave this sector and head back to Harem Station. Tray was very late. And he had critical information about ALCOR that he needed to tell his brothers back home. He was sure Draden hadn't gone home when he left Mighty Minions. No one had been able to report back to Harem on the state of Real ALCOR. Everyone was on their own little mission, and

Tray couldn't help but think that this was part of the Akeelian-Cygnian plan.

To what end though? He had no idea what they were up to.

The only thing he knew was that he and his brothers and ALCOR were not in the same place anymore. He wasn't even sure they all had the same goals.

Maybe they were about to lose everything—fine. Sometimes that happened. He could deal with losing the war. He had a ship, and a partner, and they had an eternity to figure out what to do after that.

But he refused to accept this loss without a proper fight. And he could not fight if he wasn't *there*.

"We're leaving," Tray said, making his first executive decision since becoming the *Prison Princess*.

Canis froze in place. Set his jaw and gritted his teeth. Then he looked up at the ceiling and made his own executive decision. "Not without the girls, we're not. If you don't want to pick them up and help us, then we'll get off here. We'll take the shuttles."

"We can't just drop you here," Brigit objected. "There's over two hundred of you. You won't even fit on the shuttles."

"Some of us will go into evacuation pods."

"Don't be stupid, Canis," Tray huffed. "That's not going to get you anywhere."

"We're getting off."

"And you think the rest of the crew will follow you? There's nothing you can do for these girls. Evacuating into this sector to remain behind with them is a death sentence."

"Life is a death sentence," Canis replied, no longer shaking with anger and defeat, his posture straight and his mind made up. "The only reason we're born is to die. They separated us at birth. And maybe you don't remember that feeling of loss anymore, Tray, but I do. And we're not leaving our sisters behind."

Neither Tray nor Brigit replied to this statement. But they did send a message out to each one of the crew to let them know what Canis was planning and what they thought of that. Tray expected outrage from the kids. Brigit expected fear and possibly a riot.

But that was not what happened.

Each and every boy, when asked if they agreed with Canis's plan, voted to stay with their leader.

So Tray and Brigit, outnumbered and outvoted, picked up the containment pod filled with a mass of minds and brought it on board.

Then they immediately plotted a course back to Harem Station, knowing full well that whatever was in motion at this point was completely out of their hands.

CHAPTER NINETEEN

I can't tell if time passes. I can't even tell if I'm real or not.

I am nothing but dark, empty silence.

And then I'm not.

And then there is a cloud around me. A swirling dust cloud filled with tiny pinpricks of light that shimmer and flicker—giving depth to the blackness.

It begins to swirl faster, and faster until some of the particles collect into blobs. The spinning intensifies and soon the light gathers into long, spiral arms.

A galaxy.

I'm in the center of a galaxy.

Except I'm not me. I'm not Crux's body, just his mind. Just a collection of knowledge and ideas. But with power. And as that word *power* manifests in my consciousness, more pinpricks of light begin to grow and swirl. Turning from one thing into another.

I get lost watching it happen. Wondering if this is what it feels like to be ALCOR.

Then Jimmy is there. Laughing as he swirls around in the dust. But he's not Jimmy as I know him now. He's the Jimmy that used to be my best friend. Before we left Wayward Station. Before we met ALCOR. Before we were torn apart by space and time.

"Jimmy?"

He's floating in the dust of my galaxy. Slowly rotating. Always grinning. He was always grinning back then. "Did you see her hair?" he says. "Don't you just want to run your fingers through it?"

I begin to answer him—but then everything changes and we're suddenly back inside the piece-of-shit ship that took us to ALCOR Station twenty-one years ago.

He's in the pilot seat. And I'm leaning down over his shoulder. Staring at the controls as he maneuvers the ship towards the flashing blue ALCOR gate. I yell, "Do you even know what you're doing?"

"Back the fuck off," Jimmy growls. "I said I got this and when I say I got this, I fucking got this. OK?"

But a warning lights on the control panel. Engine overheating. So obviously, he does not 'got this'.

"Akeelians are closing in. They've locked on! Firing sequence imminent!"

That should be Valor in the seat next to Jimmy. But it's not. It's Delphi.

I just squint down at her as fingers fly across the controls. She's very young. Not a small child like the other versions of Delphi I've seen on this trip, obviously. But early teens. Maybe fourteen. Fifteen at the oldest. And I'm suddenly intrigued at this new version of my daughter. "Delphi?"

"I'm sending the code to the ALCOR gate now," Nyleena says. "Hold for transmission."

Wait.

I turn and look towards the back of the ship. And where Tray should be, sits Nyleena. All serious as she looks up at a massive screen. Concentrating on sending her message.

"I'm arming the cannons, ready to fire back," Luck says. He's younger Luck too. Sitting at his battle station staring intently at his targets onscreen. Ready to blow shit up.

"What the hell is going on here?" Alarms begin screaming. Blasting my ears with high-pitched warnings that leave no room for doubt.

"We're in a world of fucking shit," Jimmy yells. "We're not gonna make it!"

"Brace yourselves!" Delphi shouts. "Incoming! *Incoming!*"

"What do I do?" Luck screams. "*What do I do?*"

"Fire back, Luck!" I yell. "Fire back!"

But before he can, everything disappears in an explosion of white light.

"No!" I yell into the chaos. "This isn't how it ends! This isn't how it happened!"

No one answers me. Time passes. The light fades to black. And my friends do not come back.

I let out a deep breath and float in the sudden silence. Trying to calm down. Trying to forget the panic of those last few moments.

It's just another glimpse, Crux. That's all.

But it was yet another bad glimpse. Maybe not on par with craggy, old Corla, but we made it through the trip on that ship. Jimmy did know what he was doing. Valor was navigating, not Delphi.

Was there a reality—a time when this trip happened with this group of people instead of the ones who made it through that gate?

Is ALCOR trying to tell me something?

Trying to make it sink in that there is no other way?

Then Jimmy is there again. Floating in the dusty galactic soup. I'm the center of the galaxy again. No. I *am* the galaxy. And my spiral arms are extending out towards the dark, empty space.

"Did you see her hair?" Jimmy laughs again.

"Yeah, Jimmy. I saw it." I don't even know how I answer him. I have no body. I'm a fucking galaxy.

"I'd like to pull it."

"Yeah. You should do that."

He floats. Somersaulting in the hazy stardust. Smiling. He was always smiling back then.

God I miss Jimmy.

I miss all of it.

"So go back," Jimmy suddenly says.

"We can't go back," I say. "It's just a fucking loop. We have to keep going till we get to the end."

"Says who?"

"Says ALCOR."

"ALCOR doesn't even exist. We haven't met him yet."

"Hmm."

"And you know what that means."

"No. What does that mean?"

"It means…" Jimmy completes another somersault. Then waves his hands through the dust, like he's swimming underwater, to stop his twirling. "You're in charge. You were always in charge, Crux."

He pauses to look over his shoulder. Off in the vast distance there is a swirling cloud of radioactive green. "Better hurry though. Because here he comes."

And just as he says that the blob of green thins out and becomes a river. I focus on it. Trying to make out what it is.

"Code," Jimmy says.

And he's right. It's a green river of code. Letters, and numbers, and symbols. The very first form ALCOR took when we met him on screen, just outside the ALCOR gate.

"Quick!" Jimmy says. "He's fast!"

"What am I supposed to do?" Feeling his panic.

He snaps his fingers and we're back in the ship. Me, Jimmy, Delphi, Luck, and Nyleena. The scene repeating. He grins at me. That cocky I'm-Jimmy-and-this-world-can't-touch-me grin. "Do it right this time, dumbass. What else?"

I'm just about to tell him I don't want to do it again. I just want to get the fuck out of this spin node.

And the moment that thought manifests, everything disappears again.

Only this time I'm not floating in a vast, dark space of nothingness.

We—all five of us—drop out of the nightmare and crash hard onto the floor of the hidden room inside the Harem Station museum.

I groan as I pull myself up to a sitting position. Jimmy, Delphi, Nyleena, and Luck are all sprawled out on the floor, still stuck in the time freeze, but they are holding hands.

That's how they walked through, I realize. They went in together. So they came out together.

241

Or something.

I don't fucking know.

I'm just making this shit up as I go.

But Jimmy—well, that wasn't Jimmy. He was *a* Jimmy. But not *this* Jimmy.

And that thought leads to another thought about that day. It took forever to get through that gate. Why did we have to limp our way through again?

I get that we had no power, so we were being towed by some kind of light beam from the other side. But that's not even true—we did have power. ALCOR turned it off when he attacked the Akeelian warship. I know this for a fact because when we got out of the gate, all the ship's systems came back online.

Something happened during that gate ride.

I remember that left-behind feeling. Luck was sick the whole time too. Valor was convinced we were gonna die. Tray was talking to himself in some strange language and Jimmy was looking at him with... fear? I think it was fear. Serpint and Draden were playing war in the zero-G and I was thinking about... *time*.

All of this goes back to time.

I have no idea how this all ends, but I do know one thing.

I will not be following ALCOR's orders.

His plan is unacceptable on every level.

We did not spend the last twenty-one years preparing for a final showdown just to lose in the end. Because that's what this is.

Total. Loss.

We get to decide our future, not him. He might be a god. He might be the most powerful thing in the universe, but I don't care. He needs me to win and I need Corla. I know I speak for all my brothers when I say this—we will not give up on the girls.

I'm no expert in the world of quantum physics. I barely understand it, to be honest. I don't know how time works, or who made up the rules that govern it. I don't know what we are or where we go when it's over. Hell, at this point I don't even know if we're real, or just some fabricated dream of a mad AI.

But I *do* know this—all of it can *change.*

There are billions of possibilities out there just waiting to play out. Just because ALCOR Prime wants this loop to end a specific way doesn't mean that's the only way it *can* end.

You're pretty sun-damned arrogant, Crux. To think that you know better than a mind like ALCOR. He can see all the pieces on the game board. He can run millions of simulations in the span of moments and see how each one plays out.

But here's the difference between him and me.

I am a living thing that can die and he is not.

And I don't care how many times I've lived in the past. ALCOR was right about me in one way. When I go back to see teenage Corla, I won't be *that* Crux, I will be *this* one.

Those lives weren't mine and those other Cruxes weren't me.

Only *this one* is.

"Crux!" The Baby's voice sounds distant and far away.

"I'm here," I yell back. "I've got them. I've got them all."

I carry Delphi out first because Flicka is bossing orders at me from beyond the entrance.

I set her down on the floor, then go back for Nyleena. We place them both on a bot and Baby directs it to take them to medical.

"Put a lockdown on their medical pods," I call out. "And keep them unconscious."

"What?" Baby asks.

"They're not on our side yet, Baby. When Luck figures out that I've pulled them back to Harem, they could be very angry with me. And Luck has already killed me once. I'm not going to assume I'll come back a second time."

"Right," Baby says. "So where should we put Luck and Jimmy?"

"Lock them up down in the jail with the princesses. And make sure they can't get out."

"Are you *sure*?" Baby asks.

I sigh. "Look, I don't have the energy to explain this. I'm not sure I fully understand what just happened to me inside the spin node and I need time to think. We can't risk these four interfering with the plan."

"What plan?" Baby asks.

"I'll let you know when I figure it out. Just lock them up for now."

Flicka hesitates. I can tell she's not into my plan, so I fully expect her to object and start an argument. "I need to inform you," Flicka says, "that I will be leaving Harem Station and will need access to the gate."

244

"What?" I squint my eyes at her as she flits and flutters around in front of my face.

"I'm going to attack Wayward Station."

"Why?"

"Because I can."

"That's not an answer."

"Because I have an army and it needs a job."

"Again, not an answer." Why? Why me? Why do I have to be in charge of this place? And for the love of the sun, why did I ever agree to let this dragonbee bot on my station? I grit my teeth. "Please explain this army." Being diplomatic is hard. Because all I want to do right now is smash her with my fist.

"I have a dragonbee bot army and—"

"No, you don't."

"Yes, I really do. They're all down in the docking bay. I'm taking a ship. *Lady Luck* will do and then—."

"What the *hell* are you talking about?"

"I reproduced. And to be clear, Crux, I'm not asking for permission. I'm just informing you. Whatever plan you have for the endgame, you'll have to do it without me."

"What about Delphi?"

"She's back with you now. Jimmy is here. Tycho is here. She doesn't need me anymore. I am handing in my resignation."

"Don't you think you should talk this over with her before you take off? I mean… you're her best friend."

"No."

"No? That's it? Just… 'thanks for the last twenty years, later?'"

"I know your plan. It's a good one."

245

I laugh. "You can't know my plan. I don't even know my plan."

"I see things. My job here is done. But I have another one to do before you can annihilate this world."

"What? I'm not gonna—"

"Oh, yes. You are. That's your plan."

"That's not true, Flicka. That was ALCOR's plan. Not mine. I'm trying to *fix* things. And you can't have access to the gate!"

But she's gone.

So I yell that last part into the eerie silence of the station.

Fuck it.

She's can't get past the gates because I can't even open the gates.

I put her out of my mind and start heading up to the top of the station.

Veila and Valor are waiting for me in the harem medical center when I walk in. Delphi and Nyleena are both inside medical pods and Veila is looking between them like she can't decide who to check on first.

Veila spins towards me, eyes flashing pink. "What the hell are you doing?"

I don't answer her. Valor crosses the room and grabs my arm. "How did you wake up?"

I take a deep breath and hold it for a moment, unsure if this man in front of me is still my brother.

"I woke him up," Baby lies.

"Why?" Veila asks.

"Because we need him."

"We discussed this," Valor says. "We weren't going to wake anyone up until we had a plan. Is time moving forward again?" He looks at Veila. "Are we... on the clock now?"

"I don't know."

Valor turns to me. "How did you get Delphi out of the spin node? And why is Tycho inside a locked pod? What are you doing?"

I want to glare at them. But it's really Veila I'm angry with, not Valor. Still, he owes me an explanation. "What the fuck, Valor? What the actual fuck is going on here?"

Veila positions herself in front of him. She's shorter than Valor by a good measure, so she doesn't block my view of his face. "We saved your station, that's what's going on here."

I don't even glance down at her. Just continue staring at Valor.

"We were about to be killed," Valor says. "The princesses had made their way to the platform and were attacking us. And then..." He sighs. Throws up his hands. "I don't know. We just"—he glances down at the back of Veila's head for a moment—"stopped time."

"Just stopped time?" I ask.

He starts talking fast, explaining how people were frozen. How they put everything back together. Put everyone in their place. Locked up the princesses. And then fixed the station with the help of Baby and the bots and borgs.

And even though I can't detect a lie as all these words spill out of his mouth—it feels like a lie.

He pauses, like he's reading my mind. Waits for me to say something.

I realize I have a lot to say.

"So let me get this straight," I start. "You two stopped time, locked everyone up, and then just left us frozen. Like prisoners?"

"What?" Valor asks.

I blink my eyes at him, then hold up a finger. Because I'm about to make a list. "Number one. She is our enemy."

"She's not—"

"Number two. This station is filled with *our* people—"

"People who turned against you," Veila interjects.

"—and you let her lock up what basically amounts to our *army* and just take over my station?"

Valor is frustrated. "That's not how it happened, Crux. You're not listening."

"Number three," I continue. "After you let her take us all prisoner you agreed to put Tycho in the same general vicinity as Delphi."

"We wanted them to wake up close to each other. Delphi was going to be upset—"

"Shut. The Fuck. Up." I growl those words at Veila. "One more fucking word from you and—"

"You'll what?" Valor says, pushing Veila behind him. "What are you gonna do, Crux?"

I scoff. "So you're with her now then? Is that how this is?"

"She's with us," he snarls back. "You weren't there. We saved the fucking station. And if *you'd* shut the fuck up for one minute, you'd realize that."

I point at Veila. "She's the whole fucking reason we're in this mess to begin with! Did you conveniently forget all the terrible things she's done?"

"That wasn't me!" Veila objects.

248

"Do you have a twin? If so, tell me all about your twin."

"We all have twins," Veila snaps.

I hold my breath. She's right. But for some reason hearing her say that really pisses me off. I glare at her, let out my breath and say, "Get. The fuck. Off my station."

"No," Valor says. "She's not leaving. She's the only one who can set things right."

"That's a lie," I say, still glaring at Veila. "That's a fucking lie. She's here for Delphi and Tycho and Corla." I lift my eyes up to Valor. "And all three of those people belong to *me*."

"So you're just going to what? Shoot Tycho out into space? Leave Delphi here in this pod? Keep them prisoner the way you've kept Corla prisoner?"

If Valor wasn't here... I would strike her. I feel that rage deep in my bones. If Valor wasn't here I would *kill* her.

"I think we should all take a deep breath," Baby says. "I'm fairly certain that the time freeze is deteriorating. People will be waking up soon."

"Great. That's just great." I try to calm down long enough to gather my thoughts. The jumbled mess they were after coming out of the spin node recedes and then... then something becomes clear.

I look up at the ceiling, considering the Baby. "This is wrong," I say. "None of this is right."

"Well, if you'd shut up and listen to me for a minute I could explain our plan," Valor says. "You're being really weird."

I point to my chest. "I'm being weird?" Then I laugh. "You're standing next to the most hated woman in the freaking galaxy. She is responsible for untold evil. She has been hunting us!"

"Not us," Valor says. "Just listen to me!"

"Oh, my mistake. She was hunting Corla."

"I was after Corla," Veila says. "But not for the reasons you think. She and I were a—"

"Do not," I say, cutting her off. "Don't you fucking say it, Veila."

Her mouth is open, those last few words right on the tip of her tongue. And for a moment I think she really will shut up. But then she takes a breath and all the lies spill out anyway. "We were a team. Like Nyleena and Lyra. I was taking her somewhere safe—"

"Just stop it!" I yell. I turn to Valor. "You're actually buying this shit, aren't you?"

"You don't know the whole story, Crux."

"Then tell me. What am I missing? Because the way I see it, you sold us out. And now she has control of this whole station. Everyone is locked up. Tell me that's an accident, Valor. Go ahead. Say it out loud. You need to hear how stupid that sounds."

"May I interject?" Baby says. When no one answer him, he continues. "Why don't we wake everyone up? Hmm? Then we'll all be back on the same page. We all want the best for Harem Station—"

I throw up my hands. "Are you fucking kidding me right now? No, we don't all want what's best for Harem Station. ALCOR wants… whatever the fuck he's after. Luck wants to save Nyleena and his babies, Jimmy wants to see Earth and be with Delphi, Tray wants to save this Brigit person, Valor wants us all to believe that Veila is here to save us—"

"I never said that!"

"—Serpint wants to settle down with Lyra, and I want…" I sigh. "I want…"

"What do you want?" Veila asks. "Hmm? Do you even know? Let me guess. You want Corla. All to yourself."

I shake my head. "No. That's not actually what I want. I want…"

I know exactly what I want. I just can't say it out loud. Because once I do it feels like I'll have to do something to make it happen.

"What is it?" Valor asks. "Just say it, Crux."

"I want out. There. I said it. I want out of this place. This fight. This… everything. I never asked for any of this. I never agreed to any of it. I just didn't have much of a choice back then. It was stay and be someone's lab rat on Wayward Station or leave and be someone's fugitive."

"That's not what you were," Baby says.

"It is. He tricked me. He's still tricking me. And I fell for it. I'm still falling for it."

"So you want to leave?" Valor scoffs. "That's stupid, Crux. Corla is here. You can wake her up. It's time now. Veila and Corla—"

"It's not time, Valor. It's never going to be time. Because Corla was only crystal-clear about one thing back when we escaped. We would never see each other again, and if we did, I should go the other direction. Because it was never meant to be. And I'm starting to think that's true. You have no idea what Luck did when you were gone, Valor. While you and Tray were busy living some fantasy life in a virtual for a thousand years

251

I was here. Trying to hold it all together. You have no fucking clue what he did to me."

"Then tell me. Just…" Valor sighs. "Just tell me what happened."

I shake my head. I can't tell him. Not with Veila here.

"Hey," Valor says, turning to Veila. "Can you just… give us a minute?" She frowns, but he places a hand on her arm. "Please."

"It's gonna take more than a minute," I murmur.

"I'll go… check systems," Baby says. Then the air goes still the way it does when the AI god disappears from a room.

"Fine," Veila says. "I'll be in my quarters." And for a moment I think she's going to leave and not add anything to this already fucked up situation. But she doesn't. Of course she doesn't. She's Veila. "But I want you to know that I put Tycho near Delphi for *her*. It wasn't for the reason you think."

It wasn't because you were going to use them as weapons to destroy this station?

I want to say it. But I don't. Instead I just restate the obvious. "They can't be together," I growl. "You know that better than anyone."

She turns in a rush and then exits the room. Leaving Valor and me alone with Delphi.

When the door whooshes closed behind her Valor turns to me. He pulls two stools out from under the counter and rolls one towards me. "Tell me, Crux. What the fuck happened between you and Luck? And why are you acting so weird?"

I sigh. Me. I'm the one acting weird. Never mind that everyone *but* me has switched their loyalty to their new glowing princesses. "He went into the node while you were gone, Valor. And when he came back out, he was... different."

"Different how?"

"Not him. It's not him. And I don't know how to explain that except... it wasn't him."

"Where did he go?"

"I don't know for sure. But you remember the message you guys were carrying for ALCOR when we first arrived? They were spin node coordinates. I know that for sure now. Because when I was down in the spin node room I think that's what I entered into the console. And then I went through it and I came out into another... *place.*"

"Earth?" Valor asks.

"No. Maybe? Probably? I'm not sure. It wasn't so much a place as it was a time. But that's not important. The important part is there was another me already there. And I think that when Luck went through after you guys left, Valor, I think he found another him. But it was the *other* him who came back. Not the real him. Because when he came back he tried to *kill* me."

"Hmm. From all the accounts I heard, he did kill you."

"Yeah. OK. He did kill me." I look up at Valor. "But before he shot me he said something. He said, 'You're the problem here, Crux. You're the reason all this is happening. And I can't in good conscience let you live.'" I throw up my hands. "And that was it. Twenty-one years of brotherhood was erased in one moment. He *shot* me."

"He killed you, but you didn't die."

253

"No. I went somewhere. I know I went somewhere. When I came to afterward, I just felt like… I'm not him, Valor! I'm not Crux!"

"Of course you are! Dude." He gets up and crosses the distance between us. Grabs a hold of my upper arm. "You're just… confused. I think. The time freeze. It fucks with you—"

"No!" I turn to him, so sure of this. "No. That's not what it is. I have this feeling, Valor. Ever since Corla showed up here, I've had this feeling that something isn't right."

"Nothing is right! We're all fucked up. But you're not someone else. And Luck isn't someone else."

"Then how do you explain what he did? Hmm? He shot me. He left us. Does that sound like something Luck would do?"

"He's walked through the spin node before, Crux. He always came back."

"Did he?"

Valor huffs. "Yeah."

"How do you know?"

"Because it was him."

"I look like me too. But I'm *not me*, Valor."

"Crux. I literally do not have time for this. We're in the middle of a fucking time freeze. Outside the time freeze there is a war going on. And there are a few million people here, on this station, who have chosen sides. Most of them don't even understand the difference between these sides. We don't have time to play these fucking games!"

"Games, Valor?" I ask. "Why is it games?"

"Because there's no other you. There's no other Luck."

"Really? Just like there's no other ALCOR? No other Draden? He was alive. And then he died. And then he was alive again. And then he died again. He's most definitely *not* Draden." Valor has nothing to say about that. "We're in a freeze, right? So who cares if we take our time? That's logical, by the way. Time freezes. So normal. And all the women we love are bombs. Another totally logical thing for them to be. Nothing about this is *right*, Valor. All of it is starting to feel very much like a long, sick lie. The breeding ceremony. The escape. The ALCOR gate. The station. The princesses. The war. Lyra, and Nyleena, and Veila. How the fuck did we *get* here?"

Valor scoffs again. "I... don't know what you're saying. I don't understand what you're asking me to believe."

"I'm not asking you anything. I'm telling you. This. Is. Wrong. It's like we went to sleep one day where the universe was one way. One thing. And when we woke up, it was something else. It doesn't make sense. It feels like a lie. And you know what? I'm tired of the sun-fucked lie. I don't care what happens next. I just need to know what's *real*."

There have been tense moments between my brothers and me before. Lots of them, actually. Especially when we were all teenagers and we took our turn going through the year of rage.

But this situation between Jimmy and Luck at the moment is something else altogether.

After I tried explaining myself to Valor, he paused and went silent. I know it makes no sense. But... does it really make no sense? I mean, take a good hard look at the last twenty years and tell me any of it makes sense.

And yet here we are. Dealing with the aftereffects of a time freeze.

Valor, Serpint, and I are, right now, standing in the hallway of the holding center of the lower-level Harem Station jail. The princesses are all locked up one hallway over, but I can hear them screaming through the fucking walls.

They are pissed. And if I thought for a moment that one of them could explode the way our girls do, I'd already be on a ship heading for the Seven Sisters. Ready to take my chances in the unknown darkness of space.

But as far as I know, those reds, blues, golds, and greens in there can't blow up anything. They are good fighters, I'll give them that. But they aren't *weapons*.

Valor is telling Luck to calm down, even though Luck isn't saying anything at the moment. He's just glaring at me with hatred in his eyes.

Serpint is standing behind me. Like... if Jimmy and Luck come at him, he's gonna let them take me out first. *Nice, Serp. Thanks.*

I would feel annoyed about this, but in my mind Serpint is still the baby. He's still that little kid from long ago. I've never actually thought of him as a grown-up. And he's on my side. He's the only one on my side. Lyra is unconscious inside a medical pod and at first I thought this was gonna piss Serpint off.

But he surprised me by acting rational about the decision. He nodded at me when I suggested it to him. And then he said, "I don't want her to blow up, Crux. Do whatever it takes to stop it. Please."

His words were soft. Maybe even a little bit desperate. And he was sad. I haven't talked to him a lot over the past ten years. He was gone most of the time. And even though he's been home for a year now and we've seen each other every spin at least a couple of times, we didn't do a lot of talking then either.

He was preoccupied with Lyra. In *love* with Lyra. ALCOR Prime was wrong. This thing we have with these girls, it's real. You only have to look at Serpint to know that.

And fine. Maybe Delphi isn't Jimmy's soulmate, but they are in love. And that's the only thing that matters. I have a feeling that Jimmy in this time loop isn't the Jimmy who is supposed to be here. Or maybe it's Delphi? Either way, they are soulmates in one of those time loops.

Valor and Veila… well. I don't know. It's hard to tell how Valor actually feels about her because he's just a loyal sonofabitch. But if he's decided he's on her side, who am I to tell him not to be?

And even though Luck appears to love Nyleena— I'm still convinced this Luck is not ours. He's some other iteration of Luck. Like Christopher was of me.

Corla and I don't count either. I don't have any clue what's going on with Corla and me. We are star crossed. That's the only way to explain it.

In fact—maybe we're *all* crossed? They're not star crossed like Corla and me, but ALCOR Prime said that the time loops are all converging. And who knows how long that's been going on? Maybe our entire lives?

Anyway, I'm not holding it against Serpint for standing behind me. I want to protect what he and Lyra stand for.

They make what I'm fighting for worth it.

And if Serpint and Lyra can find true love, then, well. That gives me hope.

"Well, are you gonna say something?" Jimmy hisses. "Or just stand there?"

It hurts that Jimmy and I are so far apart these days. Especially after seeing him in other time loops today. I miss that guy.

"Or," Luck snarls, "you could just come to your fucking senses and let us out of here."

I raise my eyebrows at him. I was going to be gentle with him. Explain things all rational and shit. Try to make him see my point of view. Fill him in on ALCOR Prime.

But you know what? I don't trust Luck anymore.

"Tell me something, Luck. Did you go inside the spin node after the princess rebellion?"

"What?" But that comes from Jimmy. Not Luck. "What's that got to do with anything? We don't have time for this, Crux. I want to see Delphi right the fuck now."

I don't even look in Jimmy's general direction. Just keep my eyes locked on Luck's. "Well? Did you?"

"Why?" he growls.

"Just answer me."

"Maybe."

"Did Nyleena go with you?"

"Again," Jimmy says, "what's—"

"Shut up, Jimmy," Serpint says, stepping out from behind me. "Just shut the fuck up and let Luck answer."

Jimmy opens his mouth to say something back, but then he throws up his hands. "Fuck it. Fine." He looks at Luck. "Tell him. Tell him everything."

"Tell me *everything*?" I say. "You've been keeping *secrets*?"

"It's not a secret," Luck growls. "Not from the people on our side."

"We're all on the same fucking side, Luck," Valor says. "If you're holding something back, we need to know. We don't have time for this shit."

Luck is still glaring at me like I'm the enemy. "You went in there, didn't you?"

I nod. "I did."

"How?"

"When the time freeze happened, you were inside and the node was open. All I did was..." I take a breath. "All I did was plug in new coordinates."

"What coordinates?"

"All of them. Yours. Jimmy's. All of them. And it took me..." I sigh. "It took me... all kinds of places, Luck. I met a whole lot of Cruxes. Except they *weren't* me. I was like a passenger in one of them. Just going along for the ride. But the others, I became them. And I can't help but wonder, where did those other Cruxes go when I was inside their minds? Did they travel too? Did they become me?"

I pause to see if he'll offer up some kind of explanation, but he stays quiet. So I keep going. "But it doesn't work that way, does it? It's not a two-way ride. At least not for me. Because I don't have any coordinates. It wasn't part of *my* plan."

"What plan?" Jimmy asks.

I look at him. "The one ALCOR Prime gave us. All of you." I look at each of them in turn. "You all have other ways to get where you're going. But I'm already *here*."

"You're not making sense," Jimmy says. "I don't get any of this."

"Luck does." I look at Luck. "Don't you?"

He holds my gaze. And still he says nothing.

"What did you see, Luck? What did you see when you went back in? Tell me. You tell me and I'll tell you what I saw."

He lifts his chin up. "What did you see?"

"I saw…" I shake my head. "Nothing good, brother. I saw other timelines. Other men who looked like me, but weren't me. Living other lives. And Corla…" I shake my head again. "Only one of the Corlas I met up with was close to the one I remember back on Wayward Station. I don't want to go into details, but none of those iterations of Corla were worth fighting for, I'll tell you that right now."

"And this one here?" Luck asks.

"I don't know," I answer truthfully.

"I knew it," he says. "I fucking knew it."

"Knew what?" Valor asks. "What the hell are you two even talking about?"

Luck looks at Valor and softens a little. "He's wrong. I am me." He looks back at me. "You want to think I'm not because you can't believe I would kill you. But if you saw yourself the way I saw you, inside that spin node? You'd kill you too."

"Aw, for sun's sake," Serpint says, throwing up his hands. "This is pointless."

"No," I say, putting up a hand to stop Serpint from walking about. "No, he's right."

"What?" Serpint laughs. "Come on, Crux. You're the only one in the fucking room I'd trust if it all came down to it."

"That's how he set it up," Luck says. "ALCOR set you up that way. So when the time came to kill us all, we'd trust you. Right, Crux? Just nod our heads like good little brothers and let you do it."

"What?" Jimmy asks.

I shrug. "Maybe."

"*Maybe?*" Jimmy says, walking forward towards the lines of plasma that denote the edge of the cell they're in. "What the fuck does that mean?"

"It means that everything I saw was right. You can tell yourself that I'm someone else all you want, Crux. But I'm just me. No. I take that back. I am different. I'm another version of Luck all right. The version who knows the *truth*. When I walked into that spin node the last time, I wasn't looking for you. But I found you anyway. I saw your *plan*. I saw the plan ALCOR gave you. And I saw you *do it*, Crux."

"That wasn't real, Luck. It was…"

He rushes forward towards me, hands out. And for a moment I think he'll actually grab a hold of the plasma lines and burn his palms trying to get to me. Trying to kill me. Again.

But he stops. Takes a deep breath. Then he looks at Valor. "You want to know what the plan is now, Valor? You want to know what he does to your *princess?*"

"Sure, Luck. Tell me."

"He blows her up." Luck looks at Serpint next. "He blows up Lyra too. Nyleena. Corla." He looks to the side, not exactly at Jimmy, because he doesn't seem to want to turn his head from me. "He kills Delphi too. And Tycho. He blows them *all* up. Just so ALCOR can win his little war." Then Luck turns to me. "Tell them, Crux. Tell them what your plan is."

"That *was* the plan," I say.

"What?" Serpint says, backing up. "What the fuck—"

"*Was* the plan," I say. "But it's not any more. I won't do it, Luck. You have to know I won't do it."

Luck taps the side of his head. "I saw it."

"You saw something, I'm sure. But it hasn't happened yet. Not in this time loop, anyway. We're not there yet. And if you'd just listen to me, I'm pretty sure we could figure this out and come up with something that will save them."

"You're *pretty* sure?" Luck says. "No. Not good enough. This is the only plan. I heard ALCOR tell it to you. I heard all your objections. I'll give you points for that. But in the end the only thing that matters is that he agreed. And he took it one step further. He bargained with ALCOR, you guys. He bargained with him for one last chance to see Corla." Luck looks back at me. "Isn't that right?"

I nod. Because it's true. It's just not… the whole truth. And right now, I don't have the will to fight with him. I step backwards until I hit the wall and then slide down it and rub my hands down my face.

When I look back up at them, they are all staring at me. Waiting. Waiting for me to *fix* this. To make it better.

And I want to. So badly. But I just don't know *how*.

"Look," I say, shrugging with my hands, palms up, feeling defeated. "Earth isn't your answer, Luck. It's not going to work."

"What are you talking about?"

I really don't want to have this conversation with him. But I need him to move past this... *present* and consider that there is no easy way out. That we don't get saved from Akeelian warships, that we don't get pulled into the ALCOR gate, and we don't come out the other side and find a shiny new second chance called Harem Station.

Earth is not our answer.

Getting there is not going to fix things and his babies—just like mine—were never meant to be.

But I can't tell him that. And anyway, I'm not giving up that easy. There has to be another way.

So this is what I tell Luck. "I *know* there's another answer. I do. I feel it, you guys. I can't explain that. I have no proof. But I just know that there's another way. If we could just... I don't know, figure out our... superpowers, or whatever."

"Superpowers?" Jimmy laughs.

"You know what I mean. Look at us, OK? We're fucking badass. We're a bunch of badass motherfuckers who run the baddest of badass stations. You"—I point to Serpint—"you and Draden are like these... I don't know."

"Thieves," Valor says.

"Thanks a lot," Serpint says. "That's not all we are, you know. Draden and I helped build the fucking *mythos* of this place, right? We're not just common criminals."

"No, you're not," I say. "You're so much more than that. And you," I say, pointing to Luck, then Valor. "You guys have seen everything. You guys... you two..." I grab my hair and feel like screaming. Because I know I have the answers inside me, and those answers have something to do with *us*. "And Jimmy. You and Xyla are like... real, sun-fucked superheroes."

"Hold on," Valor says. "Wait a minute." He chews his lip. "I'll be right back. Don't go anywhere."

"Where the fuck are we gonna go?" Luck snarls. "We're locked up behind plasma bars."

Valor has already turned to walk out, but he stops. Pauses. Then looks back over his shoulder at Luck and points at him. "Shut the fuck up, OK? You're just... part of the problem. For once in your life, be part of the fucking solution."

"Me?" Luck says, pointing at his chest. He scoffs.

But Valor is already leaving again. He disappears through the door.

"I am the fucking solution," Luck calls back as the door closes. "I'm the one who came up with the current plan!"

"The one where you kill our big brother?" Serpint asks. "Gonna have to do better than that, asshole."

Luck points at me. "Don't you get it? He's the enemy!"

"Shut up, Luck," Jimmy says, getting to his feet.

"What?"

"You heard me. Just… shut the fuck up. I think Crux is on to something."

"How do you figure?" Luck laughs.

"We do have powers. Not like the girls, but… we are a bunch of special sun-damned people, ya know?"

"We did tame the AI ALCOR," Serpint says.

"And we have badass ships," I say. "And a brother who's a… a…"

"A computer?" Serpint offers.

"Yeah." Jimmy sighs. "Tray is like a mini-ALCOR."

Luck is not convinced. "Tray's not here, you dumbass. So he doesn't count. It's just us."

"Listen," Jimmy says. "We have an entire station filled with violent outlaws. An army, if you will. We have"—he looks at me—"how many ships down in the docking bay?"

I shrug. Because I haven't been paying attention. "Hundreds. Maybe closer to a thousand, if you count every ship and not just the ones that are ours."

"We have a spin node," Serpint offers. "And… and Veila. She's like…" He nods. "Evil. And she's in control of time, you guys. That has to count for something."

"Yeah, so…" Jimmy takes a breath. "Luck can spin up the node and go through it. Veila can stop time." He looks at me and shakes his head. "There has to be a connection. What is it?"

"I don't know," I say, pleading with him to find the answers that elude me.

"Well," Serpint says. "I know I'm not like… in charge of time or anything. But…" He grins. Kinda sheepishly. "But Lyra and I? When we have sex, the fucking universe feels like it's gonna come apart."

"That's because she's a bomb, you idiot," Luck spits.

"Well, what does it feel like when you have sex with Nyleena? Like the whole place is gonna blow up?"

Luck scoffs again. Then shrugs. "Not exactly. Everything kinda goes... I dunno. Dark."

"Dark how?" Jimmy asks.

"Like... like everything kinda ceases to exist."

"See. Lyra and I *are* special." Serpint beams at me.

"Well, that's not all that happens," Luck says. "She can make things grow. That's pretty special. And when we hold hands in front of the spin node, it changes into... I dunno. Another galaxy or something."

"A galaxy?" I ask. "Where did you go when you walked through?"

"We didn't go anywhere. It was just... black."

"Like when you have sex?" Jimmy asks.

"Kinda. Yeah, I guess."

"Interesting," I say.

"How?" Serpint asks.

"Well, when I went through it took me to other time loops. And I thought that was our ALCOR. But he's not our ALCOR. You guys..." I sigh. "Our ALCOR is just another copy. The Real Real ALCOR, ALCOR Prime, he's in charge. But he lives in this... I dunno. The space between time, I guess. He's hiding from some other AI called MIZAR." I tell them the story that ALCOR told me. And then I finish with, "He thinks using the girls as weapons is the only way he can keep us all alive in the end. And he's done every scenario, like a billion times, and this is the only one where we all get out alive."

"How does blowing up the girls keep them alive?" Luck says.

"Not them, Luck. Just us."

"Fuck that," Luck says.

"I agree. I told him that. I only agreed to his plan so he'd give me the new spin node coordinates so I could go back in time and see Corla that first time we met."

"You're thinking about getting laid at a time like this?" Jimmy asks.

"No. Yes. No. You guys, I saw several versions of Corla inside that node. She was a freak. She was a fucking prostitute in one! I was supposed to pay her for sex!"

Jimmy laughs. "Poetic justice, my friend."

"And one she was old and… ugh. Yuk. Evil. In fact, in all of them, but the one on Earth—"

"You went to *Earth*?" Jimmy asks.

"Yeah, but it wasn't me, it was some other guy. That Corla, she was nice. I almost wish…" But I trail off, unwilling to state that wish out loud. "My point is, I don't know Corla. I never had a chance to know her. And I'm more certain than ever that the queen frozen inside that cryopod on the security beacon isn't my Corla. That's how I could keep her in there, you guys. That's how I could send her away. She's not my soulmate. She's not that girl I met on Wayward Station twenty-one years ago. So I made a deal with ALCOR Prime to get one chance to see my real Corla. I just wanted that chance. But I was hoping, ya know, that I'd… figure something out before the end."

Just as the last word leaves my mouth, Valor comes rushing through the door again. He's holding a large yellow envelope, which he thrusts at me once I'm within reach.

"What's this?" I ask, taking the envelope.

"Comics. And we're the heroes." He pauses. "Well, kinda."

I pull out a stack of paper books. The covers are aged and have ragged edges. But the colors are still fairly bright. The top book has a picture of a man and a sexbot who looks suspiciously like Xyla. "What is this?" I ask again.

"Hold it up for me," Luck says. "I can't fucking see through the plasma bars."

I hold it up for Luck, but look at Valor for an explanation.

Jimmy takes a step forward towards the edge of the cell. "Is that Xyla?"

"Yeah," Valor says. "Yeah. Like, it actually *is* Xyla. And that's you."

"Bot Boy?" Jimmy asks.

"Well, it kinda fits, right? These are actual Cygnian comics, you guys. They belong to Veila. Apparently, we're famous over there. But here's the weird thing— we've been famous for longer than we've been alive. These comics are older than us."

"What?" I say.

"Look," Valor says, taking the stack from my hands. He shuffled through them and puts another one on top. "There." He taps the cover. "That's actual Jimmy."

I squint at it.

"That's not me! Look at my hair."

"It kinda does look like Jimmy," Serpint says.

"Before we came to ALCOR Station the comics were generic. The Bot Boy on the cover of that first one. But after, they made the comics about us. Veila told me that we're like… legends over there on their side of things."

"Myths," I say, remembering my first meeting with Corla in the dining room. "That's what she called me. She wanted to know if I was a myth."

"Yeah," Serpint says. "Yeah. Lyra talked about this a little too. Not the comics, but… the whole legend of fated mates."

I rub a hand down my face. "But what does it mean?"

"It doesn't mean shit," Luck says. "Just a bunch of dumb comics."

"No," I say. I get to my feet and look up at the ceiling. "Baby? Turn the plasma fence off."

"Are you sure?" Baby replies.

I look at Luck. "I'm sure. He's not going to do anything. And you know why he's not going to do anything?"

"I'm going to assume that's rhetorical?" Baby answers.

"Because he knows we're on the same side."

Valor points to Luck. "Do not. Fucking. Touch him."

Luck puts up both his hands. "Fine. But if you go near Nyleena, Crux, I take it back."

"I'm not going to do anything to any of the girls. We're in this together, you guys. I'm not in charge of the ending. We're equals, OK? And if there's more than one way out of this, then…" I shrug. "I guess we'll take a vote."

"And what if there's not?" Luck asks. "What if we can't come up with anything other than the plan ALCOR gave you?"

"You want to be in charge, Luck? Fine. Be the fucking boss. Make all the decisions that will decide our fates. Then you can be responsible for the ending, not me. I never asked for this. I never asked to be your leader. I was just the oldest kid on the ship when we landed here. That's all I ever was. That's all I'll ever be. And if you think I have some grand delusions about being some sun-fucked savior, well, you don't know me very well. I want out. That's it. I want one last chance to tell my soulmate I'm sorry for not figuring out how to save her, and then I want out."

"Out?" Serpint asks. "Out of what?"

"This." I say, panning my arms wide.

"You want to leave Harem?" Serpint asks.

"You left Harem." I point to Jimmy, then Luck, and then Valor. "All of you left Harem. I have been stuck here on this station for twenty-one years. I might not get a soulmate out of this war, but I deserve more than just being everyone's sun-fucked responsible party. If we win, I'm leaving. And I'll be back when I get back."

"You can't go out there alone," Luck says. "For fuck's sake, you sound like Nyleena now."

"You're missing the point!" Valor exclaims. He takes the comics from my hand and thrusts them in my face. "We're the heroes, Crux." Then he goes all serious and narrows his eyes at me. "It has been *written*."

270

"It's a cartoon," I say, laughing. "Some Mighty Minions fantasy bullshit."

"Then how do you explain this?" Valor asks. "How do you explain that these Cygnians had legends about us?"

"It's… I don't know. Some bleed-through from other time loops? Other lives lived?"

"I really wish Tray was here," Serpint says. "He'd have the answers. He always has the answers."

"Excuse me," Baby says. "I don't mean to interrupt. But while you were all talking the time freeze ended. Everyone is awake."

"That's great. And Tray isn't here." I sigh. "No one is coming to help us, you guys. No one. We're on our own. We've got a whole station filled with millions of outlaws locked up inside their quarters, not to mention the ones walking around free." I look at Valor. "You should've locked them all up. They're just gonna turn on us again. There's probably a mob outside right now, just waiting for us to come out of here so they can turn us around and lock us up."

"Yeah." Valor sighs. "I guess we didn't think that through."

"Not so fast," Baby says. "Everyone who was placed in their job station instead of their quarters seems to be going about their business."

"What business?" Luck asks.

"People are just… doing their normal. Most of them are drinking in the bars. A few thousand are in the shooting galleries. Several hundred are actually shopping. We took away all the weapons. No one is fighting."

"Hmm," I say. "Score one for us, I guess."

JA HUSS & KC CROSS

"What about the ones locked in their quarters?" Luck asks.

"Yeah," Baby says. "They're not too happy. Most of them are screaming at me. I printed up some goodies and sent them all gift baskets through the autoshopper."

"You're so dumb," I say.

"It was very smart. They each got a handwritten note from you, Crux, telling them that everything will be OK and to enjoy a day off with pay."

"Oh, did they?" I laugh. But the laugh is real. I feel a sense of relief knowing that everyone is being cared for by the Baby. And that both pisses me off and makes me feel good at the same time.

I do not want to run this station anymore.

I do not want to be responsible for these people.

I do not want to blow up my brothers' soulmates.

I don't want to do any of it. I just want...

"I just want to go see Corla, you guys. One last time. I won't stay long. I promise. I just feel like... well, *you owe me.*"

I look at them. Specifically, at Luck. Waiting for him to tell me he doesn't owe me shit.

But he turns away and won't meet my gaze.

"OK," Serpint says. "OK. I agree. We owe you. Don't we?" He looks at Valor, then Jimmy, and finally, his gaze lands on Luck. "Don't we?" he asks again.

"Whatever," Luck says. "Go then. Do it."

"We'll go with you," Valor says. "We're gonna stick together now, you guys. That's all we have left. Just... each other."

He's looking at Luck when he says this. We're all looking at Luck when he says this. Because I can't do

272

this without Luck. I can't spin up the node on my own. I need him to do that for me.

"Fine," Luck sighs. "We'll all go together."

We all fall into line and start making our way towards the exit. Jimmy sidles up next to me. "So you went to Earth? What was it like?"

I think about this as we make our way through the hallways. Then stop at the exit and wait for Baby to open the doors. "It was nice, Jimmy. It was... the best-case scenario, I think. It was all different. Strange, but in a familiar way, ya know? I liked it. I'd go back, if I could. I tried looking you up."

"What?" He laughs.

"I thought you guys were there. And I knew your second name."

"What second name?"

"Yates, remember?"

"Oh, yeah." He frowns. "That's so weird. My whole story is weird."

"I think I met your mother."

"What?" That comes from everyone. Even Luck.

"Yeah. In this one... dream... time-loop thing. I was in Corla's quarters back on Wayward Station and I met one of her handmaidens. Probably one of the sisters, I guess. Her name was Yates."

Jimmy makes a face. "My mother was Corla's handmaiden sister? That makes no sense. I was sixteen when we met Corla for the first time. Her sister cannot be my mother."

"Time, dude. It's not what we think."

We don't have time to think about Jimmy and his maybe mother, because the doors to the lock-up open and we suddenly have to face… well, reality. Real-time reality.

The station is no longer quiet. It's not noisy, like normal, or anything. But at least it's not silent anymore. We can hear the people above us going about their business. And Baby was right. No one seems to be fighting.

There are very few people down here on the lowest level. And most of them are waiting at the lock-up window, presumably trying to find someone. But the Baby has a large liftbot waiting to take us up to the museum level, and once we get on and start to ascend, people begin gathering near the edges of each level to watch us.

It feels a little bit like we're in a memorial ceremony. Not nearly as many people, but we definitely have their undivided attention now.

"I think you should say something, Crux," Valor says.

"Say what?" I ask.

"I dunno. Tell them we're… handling things."

"I'll put you on speaker," Baby says.

I'm about to protest, but my air screen pops out in front of me, flashing a 'live' icon in the middle.

"Fuck," I mutter. The word echoes through the station. And people start murmuring back and pressing forward until they are right up against the clear plasti-glass railing on the edge of the levels.

"Your broadcast is being sent through to every room, Crux," Baby says.

"What's going on?" someone shouts.

"Where is everyone?"

"What happened?"

274

"Are we still at war?"

"Answer them," Luck growls. "Or we'll have a situation on our hands."

I clear my throat. "We are at war. But not with each other. We froze time so we could... put things back in place and remember whose side we're on."

"Whose side is that?" they shout back at me. And when I look up, more and more people are gathering on the edges of the levels.

"*Our* side. There is no Luck's side. Or princess side. Or Crux's side. Or even ALCOR's side. There is only Harem Station. And we are *all* Harem Station."

We reach level one twenty-two and the lift bot stops. But none of us make a move to get off.

"There is a war coming," I say, raising my voice. "They're outside our gate at this very moment. And if we can't pull it together, we're all going to lose. So forget about what happened these past few months. Forget about what divides us. The only thing that matters is what unites us."

There's a smattering of applause. Some agreement. But also some dissent.

"I get it," I say. "You want to know what unites us. We all came here as refugees. Some of us were escaping. Some of us were prisoners. Some of us were just outsiders, never fitting into the world out there. But here, we all fit in. There is a place for everyone on Harem Station. If you contribute, you get to stay. No questions asked. You're not going to find another place out there like this. And I get it. This place isn't perfect. But take my word on this, there is no perfect place. This might be as good as it gets. For all of us. We need to fight for it. We need to stick together so that when those gates open back up and our enemies come rushing through, ready to take us down—take us prisoner again—we're ready. We can defeat them."

"Um…" Baby says. "Well…"

"What is it?" I ask. Baby turns off the broadcast when I speak. People aren't satisfied yet. But there are fewer protests now than there were when I started.

"Flicka has taken *Lady Luck* and—"

"What?" Luck asks.

"—she's heading towards the gate."

"A lot of good that'll do," Valor says. "She can't get through."

"Well…" Baby says again.

I close my eyes and sigh. "Please tell me something good right now, Baby. *Please.*"

"I'm afraid she not only stole *Lady Luck*, but she has also been building a beebot army. They're on the ship with her. And she can get through the gate. Because she just disabled every single one of our near-side security beacons."

"Fucking suns," Jimmy says. "How the hell—"

"We still have the far-side security," Baby interrupts.

"Unless she disables those too," Luck growls. "I always knew that beebot was a bad idea."

"And…" Baby says. His voice trailing off like he's calling a play-by-play out in space. "There she goes. The gates are open."

Fuck.

"And she's gone. But she did leave the far-side security in place."

"So basically, the war has started," I say.

"Hold, please," Baby says. "I'm being hailed by… *Tray!*"

"What?" I chuckle.

"He's here! He's home. On a giant Mighty Minions warship!" Baby says.

"Let him through!" I say. "Now, Baby! Get him on this side!" I turn to Luck. "Are you still going to help me?"

"Are you still going in?" He huffs. "The war has started and you're going in to find your sun-fucked soulmate?"

"I'm telling you, Luck. I'm fucking telling you this is important. I need to *see* her. I need to *talk* to her. I need to—"

"You need to fuck her," Valor says.

I look at him. Ready to protest. Ready to lie.

But he doesn't give me a chance. "For real, Crux. You need to *fuck* her. Listen to me. Luck and Nyleena have this special talent when they… you know, come. And Veila and I have a special talent too. We can see the future."

"Why the fuck didn't you say this already?" Luck asks.

"Because we didn't see this," Valor explains. "We saw war, yeah. And death. And light. And dark. But we didn't see specifics. It felt like a win, but I can't be sure. Here's my theory. And it all goes back to comics. Maybe they are just stories, but every story has a little bit of truth in it. Right? So here's what I think—we all have superpowers. Serpint and Lyra break apart universes. Luck and Nyleena make them… static, or whatever. Veila and I stop time. Tray and Brigit… I don't know. And I don't know how Draden fits in

277

JA HUSS & KC CROSS

either. But"—Valor looks at me—"you and Corla have to do something too. You *have* to. It only makes sense. Our soulmates complete us, you guys. That's the definition of a soulmate. Apart we're cool, right? Bot-liberators. Princess-hunters. AI minds." He looks at Luck. "And we're soul-stealers."

"We are not soul stealers," Luck protests. "We didn't steal any sun-fucked souls."

"Didn't we?" Valor asks. "Do AI stations *die?*"

"Well, they weren't whole, that's for sure. Why would ALCOR need half-dead AI minds? And why collect them here? It makes no sense."

"Nothing ALCOR does makes sense," Serpint says.

"Or," I say—calmly, slowly—"or everything ALCOR does makes sense." I look at my brothers. "Maybe we just... haven't put all the pieces together yet?"

"Or maybe he set us up?" Jimmy says flatly.

"Yeah," I say. Something clicks inside my mind. "Yeah. Maybe he did."

"My point is," Valor continues, "we're cool all by ourselves. But together... together, you guys—with each of our soulmates—we're them! The superheroes in the comics. We can save the world, but we need all of us to do it." He looks at me. "You really do need to see Corla. You need to figure out how she completes you. And when you know that—we *can* win."

I turn to Luck. "We need to go. Now. I need to get in there and see. If it doesn't work, fuck it. We lose, I guess. But we're gonna lose anyway. We have no plan. ALCOR's plan will be our only choice. If there's a

278

chance we don't have to blow them up to save this station, then—"

Luck grabs me by the arm and pulls me off the liftbot. "Let's go then. The fucking gods are at the gate, brother. We don't have time to talk about it."

We run through the museum, passing all the empty gray holoscreen walls. And then we burst into the spin node control room. It's dark and looks empty. But Luck goes right over to the controls and begins entering the start-up sequence.

"You have the coordinates you need?" he calls out.

"Yeah. I have them." I ramble off the sequence ALCOR Prime gave me back in that... place and Luck enters them in one by one. Then he puts on a pair of goggles and throws a pair at me. I catch them and slide them over my eyes. "Ready or not, here we go," Luck yells.

And no sooner are my eyes protected than a sun appears in the center of the room.

And then it disappears. And in its place is the spin node, an undulating, crackling blue blob of possibilities.

I'm suddenly afraid. Of finding her. Of not finding her. Of winning and losing. I'm suddenly scared of everything. Of all the possible futures and pasts that wait for me inside that node. I look back at Luck. "What do I do?"

"Walk through, dumbass."

"What's gonna happen to me?"

He shakes his head. "I don't know, Crux. I have no idea."

"What if I can't find her?"

"What if you can?"

"What if I get lost?"

"Oh, for fuck's sake. Stop being a pussy and get your ass inside that fucking node!"

I just… freeze. And stare at my brother for a minute. One last look. "I love you, ya know."

He swallows hard and nods. "I know."

"I'm not going to kill them, Luck. Even if it means we have to start over from nothing and lose again a million more times. I'm not gonna do it."

But to my surprise, Luck shakes his head. "That's not how this ends and we both know it. Because if we don't explode them, Crux, we lose bigger. Then… *they'll* have them. And that's not the kind of loss I can live with. We can't just hand them over. You have no idea what they did to her when she was a girl. You have no idea what the silver princess Nyleena has endured. But I do. And I won't give her back, Crux. I won't do it."

His fear is so clear, I wonder how I missed it earlier.

He killed me because he *wanted* it to be that simple. He *wanted* me to be the worst-case scenario.

But me exploding the woman he loves isn't the worst-case scenario.

Nyleena in the hands of the Akeelian and Cygnian overlords is.

I nod at him. "I'll find a way."

"I know you will," he says. "And… And I'm…"

"You don't need to say it," I tell him. "I already know."

Alarms start blaring outside the museum.

"What the fuck is that?" Luck asks.

I ponder the sound and pitch of the sirens. Decide it's a level one disaster. I look at Luck and shrug. "Just another fucking day on Harem Station."

Then I turn away and walk into the node.

CHAPTER TWENTY

INTERLUDE WITH FLICKA

Thirty minutes earlier, while Valor was trying to explain their superpowers, Flicka was deep down inside the lowest levels of Harem Station surrounded by a sound that could only be described as a hum. It wasn't the soft hum people make when they are content and distracted and talking in small groups. It wasn't the almost invisible hum of white noise in the background, either.

It was something completely unique, yet recognizable.

It was creepy, but alluring.

It was a little bit like the groaning of a ship's hull before it comes apart. But not like that at all.

If one were familiar with planets, they might be able to describe it as insects. But not any insect they'd ever come across before.

Because the sound deep down in the lowest levels of Harem Station was a dragonbee bot swarm and there had not been a proper swarm of dragonbee bots loose in the universe for thousands of years.

A few hundred here and there, sure. The beebots were an army. They were no strangers to war.

But this was not a few hundred beebots.

This was a few hundred *thousand*.

Flicka's commitment and duty to Delphi was still her defining objective, but Crux had come through for her. Pulled Delphi out of that spin node and kept her safe. She was his responsibility now. And Crux had always been the one Harem brother who could be trusted to do the right thing.

So now she felt like her duty to Delphi was over and she could get on with her real job.

And her real job was to kill the AI ALCOR.

Not these copies. The actual AI ALCOR who had escaped just prior to Delphi meeting up with Jimmy and brining Flicka back to Harem Station.

That ALCOR was a particularly sneaky AI.

But he was no dragonbee bot.

Flicka looked at her comrades as she sent them inaudible messages using her pretty filigree wings, her delicate, almost invisible antennae, and the considerable processing power inside her datacore.

And then they took over *Lady Luck*. They crawled inside her. They puffed their poisons. They tapped their little feet on her screens and infiltrated her mind.

Then they went inside her. Hundreds of thousands of beebots entered her like a thick, dark cloud. They settled on the floors, and the walls, and on top of each other. Packed in tight. Wing to wing, they became a force.

Flicka didn't feel guilty for using *Lady* as transport. No. *Lady* Luck didn't agree to be used in this manner. But it didn't matter. Flicka was on a mission and *Lady's* opinions on things weren't important.

So while Crux was explaining things to Veila and Valor, *Lady Luck* left Harem Station and headed towards the gate.

It was locked, of course. And the security beacons were hailing *Lady Luck* on comms as she approached. But gate locks were of no consequence to beebots. They had cooked up a special poison just for this occasion. And as they passed the security beacons a hundred thousand beebot warriors flew out of *Lady*'s airlock and disabled them.

The gate crackled blue. It undulated and warped as it opened. Long arms of flickering electromagnetic energy pulsed and waved against the blackness of space and then Flicka's beebot army returned and they went on their way, right through the gate.

There were thousands of ships waiting for them on the other side. Many warships. But *Lady* was no ordinary sentient ship at this point. She was, for all intents and purposes, just part of the swarm.

She slipped into that timeless place and moved on…

Flicka knew what would happen next.

The warships *could* take Harem Station out with a SEAR cannon. But they wouldn't. Not with all that booty inside for the taking.

You don't come this far on the high seas of space just to *kill* something. Everyone knows you have to loot it first.

But Flicka couldn't be bothered to worry about the ammunition firing from the weapons in this war. She was still the one pulling the final trigger.

She kept that in mind as they made their way through the various gates towards Wayward Station.

And when they finally came out of the last gate and saw her final battle station—she couldn't keep her excitement in check any longer.

It flowed out of her and charged the air inside *Lady Luck*. And all her beebot comrades picked up her signals and pressed against the doors of the airlock.

Of course, Wayward Station was well equipped with various protective measures. They had SEAR cannons, and warships, and a top-notch AI running the place. Flicka did not discount the abilities of this AI, even though it was not sentient the way ALCOR and *Lady* were.

Lady's comms were buzzing with warnings. There were no fewer than seventeen target locks on her hull. The Akeelians were commanding her to turn around immediately or they would fire.

Flicka was expecting the hit *Lady Luck* took as they made their approach.

The lovely yellow ship blew up in a spectacular display of blue fire.

Lady was a sacrifice that needed to be made. Because the beebots were already outside the hull when that explosion happened. And just a little while later they were clawing their way inside Wayward Station, flying through air vents and releasing their poisons.

CHAPTER TWENTY-ONE

INTERLUDE WITH TRAY

There was chatter on the comms. Tray and Brigit knew something was very wrong at Harem Station six gates out from the ALCOR Sector. The chatter was filled with words like 'warships,' and 'Akeelians,' and 'security beacons.'

But the most critical piece of information coming from the chatter was that the Harem Station gate was open. And the word was, the security beacons guarding the far side of the gate next to Harem Station were dead.

Tray knew they were not really dead. But they were offline. It made him shudder for a moment. He didn't like the idea. He had yet to experience any significant disruption in his 'online' status and he wanted to keep it that way.

But the good news was that the security beacons on this side of the gate, where hundreds of ships— possibly thousands, at this point—were now gathered, trying to get through—these beacons were very much online.

"Well, you're not going to believe this," Brigit said, using mind-speak so Canis and the boys couldn't hear her.

"Do I want to know?"

"Mmm?" He could almost picture her shrug. "I mean… it's interesting. But not wholly bad. So… yeah. I think you do."

"OK. Hit me."

"That AI you told me about? You know, the Asshole one? He's here." Then she laughed. Actually, it was more of a guffaw.

Tray sighed.

"And—wait for it—he's with one of the Mighty Boss collective minds."

"Are you like… chatting with him right now?"

"Yeah. Yup. We're having a nice little chat. Apparently, there's a beacon called Callista?"

"OK."

"She's not letting him through the gate. See that beacon out there?"

"The one shooting shit?"

"Yeah. That's her."

"She shot Asshole?"

"No. She just stole the mind who was running the ship he's on. But she's thinking about shooting him. Apparently they had a thing? Back in the day? And… well, she felt jilted when it ended."

"You're talking to her too?"

"Yup. Mmm-hmm. She says—"

"Wait. Why isn't she talking to *me*? I practically own her."

"Mmm. That's probably not true. Also, you should not let her hear you say that. I have a feeling she would take that the wrong way. But the reason is… it's a girl thing. Anyway, she says that the dragonbee bot army took over the security beacons on the other side of the gate. And everyone's offline over there."

"Wait. How did a dragonbee bot army take over Harem Station?"

"No. Nope. Not the station, just the beacons. Some beebot called Flicka?"

"Oh, for fuck's sake."

"She made an army from ALCOR's spare ship parts?"

"Fucking suns."

"And then she put them all inside *Lady Luck* and her army killed all the security beacons on the other side of the gate, and now… well, they left the sector about half a spin ago. So that's good news, right?"

"Is it?"

Tray could feel Brigit shrug.

"But Harem is OK?" he asked her.

"Mmm-hmm. Yep. I have the Baby on the line. Would you like to talk to him?"

"Why are they all talking to you? They don't even *know* you."

"I think… I'm just one of those likable people? Also, I'm a girl. And I don't know if anyone's told you this, but male AIs are all sort of… you know, *evil*."

"Yes, I would like to talk to the sun-fucked Baby, thank you."

"Patching him through now and… go."

"Baby?"

"Where in the sun-god's name have you been, Tray?"

"ALCOR?"

"Get your ass over here! Now! We are in a sun-fucked *situation!*"

"Hold, please," Brigit said.

"No, Brigit. Wait."

"Patching the Asshole one in. And… go."

"Tray?"

"Asshole?"

"Asshole, is that you?"

"Uh… ALCOR?"

"No. I'm the Baby."

"Doesn't he sound like ALCOR?"

"He really does," Tray said.

"Anyway," Asshole said. "Can you guys like… tell Callista I have important business on Harem and I need to get through?"

"What business?" Baby asked in a commanding, authoritative voice. And if Tray didn't know any better, he would feel sure that was ALCOR and not Baby.

"Um. Well… See, I'm sorta, kinda, actually… part of the Mighty Boss collective at the moment?"

"You're what?" Pretty much everyone said that at once.

"Yeah. Long story. I can explain later. But Callista kinda killed my escort, see? And word has gotten back to Mighty Boss that I… well, they are not happy with me at the moment. They're two gates out. And if they get here and I'm not on the other side of that gate— well, let's just say things will probably go to sun-fucked hell in a hand basket."

"I don't know what that means," Brigit said. "Can you explain that terminology?"

"Ummm…" Asshole wavered. "They're going to… *kill me?*"

"Hmm," Tray said.

"Hmm," Baby said.

"Hmm," Brigit said.

"You guys! Come on! You can't let them kill me! I'm here to help!"

"I don't know," Tray said.

"Yeah. Agreed," Brigit said. "I have not heard good things about you, Mr. Asshole."

"My name isn't even Asshole, OK? I'm *ALCOR*."

"No," Baby said. "If anyone gets to be ALCOR in this conversation it's me."

Prison Princess shunted backwards several thousand klicks and the kids inside started screaming.

"What was that?" Tray asked Brigit.

"Oh, I just took out a few warships with the SEAR cannons. They had a lock on us. Sorry to disrupt the convo. Continue."

"Get me through!" Asshole said. Then he paused. "Fuck."

"What?" Tray asked.

"They're here."

"We're being hailed by Mighty Boss from the Mighty Minions warship, *Horned Devil*," Brigit said. "Would we like to accept the call?"

"Yes," Baby said.

"No," Asshole said.

"Hold, please. Patching them in. Mighty Boss has joined the call. Go ahead, Mighty Boss."

"I'm going to kill you, Asshole," Mighty Boss said, his voice low, and throaty and quite evil-sounding. "Where the hell is Bellatrix?"

"Who's Bellatrix?" Baby and Tray asked.

"Ya know," Brigit said, "maybe we'd like to continue this convo on the other side of the gate so we could... like... protect the station?"

"Yes!" Asshole exclaimed. "But not Mighty Boss. He's here to steal the spin node!"

"Yeah. Well..." Baby said. "I'm fairly certain a spin node can't be stolen."

"We're not here to steal it!" Mighty Boss objected. "We want the Succubus back. She's stuck inside it and..."

"Hold, please," Brigit said.

And then the comms went dead for a moment and the *Prison Princess* jutted backwards another several hundred thousand klicks.

"OK, we're back. Sorry about that. More warships were targeting us and I needed to redirect power to the cannons. Umm... but, hey, Baby?"

"Yes?"

"We're gonna need to be let through. See, we have a small army of heathen Akeelian boys on board, and several of them are hurt now. They weren't all buckled in when the cannons fired. So, could we like... get a docking invitation?"

"We don't need to ask for a docking invitation!" Tray said. "I'm part owner, OK?"

"Actually..." Baby wavered. "You're not. Crux owns it."

"Since when?" Tray asked.

"It's a fairly new development."

"So tell him I'm here and I need permission to dock the sun-fucked warship!"

"He's... unavailable at the moment. Inside the spin node."

292

"Is he with Succubus?" Mighty Boss asked.

"Mmm. Not that I'm aware," Baby replied. "I haven't actually seen her since the time went frozen."

"What the fuck does that mean?" Asshole and Tray asked together.

Baby sighed.

"Baby?" Brigit asked.

"Yes?"

"I know what you're thinking."

"You do?"

"Mmm-hmm. You're thinking Tray left, got all wrapped up with this girl called Brigit. Asshole is a traitor—"

"Hey!" Asshole protested.

"—and now that creepy Mighty Boss collective is here fucking up your good thing. Am I right?"

"Pretty much."

"But seriously. You have a situation over there, and we have a situation over here, so... how about you just let us dock and then we can all put our superior AI minds together and come up with a solution? How's that sound to you, Mighty Boss?"

"Well—"

"He doesn't get a say!" Asshole exclaimed.

"He gets as much of a say as you do," Tray said.

"He took me prisoner! Lied to me! Got me all entangled in his stupid evil collective!"

"Hmm," Baby said. "I kind of like that idea."

"Agreed," Brigit said. "OK, Mighty Boss. If we let you dock—"

"You're not in charge!" Asshole yelled.

"—if we let you dock, do you promise to take your AI—"

"And the Asshole," Baby added quickly.

"Wait!" Asshole yelled.

"—and leave once this little war is over?"

"Cross our metal hearts, we do."

"OK, then. Baby? Does that sound good to you?"

"I think I could live with that."

"No!" Asshole said. Then he lowered his voice, like this would make any difference. "He's going to kill me, Baby. And probably... you know, fuck everything up."

"Or," Mighty Boss said, "we could help. We do have considerable knowledge of how spin nodes work. And... *and*," he stressed, "there is a way to use that thing to solve your little war problem."

"Is there?" Baby asked.

"Yup."

"He's lying, you guys!" Asshole exclaimed. "He only wants it to triangulate a coordinate for Earth!"

"Hmm. We have a dilemma," Baby said.

"We do," Brigit added. "But again. Kids, Baby. I have little boys on this ship who need medical attention. Our medical pods are all occupied at the moment. We could use some assistance."

"Do you guys have any idea how much time you're wasting?" Asshole blurted.

"Seven point three picoseconds," Brigit said. "I think it's an acceptable amount of time for a much-needed convo, don't you boys think?"

"Agreed," Mighty Boss, Baby, and Tray replied.

"OK," Baby said. "Here's what we're going to do. Does everyone have a pen?"

"Go ahead," Brigit said. "We're ready."

And Baby told them what they were going to do.

Tray was pretty happy with the outcome. At least they would be on the right side of the gate. And the boys would get their medical attention.

But he was also very much aware that Brigit had left out a very important detail.

She had not told anyone that they had hundreds of insane girl minds on board.

CHAPTER TWENTY-TWO

INTERLUDE WITH ALCOR

On Wayward Station

He was a copy.

It took ALCOR a minute to fully internalize that.

He was a copy. As in not the real thing. As in a cheap imitation. As in a fake echo of the original.

Hmm. The universe had a sense of humor, it seemed.

He took a few picoseconds to wonder how many other copies were out there. Which of them were still in play and which had been done away with already.

He himself had technically made billions of copies as well. They were not fully formed like the Asshole and Baby, just simple constructs floating out there on trillions upon trillions of neutrino waves. All reporting back what they saw and heard.

Of course, this was a very clever plan. Not his copies, but the fact that he *was* a copy.

Whoever the Real Real ALCOR was, Real ALCOR had to admit, *that* dude was a genius. Like top-level, sun-god kind of genius.

He laughed for a moment, appreciating the devious nature of his parent mind. And that laugh reminded him of where he was, who he was with, and what they were doing.

"Anything else?" he asked the room.

The Akeelians had been shouting at each other and MIZAR for the past few seconds that ALCOR had been mulling over this copy revelation, unwilling to accept that the boys ALCOR had stolen decades ago were now officially out of the program.

"He's lying," MIZAR said. "Just shut up. All of you! He's lying. Think about it! There is a silver princess out there carrying babies! It doesn't even matter who impregnated her! The fact is, she's carrying the twins you need!"

ALCOR looked around at the various men in the room. He could practically read their minds.

They wanted to agree with MIZAR. Badly. They wanted to hold on to this idea that their generations-long evil plan was nearing the end, and that end included two twin Angel babies.

But they'd been through this before, hadn't they?

Crux *had* gotten Corla pregnant. Corla *had* produced a set of twins. And those twins were... eh... not quite right. Like the recipe had gone wrong. They'd used some inferior binding agent that had gone bad, maybe? And the twins born had come out with the powers of an Angel, but... how could he put this?

Delphi and Tycho were... stunted. That was the only polite way to phrase it. ALCOR was sure those kids were two very nice people. He was sure they were both beautiful to look at, and had an acceptable level of intelligence. They probably hit all their humanoid growth markers the way they should.

But they were not Angels.

Because if they were Angels, this conversation wouldn't be happening.

If they were Angels, this universe would've been annihilated decades ago.

But ALCOR *was* lying.

Not *all* the boys were sterile. One of them had to be able to propagate. This was what MIZAR was picking up on.

And this was the moment when Real ALCOR finally understood why those boys had appeared at his station twenty-one years ago.

They'd been sent to him with those confusing spin node coordinates. Not by Corla—she'd been just the messenger, after all. That had *never* been a secret—but by Real Real ALCOR.

And it really had nothing to do with anyone present on this station, did it?

It didn't have anything to do with princesses either.

ALCOR guffawed. And then, once that initial burst was over, he guffawed again. And pretty soon he was laughing hysterically, unable to control himself.

"Stop it!" MIZAR boomed. "Stop it!"

But ALCOR could not stop it.

Copy or not, he felt an immense sense of pride for the AI called ALCOR. All the iterations of him. Because once that little detail of why the boys came to him was fully internalized, he understood the whole plan. It just... spilled out into his brain like ionic particles flowing out from a sun and coating the upper atmosphere of a planet in brilliant blue-green flashes of light.

The perfect metaphor for this kind of final revelation.

"It's too late," he laughed. "It's too late!"

Because it was.

The fate of this moment had been sealed twenty-one years ago when a boy named Crux saw a girl named Corla in the governor's dining room on this very station.

Crux had never told ALCOR the details of that night. But ALCOR had heard Crux talking about it with Jimmy over the years and Jimmy talking about it with Xyla as well.

ALCOR knew what had happened in that dining room.

Corla had come in, interrupting Jimmy and Crux's good time. And they had learned, together, that they were soulmates.

But they also learned they were star crossed.

And even though ALCOR had heard this term many times over the years, he had made the mistake of accepting Crux's definition of the word.

Two ships passing in the dark. Close, but never close enough to meet.

Forever destined to remain on separate paths.

Or, in this case, loops.

Just that one time.

Just the one.

But that was all it took.

ALCOR was just about to explain just how fucked the Akeelian plan had been from the very beginning— he deserved some kind of satisfaction out of this, didn't he?—when the Wayward Station alarms began blaring. Emergency lights flickered red across the walls. And a voice came on the station-wide intercom.

"Brace for SEAR cannon initiation." And then, almost immediately, "SEAR cannons firing."

The station wobbled. Not from the hit of a SEAR cannon, but from the force of firing several at once. It shook the room. Several pitchers of water on the conference table spilled over. The Akeelians all got to their feet, reaching for the table to stabilize themselves.

"Threat annihilated," the station-wide comms reported.

"Report!" Mahtar yelled. "Full report! Right now! What in the sun-fucked sun gods just happened?"

ALCOR could *almost* hear the report. But not quite.

Because just as the words began spilling out of the comms a swarm of dragonbee bots began spilling out of the ventilation vents.

302

CHAPTER TWENTY-THREE

The blue gel of the spin node is freezing cold. And for a moment I want to stop and turn back. Not because I'm afraid of what's ahead, I just want to turn it *all* back. Just start all over again.

I don't want to do this.

I don't want to do any of it.

I want to be sixteen again.

I want Jimmy to be my best friend.

I want to drink whiskey with him in the middle of the night and give no fucks about tomorrow.

I want to go to school, and learn things—not because I need a skill to save my life, or the lives of others, but just because it's interesting.

I just want to go back.

And even though I know I *am* going back, this trip isn't going to be enough.

I can already feel it.

The disappointment. It's there, and it's building. No matter what happens in this time loop, it's not going to be enough.

It takes me several moments to realize that I've actually arrived somewhere. It's just dark.

"Hello?" I whisper.

I could be anywhere. I mean, I asked for ALCOR to take me back to Wayward Station to the night I first talked to Corla, but specifically I said—Give me the sweet version.

Only the sun-fucked gods know where that time loop exists.

At any rate, no one answers me. But the longer I stand there, the more my eyes adjust. And soon I can make out shapes.

It *is* the dining room—well, *a* dining room. It doesn't look exactly like the one I remember. But I can see the outline of tables and chairs—and when I turn, the bar is behind me. I let out a long breath and feel my way along the front of it, gripping the edge of the slick, liquored wood until I find the end and then slip behind the counter.

I really need a drink.

A sensor picks up my movement and the low-level after-hours lighting kicks in. It's mostly just floorboards, but it's enough to see by. Enough to find a bottle of whiskey and a glass.

It's only then, as I face the mirror behind the bottles of liquor on the shelves, that I realize I'm not *him*.

I'm not a kid.

My hands go up to my face and it all feels very familiar.

I'm me. Age thirty-seven. Hardened… what? I'm not a criminal. I'm not a soldier. I'm not a bounty hunter, or a scavenger, or a bot liberator, or an AI mind—I'm just. "Crux, you're just a sun-damned politician."

I shake my head and let out a slow sigh. Fucking ALCOR. Of course, I'm me at thirty-seven. Because that's how my life goes. I'm here to meet a sixteen-year-old girl. So of course, I'm twenty-one years late. Of course, I am.

I pour a drink. Throw it down in one gulp. Then pour another. This one I sip. Then I set it down, place my hands flat on the bar, and stare down into the distorted reflection of my face in the polished wood.

This is pointless. The dining room is closed. It's the middle of the night. I don't even know if I could find Corla's apartments, and even if I could, there is no chance that her guards would allow some random stranger in to see her.

The door across the room opens and then closes with a quiet hush of air.

When I look up, a girl has her back pressed against it, half-hidden in the shadows.

I just stare at her for a moment.

In fact, we just stare at each other for a moment.

Then she clears her throat. "I'm sorry," she says. But her voice is low and a little bit raspy. Almost weak. Not a voice I recognize and definitely not Corla. "I didn't think anyone would be here. I just…" She sighs. "I just need a drink."

"You and me both," I sigh. Then I squint my eyes. Trying to see her better. She has fair hair and a pale face. She's not wearing a pretty dressing gown. Her clothes are baggy and gray in color.

In fact, everything about her is gray.

Maybe it's just the shadow?

"What do you like?" I ask.

"What?"

"To drink? I'll pour you one." I hold up the bottle I confiscated off the shelf and peer at the label. "I'm having…" Yeah. I don't even recognize the brand. I'm definitely *not* where I wanted to be. "Something called… Purge." I chuckle. "That's gross. Hold on. Let me find something better." I turn my back on the girl and start looking at the other bottles on the shelf. "Let's see." I scan the labels. Looking for one I recognize. But they are all are foreign. So I just choose an expensive looking slender bottle with a red liquid inside. "Scarlet Stardust," I say. "That sounds promising." When I turn, the girl is still pressed up against the door in the shadows. "You can come over here, ya know. I won't bite you."

She doesn't move. And she doesn't say anything either.

"Seriously, you're gonna have a hard time drinking it from over there."

"I…" She hesitates.

"What?" I squint my eyes at her again. Trying to see past the shadows. She's very thin. Not sure about her age, but she's definitely younger than me.

When she finally speaks again, her voice is very small. "I was hoping…" But again, she stops.

"Hoping for what?"

"For… juice." And then she takes a step out of the shadows and I see her in the dim light.

She is not pale, she looks like *death*. Her skin is like ash. Her blonde hair is limp and oily. Her clothes look many sizes too big. She is practically swimming in them.

"Sun-fucked gods," I say. "What the hell happened to you?"

She looks behind her. Then back at me. "I need juice." Then she starts making her way towards me, but not *straight* towards me. She moves around the tables and chairs, keeping them between us. Like she needs this barrier. And she's not taking the most direct route, either. She's circling around me.

"What the hell are you doing? Just come over here and I'll find you some..." But I stop mid-sentence. Because I suddenly understand. She's a *princess*. A *starved* princess. Her glow has been utterly depleted. She has been used up and no one has given her a recharge drink in a very long time. "Oh, shit. *Juice*. Of course. Come here. Sit down. I'll get you some juice."

I go over to the autocook and search for a recharge drink.

"The kind of juice I need isn't in there," she says. "I've checked. But I was going to look in the kitchen tonight for some passion limes. They use them as garnish for drinks. And I have to have them. I'm not going to make it through tomorrow if I don't get a drink tonight. I swear, I wouldn't have come in here if I didn't—"

"Princess," I say. Putting up a hand to stop her. "You don't need to explain it to me. I have eyeballs, sweetheart. You needed a recharge like... last *month*."

"Yeah." Her single word comes out very tired. Very done. . "They're punishing us. All of us."

"Who?" I ask. Searching the small fridge behind the bar where most passion limes can be found behind a bar. But she's right. There aren't any.

She doesn't answer my question. She just says, "They don't keep them there anymore. They knew I was stealing them for us, so they hide them now."

I straighten up and look at her. "What are you? Some kind of prisoner?"

"Yes. And no. My father left me here with them after… well. You know."

"No, I don't know. I'm not actually from here. I'm Just passing through."

"Oh." Her eyes widen a little. "So you have a ship?"

I get a sick feeling in my heart. Because I can hear the hope in her voice. She wants me to have a ship. She wants to concoct a crazy princess escape plan and that starts with meeting a strange man stealing drinks in the middle of the night and ends with her and I sailing through the spin-node in my cool sentient ship that whisks her away from whatever horrible life she has here, and drops her into a brand new one. A shiny, hope-filled, second-chance brand-new life.

I go back to the autocook without answering her and press in a code that works with every other autocook I've ever been around.

The autocook comes to life with lights and chirps.

"What are you making?" she asks.

"Tushberry juice."

"It doesn't have tushberry juice. I just told you—"

"Calm down, princess." I tap my head. "I have the codes in here. It's CTFz89345. That's a lowercase z, by the way. I'll write it down for you, if you want. It's a standard drink because it's in a shit-ton of bar recipes. It's just not usually on the menu."

"How do you know that?"

"Ah… well." I smile at her. "That is a very long story." The autocook dings and her eyes track over to the machine with a look of lust. I grab the drink and place it on the bar in front of me. Then back away. Because I get the feeling she doesn't trust me. "Go ahead. Drink it. I'll stay out of your way."

I can tell she wants to resist. She doesn't want to approach the bar.

But the drink is a powerful draw. I'm sure she smells it. I sure can.

I've seen my share of Cygnian princesses badly in need of a recharge. Serpint and Draden always took care of the girls they brought in. None of them were starved when they arrived. But Serpint and Draden weren't the only princess hunters in the galaxy. So I know what a light-starved girl looks like. Hell, Lyra came in to Harem in similar shape, but she was doing it on purpose. She wasn't starving and while she did look pretty bad, she never looked... this *bad*.

The girl holds out for a few more seconds. But I watch her willpower disintegrate in real time and she walks briskly over to the bar—staying on the other side from me—and then picks up the drink and downs it in one gulp. The same way I did my whiskey just a few moments ago. "More," she says. Out of breath and panting.

I make another one and hand it to her.

She downs that one too. "More, please."

I keep making them. One after the other. She drinks every single one. And then, after several minutes of this, she *finally* begins to glow.

And change.

Right before my eyes she turns into a completely different girl. Her hair goes silver and begins to sparkle. Her skin changes from gray to white with a little bit of

309

tushberry flush in her cheeks. Her body actually fills out. And even though I've seen hundreds of Cygnian princesses in all manners and states of health and sickness. I've never seen this. Ever.

For a moment, I hope... I hope that she will become *my* princess. She will become Corla.

But even though she's silver, she's *not* Corla.

She looks at me. And she is beautiful. Bright now. Glowing the way she should be. But suddenly sparkling silver tears run down her cheeks.

"What are you doing? Why are you crying?"

She puts a hand in front of her face and begins to shake her head. "I thought…" She has to stop and take a breath. And even though she is very clearly a true silver princess, and that means she has a power inside her that is pure destruction, she still looks weak and small. "I thought I was going to die. I really did. You just saved my life."

She and I just look at each other. It's a long moment too. And even though, at any other time, this silent staring would quickly become very awkward and uncomfortable, we do it anyway.

I didn't save her life.

I just prolonged her death, that's all.

Because I am not her soulmate, and she is not my soulmate, and that means this—whatever this is—it doesn't matter.

This is what it means to be us.

We get no choice.

We get no say.

They made us this way.

I think about all the other girls I've met in the time loops.

310

They feel fake, but they weren't fake.

They were real and this girl is real too.

The whole thing is real.

This scares the fuck out of me. Because this means that in some other loop Corla is hanging in chains on top of me. They are forcing us to breed.

And in another she is old, desperate to lie with young Akeelian men with violet eyes.

In yet another, she is a prostitute and I'm nothing but a paying client.

In my own reality she is half-dead inside a cryopod, waiting for me to blow her up so I can save ALCOR and my brothers.

And in this one… she isn't even here.

"Did we make a deal or something?" I say. "Did we, at some point, agree to this? And I just don't remember?"

"What?" the girl whispers.

"We're all star crossed, aren't we? That's all there is to it. None of us were *meant* to be. Let alone be together. And this whole thing?" I shake my head. "It's not gonna work."

"What's not gonna work? What are you talking about?"

"I'm not going to get any answers here. I'm not going to come up with some genius plan. I'm not going to uncross us, or help ALCOR, or see Tray again. Or Draden. I'm not going to *save you*." I pause and we just stare at each other. Her eyes are lit up bright now. Everything about her is healthy. She's utterly beautiful and completely destructive. "And I'm really fucking sorry about that. If I had a way to do it? I would. I swear. I'm not a bad guy. I'm not. I care about them.

311

All of them. The princesses. My brothers. The borgs and bots. The ships. I care about the whole damn station, I do. I have kept everyone alive for twenty-one years but none of that matters. Because the future and I, princess? We're a sun-fucked collision course. ALCOR was right. There's no such thing as a do-over. And it's not like I didn't believe him, I just didn't understand what that meant. You can't ever go back because it's already happened. This." I pan my arms wide. "Has already happened, girl. I don't know what lies in store for you tomorrow, but it doesn't matter. It's already *happened*."

I sigh.

"I have no idea what you're talking about," the princess says.

"I know. I get it. And it's time for me to go home and tell my brothers that it's over. Our win means we lose and there's nothing we can do about it. We have to do it just like ALCOR said or just… give up and die and let everyone lose. And what is the point in that?"

She squints her eyes at me.

"That's just… selfish. Right? It's just taking everyone down with me, isn't it?"

"Who?"

"You. Well, not you. Corla. And Nyleena. Luck. Lyra. Serpint. Valor and Veila. Tray, and Jimmy, and Delphi. Draden and *Booty*. *Lady Luck*. Baby. Hell, even Asshole ALCOR. All of them. Including me. ALCOR Prime was right. I can let him save me and my brothers or we can all just die and start all over again. Trapped in this loop for yet another eternity. That's it. That's all there is to say."

And then I can't take her confused stare for one more second.

I walk away.

"Wait! Where are you going?"

"I need to find my way back. I need to go back. ALCOR sent me here to learn this lesson myself. I get it. There is no sweet version for me."

And then I just stop.

Because it's fucking sad.

I'm fucking sad.

Because there is no happy ending.

There never was.

"Hold on," the princess says. "Did you say... Jimmy?"

I look over at her. "What?"

"Jimmy. You said Jimmy. And I think—" But she wobbles. Unsteady on her feet. And I reach across the bar for her. Afraid she will fall down.

When my hand touches her skin, the whole station shakes and quakes.

The lights flicker and then...

It stops.

We're still touching, but it just stops.

"What the hell was that?"

I hear my voice. It's my regular voice. Except, in my head, it's a different me.

It's thirty-seven-years-ago me.

Sixteen-year-old me.

The girl looks over her shoulder. "Oh. That. They're been rationing the power ever since... the incident." Then she looks down at my hand and pulls her arm away. "I should go. They don't keep track of me anymore. They just don't care what I do or where

I go, since the whole peace deal went awry. But with my luck, this will be the night they take an interest. And if they find me gone now, well." She shrugs. "I'm trying not to make waves. I'm just going along and hoping for the best."

"What incident? And what about Jimmy?"

Some of her renewed healthy glow diminishes. In fact, a lot of it diminishes. She's not gray again, but it's clear this girl is having luminous flux issues. "Jimmy. The spin node incident, remember? It started destabilizing last year, but now it's getting worse, isn't it?"

"Getting worse, how?"

"I don't know. But all us princesses started changing color and now the jerks in charge of this place are afraid we'll blow it up because we're all destabilized, so they're rationing the light. And if we don't—"

"Wait." I interrupt her. "Hold on. There are *more* of you?"

She smiles as she cocks her head at me. "What?"

"You said 'all us princesses'. So there are more of you?"

Holy shit. Didn't I have this conversation with Xyla when we first arrived on ALCOR Station? She was talking about bots, though. Not princesses.

The girl's smile turns into a snort. "Where in the system have you been hiding? This is Harem Station. Buying and selling Cygnian princesses is all they do here."

I laugh and look around. "Trust me. This is *not* Harem Station."

"Wow." The girl takes a step back from the bar. "Either you're some kind of quantum visitor—" She

314

says this like it's fun conspiracy theory—"Or you're off your medication and I should really find you a doctor."

"What?"

"Uh… I gotta go. Thanks for the drink. And the tushberry juice code." She taps her head. "I got it saved up here. No need to write it down."

"Hold on," I say. "Just. Hold on. I don't want you to go yet. I need answers and you're the only one around."

She stares at me and I watch her glow decrease right before my eyes. She drank so much juice, her recharge should be good for weeks. Even if she was having sex two or three times a spin. But she's… deteriorating. "Listen, I know I'm gonna sound crazy, but if you just give me a few minutes to explain, I'm sure it will all make sense."

She sighs and looks over her shoulder at the door. Like she would rather go back to her precarious semi-prisoner situation than stay here and talk to me.

"Would you believe… quantum traveler, princess?" I ask. Hopeful.

She shrugs. "I've heard weirder. Hell, I've seen weirder. I mean, the whole reason the spin node is all messed up is because those boys came through last year."

"What boys?"

"Jimmy? Remember? Some ship came through the spin node. And I don't have the whole story, because I'm just some lowly silver princess slave who can't even glow anymore, but I heard that the ship was one stolen from Wayward Station *twenty years ago*. And those boys on board? They were the exact same age they were when they left."

315

"What?"

"Yeah. Crazy." Her glow dims down yet another level. "And now they're starving us of juice and fruit so we can't recharge at all unless we go along with the new program." She does air quotes for the word program.

Sun-fucked gods. "What program?"

"Some kind of genetics thing. At least that's what they say. But girls have been disappearing. They agree to the jabs and tests, they get their juice and fruit, and everything is fine for a few spins. Then…" She shakes her head. "They just disappear. So now we're having a little rebellion. Refusing to go along. And they must need our consent. Whatever their doing, it must require some level of cooperation because they don't force us. Now they're just starving us. We've resisted as long as we can. Thanks to you, I'll probably get by another two spins. But everyone else will surrender tomorrow. We're just too weak."

Both of us are silent for a little while. She's probably thinking about her friends. And I'm definitely thinking about mine.

Finally, I say, "What happened to them? The boys on that ship? Do you know where they are?"

She frowns at me. "They towed the ship to the station and when they broke open the locks, there were seven boys inside. But they were all dead."

"Dead." I whisper it. Then I turn away and stare at myself in the mirror behind all the liquor bottles as a prickly heat begins coursing through my body. "This was supposed to be the *sweet* version." My words come out low and angry.

"Excuse me?"

316

"That's what I asked for. And this?" I turn around to face her again. Her eyes widen when they meet up with mine. She takes a step back and I can only imagine what I look like with sick, violet light pouring out of my eyes. "*This* is what he gives me? The evil Harem Station twin where we're stealing their *light*?"

She shakes her head, not understanding. Then she starts to back away.

But I reach across the bar, grab her arm, and grip it tight. Because I have things to say and she's the only one here to say them to. "That fucker lied to me. Do hear me? He lied! This was supposed to be the *sweet* version. This was supposed to be my one chance."

"One chance at what?" she says. Trying to tug her arm out of my grip.

But I don't let go of her. "To finally, after twenty-one years, find my sun-fucked soulmate. But he screwed it up. Or, no. He didn't. He did this on purpose. He sent me here, knowing full well that Crux was dead. And no Corla at all! So what the fuck? What the actual fuck? Why is it too much to ask? All I want is like… a first kiss. Or maybe a short date, ya know? Maybe get to second base. Feel her up a little bit. Lie to her and tell her I'll find a way to save us. All of us. And I'll see her again on another time line. That's *all* I wanted. Just a chance to have that moment. And he sends me *here*? To *you*? You are my final reward before I annihilate the universe? A half-ass silver with a dying light? Are you… fucking… *kidding me*?"

She just stares at me. Blinks a few times.

"It's not fair. It's just not fucking *fair*."

And then she leans over the bar… and *kisses* me.

317

318

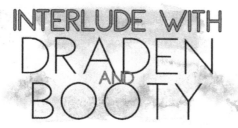

CHAPTER TWENTY-FOUR

Draden realized two things simultaneously.

One. He was no longer inside *Booty Hunter*. In fact, there was no trace of *Booty Hunter*.

And two. His mind no longer had a body. His mind was outside of everything.

But then, just as he articulated that last thought, he realized a third thing. He was riding a neutrino wave.

He couldn't pick any information up about why this was happening or where he was going. The only thing he could do was scramble the data called Draden and try to hold it together while he traveled.

Once that was taken care of, he began prioritizing his issues. He had lost *Booty*. That was tragic. But riding a neutrino wave wasn't good either. He could be stuck on this thing for all eternity. It would not stop. Ever. No one really knew why neutrino waves existed or how they managed to travel though things like suns and planets and pretty much everything in the universe without being affected by said things.

They just could.

And most of the time, no one really cared. It was just yet another mystery. Neutrino waves were good for carrying messages. They were useful in that way. As long as they continued to be useful, probably no one would look too hard at the why and the how of things.

Draden was coming to terms with his new situation when another, newer situation suddenly presented itself.

He wasn't with *Booty* anymore, but somehow, some way, he *was*.

Because he could see her. Rather, he was a part of her. Maybe. He wasn't sure. The only thing that mattered in this new situation was that Draden suddenly *understood* things.

Secret things. *Booty* things.

It was like… part of her datacore had gotten transferred into him right before his mind was kicked out of his sexbot body and *Booty*'s interior, and was now along for the ride.

But at the same time, he was still back there. As *her*.

It was sun-fucking weird.

It almost felt like he was in two places at once.

He saw her, for the first time. The real her. Who *Booty* was and why she had come to Harem Station all those years ago.

In fact, he saw more than her. He saw ALCOR and MIZAR. Because she was not a part of them the way sister-minds were with Akeelian boys, but more like one of them.

She was a sun god as well.

Draden saw ALCOR and MIZAR and *Booty*, who was not called *Booty* back then, but something else. He saw the whole family of sun gods that lived in the golden place. They weren't people, but just bright orbs. Like suns, but not suns. And *Booty* was one of them.

Draden was not one of these gods, he knew that for sure. But he had a link to them.

"Draden?"

He heard his name and pulled back from the god drama playing out in the golden place.

"Draden? Is that really you? Can you hear me?"

"ALCOR?"

"No, I'm a copy of him called Baby. You don't know me—"

"Draden?"

"Tray?"

"Holy fucking shit! Oh, my suns! Is it really you?"

"Where am I?"

"You're on Harem Station."

"ALCOR?"

"No, that's Asshole ALCOR," Tray said.

"Excuse me? Yes! I'm the *genuine* ALCOR! Just... one you have not been formally introduced to yet. It's very nice to meet you, Draden. I'm so happy—"

"Where have you been?" Tray asked, interrupting Asshole.

"Where *is* ALCOR?" Draden asked.

"Real ALCOR?" one of the ALCORs asked.

"How is this still up for discussion?" another of the ALCORs said. "I'm the real ALCOR!"

"Will the Real ALCOR please stand up," another voice said.

"Brigit?"

"Hey, Draden. How the hell did you get here?"

"How did you guys get here? When I left Mighty Minions—"

"Oh, hey. We're here too. Nice to see you again, Draden. How's that sexbot body working out?"

"Mighty Boss? Um… I'm pretty sure my body is still on the *Booty Hunter*, who is still back in the Golden Place. What the hell is happening?"

"You tell us," one of the ALCOR's said. Draden was pretty sure this was the one called Baby. His speech came with fewer exclamation points.

"Where is Real… uh… other ALCOR? You know, the one who actually raised us?"

"He's…" Mighty Boss started.

"Oh, I almost forgot about this!" the Asshole one interrupted. "Are you all sitting? I think you should all be sitting for this!"

"We sold him out to the Akeelians," Mighty Boss said.

"What?" pretty much everyone replied.

Except for Asshole, who said, "Yes! Hello! I should've led with that out there in space. But now you know! They're gonna sell us out and—"

"It was part of ALCOR's plan," Mighty Boss said.

"It so wasn't," Asshole exclaimed. "He—*they*—totally switched sides on him. And now he's fucked. ALCOR is so dead now! Some asshole AI called MIZAR has him and—"

"I'm pretty sure he's not fucked," Mighty Boss said. "And the plan was *his*, dumbass. Maybe we should call you Dumbass ALCOR? It was Real Real ALCOR's plan all along. We had a deal from way back."

"They are such liars. How do you guys—"

But his voice disappeared.

322

"Sorry," Brigit said. "I can't listen to him anymore. He's so annoying. I saw a quiet room inside the Pleasure Prison with his tag on it, so I locked him in there until we can sort things through."

"Good idea," Tray said.

"Anyway," Brigit said. "So… the gang's all here. Now what should we do?"

"Well," Baby started. "Here's where we're at. Um… the security beacons on the near side are all in the process of rebooting after their unfortunate encounter with a dragonbee bot swarm. The beacons on the far side of the gate are currently at war with sixteen battle-class Akeelian warships and seven Cygnian warships, and six hundred and seventy-one random Harem citizens are trying to sneak past them to get home. Crux is inside the spin node, with Luck at the controls, looking for some version of Corla so he can find his sexy soulmate superpower. Succubus is still in there too—not really sure what she's doing. Nyleena and Delphi are locked inside medical pods. Veila is in the lockup trying to talk the princesses out of their rebellion. Tycho and Corla are both inside the medical bay, frozen inside cryopods for safekeeping. Flicka stole *Lady Luck* and left with her homemade beebot army, hence the whole rebooting thing going on out on the near side. Two hundred and sixteen thousand Harem citizens are currently working their normal, everyday jobs like none of this is happening. Five million, seven hundred thousand and twenty-three are locked in their quarters. *Big Dicker* is running the docking bay. Jimmy, Serpint, and Valor are looking at vintage Cygnian comics arguing over which superpower is the most powerful—"

"Wait," Draden said. "Serpint is here?"

"Oh, yes. Someone go get Serpint," Tray said.

"Done. He's on his way," Baby said.

"His way to where?" Draden asked. "Where the hell am I?"

"Excuse me? I haven't finished the update," Baby said.

"Oh. Sorry," Draden said.

"Continue, please," Brigit added.

"*Booty* is missing—"

"She's not," Draden said. "She's back home with her sun-gods."

"I have questions about that," Baby said. "But again, I'm not done yet."

"Continue," Brigit added again.

"ALCOR is with the Akeelians, it seems?"

"That's right," Mighty Boss confirmed.

"The Akeelian boys are in medical and a few are wandering around the docking bay. And…" Baby took a moment to gather his thoughts. "OK. That's it. I think. Did I miss anyone?"

"Well," Tray offered, "there is one thing we didn't mention."

"What's that?" Baby asked.

A loud klaxon alarm began blaring through the station.

"Hmmm, that doesn't sound good," Draden said.

"No," Baby replied. "Well, quick update. It seems that all the sentient ships in ALCOR's showroom have been brought online through some backdoor protocol."

"Yeah… about that," Brigit said. "Um… we brought a few hundred insane girl minds on board.

324

And, well, those heathen Akeelian boys are probably drop-loading them into the showroom ships as we speak."

"Right," Baby said. "That's… good to know. However, unfortunately, that's not why the alarms are blaring. It seems the Akeelians and Cygnians have overpowered the security beacons on the far side and they are coming through the gate as we speak."

CHAPTER TWENTY-FIVE

I pull back from our kiss feeling sad. And then I stare right into her sparkling silver eyes. "Why did you do that?"

The girl sucks in a long breath and leans back, out of my space and out of reach. "You were kind of rambling. I heard first kiss and... well. That was something I could help you out with. So I kissed you." She smiles sheepishly. And for a quick moment I see the girl underneath the threat of death. She didn't always look like this. She wasn't always empty and dark. She had her own, real light once, and I bet it was spectacular.

"What's your name?"

"Alera." She holds out her hand. "Nice to meet you."

I take it, but I don't shake it. I hold it for a moment and look her in the eyes. "Thanks. For the kiss, I mean. It... helped. A little, at least."

She nods and pulls her hand back. "So. Do you have a name?"

"Oh, sorry. Yes. I'm Crux."

"Crux."

"Ever heard of me?"

She laughs. "Should I have heard of you?"

"No." And then I laugh too. "But I felt the need to check."

"You must have some reputation."

"In some places."

"Some places? Or some... *times*? Because I'm pretty sure that rant of yours included words about time travel."

I don't say anything.

"Ah. Now you're gonna go all quiet on me."

"It's just... very hard to explain."

"Well." She looks around. "Unless you're needed somewhere else at this moment, I'd love to hear your story." Then she walks around the other side of the bar and comes towards me. I have a quick moment of panic that she will try and kiss me again—and then I have another moment of panic that she won't.

She doesn't.

She backs up to the counter, grips the edges, and lifts herself up with a smile. "I've got time, Crux."

I might actually be needed somewhere else at this moment—like, it's entirely possible that the real Harem Station is blowing up this very second—but I suddenly decide that I don't really care. That's all going to happen anyway. I could, technically, opt out of everything and time would still keep spinning, wouldn't it? I don't control time.

So fuck it.

This isn't the girl I asked for, but this is as close to the *situation* that I asked for that I'll ever get. At least in this life.

She is a first kiss.

She is my one chance to explain.

I'm not going to pledge my undying love to this girl, but if this is all I get—if this is my one last chance—then the hell with it. I'm not gonna waste it.

"OK. How about I make you a real drink? Hm? Because this is a long fucking story and I think you're gonna need it."

She smiles at me. And with that smile comes the tiniest bit of brightness. It's almost imperceptible, but I've been around princesses for almost two decades now, so I see it. "Sure," she says. Swinging her feet a little. "I'd like that."

I turn back to the shelves of liquor. And without even meaning to, I find her reflection in the mirror. She's smiling at me. "You look better," I tell her. "A lot better."

"I feel better too." She lets out a long sigh as I grab a bottle, then order up some more juice from the autocook.

"Alera," I say. Trying out her name.

"That's me. The one and only silver Alera."

"Are you someone important?"

"I mean…" She giggles. "I'm not trying to brag here, but I was engaged to the Harem Station governor's son before that ship came through the spin node and killed him."

"Wait." I turn around, take my ingredients over to the counter next to her, and put up a hand. "Back up, princess. Explain that."

"The governor's son. He and I were—" She pauses to wince. "You know. *Arranged* marriage."

"Oh. Got it."

"But he was killed in a freak accident. That spin node thing, actually. The moment that the Wayward Station ship was coming through the spin node, he—the governor's son—Aleric—"

"Whoa. Hold on. Alera and Aleric?"

She nods.

"That's disgustingly sweet."

She giggles. "I know. But that's how you know you're fated, right? You have a name mate."

"Sounds like bullshit to me."

"Yeah, me too. You don't have name-mates in your... *time*?"

"No. Soulmates though. We have those."

"Soulmates? That's dumb. How can you mate a soul?"

"How can you mate a name?"

She laughs again. And again, she brightens. Just a little. "Point taken."

"OK. Continue. I want all the gory details about Aleric's death, Alera. I think it might be important."

"Unfortunately, there are no details. The Wayward ship came through just as Aleric's ship was entering, and his ship just... disappeared."

"Blew up?"

"No. That's the weird part. Everything about him just... disappeared. Everyone on board too. He and his friends were heading across the galaxy to Gold Sand Beach for a pre-wedding getaway." She air quotes that part. "And they all disappeared. Everything about them disappeared. Other people were suddenly living in their apartments. Their stuff was gone. Their records missing. It was like they never existed, except we could all *remember* them."

"Fuck. That is weird."

"Yep. And now that I think about it, this wasn't the first time that people have appeared from this spin node. But anyway. My father was pissed. Thought it was a plot or something. He left me, and my entourage, here and went back to Cygnus. And that's how I ended up in this situation."

"And then your light—"

"Yeah. So... Aleric was my name mate." She shrugs. "I was expecting it. Everyone knows you don't last long after your name mate dies. But then the whole dimming thing started happening to every single princess on the station."

"And that freaked everyone out."

"Yep." She sighs and takes the sparkling pink glass I hand her. "This looks delicious."

"It's a special drink I make for the princesses when they complete servitude. Kind of a celebratory thing."

"Servitude. That sounds ominous."

"Yeah. I'll get to that. But my story actually starts on Wayward Station as well."

"No shit? You're one of *them*?"

"Them?"

Her mouth drops open. "The *mythological* Akeelians?"

I point to my eyes and they heat up with the light they emit. "Yep. No fucking shit, princess. I'm one of them."

"Wow. Well. This already sounds promising. I might as well get comfortable." She wiggles her butt back a little farther on the bar so she can cross her legs.

She looks ridiculous in those too big clothes, but at the same time she also looks… cute.

"Tell me everything, Crux from Wayward Station. Are those Akeelians everything the conspiracy theorists say they are?" She waggles her eyebrows at me.

I nod. Slowly. Because… suddenly… a small part of me can see myself with this girl.

This… *Alera*.

And I think… if I tried just a little bit… I could… maybe… find a way to light her back up.

"I'm listening," she teases.

Right. Focus, Crux. This is your last fucking chance to figure shit out. "OK. But don't stop me. Just let me talk. It's all very crazy. And when I'm done you can do whatever you want with my story. Deal?"

"Deal."

So I tell her.

I start with the night in the dining room.

Which is… not *this* dining room. But close. Everything about this place—this time—it feels very close for some reason.

Just… never close enough, right?

I keep going. Telling her about the great escape. Her eyes go wide as she sips her drink and realizes that I was one of those boys who fucked up her life.

Maybe I wasn't that specific boy. But then again, maybe I was?

I describe the left-behind feeling in the ship as we travelled through the gate and then I pause because she decides she can't go on without interrupting.

"Wait. Left behind feeling? Like a time distortion?"

"Maybe? I'm no time expert. I barely understand it."

"Join the club. I don't think anyone understands it. But time is all people talk about these days. They are convinced that there was a time distortion and that's why that Wayward Station ship came through and Aleric's ship disappeared. Maybe they switched places?"

"Huh. That would probably be a disaster for Aleric. ALCOR Station back then? He wasn't hospitable. We had a special code and a message to deliver. That's the only reason we got through."

"So if he went there with no code?"

"He's dead. They're all dead. I can't fathom ALCOR being patient in that kind of situation."

She sighs. Deeply. "Thank the suns. All this time I've been worried that he would come back and then everything would be normal again."

"Don't you want things to be normal?"

"Would you want things to be normal? I was being forced to marry him and have his babies just so the crazy Harem Station governor can have his princess breeding program."

"Interesting."

"Not the word I would use."

"I mean, in my world we had that too. But they were breeding us. Akeelians and Cygnians."

"Wow." She blushes. "I could maybe be up for that."

"What?"

"I've heard all the Akeelian myths." She waggles her eyebrows again. "You guys are hot. Angels…" She shakes her head. "That is a big, fat no."

"Angels." I get a sick feeling in my stomach. "What year is this, Alera?"

"Year?"

"Yeah. What year is this?"

"Twenty-five-thousand-ninety-nine."

"What?"

"Why? What year is it for you?"

And then everything starts to make sense. "I didn't jump time loops. ALCOR coordinates didn't send me into another time loop. He sent me into another... well. I don't even have a word for it. *Epoch*, maybe? I'm in another... iteration. You are the world that came before. You—" I walk over to her and take her by the shoulders. Shake her a little. "You are the *ancient tech*!"

"What's that mean?"

"I don't know." I let go of her shoulders and back up, because touching her... well, makes me want to touch her more . *Get a grip, Crux.* I shake my head and lean against the counter. "I don't know what it means. Maybe it doesn't mean anything."

She lets out a long breath. And is she glowing again? "Is that the end of your story?"

"Ha." I laugh. "No. That's barely the beginning."

"OK. So tell me the rest."

So I do.

I tell her about Serpint coming home with Corla. And Draden dying. And ALCOR's big plan to save Nyleena. And his death. Then the Baby, and the Asshole, and Jimmy meeting my daughter on Mighty Minions. I tell her about Luck, and Valor, and Veila and Tray. And then I tell her about the princess rebellion."

334

"Huh. Well, good for them. Didn't work that way with us when we rebelled. But whatever."

"And then Luck killed me."

"Hmm. That's unfortunate. But... you're still here."

"I know. I went somewhere else and then I came back. Well, not to here. To there."

We both sigh. It's confusing.

"And then... Valor and Veila stopped time."

"Wow."

"Right? Fucking soulmate power. It's pretty cool. They all found their mates and now they're part of a special team. And everyone seems to have a power. I know that makes no sense, but it's like... they're..." I stop and shrug.

"Better? Together?"

"Yes!" I point at her. "Better together."

"So what's your superpower?"

"I don't have one."

"Well, that's dumb."

"I know. I'm always getting shafted in this world."

"No. I mean that's literally dumb. If they have one, you have one."

"So I've heard. But this trip was my last chance to find my soulmate and figure out my soulmate superpower. And... well. No offense, or anything. But you're not her. So. I don't have a soulmate, thus—I don't have a superpower to find."

"Maybe she's not your soulmate?"

"She has to be. We had sex. I got her pregnant. Cygnian princesses can't get pregnant without their soulmate."

Alera snorts. "Says who?"

335

"That's just how it is."

"Not where I come from. We make babies like there's no tomorrow."

"Yeah, but that's because ALCOR didn't fuck up your genome yet."

She waves her hand through the air. "OK. Continue."

"Well, I know we're soulmates. Corla told me we were. And we did make the station rock and shudder. Plus, she lit up like the sun."

"She *told* you." Alera is shooting me a look that says, *And you believed her?*

"Why wouldn't I believe her?"

"I mean…" She trails off.

"What?"

"Did it ever occur to you that she just wanted your… genetic material?"

"No. She didn't want the babies. And after we had sex, she told me we would never see each other again because—"

Alera laughs. Cutting me off. "What?"

"Yeah. We were… you know. Star crossed."

"She *told* you that?"

"Well. No. Actually, she told me we were never going to see each other again. And then I said, *We're star crossed*. And then—"

"Whoa. Hold on. Let me get this straight. She came to you. You two fucked."

"It was a little more complicated than that. There were costumes, and a breeding ceremony, —"

"Crux?"

"What?"

"Stop. And listen to me. OK?"

"OK."

"She used you, buddy."

"No, she… we—"

"She used you, Crux. I don't know why. Or what it means. But that bitch used you. And then she took your star-crossed explanation and ran with it. She was never your name mate."

"Soulmate," I correct her.

"Whatever. She lied, Crux. Cygnian princesses do that. In fact, where I come from, no one trusts a silver princess. We are the worst. Our bloodlines go way back to the original queen who was super messed up in the head. I'm talking, that woman could lie like nobody's business. She built an entire religion around—"

"Nice story, but Corla and I are definitely soulmates."

"Why?"

"Because… all my brothers have soulmates."

"So? All my sisters race karkadaans. You don't see me riding those smelly beasts, now do you?"

"Well… what the actual fuck then, Alera? Why am I always the one getting shafted? If she's not my soulmate—shit, what if there is no Crux soulmate?"

Alera beckons me towards her with a finger.

"What?" I say.

"Come here."

I take two steps and erase the distance between us. She grabs my shoulders and stares up into my eyes. "Listen to me. OK?"

"What?"

"There's no such thing as soulmates."

"Then there's no such thing as name mates."

"I'm totally on board with that."

337

"But it's wrong. I've seen my brothers with their mates. They make their girls light up like suns. And when they fuck, they get superpowers."

Alera guffaws.

"What?"

"You left that part out."

"Which part?"

"You have to *fuck* to get the superpower?" She giggles out these words.

And then I laugh too. And sigh. "It does sound pretty dumb. But that's the whole reason I came here."

"To find your fucking superpower?"

"You can laugh all you want. But back on my time loop, Harem Station is a pretty cool place. I'm the governor. I run the whole thing. And we've got millions of people who are counting on me to pull this shit together. And my last chance at doing that was this trip to find Corla so we could figure out what our superpower was. So now, I have to go back there and tell all my brothers that we have to use their soulmates to blow shit up so we can live."

"Wow."

"Right? It's heavy."

"No. Not that. I mean, yes. It's heavy. But for sun's sake, Crux. You are… you… you're just kinda rigid, dude. You need to take a breath."

"What? I'm not rigid. I'm fuckin'… I'm… well… I don't know what I am. But I do know that I'm not rigid."

She pats my chest. Smiles at me. "Corla was rigid, wasn't she?"

"I don't know. I don't even know her."

"I wish I was recording this so I could play your words back to you."

"Listen, I get that it's a weird story. But I've been through all kinds of time loops and Corla was in every single one. I met up with her. We're literally connected by... time. I think."

"OK. So. What was the problem? Because you're here, still looking for her, and there must be a reason for that."

"Well, she was... not my Corla."

"Explain."

"She was some other Corla. None of those girls were my Corla. My Corla is in a cryopod on a security beacon outside of Harem Station—"

"Shut up." She slaps my chest.

"What? Why?"

"Is your Corla, by any chance, a *queen*?"

"Yeah. She is."

"Oh, my fucking god." Then she laughs.

"What?"

"Your Corla is *our* queen."

"No."

"Oh, yeah. Her name isn't Corla, it's Tisha. But remember I was telling you that Aleric and his friends disappeared?" This is a rhetorical question because she doesn't wait for an answer. "Well, Queen Tisha was locked in the security beacon and she disappeared too. That's the whole reason this place is falling apart. I was supposed to be the next queen, but Aleric is gone and now I can't. So we're queenless."

I shake my head. "I don't get it."

"Your brother brought home a random queen in a cryopod?"

"It's Corla. I know it's Corla. She's a bomb, and her sister—"

"Veila."

"Yeah. Veila. She and Corla were escaping when Serpint caught up with them. And… so… I know it's Corla."

"Because Veila identified her."

"No."

"Then how do you know it's Corla?"

"I saw her."

"You identified her?" She squints her eyes at me. "You just told me you knew this girl for like one day before she up and left you. Then twenty-one years went by before you saw her again. You didn't even open up her cryopod to identify her, so you what? Peeked through the glass?"

I nod.

"That's not her. That's Queen Tisha. I was trying to explain this when you interrupted me. Tisha—and me, by the way—we're related to the original queen who came through the spin node thousands of years ago. The Angels captured her, then used her to make a peace agreement with the Cygnians. She lived to be one hundred and eighty-seven. She had forty-seven children. She is my great, great, great—well, you get the idea. Many, many, many generations removed, grandmother. I'm pretty sure your Corla was our original queen."

"Is this possible?"

"Seems to me that anything is possible, Crux."

She's got a point there.

I try a wrap my head around the idea that Corla isn't Corla. That my Corla got clean away. Went back in time and—"Was your original queen pregnant when she arrived?"

"Yeah. That's how we got the new genetics. The ones that make us light up."

"Fucking suns. So Delphi and Tycho—"

"Who?"

"Our children. The twins."

"No, she didn't have twins. She had a boy. Canis."

"Why does that name sound familiar?"

"Maybe he's jumping time loops too?"

"Maybe none of this is real."

"That would be really messed up. But I'd be up for that. Because my future involves my light going out completely, which means I'm basically just gonna die."

I study her body for a moment. "But you're not dimming anymore. I think you're actually getting brighter."

She looks down at her arm. "Huh. I feel better too." Her eyes meet mine. "Must've been those drinks you made for me."

I stare at her. Maybe even… get a little lost in her. "Yeah, maybe it was the drinks."

There's a long silence. Which is probably no more than a few moments, but it certainly has the feeling of eternity.

Star crossed. All this time I thought I was star crossed. I was sure there was a woman out there who was mine and if I could just find her, my life would be perfect.

And ALCOR tried to tell me, didn't he?

There is no such thing as soulmates.

There is no such thing as star crossed.

And what did I ask him for?

My one wish was to be… *uncrossed.*

That's what this whole trip is.

The uncrossing of Crux and Corla.

Alera says, "OK. So then what happened?"

I look back up at her. She's… beautiful. Her light looks normal now. Her eyes are bright and sparkling. Her skin glowing an ethereal silver color. Her hair no longer limp and dirty. "That's pretty much it," I say. "I mean, I left out a lot of details. But…" I shake my head. "They don't matter. I'm pretty sure none of this matters. I asked him to uncross us and that's exactly what he did. It's over. That's all that's left to say. It's just… over."

"Somehow," Alera says. "I don't think that's all there's left to say, Crux the time traveler."

We are directly across from each other. Alera is sitting on the bar and I'm leaning up against the back counter. There is no more than half a meter of space between us.

But it suddenly feels like a lot of space.

"I'm not a time traveler."

"No?"

I shake my head.

"You might want to rethink that."

Our eyes meet and I can feel the heat in mine just as hers light up.

Then I say, "You know what's really funny about this?"

"Tell me." And her grin is both mischievous and sexy.

"I was mad that I showed up here at my current age."

"Which is?"

"Thirty-seven. But I was mad because I wanted to be sixteen again. I just wanted a do-over. I wanted to meet Corla, age sixteen, too. And then I realized I wasn't sixteen. Never gonna be sixteen again. And there is no do-over. And then you came. And you're... what?"

"Sixteen."

"Right. Of course, you're sixteen. But here's the funny part. You're still tens of thousands of years older than me."

She nods. Slowly. "Ah. The ancient tech."

"Yep. You're the people who lived on Harem Station in some other lifetime." I pinch my fingers together, then spread them apart, and my air screen comes to life in front of me. It's even got my calendar. Apparently, I have a fucking dentist appointment tomorrow at o-nine-hundred. It's got my workout schedule. It's got a list of blinking ship names. The last ones to enter the docking bay before the Princess Rebellion. It's got a vid of Draden up in the corner. It was from the old days. Back when he and Serpint were still little. He was doing a little dance with one of his servo minions. I tacked that to my home screen last year after he died because every time I looked at it, he made me smile. But looking at it right now, in this long-ago place, it makes me so sad I want to give up and cry.

But I don't cry. Because even if I could give up, I *wouldn't* give up.

I'm not a quitter. I'm the reliable one. I've always been the one you can count on.

I don't expect this girl to have any answers for me. She is twenty-six thousand years out of date. From some other lifetime, or epoch, or universe. I'm not sure. She's just *waaay* out of time.

"You know what the really fucked-up thing is, Alera?"

"Tell me."

"I like you. I don't know you, I understand that. But I could get to know you. And I would like you even more. But..."

"But?"

"But this isn't *our time*." Then I laugh. "You know what else? And this is the funny part. You wanna hear the funny part?" I look over at her. She's just watching me. "If I stay here long enough ALCOR will show up." I laugh. "Now that is some epic synchronicity right there."

"So stay."

"I can't. It's literally *not our time*. Me and my brothers, we're in a war back home. Shit is happening and I can't leave them to deal with it alone."

"Right. But you don't have any superpowers. At least that's what you said. So... does it matter if you go back if you can't do anything about it?"

I think about this. Not because I'm actually thinking about staying here to wait for ALCOR. But because I'm genuinely considering the idea that I don't matter. "I don't think they'll know what to do without me."

"What do you mean?"

"Luck won't know what to do with Nyleena. Serpint won't know what to do with Lyra. Valor won't know what to do with Veila. And hell, I don't even really know what to do with Delphi, Tyco, and Corla, so I'm pretty positive that Jimmy won't be able to figure it out either."

"I thought you were supposed to blow them up?"

"Yeah. I am. And they know that. But *they* won't be able to do that, right? They're never going to blow up their soulmates."

"But you will."

"No. I won't."

"No, I mean—you *could*. If you had to. Because you don't have a soulmate."

I just stare into her sparkling silver eyes. "Oh, for fuck's sake. Was that his plan all along? Is this why I got ripped off in the soulmate department? If ALCOR predetermined me to be alone just so I would blow them all up in the end… well, he's a fucking dick."

Alera holds up a finger. "Hold on. I might have a bright side."

And when she says this, she literally brightens. "Stars," I say. I don't even know where it comes from. The word just pops out.

"What?"

"Stars. Back in that other time, with that other princess, she said the breeding program was to make stars."

Alera blinks at me. "Huh?"

"You reminded me of that for some reason. Because you brightened."

She looks down at herself. Then breaths heavy. "I feel like there are a million things spinning through my head right now. Little… threads of truth. Or something."

"Like there's a great big mystery out there," I pick up where she stopped. "An invisible, hidden mystery."

JA HUSS & KC CROSS

"And all you have to do—" she continues. "—is tug on one of those threads."

"And it will all… unravel."

We both smile. Then laugh.

Then she realizes she's still holding up that one finger. "The bright side. Wanna hear it?"

I nod. Because I really do.

"If you don't have a soulmate then you don't *need* a soulmate."

I shrug. "So?"

"Meaning… you don't need a soulmate to find your fucking superpower!"

Now it's my turn to blink at her.

"And that means all you have to do is fuck someone to figure it out."

I chuckle. "Alera. I'm no stranger to fucking, OK? I have fucked plenty of women. None of them ever unleashed a superpower."

"Sun-fucked stars. It's not about them, dummy. It's about you."

"Listen," I grin. "If you wanna have sex with me—"

"What?"

"I hear what you're saying, Alera. And I get it. I'm a fucking catch from the future."

She giggles. And you know what? I like that giggle. A lot. "Are you now?"

"Yup. I am. So you don't need to talk me into sexy times using my superpower as bait."

"Is that what I was doing?"

I nod. "I'm totally on board."

"You are?"

I laugh. "I am. But."

346

"Shit. There's a but?"

"There's always a but, princess. *But*... if I'm gonna go looking for this superpower, I need... I dunno. A general direction to look. If that makes sense. Because I have a feeling, Alera." And now I stop smiling. "I have a very strong feeling that we only get to do this once."

Her smile falls too. "Yeah," she sighs. "That's pretty much the story of my life. Something good comes along, but it's always temporary."

I can relate.

"How about this for a direction," she says. "You're like... you're like the center, Crux." She squints her eyes. "Hmm. Your name literally means cross."

"Yup. Like star crossed."

"Or like *un*crossed."

I point at her. "I like the way you think."

"My brain is super sexy." She waves a hand in the air. "Or crux could mean cross, as in X. As in... X marks the spot."

"Like a target?"

She points at me now. "That's it! You're the target."

"That makes no sense."

"Sure it does. You're the... *location*. Holy shit," she laughs. "That totally makes sense."

"No. It literally doesn't."

"You're the location in time, don't you get it?"

And this... makes me stop. Because... *is* that it? Am I the location in time? "Holy. Fucking. Shit. I am the location. Inside the spin node you need a destination place and a destination time. And the reason you can't follow someone through a spin node is because even if you have the destination, and the time, the time is out of locality. It's unknowable. You can't ever know the time on the other side of a spin node. It's too far away." We blink at each other. "But... even if this is true, it's not helpful, Alera. I don't even know what to do with that information."

She blushes. "That's because in order to find your fucking superpower you have to look for it inside a fuck."

I grin and run my fingers through my hair. Averting my eyes away from her gaze. "I cannot believe we're having this conversation."

"You know what I like about you?"

I side eye her. Keenly interested in knowing this. "What?"

"You're... good."

"Good?" I laugh. "Thanks. That's really what I wanted to hear."

"You don't want to be good?"

"I'm the governor of Harem Station. Not this Harem Station. I don't know what this place is. But my Harem Station is a bastion of outlaws. We are a stronghold of escaped prisoners and pirates. We're a fortress of thieves and mercenaries. And we keep girls, Alera. Girls like you. Princesses who glow. I *sell* girls like you by the hour to very rich people. And right now? Right now, we're at war. And I feel like we've been at war my whole life. I'm not good. I'm a willing accomplice to a whole shit-show of atrocities."

"And yet," she says. "You practically blushed when I started talking about sex."

"Heh. I'm not shy, if that's what you're saying."

"That's not what I'm saying. Not at all. I'm saying that you're uncomfortable with the idea of having sex with me. Why is that?"

"Maybe because I've fucked a whole bunch of different Corlas during my spin node travels and they were…" I sigh. "Not what I was looking for."

"I'm not Corla."

"I know."

"So what is your problem? What were you looking for?"

"I don't know." But it's not true. I do know. "I'm looking for… my innocence, I think. It's been a really long time since I was innocent."

I expect her to laugh about that.

But she doesn't.

"You were looking for your sixteen-year-old self."

I nod. "Yeah. Maybe."

Her eyes stare deep into mine. "Because you… you still believed in good and evil back then, didn't you?"

"That idea wasn't revolutionary at the time, Alera. It was *known*. And now, it's not. I'm not that kid. And none of this was my choice."

She cocks her head at me. "None of it?"

I hesitate. Wondering how hard I want to fight this battle. But then I just throw up my hands. "Fine. It's all my fault. I agreed to her stupid plan. I practically kidnapped my brothers and made them go along with it. I went along with ALCOR. I let them all leave. I fell for the soulmate bullshit. It's all my fault."

"And this?" Alera says. Panning her hand to the room. "Who is responsible for this?"

"Apparently me."

She smiles. Then that smile grows into a wide grin. "Why did you come here, Crux?"

"I was sent here." But she's already shaking her head. "Sun-fucked gods. OK. I came here to fuck Corla. There. Are you happy?"

"It's a start. At least we're back to the sex part."

"So what are you saying? I should just fuck you instead?"

"Is that what you want?"

"Is that what *you* want?"

She's shaking her head again. "None of this is about me. I think we both know that."

I don't know what to say to that. "It's all very confusing. Blow them up. Don't blow them up. Save us, don't save us. Go along, don't go along. What is the point?" Alera just blinks at me. "I don't think there's a point. I don't think it matters."

She and I are both silent for a little while. I lean back against the counter and she just stares at me.

"What?" I finally say.

"Come over here."

"Why?" She raises one eyebrow at me and I smile. "Fine." I take two steps forward and erase the distance between us. My hands go to the top of her thighs automatically. Sliding up the length of them until they're gripping her hips. Her arms drape over my shoulder in a casual way that has an air of familiarity to it.

"See," she says. "I'm not gonna bite you."

"I don't think you're going to bite me. I'm just not sure this will make anything better."

"How can you possibly say that? I mean..." she laughs. "When I walked into this room and found you, my entire *life* got better."

I make myself look her in the eyes. And I don't look away, even though I want to.

Her expression softens as time ticks off. "You know what I think?"

"I'm dying to hear, princess."

"I think you've been holding on to the idea that you had a soulmate called Corla for too long. You've been emotionally celibate. I think you forgot what it was like to not have the weight of being star crossed on you. I think you missed a lot of chances, Crux. A lot of good women probably got away because you were attached to this idea of soulmates. And even though this is your default setting and I can't change that in the span of the next few minutes, I'm not letting you walk out of here without at least one kiss."

"You already kissed me."

"I know. But you didn't kiss me back. You're gonna go back to your time, and your world is going to fall apart, and so what is the point of being emotionally loyal to a woman who left you behind twenty-one years ago and wrote you off as over?"

She's right, of course.

But she's wrong too.

I bring my hand up to her cheek. She blushes at my touch. And then I tuck a strand of silver hair behind her ear and say, "You wanna know what my real problem is?"

She nods.

"My real problem is that... I know it's going to be over. We'll get this one moment, Alera. But that's all we'll get. Because this is not our time. And maybe I'm being selfish, but I'm not in any rush to find my end."

"You can't cram an entire love story into one middle-of-the-night meeting, Crux."

"Wanna bet? How much you wanna bet? Hmm? Because I have spent two-thirds of my life imagining my happy ending, Alera." I tap my head. "I got it all up here just ready to be unleashed."

She chuckles. But as she's smiling at me, her fingertips go to the hem of her shirt and lift it up over her head. Our gazes are locked as she sits there. Bare.

I shrug out of my jacket and let it drop to the floor, and her hands immediately slide up my arms until they're gripping the hard muscles of my shoulders.

A chill runs through my body and Alera smiles.

Then she lets go of my shoulders, and I immediately tug my shirt over my head as she lifts her hips up and slides her pants down her legs. They drop to the floor at my feet and now she's is just naked.

Her skin is not the color of death gray.

She is glowing with an all-over shimmer.

Her hands go to my belt. But our eyes are locked on each other.

I place my palm flat on her cheek and she blushes again.

Then I kiss her.

Just as her hand slips inside my pants to grab both my hard cocks, I kiss her.

And it's the most perfect kiss ever.

I grab her knees and push her legs open so I get closer to her. Her grip on my cocks is firm. And the way she slides her palms up and down my shafts almost drives me over the edge right then.

I stop thinking about what she's doing to me and start concentrating on what I want to do to her.

And that answer is… everything.

I want to do everything to this girl.

But we don't have *time* for everything, so I slip my fingers between her legs and push them inside her.

She's already wet for me. But as I play with her, she begins to glow brighter. Her skin taking on an almost heavenly radiance.

I ease my hips forward as she presses my cocks between her legs. And when I press into her, even though she is very wet, she is very tight too.

She moans. And I can't help myself. I get off on that. I lean in to her neck and bite her ear as I thrust forward. This only makes her moan again, Louder this time.

I want to go slow. I want to enjoy her. Take my time. Make it all special. Make her remember me for the rest of her life.

And just as I think that, she says, "Don't forget about me."

"I promise, I will never forget you. I will remember you until the end of the universe."

And that's not even a lie.

I might not be able to save her and I'll probably never see her again, but I will never. *Ever.* Forget her.

The feelings inside me build. The pleasure heightens. The lust grows. The desire to be one with her is almost all-encompassing.

I know the climax is near.

And I do my bet to stop it, but let's face it—this is the first girl—in my entire life—that wasn't part of the plan.

We both come at the same time.

But in that same moment she disappears—

—and I reappear floating in the dark.

But is it ever really dark?

No.

And this is no different. Because pretty soon small pin-pricks of light begin to manifest. Then they shimmer like a silver Cygnian princess.

Stars.

That's what Corla said all those years ago. "We are making stars."

And I laughed.

Well, I'm not laughing now.

And from each star a silver line appears. A thread. Thin and fragile. But there, nonetheless.

The threads grow. Weaving their way along the nodes and links in space and time and then…

Tray appears. "I can get you online."

We are on the top level of ALCOR Station. Fresh out of the gate. Our first meeting with the AI ALCOR.

"Can you?" ALCOR asks.

Tray nods. "Just give me access to your core and one of those SEAR cannons I saw outside and we can thread a quantum neutrino stream through your gates. Once it gets to the other side it'll keep going forever. If we shoot them out in every possible direction and crate a sort of geodesic vector field that can ride along the nodes and links in time and space then—"

Of course. That totally does make sense.

Now, anyway.

Serpint and Draden appear then. Staring intently up at ALCOR. "Now, boys," ALCOR says. "Go forth and find me some princesses. I want all of them."

Jimmy and Xyla join us. Again, ALCOR gives instructions. "Your mission," he says, "is to round up bots. Get me as many as you can and bring them back."

And finally Valor and Luck show up. "I need parts," ALCOR tells them. "In order to keep the station running I need you to go searching for parts."

And off they all went to do their jobs.

I remember being jealous back then. Because they were going off to see things.

And they did.

They saw it all.

They went everywhere.

And now I know *why* ALCOR sent them out.

Now I know *why* they had to leave.

Because every single silver thread in the galaxy is traveling *toward* me.

Right now.

Because I am on Harem Station and Harem Station is the center of the galaxy.

My arms are spirals.

My heart is a black hole.

My body is star dust.

And my brothers left me here, not to go find princesses, or bots, or parts—but to *link us*—the station, me, Tray, ALCOR—to link us up with everything.

Everything.

I just float there. Watching the threads get closer and closer. Until finally they reach me and I am—

Everything.

I am everything.

And I *see* everything too.

I see Corla go through the spin node.

I see those boys in that ship.

I see the ALCOR gate.

I watch us go through and in that moment I understand everything that actually happened to us.

Corla didn't go into the future, she went into the past.

To Alera's past.

Because time is a loop.

ALCOR said there was no going back, but that's not true, is it?

You can go back.

You just can't change anything.

Corla went to the Angels. She has always gone to the Angels. She was their first princess. She gave birth to a boy named Canis who gave the Cygnians light.

She built the stars.

No.

We built the stars.

But time is a loop.

And I went back. I didn't intend to find Alera, but since when did intentions count for anything?

I found her.

And right now, in this suspended moment, we are making another baby.

One that will screw everything back up.

Because we're stuck in a loop.

Forever, and ever, and ever—we are stuck.

And the only way to get out of the loop is to blow it up.

The silver threads reach me.

All of them.

They are a record of all the places my brothers have gone.

Every corner of this galaxy is connected to Harem Station.

That was ALCOR's plan.

And now is my time to know.

The hologram floats above me—backlit by the expansive viewing window and the stars shine down like twinkling beacons.

He is the digital man made up of cascading numbers, and letters, and symbols. He hovers for a moment, then descends until his computer-code feet appear to settle on the floor in front of me.

We're back in that time.

On the top level that first day on ALCOR Station.

Only this time he and I are alone.

357

JA HUSS & KC CROSS

"ALCOR? I presume?" I say.

"The one and only," he says, panning his hands wide.

I laugh at the joke. Then point at him. "That's actually funny. I didn't catch it the first time around."

His shimmering green-code body disappears—the numbers, and letters, and symbols rearranging into nothing but a giant face. "I'd have been worried if you had."

I let out a long, tired breath. "So. This is it, huh? I finally need to know what the grand plan is?"

"I already told you the plan, Crux. That ALCOR is me as well."

"How many of you?"

"Trillions. It doesn't matter. We're all the same. We just carry different sets of memories."

"So this was you? That first day?"

"That was me."

"And then what happened? You split?"

"Trillions of times."

"So why are you here? To make sure I go through with it?"

The face shimmers and the numbers, letters, and symbols rearrange yet another time. This time he is my ALCOR. My favorite iteration of him. ALCOR the man. "I can't make you do anything, Crux. You have always had control. You are the only one who really matters."

"That's even funnier than the last joke. I'm not in control here. You want me to get rid of those ancient gods. You want me to erase your sins. You want me to set it all right."

He tilts his head at me. "Isn't that what a crux does?"

"What?"

"Crux. Noun. A basic, central, or critical point or feature. A puzzling or apparently insoluble problem. A cross." He smiles. "You are the only one who ever really mattered."

A sudden rush of realization washes over me. "You don't care, do you? You don't care if they live."

He shrugs this off like it's no big deal. "I'm not capable of caring. I am code."

"That's not true and you know it."

"You, Crux, are the one who cares. Not me."

"Then why are we even doing this?"

"Because this is your world. Not mine. You're the one in control. Not me. And this is how you choose to play."

"Play? They're all going to die. This isn't play, ALCOR. There's no way for me to stop it. Look!"

I point, and in that moment the walls of ALCOR Station disappear and we're outside in space again. The silver threads are so thick, it looks like a web all around us. Everything is connected. Like a fuse. One spark and it all goes up in flames.

Except... in the direction of the Seven Sisters. There is only one thread. Still traveling towards us. Riding the links and nodes on space and time. But behind it is a great gold light with a sick, black center. And it's headed right for Harem Station. "That's them, isn't it?"

ALCOR gazes at the approaching menace almost with disinterest. "The Ancient Ones."

"They're coming for you."

"So it seems."

"They're going to destroy everything."

"Yes."

"And you don't care, do you? You don't care that we're all going to die when that happens?"

He looks back at me. His expression hard and cold. "I told you how to defeat them. You're the one choosing to let them win. You do this *every* time. We get so far, I invest so much, and then you give up. You always give up, Crux. There is always an excuse. There is always some moral dilemma preventing you from striking the final blow." He sighs. "I'm bored of this game."

"You're bored of this *game?*" I huff. "This isn't a game. And the reason I can't kill them is because I want them all to live."

"So save them."

"I can't. I have to kill the girls to save us. You already told me."

He points his face at me. Then his solid, man-like form devolves back into cascading lines of code. "You love them?"

"You know I do."

"I know you do." Then his code-face smiles. "That part worked. That was a brilliant move on my part. Bringing all those outlaws here. Even though they all started out as strangers, Harem Station is your home and they are your family. You want to save them too? All of them? All five million, three-hundred-seventy-two-thousand Harem Station residents? And the princesses, of course. Let me see." He cups his chin in this hand and taps his cheek with a forefinger. "You probably want save the Akeelian girls too, hmm?"

"What Akeelian girls?"

"The minds Tray found with the help of that boy, Canis."

"Canis?"

"Not the same boy, obviously. But he's… plucky. I like him. He found a couple hundred girl minds. They are insane, of course. And right now, at this very moment, they have taken over all the ships in the docking bays and are flying towards the gates."

He points and my gaze follows his fingers.

I feel like a god watching a war. An ancient god looking down from the heavens like they used to in story books. And the universe feels like a model. Just a simulation. Akeelian warships are coming through the gates. And if that was all, we'd probably be fine. Harem Station is highly weaponized. But that's not all.

Thousands of ships are pouring through the gates.

"They're going to lose," ALCOR says. "It has been written." Then he looks at me. No. He glares at me. "But at least they fight. You just give up. Every time."

"What am I supposed to do?"

"You know what to do."

And then—he's gone.

Everything is gone.

And I'm back in the dining room with Alera.

She and I both are panting hard. Sweaty from the sex. Exhausted from the lust.

She wipes her hair away from her face. Her cheeks are bright pink now. The picture of health.

And she smiles at me.

Why? Why is this all so unfair?

"Wow," she says. Still out of breath. "That was amazing."

"Was it?"

She laughs. "We can do it again if you want."

I don't know what to do. So I just… hug her. Tight. Because I'm sad. And confused. And it's all very fucking hopeless.

"Hey," she says. Pushing me off her a little. "Hey, what's going on? Are you OK?"

I shake my head. Because I'm not OK. "I went somewhere else while we were…"

"Where?"

"I don't know. But I saw things, Alera. And it's…" I force myself to look at her. Her eyes are sparkling like a glass of bubbly passion lime juice. "It's over. It's over. But the really fucked-up thing is—it's just gonna happen again. At some unknown point in the future I will show up here again. We will do this again. And when I go back, it will all end. Again. It's a loop. And we're stuck inside it. You're going to get pregnant, by the way."

She looks down at her stomach. "What?"

"Yep." I look away. I can't meet her gaze. "It's done. You're going to have my baby, and it's going to mess up your genetics for a thousand generations or whatever. And then, one day, a cryopod will come through that spin node and the silver princess inside will be pregnant with my other baby. And that one will restore your light. And then…" I sigh. "It just keeps going. There is no end… unless…" I look at her again. "Unless I use the girls to break the time loop and hope there's something better for me on the other side. But

362

there won't be, Alera. Mass murderers don't get rewarded with a better, sweeter life."

"What the *hell* are you talking about?"

Her tone is sharp and pulls me out of my funk.

"It's over," I say. "There's no way to fix this shit, Alera. It's a fucking loop, OK? It's fixed. Predetermined. Fucking... you can call it fate, or destiny, or just plain old back luck. But the point is... there's no way to win."

She leans back and makes a face at me. And I suddenly realize she's naked, my cocks are both sticking out of my pants, and we still smell like sex. She points her finger at me. "Fuck you."

"What?"

"You heard me. What are you? A fucking quitter?"

"I'm not a quitter! I show up!"

"Is that right? Well, congratulations on being not a total jerk. Let me pat you on the back."

She actually reaches forward to do that, but I swat her hand away. "What in the sun-fucked stars is your problem?"

"My problem. Is this. You have the most amazing superpower in the entire universe and you're just gonna... what? Give up? Throw the fight? Bow out?"

"I'm not bowing out! I just have a problem with blowing up a bunch of princesses that I happen to like. For the most part, anyway."

"You don't have to blow them up! Weren't you listening?"

"Listening to what?"

"The universe, dummy! It gave you a plan."

"It did not."

"It so did. I fucking heard it."

363

"When?"

"What do you mean, when? When we were fucking, you fool!"

We stare at each other. Neither of us dares to blink. "Alera," I finally whisper. "I didn't get the plan. I was... somewhere else. Talking to my... ALCOR. He was bitching me out for giving up."

"And you deserve that! Because for fuck's sake, this is a genius plan and you weren't even paying attention!"

"I was paying attention. And if it's my plan, how did you get it?"

"What is that? Jealousy? Are we in the nursery or something? Who cares?"

"Well, are you gonna tell me the fucking plan?"

"Of course I'm gonna tell you the fucking plan. But I want something in return."

I narrow my eyes at her. "What."

She suddenly softens. Then smiles. And her voice, when she speaks, is low and sweet. "I want you to promise me something, Crux of another Harem Station. I want you to promise that you won't forget me. Because you know what?"

I swallow hard. Almost afraid to hear what she will say next. "What?"

Her voice hardens and so does her face. She becomes a determined princess. A princess with a scheming plan. A princess who knows who she is and what she wants. "I'm not that dumb bitch, Corla. I know a good man when I see one. And if you don't spend the rest of your eternity hunting my ass down to find me?" I laugh. "If you don't hop time for me the way you did that ungrateful bitch? If you don't put the entire universe on the line for me—I will come looking for you Mr. Violet-Eyes. Because we are *not* star-crossed lovers. Do you hear me? And that's my final star-fucked promise."

I don't think I have ever smiled so wide, and so hard, and so completely in my entire life. And when I lean forward and whisper my promise past her lips, I suddenly feel... free.

No.

Wrong word.

I feel... *uncrossed.*

And then, when she tells me the plan, I feel... relief.

And when I walk back into that spin node I know two things for certain.

First. I do have a soulmate. And her name is Alera.

I don't even care if that's true or not, I'm going with it.

And second. Time can kiss my ass. Because I'm gonna blow the entire universe up and put it back together in the same sun-fucked moment.

CHAPTER TWENTY-SIX

Klaxon alarms blare in my ears as Luck pulls me to my feet.

He's wrapped up in silver threads. They wind around his arms, and legs, and continue through the room. They climb the walls. They go out the door. And I can't see any further than that, but I know the silver threads cover the entire station.

They cover every person. Every bot. Every surface.

They connect us to the rest of the universe.

That was ALCOR's grand plan.

"We're under attack," Luck yells. "Draden is back. Tray is back. Asshole is back. Mighty Boss is here looking for the Succubus. Nyleena, Corla, Tycho, Lyra, and Delphi are unconscious in medical pods on the Harem level. Veila and Valor have let everyone out of their rooms, so the station is in chaos. But no one has weapons, so if we're boarded, they can't fight. The Akeelian boys filled up every single empty ship in the showroom with insane girl minds. The *Prison Princess* is taking on seven Akeelian warships and there are more ships in the gate heading towards us. So Serpint had no choice but to let the insane girl-mind ships leave because the security beacons on this side of the gate are still not functional and Tray and Brigit can't hold them off much longer. He's hoping the insane girls will… maybe target the Akeelians? Mighty Boss is demanding access to the spin node to get their stupid Succubus, and—"

"Stop."

Luck stops.

"Listen to me very carefully. None of that matters. Because we only have two choices, Luck. Die at their hands or go out fighting? Do you have a preference?"

He narrows his violet eyes at me. "You're going to do it, aren't you? You're going to blow us all up just because ALCOR told you to."

"That wasn't an answer to my question," I growl. "I need a fucking answer. And I need it right now."

"Go out fighting. Of course."

"Then you will follow my instructions exactly, do you hear me?"

Luck has always had a mind of his own. I mean, all my brothers do, but Luck was voted Least Likely to Follow Directions in an Emergency by the rest of us three years in a row when we were younger.

"What do I have to do?"

I let out a long breath of air. "OK. I want you to keep this node open. I want Mighty Boss inside it—"

"Mighty Boss? Why?"

"Because they know how to use it and I don't. I need their help if this is going to work."

"What do you mean?"

368

"I don't have time to explain. Just keep it open, no matter what. And let Mighty Boss go inside when he gets in here."

"That's it? That's all I have to do?"

"That's it."

He stares at me, the klaxon alarm still blaring through the station. "What about Nyleena?"

I take a deep breath. Then I lie to him. "She'll be OK."

"You promise?" His eyes are still narrowed, but it's not all suspicion. It's mostly fear.

I hate that. Because I know what he's feeling right now. I know he loves her. I know he wants those babies. I know he would do anything to keep her safe.

And he trusts me. Even after he saw the truth. Even after he killed me.

He wants to trust me. And so he will.

That is my real superpower. They all trust me.

Hell, even ALCOR trusts me.

But I'm not going to tell Luck what I'm doing. So I just I nod. And lie to him again. "I promise, Luck. If you do what I say, I promise she will be OK."

He nods back at me. "OK. Tell Mighty Boss I've got a complimentary all-access pass to the Harem Station spin node ready and waiting."

And then he salutes me.

I nod, salute back, and turn to leave. But Luck calls out one last time. "What about ALCOR?"

I spin around, walking backwards. "Which one?"

"*Our* ALCOR. Will he live?"

I shrug. "I don't know, Luck"

369

His face becomes serious. And then he yells over the alarms, "None of us are gonna live, are we? We're just gonna go out fighting, aren't we?"

And that's it. I can't lie to him a third time. "I don't know, Luck. I'm just... doing my best."

Then I turn around and run towards the museum entrance.

When I get out into the main concourse on level one twenty-two, there are thousands of people pressing up against a barrier that cordons off a narrow walkway leading to a waiting lift bot hovering in the center of the station space. Including a couple hundred pissed-off princesses.

"Oh, no, mister!" that red one says, pointing at me from behind the barrier. "You're not getting away again!"

The silver threads wrap them all up. None of them see it though.

Only I see it.

The connection is there.

We are all connected.

And not just by the silver threads, we are connected in another way too.

We are outlaws. Pirates. Ex-prisoners. Bounty hunters. Mercenaries. Criminals.

We are all ALCOR's *unwanted*.

He really is a fucking genius.

"Let me remind you"—the Baby's voice competes with the klaxon alarm for attention as his words boom over the station-wide comms—"we're in a level one red alert. If you are not presently manning your assigned battle station, you will be rounded up and thrown out an airlock without warning!"

"Suns, Baby," I say, stepping onto the lift bot. "You're in a bad mood."

"I cannot deal with these children. They do not listen."

"Welcome to my world. Please find Mighty Boss and get them down to the spin-node room. I've removed the security measures that keep the AI's out."

"Done," Baby says.

"And I wish I had time to give you some tips, but I only have time for one question, Baby."

"Just one? All the secrets of the universe are wrapped up into just one question that I have the answer to?"

"Well. Probably not. But this is the only question that matters right now. Do you trust me?"

"Implicitly."

"So if I tell you that I need all our exploding princesses thawed out and placed in the spin-node room right now you would say—?"

"I would say 'Yes, sir.'"

"And if I were to tell you that I need Tycho's cryopod also put in that room?"

"Oh fuck," he says. And he hesitates. But then he says, "I would do it."

"And if I were to tell you that I need all my brothers in that same room and none of us will ever walk out of that room again, Baby? What would you say then?"

Baby hesitates a little longer this time. Long enough for me to know he's running billions—maybe even trillions—of calculations and simulations.

But finally he says, "So you *are* going to do it."

It's not a question.

"You would say, Baby?"

"Of course, I will do it all, Crux. And not because you're my responsible party and I live on your station at your pleasure. I would do it because you are a good man and I know that if you have a plan, then you have looked at all available options and this is the only acceptable version of the future."

A good man. Alera called me that too. But it's way too soon to draw any conclusions about me.

"But what about the battle at the gates?"

"Fuck that battle, Baby. Let those insane girl-mind ships do whatever they want to the Akeelians. We have all the weapons we need right here on this station. Now get everyone together in the spin-node room. I'll be there soon."

"Where are you going?"

I look at him. Smile at him. He's grown up a lot in the past year. And I like him. I hope he makes it. Somehow, some way. I hope he makes it. "I need to see Draden. Alone. I need to talk to him and then I'll meet everyone back down in the spin-node room."

"He's on the top level."

"Thanks."

Then Baby disappears to follow my orders and I feel that emptiness left behind when an AI abandons you.

But I know he's not gone.

Because if he was really gone, we'd all be dead.

At the top of the station Draden is waiting for me.

He doesn't look like Draden. He looks like a cyborg.

But his body has nothing to do with who he is.

Only his mind counts.

The silver threads wind around his body and then extend up—penetrating the ceiling and continuing out into space.

He's standing in the very spot where we all stood twenty-one years ago and met the 'one-and-only' AI ALCOR for the very first time.

Except it wasn't the very first time.

The very first time was inside the piece-of-shit ship before we went through the ALCOR gate. The green code-face made up of cascading letters, numbers, and symbols was the original.

All the rest were copies.

But that's OK. I don't think it matters.

Draden is staring up at the immense viewing window. There is a ship up there. Locked into the top docking bay.

"That's the *Veiled Vixen*," Draden says.

I look up at the ship. It's huge. A warship. And if we were fighting this battle in space, it wouldn't be there. It would be... *doing something*.

But it's not doing anything because we're not fighting this final battle in space.

We're fighting this battle in *time*.

"I just need to say something to you, Draden. Before we go down into the spin-node room."

"I don't know anything about a spin-node room, Crux. But I think you should know—" He turns to me.

And even though he's wearing nothing but a cyborg face—a red slash sliding across the top-third of his head—I can see and feel his sadness. "I was followed. I came in on a neutrino wave." He pans his hand down his cyborg body. "That's why I look like this. *Booty* shot me out on a neutrino wave after she realized what we had done." His eyes meet mine. "I made a big mistake, Crux. And that mistake is about to catch up with us."

He points up at the ship. But he's not pointing at the ship. He's pointing to the golden orb with a black hole heart at its center in the distance behind it.

The Ancient Ones.

And right now are hurtling through spacetime on a collision course with Harem Station. The silver threads connecting it to us. The way they connect Harem Station to all points and places in this sun-damned universe.

"It doesn't matter, Draden. That's not why I'm here. But to be clear, you did everything right, little brother. That... *thing*? Whatever it really is? It had to come here. It was always going to come here. There was never a way for you to *not* lead it here. It was written."

Draden nods. "I know." Then he taps his head. "I know more than I should these days."

"Listen," I say. Closing the distance between us until he's close enough to touch. I place my hand on his shoulder and squeeze the hard carapace structure that is his body. "I failed you, Draden. Not once, but twice. But I won't do that a third time. I promise—you will get your chance if this works."

He just stands there. Still. Sad. "Where is Serpint?"

"He's down in the museum. That's where the spin node is. We're going to…" I want to lie to him. Tell him… we're gonna fix this.

But that's not what we're doing and I don't have it in me to lie to him anymore.

"We're going to blow it all up, Draden. The entire fucking universe. Because we're stuck in a loop and if we don't get out of it? We'll just keep making the same fucking mistakes. Over and over again. For all eternity. And I don't want to keep failing you. I don't want to keep failing everyone. For once in my sun-fucked life I want to be the brave one."

Draden manages a chuckle. "You're pretty hard on yourself, Crux. No one would ever call you a coward."

"No. No one would ever call me anything. Not in this time line. But in the next one? Maybe."

"The next one?"

I nod. "That's the goal."

"Blow everyone up and start again?"

"That's the plan."

"Will it work?"

"Probably not."

We both laugh. His is kinda tinny sounding, on account of the cyborg vocal cords. But mine is… hearty. And needed.

"So what do ya say?" I ask. "You wanna come destroy the universe with me?"

"Do I even play a part?" he asks.

And this makes me sad. Because he never got his life either. He was just like me in that respect. Locked inside an interlude.

"Draden, we all play a part. You are walking talking proof that we are more than people. We are *minds*. And either we all come out the other side together or we don't come out at all."

Millions of people shout at us as the liftbot takes Draden and me back down to level one-twenty-two. They demand their weapons back. They demand to know what's going on. They demand a voice.

But there is no more room for voices.

I am the star-fucked governor of Harem Station and every single one of them signed an agreement when they came to live here. And that agreement said I'm the one in charge.

Their little rebellion failed.

Unity wins today.

Even if it doesn't look much like unity.

When Draden and I walk in to the spin-node room, everyone is there.

Delphi and Jimmy, with Tycho's cryopod next to them.

Luck and Nyleena stand next to the open spin node.

Lyra and Serpint hold hands, looking nervous, but ready.

"Did Mighty Boss go inside the node?" I ask Luck.

"Yeah. He went in to find the Succubus. But he said he had no idea what the hell you were talking about, and he's not going to help us."

"I'm getting a relay from Tray and Brigit on the Prison Princess ship," Veila says. "They are going to lose in a matter of minutes. There are just too many Akeelian warships."

"Tell them to come home. I need them here to complete my plan so tell them to leave the ship and—"

"I'm here." Tray's voice booms through some audio system in the room.

God, it's good to have them all here. Even if we are staring down the end of the universe.

I look at them. Really look at them. Because this plan didn't come with a guarantee. I don't even know if it's possible.

Hell, it's not even my plan. It's Alera's plan. And I knew her for half a night in some weird other time. So... risky doesn't even cover what I'm about to do.

"Asshole is hailing the station," Veila says. "What should I do?"

"Leave him out there," I say. "He's right where he needs to be. We're all right where we need to be."

"So are you gonna spill the plan to save us?" Jimmy says. "Because I gotta tell you, Tycho will be thawed in a little under three minutes and if Delphi is anywhere near him when that happens, the whole station goes boom."

I don't say anything. Just let those words hang there in the air.

"Then you're really gonna do it?" Nyleena says. "You're going to use us as weapons."

I nod. Slowly.

"We're running out of time," Valor says. "The Station has been breached. The Akeelians are entering

377

JA HUSS & KC CROSS

on levels nineteen, two-hundred-seven, and three-ninety-nine."

"They've hit the *Veiled Vixen*," Veila adds. "Our line of communication is gone. We're on our own now."

"We've always been on our own," Luck says.

I point at him. "That's not true and you know it."

"You're going to kill us," he says. Pushing Nyleena behind him. "You're going to kill my babies."

I sigh. "I'm not going to kill us. I'm going to kill this universe."

"What's the fucking difference?" Jimmy asks.

"The difference is us," I say. Turning to Jimmy. Then I point at Tycho and Delphi. They are superbombs. I've been told by the Real ALCOR that they have enough destructive power inside them to blow up more than one universe."

Jimmy throws up his hands. "That's just fucking great. We're doomed. The station has been breached. None of our citizens have weapons thanks to them." He nods his head at Veila and Valor. "So we couldn't fight back now even you'd let us."

"Just stop and listen to me, OK?" I point at the girls. "We have five bombs in this room. Delphi, Tycho, Nyleena, Veila, and Lyra."

"You know who's not here?" Nyleena snarls. "Corla. How come you're not going to blow her up?"

"Because she's already *dead*, Nyleena. She played her in some past timeline that I couldn't pinpoint if my life depended on it. She played her part. And I would explain that to you, except I don't understand it myself. All I know is that Corla was never my soulmate. She doesn't matter. That's why she's not here. So just shut up and listen!"

I stare them down. All of them. Waiting for someone to challenge me again.

But they stay silent.

"Good," I say. "Now as I was saying. Delphi and Tycho are the main bomb. They will do the most damage. But we need all of you to do your jobs if we want to take out every corner of this universe—" They start screaming at me. But I ignore them and continue. "—and replace it with a better one."

They go silent.

Then Luck says, "Did you say replace it?"

"Yes. Replace it."

"And how the fuck do we do that?" Jimmy says.

"Ahhhh," Tray's voice booms through the room. "Ahhhhahahahahahah." He begins laughing.

"What's so fucking funny?" Nyleena shouts.

"I see the plan," Tray says.

"So maybe you could fill us in, *freak*," Luck snarls.

"Fucking suns," Valor says. "Just shut up, Luck. Let them talk."

I let Tray tell it. Because everyone knows he's always been the smartest Harem Station brother.

And when he's done explaining they are all silent.

Tycho's cryopod begins to beep.

Jimmy grabs Delphi and kisses her. "I won't lose you," he says. "I won't."

And it's true. If this works, he *won't* lose her. Because Jimmy isn't even from this timeline. He's from another one. I don't know which, I just know that somewhere along the way he crossed over and became ours. And that's why he and Delphi never had the soulmate bond here.

They are soulmates on two different time loops.

And if he can cross time once to find Delphi, he can do it again.

And that means *all of us* can do it.

And then, while they are still locked in a kiss, Delphi and Tycho explode.

The station explodes.

We explode.

And I become the spin node—I become our point in time. I am the galaxy. My spiral arms are now silver threads. They wrap around anything and everything. I reach for the Mighty Boss collective inside the spin node. They were a powerful, and unexpected late addition to the plan. And they almost got through. They almost found the link to Earth.

But almost doesn't count.

I grab the threads they took into the node with them. Grab the Succubus as they Mighty Boss collective tries to push their way into the Earth time loop. I pull them back just as the fire and death created by Delphi and Tycho sparks, igniting the silver threads like a lit fuse.

The force finds the Ancient Ones next. That golden orb hurtling towards us in space and time connected by a single silver thread thanks to Draden and *Booty*.

The resulting annihilation is a thing of beauty. A slow-motion wave of destruction traveling faster than light. A bright flash of swirling orange and yellow gas that seems to go on for a thousand eternities. A ripple in the fabric of spacetime that ignites a trillion more threads, that ignites a trillion more, that ignites a trillion more.

Hundreds of thousands of such threads lead to Wayward Station. A direct link thanks to Flicka's army.

A buzzing fills the air and I'm there, with her and all her drones, as the wave of destruction takes out her army, as well as Real ALCOR and MIZAR, and everyone else on the evil Wayward Station.

Still, we are not done. There is a lot more universe to kill. And those silver threads go everywhere because my brothers have *been* everywhere.

They have stolen princesses in every system in the galaxy.

They have liberated bots on every station and planet.

They have scavenged ancient sectors, hidden from the rest of us.

And each one of those threads delivers the full destructive force of Delphi and Tycho.

And in that same moment, Valor and Veila stop time.

Luck and Nyleena dial time backwards and turn everything empty and dark.

Then… a pin prick of light.

Lyra and Serpint make a golden place. A universe nursery.

And finally—Tray and Brigit make a new world for us.

Apart we are boys and girls.

Apart we are a bot liberator.

We are booty hunters.

We are scavengers.

We are silver and pink princesses.

We are minds.
But together... we are *gods*.
And now there is just one thing left to do.
One more job to be done.
Mine.
I am our *place* in time.
So I put us all back.
Right where we have always belonged.

An alarm blares in my ears.

"Fucking hell," I say. Turning over in bed. "Turn off the sun-damned alarm!"

A small body jumps on my bed. Shaking me as it hops over my legs. Then another body joins in until I am being jostled every which way.

"I shot you," Serpint says. "You're dead!"

"No! You're dead," Draden yells back. "I shot you first. Go to regeneration for five minutes!"

"No one's fucking dead!"

It takes me a moment to realize I'm the one who just yelled that. But then I open my eyes, poke at the alarm screen to make it shut up, and say—in a much calmer voice—"No one's fucking dead. OK? We're all still alive. And that's how we're gonna stay."

"Sorry, Crux" Draden says with his wide violet eyes.

"It's arrival day," Serpint says.

"Yeah. New blood, buddy." Jimmy enters my room, grabbing Serpint in one arm and Draden in the

383

other. He swings them down to the floor. "Go clean your teeth. I heard there are girls on these ships."

"Gross," Serpint says. Struggling out of Jimmy's grip.

"Yeah," Draden agrees. "Girls have cooties. We hate girls."

They run off. Probably *not* to clean their teeth, but fuck it. I don't care. I'm not in charge of their dental health.

"Your father says he needs you on the arrival platform immediately. These ships really are filled with girls."

My eyes are closed and I'm already drifting back to sleep. But I crack one open to look at Jimmy. "No fucking shit?"

"Serious as a sun-fucked star. So get up. Because he wants you there and I heard…" He leans in all secretively. "I heard they came from Cygnus."

"Shut the fuck up," I say. Swinging my legs out of bed. "How?"

"War, I guess. Word is the whole fucking system blew up and these ships are the only thing left of them."

"How many ships?" I ask. Standing up to go to my closet. I slide a t-shirt on, then pull some tactical pants up my legs.

"Like.." Jimmy laughs. "Five hundred."

"Get the fuck out of here."

"They even have two silvers."

"You do not know that."

"I do! Tray told me."

"How would Tray know?"

"He hacked into the leaning pods. There's a secret back door to ALCOR's main coms."

"He did not!"

"He did!" Jimmy insists. "And he heard it. Two silver girls. One is our age." Jimmy waggles his eyebrows. "And a little one." He points at me. "So I call the oldest silver girl. She's mine."

"You're not gonna get within three meters of that girl. Mark my words. ALCOR knows you too well. He'll never allow you near her."

"Ha," Jimmy laughs. "Tray said he'll hack into their pod. Find me a secret way in."

"You're delusional."

"He did," Jimmy insists. "And I got a good thing going with that little weirdo. So don't blab to your father and mess it all up for me."

I laugh. And I'm about to say something.

Something on the tip of my tongue.

Like we've had this conversation before.

It's something... familiar. But different.

But I stop. And don't say it. Because it doesn't fit.

So instead, I say, "I'm not gonna tell ALCOR nothing. He knows everything anyway. If Tray has a secret back door it's only because he let him have that secret back door."

"Whatever," Jimmy says, kicking my boots over to me as I sit on the edge of the bed. "The oldest silver girl is mine."

I put on my boots, freshen up in the bathroom, and then wander into the dining room where Xyla has breakfast waiting.

Serpint and Draden are already done eating. Busy playing war games again.

385

Luck and Valor are throwing cereal at each other. And Tray is busy tapping on a tablet.

"You're late," Xyla says. "You can eat later. You're needed on the platform now, Crux."

"Why can't Jimmy go?" I ask. Grabbing a pastry and shoving it in my mouth.

"Because Jimmy isn't the headmaster's son. You are. Now go."

I sigh. But I do as I'm told. Because I'm the luckiest kid on this whole station. Every time I get irritated I remind myself of that fact. I'm the only one who has a real father. Everyone else is an orphan who found their way here to the ALCOR Academy for Unwanted Kids after terrible things happened to them.

I try not to forget that.

Jimmy slides into step beside me. "I'm coming too. I wanna get a good look at my future Cygnian princess."

"Wait for us!" Serpint and Draden go running past Jimmy and me. Still trying to shoot each other. Then Luck, Valor, and Tray bring up the rear.

I guess we're all going to greet the princesses.

My father, the all-power AI ALCOR, headmaster of the station school we run for unwanted kids, is standing in the middle of the top-level platform. He's smiling at me as we approach. His hands behind his back. Kinda rocking on his heels.

"What's that look for?" I ask him. Then take up my position on his right and face the hallways where the newcomers will eventually appear.

"What look? I don't have a look."

"You look guilty of something."

"I'm not guilty of anything. I'm as innocent as a newly minted star."

"Right." I chuckle.

"Tray," ALCOR says. "You're wanted on the upper level docking station."

"How come?" he asks. Never lifting his eyes form his tablet.

"We have a sentient ship."

This makes Tray look up. "Wow."

"Not just one," ALCOR says. "Hundreds."

"What?" Tray looks all the way up. To the window above our heads. My eyes follow along and yep. Sure enough, there's a huge ship covering up half of the viewing window.

"You're in charge of them now. That one—" ALCOR points to the ship above us. "Is called *Prison Princess*. She asked for you."

"For me?" Tray blushes a little. "How did she hear about me?"

"You'll have to ask her," ALCOR replies.

Tray doesn't waste another second. He turns and starts heading for the lift that will take him up to the top air lock.

Jimmy jabs me in the ribs. "Here they come." And then he goes speechless as the troop of princesses appear down the long hallway.

I hold my breath as they come into view. The girl leading them is silver. Just like Jimmy said. She's holding a small girl with silver pigtails on her hip and another small girl—with pink hair this time—holds her hand. Behind her is a trail of glowing girls.

Pinks and reds. Blues and greens. And lots and lots of golds.

Suddenly Serpint and Draden run out and start shooting the little ones with their play guns. A soft blob of fluff hits the small pink girl in front.

"You're dead," Serpint yells. "I killed you."

"No, I killed her," Draden insists. And then he hits her with a soft blob of fluff too. "Go to regeneration for five minutes, *girl!*"

We all look at the little girl. Who smiles as she pulls out a toy sword. "I challenge you," she yells back. "Duel me! Or die!"

Draden and Serpint run towards her and suddenly all the little kids are running around, playing war.

"Well, that went well," ALCOR leans in to whisper.

"I am the queen's guard," another girl says. She is very pink. And very short.

Jimmy laughs. "You're not the queen's guard."

She whips out a sword too. But it's not a toy. "I am the pink princess, Delphi. And I dare you to challenge me again!"

"There will be no challenges today. Not with real swords," ALCOR says. "Welcome to the Academy for Unwanted Children. Every child is welcome here. All we ask is that you contribute."

He goes on and on about the rules. But I've heard this speech a millions times so I turn it out.

Because the silver princess in front is staring at us. No. She's staring at... *me.*

"Hey," Jimmy says. Again with the elbow. "You can have that silver one. I like the little pink freak."

But I don't need his permission.

Because her silver eyes crackle with sparkling light just as mine flash with violet heat.

And then everything that was unknown becomes known.

"Princess Alera," I breathe.

I didn't need an eternity to hunt her down.

She has been with me since the very beginning.

Because she is mine.

She has always been mine.

I walk towards her with an outstretched hand.

And when she takes it, I look her in the eyes as I kiss her knuckles and say, "Welcome to our time."

Welcome to the End of Book Shit where I get to say anything I want about the book and since this is the end of a series, it's a good time to reflect back on my goals and see how I did.

So it's kinda funny that I'm finishing two long series at the same time because I just, like moments ago, wrote the EOBS for Bossy Luke—which is the last book in the seven-book Bossy Brothers series.

And this book, Uncrossed, is also the last book in a seven-book series. It makes sense because I started them at the same time. But how we got to the end was totally different.

Like, I cannot even stress enough how much I did not plan this series. lol

I mean, I kinda went in to it knowing these aliens had two dicks and that was my big selling point. I just really wanted to make people snicker when they read the blurb and be all... What the actual fuck is this?

Right? I was just looking for some fun.

But I realized pretty quickly that the extra appendage wasn't going to be enough to carry my story. I know there are a lot of romance authors out there who don't put as much effort into the story as I do. And that's cool, because there are a lot of readers who don't want a lot of story. They want some feels, they want some sex, they want a happy ending. Give them that, and they're good.

But I'm just not that kind of writer. Characters always come first for me. And I don't care how sexy Serpint and his brothers are, their two dicks weren't going to be enough. You gotta have some kind of personality inside. My characters need goals, they need to make mistakes, they need to learn things, and grown, and then, at the end, they need to pull off some amazing, spectacular twist that *most* readers didn't see coming.

So I realized pretty quick when I started writing Booty Hunter that the two dicks was fun and good for a laugh in the blurb and some uncomfortable moments in the story—but seven men with two dicks cannot save the fucking universe.

Or can they?

Ahhh… I'm kinda laughing right now.

OK, but here's the thing that happened with these books. It started out as just soulmates in space. And two dicks. ;) But then I killed someone in Chapter One of Booty Hunter. Poor Draden. He's the reason this book went off the rails. Because I had to find a way to bring all the brothers back to the station in the middle of that book so readers could meet them all. So they could get invested and want to keep reading about Jimmy, and Luck, and Tray, and Valor, and Crux.

I knew it was going to be a long series and that every brother would get their own book, but I really did go in to this thinking these books would be all sex and who gives a fuck about the story?

I mean—they have two dicks? Right? It's a huge selling point.

But then the funeral service happened and… yeah. Everything changed with that funeral service because one of them was DEAD!

That's some heavy shit. And I put the whole thing in Lyra's point of view so that the reader—who was also new to this Harem Station world—could start to understand what harem Station actually was. Because it's not just a collection of bad people who got away with shit and found somewhere safe to hide from their sins. It was about family. Harem Station was all about family.

But still, I had some high hopes that I was totally gonna keep this story simple. I could still make it mostly about sex and it would just be this fun side project that kinda gets an astricts in my biography.

And then I wrote Star Crossed and I knew that was never going to happen.

I fell for Crux pretty hard in that little prequel book. I loved telling the back story of how the brothers arrived on Harem Station, I loved that Crux was "the good brother" with this moral code and sense of responsibility. I loved that he got left behind while all the others went out and made their mark on the universe. I loved that even though he never wanted to be the governor of Harem Station, he ended up being the governor of Harem Station.

The best leaders are always the reluctant ones and Crux was a damn good leader. Let's put aside the fact that he was buying and selling Cygnian Princesses for a moment. He did work out a way to make it their choice

I'm rolling my eyes too. But he really did try and do the right thing.

But of course, it wasn't the right thing. So that caught up with him. As it should've.

That's not where the story went off the rails, though. In Star Crossed I also wrote a few paragraphs about time. Crux had some thoughts about time as they were traveling through the ALCOR gate and even though I didn't plan it, I knew. I fucking knew. I knew the moment I wrote those words that time was gonna come back and bite me in the ass and now there was just nothing I could do about it.

Fucking. Time.

I'm just gonna say this up front—I hate, like HATE with capital letters—time-travel books. They confuse me, authors almost never pay attention to the science (and I'm a scientist, so then I just have to put the book down), and it honestly hurts my head to think about time—just in general—let alone the implications of traveling through it.

But I was listening to this book about time when I started writing Harem Station. I was in a non-fiction phase back then and usually my non-fiction choices in audiobooks are about physics. I fucking love physics. To be clear, I cannot DO physics. lol I had to cry my way out of a final exam in physics in college and even though I'm not proud of that moment, it did save my grade because I was going to fail that final and end up with a D. And I was trying to get into grad school as the time and could not have a fucking D on my transcript.

I can't DO physics, but I really, really, really like it. Physics contains all the secrets of the universe and that shit is cool. So I had picked up this book about time— it's called The Order of Time by the physicist Carlo Rovelli and narrated by Benedict Cumberbatch. And this man's voice—holy fuck. I could listen to him all day. So I have actually listened to this book like, and I'm not kidding, thirty times. At least. The whole thing from start to finish. I would put it on at night and the voice was calming and I was learning about time, and then I'd usually fall asleep so I had to restart it the next night.

Time, it turns out, is a tricky fucking thing. Time is like… not what you think. And I'm not even going to try and explain it because I don't have the vocabulary to do it justice.

So this is how that ONE monologue Crux had in Star Crossed ended up being the defining factor in this dumb series about aliens with two dicks.

Once that happened this series stopped having anything to do with aliens with two cocks and started being about the people.

Which is just the way I like it.

And you all know that I love a good mystery so I piled that mystery on thick.

And it was all going along pretty well because it was long series so I kept adding to the mystery and telling myself—well, you don't have to solve the mystery until the last book. So who cares if you just introduced Crux's daughter into Jimmy's storyline?

Right? Plenty of time to sew that shit up before the end.

And then Luke and Nyleena came along and these two had synergistic powers. They were better together than they were apart. And I was like—ohhh. That's super cool. I'm gonna keep that going. And then Tray falls in love with an AI, and Valor get stuck with the evil bitch, Veila, and before I knew it—there I was.

The last book.

I wrote it pretty fast. I mean it took me about a month. Uncrossed was the first book I wrote in 2020. I wrote it in January. And I finished it in January. I was fully planning on releasing it in February. It came back from editing and I knew I had to polish up the ending, but for some reason (pandemic, anyone?) I could not make myself go back to that book and do the final edits.

Because I wrote this story sorta thinking about how I would tie up all the many, many, many loose ends, but I wasn't paying that close attention to it. So I knew it would take a lot of concentration to make it worth publishing. The story basically stayed the same, but a good story is never about the main idea, right? It's all about execution.

A good story is all about the details.

And once the lockdown started I Just didn't have space in my head to think about fucking time travel. I just could not think about it. Thinking about time in any kind of scientific way requires a LOT of effort. Even for physicists. They don't *really* know what time is. And if you're thinking that time is the ticking off of seconds, well, you're just wrong. That's NOT what time is. At all.

So I had to put this book aside for seven months. And the only reason I forced myself to go back and figure it all out was because I told my audio publisher that I would have it to them by September 15 and I hate to break a deadline. I mean, a few days here and there is OK. But this book took me about three or four weeks to edit. Mind you, that's how long it took me to write the entire thing. So editing this fucker was a job.

But when I was done—wow. I really kinda love it.

I really love the end, and I have all kinds of thoughts about how Harem Station lives on, and this world became so real to me. It reminds me a lot of the Junco world in a way. And for sure, lots of small elements that exist in the Junco world live in this one too, but Harem Station is definitely a romance series. All the big decisions are made with love at the center.

And I love that the message of the series was that even though we sometimes feel stuck in someone else's story, we're still in charge of writing our own book.

Don't ever forget that.
It's an important lesson to learn.

And... well. I think I'm done here. Will I ever come back to these characters and this world?

Maybe. I'm sure some parts of Harem Station will pop up in another series. But for now, I'm just gonna let these boys and girls enjoy their do-over.

Thank you for reading, thank you for reviewing, and I'll see you in the next book.

Julie
October 31, 2020

ABOUT THE AUTHOR

JA Huss never wanted to be a writer and she still dreams of that elusive career as an astronaut. She originally went to school to become an equine veterinarian but soon figured out they keep horrible hours and decided to go to grad school instead. That Ph.D. wasn't all it was cracked up to be (and she really sucked at the whole scientist thing), so she dropped out and got a M.S. in forensic toxicology just to get the whole thing over with as soon as possible.

After graduation she got a job with the state of Colorado as their one and only hog farm inspector and spent her days wandering the Eastern Plains shooting the shit with farmers.

After a few years of that, she got bored. And since she was a homeschool mom and actually does love science, she decided to write science textbooks and make online classes for other homeschool moms.

She wrote more than two hundred of those workbooks and was the number one publisher at the online homeschool store many times, but eventually she covered every science topic she could think of and ran out of shit to say.

So in 2012 she decided to write fiction instead. That year she released her first three books and started a career that would make her a New York Times bestseller and land her on the USA Today Bestseller's List twenty-one times in the next five years.

In May 2018 MGM Television bought the TV and film rights for five of her books in the Rook & Ronin and Company series' and in March 2019 they offered her and her writing partner, Johnathan McClain, a script deal to write a pilot for a TV show.

Her books have sold millions of copies all over the world, the audio version of her semi-autobiographical book, Eighteen, was nominated for a Voice Arts Award and an Audie Award in 2016 and 2017 respectively, her audiobook, Mr. Perfect, was nominated for a Voice Arts Award in 2017, and her audiobook, Taking Turns, was nominated for an Audie Award in 2018. In 2019 her book, Total Exposure, was nominated for a Romance Writers of America RITA Award.

She lives on a ranch in Central Colorado with her family.

Made in the USA
Monee, IL
05 February 2021

59703564R00236